Daughter of Atlas

by Kirsten Corby

copyright © 2017 Kirsten Corby

ISBN 978-0692893203

Cover design by La Lima Design through selfpubbookcovers.com
Book layout by Charlie Brown, Lucky Mojo Press

5

Chapter One

At dawn on the morning of the summer solstice, a young woman came alone to the shore of the island home of the Sea Kings. She wore the linen robes of a priestess and a heavy, jeweled collar. She walked down the white beach to where the sand was flat and wet, and when the waves of the tide wet the hem of her skirts, she raised her arms and gave a high, trilling call.

Then she lowered her arms and waited.

She did not have long to wait. From out of the east, under the brightening sky, a sleek, powerful shape cut through the water, heading for the shore. Dolphins came to the Sea Priestess of Atlantis at dawn of the new season, as they had since the first long ships braved the coasts of the island home.

But there was only one. One, instead of a whole chorus of magical beasts.

The young woman hiked up her skirts and waded into the waves to greet it.

The dolphin swam up and butted gently against her flanks, whistling in greeting.

She whistled back, in the simplified version of cetacean speech that humans had to use. "Akasha," she whistled, "What has happened? Where is the pod?"

But the dolphin would not be hurried. He pulled back and circled around her in the shallow water.

"I greet you, Herata, Priestess of the Sea, Daughter of Kings," he sang.

"And I greet you, Akasha, Prince of the Waters, Terror of Sharks," the priestess replied. "But where are your kin? Has something happened? The ritual …"

Akasha rolled slightly in the water, fixing her with one deep liquid eye. "The pod is not coming," he sang. "There shall be no ritual today."

Herata was dismayed. No ritual? The Sea Priestess of Atlantis and the dolphins of Akasha's line had sung in the new season every year since the days of legend. It was one of the most sacred rites of the temple. How could the great fleets of the Sea Kings travel the oceans safely without the aid and blessing of the sea-folk?

"But why? Has something happened?"

Akasha circled her again, powerful tail threshing the water.

"Something? You tell me, priestess. Listen to the tidings I bring," Akasha sang, "and then … you tell me.

"A black tide chokes the shores of the Strait of Dawn. Fish die, dolphins leave. People on the shore go hungry. A sunken volcano poisons the waters of the Inner Sea. The ground shakes, buildings fall. In the Ocean of Suns, a great crack has opened in the bed of the deepest sea. Hot gas and filth pour out. Monsters crawl forth.

"So we leave," Akasha sang. "Always dolphins can leave; we are free people, we call the nine seas our home."

Akasha thrust his great body half out of the water and looked Herata straight in the eye. "But when the Nine Seas are filled with poison and gore, when the fish are all dead and there is nothing to eat, where then can dolphins go? Where then will we call home?"

Herata stared at him. "What are you saying?"

He sank back down, lay on the breast of the waves. "The oceans are unwell. We feel it; we see it in the lines of force that run under the waves. Harmony has been destroyed. The earth is suffering. Earth is our mother; as she goes, so go the oceans. So go the sea peoples."

"The ley lines!" Herata said. "You say the ley lines are out of balance."

"In some places, the power runs too great; the seas boil. In others, the power flows too weakly. The tides cannot turn, the waters die."

"I see," Herata whispered.

Akasha stared at her, his black eye unfathomable. "The Sea Kings control the secret lines. All know this."

"So let us sing the ritual," Herata said, almost pleading. "Let us make magic and set things to rights, together! Call the pod! We shall pray to Mother Earth for understanding."

"*No.*" Akasha croaked the word, in human speech; the sound was chilling.

"I am here not to sing with you, Daughter of Kings, but to warn you," he continued in song. "The Sea Kings take too much upon themselves. Too much power, at the cost of others, all the others. The primitive folk in the outlands and the sea peoples alike - all suffer now under the rule of the Sea Kings. Dolphins say, no more. There shall be no singing, there shall be no blessings, until the seas are calm again. I, Akasha, Prince of the Waters, say it."

He leapt up from the water, a glistening arc, twisting away from the priestess. With a splash he landed, diving deep, and then he was gone, arrowing away toward the rising sun.

"Wait!" Herata cried, splashing clumsily deeper into the water. "Come back!"

But he did not.

And so the Sea Priestess of Atlantis was left to sing the dawn solstice song alone, for the first time in living memory.

The ritual done, Herata straggled back up the beach, stunned. The dolphins had not refused the rites of Atlantis since the evil days of the Twenty Kings. She must bring these dark tidings to the Sea Kings, to all Atlantis.

Was it true, what Akasha said? Was the earth out of balance?

Cresting the dunes, she beheld the temple of the Nine Seas, her home and charge. A cluster of low, rounded buildings, scattered like shells cast up by the sea, gleaming softly in the early light, the pale seafoam marble tinged with the blush of dawn. Palm and laurel trees circled the buildings, their leaves shining in the morning light. Flowering vines climbed up the rounded pillars of the men's and women's halls. The buildings were cunningly built and situated to take advantage of the ocean breezes. The whole complex looked almost as if it had grown up on the shore itself, like a coral reef. A natural formation, at harmony with the land and sea.

Inside, the dedicants would be waiting, expecting news of the ritual safely done.

Steeling herself, Herata walked down to meet them.

At the gates of the sanctuary, acolytes met her with the ritual meal: smoked fish, fresh bread and the white wine of the Inner Sea. Numbly, she took the chalice, her gorge rising. This would be no celebration.

"Is it done, my lady?" asked Amalthea, her attendant. The girl was young and new to the temple. Looking into her large, dark-lashed eyes, Herata felt sorry that the child would have to meet the term of her service in a time of such sorrow.

"It is done, but poorly," she said, so that all could hear. No use trying to keep this secret. "The dolphins did not come."

Cries of surprise and dismay broke from the crowd.

"How can this be?" asked Lamike, a gray-haired elder of the temple, from the western shores.

Herata took a tiny bite of the smoked fish; it was like ashes in her mouth. "Akasha brought word. Dolphins sing no more with the sons of the Sea Kings. The seas are disturbed; the dolphins are unhappy."

The acolytes murmured, distressed. What could it mean? "We must send word to the capital, to the Great City," Lamike said.

"No! Not yet," Herata said firmly. "I must think on this first."

She handed back the chalice. "Continue about your duties," she told her priesthood. "The world yet turns, our work goes on. Be at peace. The burden is mine." She filled her voice with as much authority as she could muster; she was the High Priestess, they needed her strength.

Bowing to her, they drifted away, eyes troubled, voices low.

"Attend me," she said to Lamike.

The old priestess walked with her as they went deeper into the temple.

"Is there more?" Lamike asked quietly.

Herata glanced at her, impressed as always by the older woman's perception. Lamike had been in service to the temples for decades; she had terrified Herata once, as a young girl new-come to the temple's service. But as Sea Priestess, Herata had come to rely on her wisdom and quiet resolve.

"Dolphins say the leys in the deep sea beds are unbalanced. The waters grow sick; there are earthquakes, poison tides."

"Is it true?" Lamike mused.

"It must be. Even we of Atlantis do not know the wide oceans as well as the sea peoples. Dolphins do not lie."

"No. But they are … excitable," Lamike said. "Perhaps these disturbances are natural."

"Perhaps," Herata agreed. Dolphins' flightiness was, after all, legendary. "Yet I cannot think they would abandon us lest they thought they had good reason. I must see for myself."

"You mean to go into the leys?"

"Yes." Herata touched a knob on the wall, the carved eye of a giant squid. A door slid open, leading behind the sanctuary to the most guarded of rooms in the whole temple complex. The ley chamber.

"You have hardly eaten," Lamike said. "You have not the strength."

"Better this way. I must be clear for the work," Herata said. "Assist me."

They stepped into the ley chamber.

A great round room, the roof a dome of crystal, eight arched doors at the eight cardinal points. The room was empty save for the object in the center: a massive gleaming crystal, sunk to its midpoint into a socket in the floor. A ley-stone, secret glowing heart of the sea temple, seat of the Sea Kings' power. With these stones Atlantis harnessed and channeled the natural, vital energies of the living earth, using them to fuel their ever-growing society.

Herata unclasped the jeweled collar from her neck and stripped off the linen robe. Lamike helped her undo her braids and take out the fine golden wires woven within them. Naked, Herata approached the ley-stone. Sometimes, for extended work in the leys, it was best to have nothing impeding the adept's sensitivity, nothing between them and the power, not even a wisp of cloth.

"See that I am not disturbed."

Lamike bowed and withdrew.

Herata breathed deeply, regulating her heart and breath, preparing her body for the encounter with power. When she was ready, she touched the stone.

It flickered to life, shining like a lamp as she called the power forth. She could feel the vibration under her fingers, the stone brimming with the energies that fueled life itself.

Closing her eyes, she opened her mind to the power.

Like a rising tide it came into her: warmth, tingling, a sense of movement, as if the stone itself were alive – which, in a sense of course it was, full of energy as all things in the world were, biological or not. Sometimes the stones even spoke to their users – but only the oldest ones, at the most sacred sites. This crystal had never spoken.

For a long moment, she rested this way, flesh in stone, stone in flesh, harmonizing her own energies to that of the crystal. Then, when she was ready, she extended her awareness out.

Ah, she could feel them, the ley lines, like hot wires across the surface of her mind – the lines of force where the natural powers of the earth ran, straight as plumb lines across the world and back, carriers of the vital force of the planet itself. The leys carried the power – *aum*, the adepts called it – just as veins carried the blood of a mammal, or rivers the waters of the world. An exquisite sensitivity to this *aum* was the particular gift of the Atlantean race. With it they had developed the crystals, to take the power, store it, and use it to light their houses, power their sleek ships, to heal the sick and aid the crops to grow, to speak across great distances. Alone among the peoples of the world the Atlanteans had this knowledge, and it had made them rulers of the world, Kings of the Nine Seas and of all the shores they touched. So had it been for many generations.

This particular ley-stone lay at a junction point of three lines, going north to the Great City, south across the open sea, northwest to Olmec lands from whence Lamike came, and northeast across the cold seas to the Misty Isles, land of great power and magic. The temple was here because the junction was here. The adepts used the power as it came, and the movements of the mother earth's life energy were sometimes a mystery, even now.

Herata hung for a long moment, her mind in the crystal, feeling the leys stretching beyond her perceptions, all the way around the world and back. These three leys joined up with others from distant lands, merging and branching like a spider's web, the web of life. Mere distance was no barrier to an adept of the Atlantean way.

Kneeling by the crystal, her body in repose acquired by long years of training, Herata sent her consciousness out along the Olmec ley, away from the temple to the west and north.

She let the power carry her. The *aum* moved, traveling along the lines of force like blood in the veins, pulled by the tides of the moon, pushed by the heat of the sun. In this way the adepts communicated and kept the ever-expanding empire of the Sea Kings together.

Waves of power passed over her, through her, as her mind sang along the leys, carrying hints and messages of distant lands like snippets of dream: the warmth of the island sun in the Inner Sea, a snatch of song from the tiny Forest People in the far south of the Great Land, a breath of bracing cold from the high mountains in the easternmost east. Morning, noon, midnight; winter and summer; growth and repose, all commingled in the leys. All were one in the leys.

For a moment she was almost overcome by it: the joy, the ecstasy of union with the great breathing body of life, the mother earth, and all the creatures upon it. For a moment she ceased to be Herata at all and became simply a life, Life, ever-burgeoning, never dying, inexhaustible life on the blue planet under the sun and stars.

But only for a moment. The discipline of long years called her back to herself, recalled her body kneeling cold and alone in the temple by the sea – and with it, her task. This was the greatest danger to the ley-walkers, this all-consuming joy. Occasionally an adept would be found lying cold and lifeless beside their stone, their spirit gone, merged into the exalted oneness of the leys. Long years of training and hardship lay behind an adept's first encounter with a crystal.

No, there was work to be done. She pushed on, up the Olmec ley, to the city on the plain where Lamike's people lived.

The city hummed, buzzed, a bright shoal of power and life in the net. The Olmecs had been clients of Atlantis for generations; they too lived the Atlantean way. The city was old, prosperous, rich with strength and knowledge, its citizens healthy and wise. It gleamed in the web, a glowing jewel, almost as bright as the Great City, Poseidonis.

All was well here. Herata moved on.

The leys merged and split in Tiotiwakan, moving north and south, up to the northern continent, down to the south, west to the Ocean of Suns. A brilliant line pulsed southwest toward the hidden City in the Clouds, a major node and seat of great wisdom and learning. Herata thought about going there, but decided against it. What she sought would not be there.

She was unsure quite *what* she sought – but she would know it when she saw it.

Instead she shunted northwestward to the cold but bountiful lands on the extreme northwest of the northern continent. Here Atlantis was building a new colony. The native people were still simple hunters and fishermen, primitive and superstitious, easily overawed by the Sea King's magic. Soon they would come to see the strength in the Atlantean way, and the gifts it brought – warm homes, enough food, education for their children in the majesty and might of the Sea Kings. Their land was rugged but fertile, rich with lush forests and cold rivers running with fish. They were not warlike people. They put up no resistance to the shining marble city being built on the banks of their wild river.

And here, she found what she feared.

The leys powering the marble city hummed shrilly, vibrating at a dangerous rate. Power was being sucked from all quarters into the nodes at the center of the city. Little was going back out. Herata could feel it, like a deadly whirlpool, a ghastly, burning hole in the symmetry of the web, sucking *aum* in and down, consuming it.

Consuming *her*. A soundless cry ripped through her as the torrential flow of power caught her, snatching her along like a leaf in a raging river.

Far away, in the temple, her body jerked and moaned as its link with her mind was disrupted.

Struggling helplessly, Herata was carried along by the titanic flow of *aum*. Sounds and images assaulted her: the traffic of the leys, the uses to which the *aum* was being put. A woman screamed in a difficult labor; power was used to dull her pain and still her thrashing struggles. Men swarmed over the half-constructed stages of a tall stepped building; power was used to lift the mighty blocks of stone. *Aum* was used to hold fast the stones of a dam blocking a swift, white river; the stones throbbed with the strain. Other things she could hardly understand: booming sounds, flashes of light, a sort of fountain in a plaza where *aum* was made visible and spewed endlessly into the empty air. And all were dead ends in the web, wastage, sinks of power where nothing was given back to the earth. All unnecessary, useless, dangerous! There were herbs to ease the pain of labor, and machines to lift the blocks of stone. A river that fast should never be dammed. The white city was burning *aum* like candle wax.

And still the massive flow swept her along. Tumbling, dazed, she passed through a crystal that throbbed with an obscene load of power. She screamed with pain at its burning touch. She felt a flash of searing heat, the stink of ozone.

And then, like a seed squirted from a wet hand, she was out, past the white city, shunted somehow to a deep ley that went from the cold lands into the Ocean of Suns.

She simply coasted, exhausted, letting the natural flow of the ley-line carry her along.

Back in the temple, her body slumped neglected against the crystal.

What was that city? Who was its King? Who kept its temples, its engorged ley-stones? How could they do that? That was not the Atlantean way!

The power of the earth belonged equally to all life, to everything that lived on the body of the Mother. All life relied on the natural flow of earth-power; it *was* life, the stuff of life itself. There was only so much to go around. It came from the body of the earth and returned to it. When it was gone, squandered, all life was decreased.

The whole empire of Atlantis was built upon the even flow of *aum*. When it was damned, blocked, wasted, the empire itself trembled.

Coasting along the ocean ley, her weakened mind and spirit churning, Herata knew this beyond a doubt. She could feel it.

A new flash of pain wracked her. But this one was an old pain, one she knew. Her body, leagues away in the Sea Temple, was growing dangerously weak. She must return.

But not by that way! She would never touch the nodes of that city again! Instead, she shunted herself as soon as she could southeast, across miles of ocean, up the coast to the City of Clouds, basking for a moment in its cool, pearl-like vibrations, its even flows of energy, like a beautiful heart beating. This was what an Atlantean city should feel like!

Stepping down through many junctions, she turned her awareness east, and home.

But the way was not as easy as she hoped. High in the dry, ancient plains of the southern continent, where the power should flow fast and clean in the thin air, the ley narrowed, slowed, began to stutter. Herata felt a dreadful heavy sensation as she struggled to send her consciousness on up the line, like when one tried to run in a nightmare, and could not. The power was faltering here. The earth had no life to give; it had been sucked dry. The plains were dying, the grass shriveling, the soil drying up and blowing away.

She should have known. The fragile places of the world would be the first to go. All life was a web, a balance. Power gorged one place meant power gone in another.

It was too late to go back, too far. She did not have the strength. If she tried another way she would be lost in the web. She had no choice but to push on.

In the temple, her body had long since ceased breathing.

Struggling, her mind released a faint cry, hoping someone somewhere in the web would hear her, and respond. The ley stuttered on.

And then, it was as if something came down the line and grabbed her, something strong and warm, and familiar, drawing her on.

Lamike! Herata screamed, soundlessly.

Hurry! The old priestess said with a dreadful urgency that echoed down the line.

Together they struggled on, linked in thought, the old woman lending her strength to the young. Down the opposite length of the continent, where the earthpower swelled strong under the roots of the mighty forests, then into the sea, and home.

Fear goading her, with a sudden burst of strength Herata slammed back through her own crystal, and back into herself.

A rush of agonizing sensation, a feeling of suffocating confinement in the prison of bone and flesh. Air. There was no air!

Herata opened her eyes and convulsed, coughing, on the floor of her own ley chamber.

"Where were you?!" Lamike cried, stumbling away from the glowing stone. "We almost lost you!"

The marble of the floor seemed to suck the last thread of life out of Herata's weakened body. "C-cold," she gasped. "Cold."

"Attend us!" Lamike cried to the hovering group of priests at the doorway.

Herata was wrapped in woolen blankets and carried to her rooms. The temple healers dosed her with fortified wine and tucked heated bricks around her in bed. They forced soup into her. The life had almost been sucked right out of her; she needed food to recover, even if it outraged her heightened senses. Her weak protests did nothing to deter them.

"Why did you do this?" Lamike asked from beside her bedside. Her dark eyes were huge with worry. "What did you see?"

"Later!" Meilikki, the senior healer, said firmly. "She needs to sleep."

Cocooned in the mound of heated woolens, Herata felt warmth returning to her limbs. Sleep began to claim her.

But she groped weakly for Lamike's arm, pulled her down.

"The dolphins are right!" she whispered.

Chapter Two

Herata slept for a day and a night. She woke blearily the next morning, her eyes grainy and hot. She stretched hesitantly; the very tendons in her flesh felt loose and weak. She wondered if Meilikki had dosed her soup to keep her down. Sleep was the best cure for crystal exhaustion.

But no. Her fatigue was genuine. She had come very close to dying.

The morning light slanted through the windows of her apartment. Following it, she crept to the terrace outside her rooms, turning her face to the sun, grateful to still be able to feel its warmth. Amalthea, silent and terrified, brought her breakfast. Gods knew what rumors were circulating among the acolytes. Nothing like this had happened in the temple of the Nine Seas since the Silver Age of Atlantis.

Herata picked listlessly at her food. Truth was, nothing much of anything had happened at the temple for as long as she could remember.

She had hated it when she first came here, years ago as a girl from the Great City: the endless round of rituals, morning and evening always the same, the dawn songs and the dusk songs. She had hated the quiet after the bustling life of the imperial capital, hated the endless tasks: cleaning the sanctuary, tending the gardens, one day just like another, for years on end. Mindless, repetitive, pedestrian. Nothing like her father's glittering court in Poseidonis, where learned men and barbarians alike came from across the wide world.

But with time and study she found the wisdom in it: the perfect symmetry of the days mirroring a greater perfection, like the branching arms of a tree, programmed by some hidden order in the seed even before it fell, an order like the circling of the stars around the pole. As above, so below. The temples were the still points in the whirling cosmos of the empire. It had always been so.

At length she came to find her part in it, as she was required. She no longer thought of the Great City or her life of wealth and pleasure in the

Sea Kings' courts, now only dimly remembered, years in the past.

So when the old Sea Priestess had passed beyond the veil a year ago, the signs had pointed to Herata as her successor. And she had taken up that burden as was her duty: to mind the temple and keep its ancient ways, ever the same, days following days like the stars around the pole.

She had let the long quiet of the temple lull her. She had been too comfortable, too withdrawn in the dreamy days and silent nights. She had not thought about the outside world in a long time.

Too long a time. She pushed the food away, disgusted. She should have known what was going on in the colonies, should have noticed. She was Sea Priestess after all; events across the wide waters were her charge. But she had not raised her eyes from her own shores for many moons, content with her portion in the temple.

Well, no longer. She was a priestess of Atlantis and a Sea King's daughter, and it was time she paid a visit to court.

"Make ready the galley," she told Amalthea. "I travel to the Great City."

Meilikki gently tried to remonstrate with her as the arrangements were made.

"You are not well," she said. "You need rest now, not travel."

"I can rest on the journey up," Herata said, picking through her clothes for something fine enough to wear to court. She did not tell the healer about the twinges of pain in her joints, the shortness of breath. She did not have to.

"Whatever it is," Meilikki said, taking a stiff brocaded gown from her trembling hands and smoothly folding it, "has been going on this long. It can wait until you recover."

Herata remembered the dying soil of the high mountain plains, blowing in the wind. "No," she said. "I don't think it can. Now leave me!"

Meilikki bowed silently and withdrew.

It was a short journey by ship from the Sea Temple on the southern tip of Atlantis to the Great City at the foot of the mountains to the north. Herata sat bundled in a woolen throw as the galley swept up the coast toward the city's harbor mouth. They sailed against the wind and the ship's engines throbbed, powered by the glowing crystal set in its prow.

Herata was nervous. It was a long time since she had been to the Great City; a long time since she had spoken with her father. She was uncertain what to expect.

But she had had the galley rigged with the green sail which signified her rank and her Nome. The court would know she was coming.

The sun was high over the island home by the time they came to the

Pillars of Atlas, entrance to the great realm of the Sea Kings. Atop the ramparts of a deep-water bay sat two titanic gleaming ziggurats of purest crystal, glowing like pearls in the rays of the sun. At night they were fired by massive flows of *aum*, visible across the Ocean of Storms for many leagues. Thus all would know they were come unto the presence of the Sea Kings.

Herata looked at them and wondered, for the first time, how much power was wasted keeping those bragging lights aflame.

Between the ziggurats the living rock of the cliffs was cut into a deep, high-sided canal, which shot arrow-straight inland for many stadia, to Atlantis the City, on the Plains of Gold at the foot of the Atlas Mountains. Herata's galley backed and turned, maneuvering among many ships large and small from across the world, each jockeying to be the first into the canal. Herata ordered the sail raised; her sigil blazed bright in cloth-of-gold. Other, smaller ships gave way before her.

She felt a thrill of excitement. The Great City! She had grown up there, spent her childhood running along the arched bridges over the great canals, climbing the walls of gold and oricalch, eating the foods and playing with the baubles of a hundred lands. But she had not been back since before her woman's blood came upon her.

Plugged into an *aum* current running under the canal, her galley sailed smoothly inward. The high walls of stone surrounded them, cutting off the light. As they sailed, she studied the mighty carvings on the stone sides of the canals. They depicted the deeds of Sea Kings from ages past; the raising of the Great City, the carving of the canal. The discovery of oricalch, which when fused into a growing crystal made it hold and absorb the elusive earthpower, and so powered the entire Atlantean empire.

Here were the journeys of Prince Gavran the Navigator, who divined the secret of longitude back in the earliest days, and set the Sea Kings on their great quest around the world. Here the Sea Kings of the Silver Age conquered the savage tribes of black-headed people in the farthest east. There the Sea Queen Elissa established the city of Tharsis at the cost of her own life, anchoring the trades in tin, gold, and spices that had enriched the coffers of the island home.

A very great history, the story of a mighty people. Herata had learned these stories as a child in the nursery; she had sung the deathsongs of these kings in ceremony countless times. The Sea Kings of Atlantis were lords of the world, made so by their wisdom and their strength in arms. But, Herata wondered, did that give them the right to spend the wealth of that world with abandon?

She thought on these things as her galley worked its way though the locks of the mighty canal and slowly approached the Great City.

Shortly they reached the outer harbor. A vast ring of water, leagues in diameter that completely surrounded and enclosed the City, it was fronted by bristling quays of black and white stone. Beyond crowded a bustling waterfront, full of races and goods from every corner of the world: from black-headed Han to the savage blond poet-warriors of the coldest north, from wine of Thera to ancient singing-stones of the Island of the Dreaming in the southern ocean. Stevedores chanted their work-songs, merchants hawked their wares, beggars shook their alms-bowls, and singers from many lands told the tales of their people, hoping to please a lord of Atlantis and thus earn a spot in a fine hall for a night or a season. The Great City, glory of glories, navel of the world.

Enclosed within the waterfront, the city nested in rings like the garden of heaven, circled by canals, bordered by walls of precious metals, each finer than the last, until they reached the innermost portion, the center of the circle. Here were the sacred precincts where lay the ancestral halls of the Nomes of Atlantis, the temple of Poseidon, and the palace of the High King. Herata would meet her father here.

Once docked, Herata and her attendants transferred to a gondola sent by the palace. The canals that linked the channels of the city were the quickest way to travel from ring to ring.

Herata tried to compose her mind as the gondola glided up the canal. What would she find at court? What did the kings think of the white city, swollen with power on the shores of the north sea? Were her concerns genuine, or the phantasm of *aum*-fatigue?

No! She knew what she had seen, what she had felt. She was the priestess of the Nine Seas; the Kings must heed her words.

She would speak to her father first. He was a great King, lord of the Nome of the Salmon, of proud and ancient lineage. She was his only child. He would listen to her.

They were not challenged as they made their way to the central ring of the city, the sacred district; Herata's banner on the prow of the gondola proclaimed her royal blood. The gondola slid to a stop at the quay of the Salmon Nome.

White steps rose from the water to a many-pillared hall. Crystal lights glowed, braziers smoked with sweet perfume. Herata had sent word ahead; her ancestral house was ready to greet her.

"My lady." An old woman, iron gray of hair but straight of back, bowed to greet her. "The Daughter of our King is welcome in this hall."

"Is it ... Hecuba?" asked Herata, amazed. The steward had seemed ancient even when Herata lived as a child in her father's house.

"You honor me with your remembrance, my lady," said the crone, pleased.

"How could I forget the one who used to dose me with fish oil when I coughed and sing me to sleep afterwards?" Herata asked, and they embraced.

"We have readied your mother's rooms for your stay here ... if that is acceptable?" Hecuba asked, with a hint of hesitation.

Herata's mother was long gone from her father's house. She left shortly after Herata went to the temple. "Certainly," Herata said, though it made her feel a little strange. But she could hardly stay in her childhood cubby; she was a High Priestess of Atlantis and had some standards to maintain after all. Her mother's rooms were beautifully painted with frescoes in the style of the Inner Sea.

"Is my father in attendance?" she asked Hecuba led her deeper into the house.

"Indeed, he is!" a deep voice suddenly boomed out from the far doorway. Herata beheld her father, the Sea King of the Salmon Nome of Atlantis.

"My daughter!" he said, beaming as he strode into the room. "Too long has it been, my girl." He grabbed his only child in an enveloping hug.

King Herodian was a huge man, strong-browed like all the noble race and heavily muscled from a youth of rowing primitive galleys around the waters of the Inner Sea. He had given Herata her dark, wiry hair and ruddy skin. Her sea-green eyes were the gift of her departed mother.

Herodian was dressed in a kilt of finest linen and a broad collar of kingly gold and oricalch. His hair and beard, salted with gray, flowed down his naked chest. Herata felt overwhelmed by his embrace. She had almost forgotten how big a man he was, how mighty. Even now he could probably pick her up with one hand.

"Greetings, Majesty," she said.

"Child, child, none of that!" he said. "This is not the throne room. And it has been a long time since I have seen you."

"Hello, Father," she said instead, blushing. He roared with laughter.

"Let me see you!" He stood back to survey her, her simple but fine robes, her hair dressed in the style of the priesthood. "My little minnow, all grown up and a great priestess now!"

Somewhat teasingly, he stepped back and bowed, hands together in the position of honor.

"Welcome, my Lady of the Nine Seas," he said, "to the Hall of the Salmon in the Great City. We are at the service of your wisdom."

"I thank you," Herata said, trying to attain an air of gravity. He seemed so amused by her. Would he listen to the words she brought?

"Oh! So serious!" he said, making a comical face. "You have not come just to visit your poor old father, then, have you?"

"No, Father, I ..." She stumbled to a stop, tongue-tied. Now that she had come to it, she had no idea what to say to this man, her father, a virtual stranger.

He regarded her with a quizzical look – humor, but something also of sorrow, too. "Well," he said. "It has been too long, minnow."

Herata only nodded, overcome.

There was a moment's awkward silence.

"Have you eaten, my lady?" Hecuba asked into it.

"No," Herata said, relieved to take refuge in the rituals of politeness.

"Then by all means," Herodian said, "come."

And so Herata broke bread with her father for the first time in years. They talked of trivial things: family matters, cousins, who wedded whom, which children had been sent to serve in distant colonies. Herata did not discuss her mission. She wanted to take the measure of this man, the Sea King, first.

"Tell me, Herata," King Herodian asked at the end of the meal, as they lingered over wine. "The temple. Are you happy there?"

She was surprised by the question. It mirrored her thoughts of the morning. "Yes, Father, I am," she said stoutly. "The work is important, and I love my brothers and sisters in the order. It is ... a very serene existence. Who would not be?"

"Do you not miss the City? You cried when we sent you away," he said.

"I was just a child!" she said, amused. "I did not understand. But now I know my duty, and do it. As you do yours, Father."

"Of course," he said, as if retreating.

"That's not why I'm here!" she said. "Not at all!"

He studied her curiously. "Then why are you here, daughter?"

She took a deep breath. "I have tidings," she answered. "Of the business of the Nome, and of all Atlantis."

He nodded. "I sit in counsel this afternoon," he said formally. "You may bring your tidings there."

Herata bowed her head in assent, obscurely relieved that she did not have to speak immediately.

And so Herata attended her father as he held audience, hearing the grievances of people of the Salmon Nome from all over the world, some sent in by crystal. She hoped to hear more of the broad doings in the world, see if any of her fears were confirmed, if additional evidence arrived to support her story before she presented it to her father.

But it was all terribly ordinary: fishing rights, border disputes, requests from distant colonies for more supplies, more crystals and those trained to work them. Herata tried not to fidget, growing bored. Again she was glad that she had been sent to the temple, where she could turn her thoughts to greater things, instead of trained to service of the Nome.

Herodian noticed her annoyance and called a short recess.

"This is what it means to be King," he said, amused, pouring her a drink of watered wine. "It is not all pageants and triumphs."

"I know," she said, a little embarrassed that he could see through her so easily. "And keeping the Temple is not all dancing and flowers. But I feel I am better suited for that than this."

"Perhaps," he said. "But one day you might be called upon to rule the Nome. Ours is no hereditary kingship as the outlanders have; we know honor and ability do not always run true in the blood. But even so, you are of the old blood of the Salmon, and *aumvre* besides – gifted with the sight. That counts for something. If anything were to happen to me, you might be elected to the Salmon Throne."

"Nothing's going to happen!" Herata said, surprised and alarmed. Her father was still hale, and Atlantis was not a barbarian land where the king was slaughtered when his eyesight shortened or his hair first showed a strand of gray.

"Perhaps not. But one day you may be called to serve Atlantis in a different way."

Uncomfortable, she turned away, idly shifting through some papers on a table. It was Herodian who had installed her in Nine Seas temple, she thought with resentment. Would he yank her out again, now that it was home?

She came across a map, marked with the holdings and colonies of all the Nomes across the nine seas. She studied it.

The Sea Kings had spread across much of the world, both from the Ocean of Storms to the Straits of the Dawn. They occupied warm coasts and fertile river valleys far inland, leaving the dusty plains to rude tribesmen and savages, demanding only tribute. The Sea Kings were sailors and merchants, not farmers or sheepherders. From the cold islands off the coast of the Han, to the tropical atolls in the Ocean of Suns, the Atlantean empire girded the world.

She noticed a glyph marking the far northwest shore of the northern continent. She recognized it: the white city of her vision.

She turned to her father. "What city is this?"

He glanced at the map. "Ilethelme," he said, "a new colony. Of Orca Nome."

Looking over the map, she found other cities marked by similar glyphs. One was near the dry, dying plains of the southern continent.

"And these?"

"All new colonies," Herodian said. "Within the last ten years."

"Are any of our Nome?" she asked.

He pointed to a cluster of islands in the Inner Sea. "Here, Antikythera." He looked at her speculatively. "So now we learn why you have come."

She looked up, surprised by his perspicacity. He met her with a level gaze.

She pointed at Ilethelme. "They are using too much *aum*," she said. "Here, too," pointing to the southern continent.

"How do you know?"

"I have seen it."

"When have you been to Ilethelme?"

"While ley-walking."

He arched an eyebrow.

"I felt it!" Herata repeated. "I was there!"

"In vision only," Herodian said.

"No, it is not like that, I was *there*." She looked at him, frustrated. He was not a ley-worker, he did not understand.

He shrugged. "Tell me," he said.

So she did, speaking of her journey through the swollen nodes of the white city, Ilethelme, and of her struggles in the dry mountain plains.

"I almost did not make it back," she said.

Herodian took her chin into his hand, lifted it to look into her eyes. "So you have the crystal sickness. Yes, I could see you were not well."

Herata blushed; she had hoped she was hiding it better.

"Are you sure these things are not a fever dream of the sickness?"

"Yes! I tell you, Father, the leys are out of balance. The degradation will only grow worse."

"These colonies have the approval of the Council," he said. "The cities prosper. All is in order and is proceeding according to plan."

"Then the plan needs to be changed," Herata insisted.

He frowned at her. "This all has the blessing of the High Temple," he said. "You need not worry."

"It is not I who am worried," Herata said. "And it is not I who brings this warning. It is the dolphins. Akasha's pod did not appear for the solstice ceremony."

That got his attention. "Tell me!"

She told him what the dolphins had seen, and of their ultimatum. Such a demand had never been made in all the generations the sea folk and the Sea Kings had shared the ocean waves.

"So I had to sing the ritual alone." Her voice trembled at the memory of the utter aloneness she had felt, and the fear. "Then I went into the leys and I searched. And I saw it too. The imbalances. I barely lived to tell of it."

The look on the king's face was hard to read. He had not a smidgen of the power; he could never really understand. "Can it be so bad?"

"The Council must be told. I came as soon as I could."

"You have tired yourself," he said gently. "You should rest. I will look into these matters and see what the Council says."

"Thank you," she said gratefully. It was what she had hoped for.

"Now, I will send you my personal physician. You must recover your strength. And perhaps I will have a diversion for you tomorrow, if you are well."

He called for servants to see her to her chambers and to bring his physician to attend her. She did not see him for the rest of the day.

Herata spent the next day being bathed, massaged, smudged and needled by the King's physician and his staff. With some relief, she submitted herself to their ministrations, glad to let go of the fear that had shadowed her. She had done her duty, and informed her King. Events would now move beyond her.

While lying on a great slab of leystone bathed in a very small trickle of *aum*, enough to invigorate and not drain her, she was consulted upon dress styles by Hecuba and a succession of handmaids.

"Perhaps the silk," Hecuba said. "It would bring out the color of my lady's eyes."

Herata rolled over, stretching on the warm, humming stone. "But what is this for?" she asked, amused. She had not been this fussed over since – well, since she was a little child in her father's house. Life in the temple was comfortable, even beautiful, but simple, geared toward useful work and the contemplation of higher things.

"His Majesty has invited you to dinner with some dignitaries of the Nome," Hecuba said. "If you are well enough, of course."

"Thank you, I think I shall be." Herodian's doctor, a wizened little man of the Han, was highly skilled. She began to feel strong again. And she had not been to a feast in the Great City for crystal's years! "Let me see the cloth-of-silver."

That evening, the hall of the Salmon Nome blazed with rainbow light, pure *aum* refracted through a thousand tiny crystal lamps. The scents of spikenard and lotus wafted through the air. Music thrummed from bands of players hidden subtly in shadowed corners. From all corners of the city, by gondola and sedan chair, guests of the Salmon King flocked to the

Hall.

In her mother's old chambers, Herata studied herself in the looking glass. She had to admit, she was pleased. One of Hecuba's women had curled her hair and piled it high on her head in the latest style, with a few strands falling playfully down. She wore a one-shoulder gown of subtle dark green silk, simply yet exquisitely tailored. Its sheen picked up her eyes and made them shine like emeralds. The look was completed with glittering jewels of finest craft, tribute from the wild but gifted horsemen of the central plains.

"Oh, my lady, you truly look like a princess!" Amalthea gushed.

Herata caressed the girl's shoulder, touched. "Have them find something for you too, and you can attend me."

Amalthea squealed with delight and scurried off with the slaves.

In the Great Hall of the House of the Salmon, the doorkeeper introduced Herata to the assembled guests by her full ceremonial titles as "Daughter of the Salmon King, High Priestess of the Earth Our Mother, Keeper of the Radiant Stone, Mistress of the Nine Seas," etc. All those assembled lifted their hands to her in the traditional gesture of honor and respect, and her father came forth himself to greet her and hand her down the steps.

"You look radiant, my dear," he murmured as the assembled guests were presented to her, her kin and clients from all over the empire. Herata only nodded and murmured, having to use all her concentration to remember the barrage of names and titles.

People of every race were represented there, of every color and style of dress, but who all accepted one thing: the rule of the Kings of Atlantis. Only under the Sea Kings did the tribes of men come together in harmony. In the outland there was nothing but toil and strife, clan against clan, king against king. Atlantis brought peace; all wise men knew this.

Contemplating this panoply of humanity, Herata was humbled by this realization of the strength and purpose of Atlantis. Yes, she thought, she should get out of the temple more often. Cloistered inside its *tenemos*, its sacred precinct, it was easy to forget that the adepts served, and were part of, a much wider world.

A gong sounded. The dinner was served.

Herodian placed Herata on his couch, at his right hand, where he would place his queen, or his heir, if he had one. Herata was honored, but it made her uneasy. The King had no claim on her; she was sworn to the service of the temples. Child or no, she was not the Sea King's heir.

The theme of the banquet was a sampling of food from every land where the Salmon Nome held sway. A rice dish from the Islands of the Dawn, maize from Tiotiwakan, richly roasted ground nuts and braised eland from the Great Land. Eels from the warm waters of the Inner Sea. Mutton roasted with honey and mint from the Misty Isles.

The final course was rich red slabs of gleaming salmon, fresh from the waters of Atlantis itself, smoked with fires made from the nine woods of wisdom. A reverent hush descended on the crowd as the platters were lifted high for the King's approval; rare was the occasion when the kin of Salmon Nome ate their totemic beast. And when they did, all remembered the story of the great Salmon of Wisdom, which had taught the first Kings of Atlantis the secrets of many things and the spells to unlock them, in the eldest time.

King Herodian stood and raised his cup of wine. "To Salmon Nome!"

The crowd responded, "To Salmon Nome!" lifting their cups in salute. Herodian drank deep, the guests cheered, and with this sign of approval the platters were delivered to the tables.

"Had I known you were going to serve the fish, I would have left more room," Herata said ruefully. "I fear I cannot eat another bite!"

"Ah, but you must eat it," Herodian said. "Just one bite. It will make you strong."

In the end, she ate more than one – many more, for she loved salmon but only rarely ate it. It began to feel like a festival to her.

After the last course was served, the couches were cleared away and the guests were free to stroll and mingle, while entertained by roving musicians and acrobats. Wine flowed freely while wild strains of music clashed and mingled. It was the time when a party began to get looser, wilder, even a little dangerous. In the colonies, women would often be sent from the room. But no one told the free women of Atlantis when to leave or where to go.

Herata strolled among the revelers, feeling a little giddy. The wine in her cup never seemed to go down, though she drank liberally. She had not had this much fun in … years. It had been years.

"Daughter!" Her father beckoned her from across the room, and she went to him. "I have someone I'd like you to meet."

Beside him stood a blond young man with the sun-kissed look of the Inner Sea about him.

"May I present Branek, prince of Lacaon."

Herata nodded.

"Branek, my only child and High Priestess of Nine Seas Temple: Herata of Atlantis."

"How do you do," Herata said politely. She extended her hand.

He took it. "My lady."

Branek was tall, as was the way of his kind, and his shoulders and chest were broad and strong, the mark of a man who spent his days hauling lines and nets on the waters of the wine-dark sea. His skin was tanned a ruddy bronze; fine lines around his eyes bespoke laughter and days of squinting into the bright ocean sun. He was dressed in a wondrously pleated kilt of Keftian linen, and his wrists were heavy with bracelets and bands, giving a gloriously barbaric effect.

"What a pleasure to meet the mistress of the holy temple," the island prince said. "When I came to the Great City I did not hope to be so fortunate."

"You flatter me," Herata said, feeling obscurely pleased. His eyes were extraordinarily blue. They caught and held hers. He hadn't let go of her hand.

"Not at all," he said. "In fact I hope you will allow me the honor of making an offering at the temple while I am on the island."

"But of course. All kin of the Salmon Nome are welcome."

"Even one half-barbarian?" he asked.

"Branek's mother was one of the wild women of Colchis," the King offered. "Taken in tribute. His father, of course, is king of Lacaon."

"How fascinating," Herata said. "Did she teach you to ride?"

"Yes," Branek said, "but I haven't much use for it at Lacaon. The island is steep and there's not much place to go but the beaches."

"My mother is also of outland race," Herata offered. "From the Misty Isles."

"May I greet her?" the prince asked politely.

Herata glanced at her father; he shrugged. It was hardly a secret.

"Alas, she is not here," Herata said. "My parents discontinued their association long ago. Mother retired to a temple in the Cloud City. But I'm sure, were she here, she would be delighted to make the acquaintance of such a fine prince."

"Now you flatter me," Branek said smoothly.

He had extraordinarily pretty manners for a colonial. And his accent in the king's speech was excellent.

"Prince Branek will be here for some months," Herodian offered. "Perhaps you could show him the sights of the City before you return to the temple."

Prince Branek smiled engagingly. Herata looked at him, at her father, smiling at her encouragingly, at the glittering party around them, and a sudden, horrid suspicion blossomed in her mind.

Her hand clenched convulsively around her wine goblet. How dare he! Father or no, king or no – she was an adult woman and a priestess and her life was her own to do with as she chose.

Well, easy enough to scuttle that plan, with a little dollop of unvarnished truth.

"A lovely thought, Father, but I fear I will not have time, as I must address the Council – as we discussed?"

"Address the Council?" Herodian said with an edge in his voice. "You? Is that perhaps not a bit premature, my dear?"

"No, indeed, Majesty, for I fear time is short, and if you will not address my concerns, then I must seek other avenues."

She stared at her father, eyes boring into him, using the gaze she had perfected for disciplining willful novices. The King's expression grew darker; the tension stretched between them, suddenly electric.

"I should leave you to your discussions," Prince Branek, no dullard, said hastily. "If you will excuse me?"

"No, not necessary – " Herodian started to say, but Branek bowed and withdrew.

Herodian looked positively thunderous. Herata smiled to herself behind the rim of her cup, but her heart was pounding.

"With me," the King said to her, and he looked so angry that she began to feel a little afraid as they withdrew to a private chamber.

"You are a princess of the blood, and I had not imagined that you could act so churlishly," Herodian fumed when they were alone.

"And I would not imagine that you would put me on the market like a side of beef before I had even unpacked my things!" Herata retorted.

"You are not 'on the market'!" Herodian said.

"No? This party? These clothes? A colonial prince?" She banged her cup down on a table before she threw it against a wall. "I am astonished you did not show him my teeth!"

"That is enough!" the King barked.

"No, it's not!" Herata cried, just as agitated. "I have a life of my own and I am not a bauble you can use to bribe the loyalty of barbarian warlords. It is you who installed me in the temple – you bought my position there with slaves and gold! And now that I have made a life there for myself at last, you would take it away again?" She was so angry, she was shaking.

The murderous look on the king's face softened. He put his hands on her shoulders and though she tried to twist away, his huge hands held her fast.

"There, there, child, enough," he said. "I have made no plans for your disposition in your absence, you have my word on it. But when we heard that you were coming, I thought …." He trailed off.

"Thought what?"

"It was your mother's wish that you be sent up to religious life," he said carefully, beginning again. "I allowed it to please her. Aglaia always was overly pious. I had expected we would have many more children, but

… that was not to be.

"I have come to regret sending you to temple these past years. But the choice was made."

"So why –"

"I was glad when I got word that you were coming to the city. At last, I thought, I could tell you what I felt. I want you to know, Herata, that there are other choices, other ways of life. A world outside the *tenemos* – if you wish to take it."

Herata began to feel a fool. She had been worked up over nothing.

"So you don't have a contract with Lacaon?"

He laughed. "No, indeed. I hope you realize I would never be so presumptuous!"

He took a sip of wine. "Though the young prince would be a good friend to make. He is brilliant and well-liked; he will go far in the councils of power. I can see it."

"You like him," Herata said.

"More to the point, I think he likes you," Herodian said. "You know, daughter, there are other satisfactions in life than serving the gods. More … personal satisfactions."

Herata felt herself blushing. "Really, father!"

The king threw back his head and laughed. "I would be well pleased, Herata, if you could make a happier home for yourself than I did. A man always wants his child to do better than he did himself.

"But the choice is yours. Come, we must return."

The evening was winding down when they returned to the feast hall. The hidden musicians were playing slow, soothing numbers, and the wine was well watered. Herata amused herself by picking over a tray of sweet-meats as the guests said their farewells to the king.

"My lady," a voice said from over her shoulder.

She turned. It was the prince, Branek.

"Before I left, I only wanted to say … I hope you will forgive me if I did anything this evening to offend you."

She was surprised, and pleased. "I wasn't offended. Well, not by *you*."

He smiled, shook his head a little, quizzically, not understanding. His thick long hair was as gold as the fillet that bound it back.

"Do not worry," Herata said. "I have been pleased to make your acquaintance."

"I hope I did not interrupt your business with the King your father," he said.

Herata frowned. "I fear my business with my father may be in abeyance." It occurred to her that her father really did not want her to speak to the Council.

"If it is not an imposition, my lady … perhaps I may be of assistance?" She studied him. Could he?

"Tell me, my lord, do you walk the leys?'

"I'm sorry?" he said.

"Do you draw *aum* in Lacaon? Does your city run from earthpower?"

"Why yes," he said, a little surprised. "We have had the stone-craft now for some generations. Since not long after the Sea Kings first discovered our island."

"And you yourself, do you work the stones?"

"No, regretfully. Though I have heard it is wonderful to touch the power directly. It is my aunt and my sister who are the adepts. In our family, the gift seems to run in the female line."

"That is not uncommon," Herata said. "And how are they managing, your aunt and your sister?"

"Why, fine," Branek said. "As far as I know."

"No headaches?" Herata asked. "No fevers? Nightmares?"

He frowned. "They do not suffer the crystal sickness, if that is what you are asking. We run an honorable temple."

"Of course. But I have had reports of disturbances in the leys. From widely spread locations. I was wondering if you had heard of any such in the Inner Sea."

"Not that I can recall." He furrowed his brow. "Ah, there was an earthquake last year, in the northern islands of the chain. But there are always earthquakes in the Inner Sea."

"Yes," Herata said thoughtfully. That was hardly conclusive.

"In fact," Branek said, "earthquake control is one of the uses to which our crystals are put."

That sharpened her interest. "How is that accomplished?" she asked. She had never heard of that use before.

He smiled and shook his head. "I'm afraid I wouldn't know."

"It must take a lot of power."

"It does, yes."

"It sounds dangerous."

He shook his head. "I don't think so. Not more so than any *aum* work. We obey the ancient laws."

"But the laws say nothing of earthquakes," Herata pressed.

He shrugged. "This is all I know. For more, you would have to ask my sister."

"Perhaps I shall," Herata said. She could send her a message by crystal.

"Her name is Laodice, of White Mare Temple," Branek said. "I shall tell her to expect you. I hope she can be of some assistance."

"Perhaps she will." She should check with other temples in the Nome, as well, she thought. She couldn't be the only one who noticed the imbalance.

"I hope it is not serious?" the prince said politely.

"I don't know," Herata said honestly.

"Serious enough to take to the Council of Kings," he guessed.

She gave him a narrow look. He was a quick one. "Maybe."

"That is grim news, my lady, if it is true," he said, lowering his voice.

"Do not speak of it!" Herata cautioned. "Not yet. I must speak with the Five Kings first. If they will hear me."

"Of course." Prince Branek looked around at the rapidly thinning hall. "I could wish this symposion had taken place at my father's townhouse," he said.

"Why?" Herata asked, puzzled.

"Because then I would have the honor of seeing you home, my lady," he said.

Herata felt herself blushing again. "You are trying to change the subject," she demurred.

"Only to end the evening on a happier note," he said. His blue eyes caught hers, held them effortlessly.

"May I call on you again, my lady?"

She would be in the city for some days before she could meet with the Five. And she could ask him more about the strange uses of *aum* in the colonies.

"Yes," she said, "You may."

He bowed over her hand like a courtier of the High King. "I shall look forward to it!"

Herodian would be pleased.

Chapter Three

Herata paid for her festival the next day, sleeping late into the morning, and waking with her head feeling as if it had been scoured out with sand. She took a long bath, and Hecuba sent her a ghastly concoction of herbs and salts. She managed to choke it down, and after a while she did feel better.

King Herodian was in session with his advisors; Herata hoped they were discussing her news. She would not bother or distract them. Instead she called for Amalthea and went out into the city.

The Hall of the Salmon was in the holy precinct in the center of the city. Taking a high, arched bridge, they crossed over the innermost canal and descended into the second ring of the city.

Here lived prosperous merchants and scholars in fine townhouses of white marble along wide, tree-lined streets. The great Academy of Atlantis was here, where students came from all corners of empire to study with the finest thinkers and artists in the realms. Small shops vending the riches of the world and tiny, exclusive eateries lined the smaller streets.

And everywhere *aum* was in use, in open current and stored in crystals for remote use, powering the very life of the Great City. *Aum* lit the lamps in stores and homes; *aum* heated trays of food in restaurants. *Aum* inscribed crystals with letters and bills and great works of literature in the Academy alike. At one street corner they found a fountain, cascades of water flowing over crystals glowing with pure, unmediated *aum*, golden clear.

"So beautiful!" Amalthea cried.

"But wasteful," Herata said. The same effect could be achieved with plain glass and ordinary electric light. It was as if she was suddenly seeing everything with new eyes. *Aum* was everywhere, being squandered on the most trivial uses. When she watched a musician in a café play an *aum*-based instrument – tuned, colored crystals infused with different elements – a part of her thrilled to the skill and craft of the Sea Kings, who had created such wonders. But another part remembered the choking sensation of trying to travel the dying ley in the southern mountains.

"Can't you feel it?" she asked Amalthea.

The girl closed her eyes, took a deep breath. "It is unlike anything I ever felt," she said happily. "It feels -- alive!"

Herata could feel that, too, of course: the whole great city-organism, brimming with life, energy, motion: the energy-body of the Great City, made of the collective energies of all the inhabitants and all their works. But to Herata it felt – manic: too fast, too alive, like a man who had chewed too many coca leaves and whose heart was fluttering under the strain. A man who would soon crash and plunge into a black, dreamless, drug-addled sleep.

"Come," she told Amalthea, "let us go back."

The girl was sore disappointed. But Herata had bigger concerns. She would visit the Great Temple of Poseidon in the inner ring, the holy of holies, and take the measure of its currents. The very heart of Atlantis the Empire. How did it beat?

They turned back toward the sacred precinct. The bridge over the canal was crowded; some fine lord's retinue was hogging the way.

"Make way for the Lady Herata, Priestess of the Nine Seas!" her bearers shouted as they jostled forward through the crowd. Herata reached down from the palanquin to quiet them.

"No," she said, "let them pass." She was not comfortable with such a display; it was not the way of the temples to put oneself forward so.

But at their call, the column of richly dressed men clogging the bridge came to a stop and parted. A blond man in blinding white linen came forth.

"Prince Branek!" Herata said, surprised but pleased.

He bowed over her hand. "My Lady of Nine Seas."

He looked remarkably hale for one who had drank as much and celebrated as late as they all had last night. His gold ornaments gleamed richly in the afternoon sun. Herata suddenly felt shy; she was dressed in a gown of good but plain cloth, and she was never at her best after a head full of wine.

"How pleasant to renew our acquaintance this fine day," Herata said.

"The pleasure is all mine," Prince Branek said. His hand cupped hers caressingly until she hastily withdrew it.

A knowing smile crinkled the corners of his eyes. Oh, he was a smooth one. How many fine ladies had he charmed with that pretty tongue and those blue eyes? Herata retreated into the shadows of her palanquin, trying to hide her blush.

He seemed to take pity on her, stepping back and gesturing to the shores of the sacred precinct beyond the bridge. "My men and I were hoping to visit the Poseideion," he said. "May we see you on your way?"

"We are going to the temple as well," Herata said, somewhat surprised. Outlanders were seldom permitted entrance to the holy of holies. It was unlikely he would be allowed to make offerings, half-barbarian as he was.

But he smiled, more genuinely this time. "Then by all means, let us go together!"

His men spread out around them, and he walked beside her palanquin as they went.

"I must thank you and your father for a most excellent entertainment yesterday," the prince said politely.

Herata eyed him. "Even the impromptu bits?" she asked. Her behavior last night really had been beyond the pale, she mused, arguing with the King in front of his subjects.

He had the grace, or the wit, to look abashed. "Again, my lady, I can only hope I did nothing in my outland ignorance to offend you yesternight," he said.

"At least you did not ask to check my teeth like a horse's," Herata said, without thinking, and then clapped her hand over her mouth, appalled. Beside her in the palanquin Amalthea gasped at the coarse remark.

But Prince Branek laughed, a full-bodied laugh of genuine amusement.

"Yes, indeed," he said, grinning. "I know just what you mean. I am but a poor colonial, but I think every unmarried merchant's and priest's daughter in the Great City has already been paraded in front of my townhouse."

"That is not why I am in the Great City," Herata said, face flaming. Herodian would just disown her if he heard!

The prince looked at her, and for a moment something besides amusement came into his eyes, something altogether darker and hotter. "A pity," he said.

Herata took refuge behind her hangings, completely flummoxed. A silence grew between them.

Their party wound its way through the fantastical gardens that decorated the sacred precinct, heading towards the temple complex. Perfumed trees from a hundred lands shaded them. Precious jewels decorated the stone tiles of the walkways. The lanes were cunningly laid out so that, no matter how they meandered, the Poseideion, the great temple of Atlantis, lay always visible before them, a gleaming marble pile at the very heart of the city.

"Why have you come, then?" the prince asked at last.

Herata gave him a narrow look, hardly trusting her tongue.

"Ah, your business with the Council," he said. "Forgive me; I have overstepped myself."

"Are you enjoying your time in the Great City?' she asked him, trying to change the subject.

His eyes lit up at the question. Their eyes were just on a level as he walked beside her chair.

"Indeed, it is finer than I ever dreamed of, finer than my father could ever describe. I have seen more strange and wonderful things in a fortnight than I saw in my whole life in Lacaon. Atlantis is truly the heart of the world."

"It is that," Herata agreed.

"You were raised here?" the prince asked.

"Yes, until I was sent to the temples."

"I wonder that you could bear to leave it," he said, gesturing at the splendors all around them – the rare blooms from distant lands, protected by crystal domes, the fountains where water was made to flow uphill, the gems and veins of orichalc that gleamed in every stone and wall.

"I couldn't," Herata whispered. All those years ago, when she was just a girl, she had thought she might die when she was first sent away. But that had only been a child's fancy, born of loneliness and confusion. She shrugged the memory off. "But it was my duty."

Branek sighed. "As it is my duty soon to return to Lacaon, and spend my life herding sheep and marking tribute to the Nome. Still, I count myself blessed to have tasted the Great City at all, and its many delights."

He gave her a sidelong look that evoked a strange fluttering feeling in Herata's breast. He was teasing her again – or was he?

Their party came around a final turn in the path, and Poseidon's temple lay revealed before them.

Branek let out his breath in an audible gasp, and as one he and his men knelt and made obeisance to the god's most holy house.

A vast pyramid of gleaming white marble, the perfect shape which did honor to the gods. At its summit, towering over the cityscape, a gracious pillared hall, its rooms open to the sky and the seawinds. Within dwelled the very presence of the god Poseidon, lord of the Nine Seas and father to the race of kings.

Once, Herata knew, in the oldest time, this had been a temple of the Earth Mother. But when the kings of old began to learn the ways of science and used that knowledge to seek other lands, the friendship of the Great Husband, the Ocean, mate of the Earth, was sought. And under his favor the Sea Kings had prospered ever since.

Slowly, reverently, their party crossed the vast white plaza in front of the pyramid. Herata touched the prince's arm and indicated to him the marble flagstones, which held a secret of Poseidonis. Somehow, whether by great art or true magic, they had been laid out in such a manner that the natural veins and colors in the stone, when viewed from a distance, figured a map of the world, with Atlantis at its center. Colored gems indicated the location of Atlantean colonies, and the major cities of tributary kings.

Prince Branek and his men seemed truly awed, standing in the very presence of empire, the wellspring of Atlantean power. The wind whistled across the plaza, bringing the smell of the sea and the cry of sea-birds: the god's presence seemed manifest around them.

Herata knew, but she did not say, that the plaza had been expressly designed to evoke that very feeling. Seeing the wonder in the islanders' eyes, she did not want to spoil it for them.

"Even to come this far, to see the holy pyramid, is enough," Prince Branek said. The breeze lifted the heavy golden locks of his hair, like a caress.

Herata regarded him. Alone, he would surely be turned away from the temple, even though he was a prince in his own land. But she was an elder of the faith, and the holy of holies was not forbidden to her.

"Come with me," she said, slipping out of her palanquin and holding out her hand.

He stared at her, eyes wide. "Truly?"

"Of course. You are my guest."

He took her hand, and they proceeded toward the looming steps of the pyramid.

Crowds of worshipers thronged around them. Sweet clouds of incense billowed from the braziers at which outlanders were allowed to make their offerings. Herata secured flowers and incense from a novice in a yellow robe. Even she, high priestess of her own temple, should not go empty-handed into the house of the god. She took enough for Prince Branek as well.

Together, they ascended the thousand steps of the pyramid.

As they climbed, Herata felt herself slipping into trance. The wind sang and muttered in her ears, speaking secrets she had not yet learned. Beside her, she felt the prince of Lacaon tense with excitement.

At the door to the temple, attendants slid forward to bar the prince's passage, then ghosted aside at her wordless signal. Recognizing her, they let her and her guest pass into the presence of the god.

The words of Queen Thais's ancient *Hymn to Poseidon* moved up through her, out her mouth as song. This was her god, her spouse, the energy to which she had devoted her life. Lord of the Nine Seas as she was Lady, father of the race of kings, her ancestor. Guardian of the empire, it was to him that all Atlanteans turned at need, or in joy. The god's icon of white marble rose before them, in his magical chariot pulled by sea serpents. Not presence but image, still the statue was the focus of the love and devotion of thousands of souls across the Nine Seas.

Carried away by song, Herata made her offerings, laying the flowers at the foot of the statue and casting the incense in the eternal fire. This was all that was required; blood sacrifice was no longer made in the cult of Atlantis.

Beside her, whispering the words of the hymn after her, Prince Branek did the same.

Watching him, Herata suddenly saw the statue and the temple with new eyes, as if she too were seeing it for the first time. The huge statue, so perfect of form and detail that the god looked as if he might step down from the chariot at any moment. The mighty temple-pyramid, a man-made mountain of stone, built to arcane perfection with the aid of crystal science. And surrounding it, the Great City, sitting astride the byways of all the earth, rich with the wealth of the Nine Seas, walled with gold and orichalc, glistening with the power of crystals. Looking through the pillars of the god's hall, she saw the vista of the city and the Plains of Gold beyond. The sight snatched her breath away, as it had not since she was a tiny child and had been carried up these steps to be presented to the god.

And seeing it thus, she remembered suddenly, piercingly, why she had come here. The leys! The flow of earthpower in the cities of the empire. Standing at the apex of the temple, in the exact center of the city, at the heart of the island home, she could feel the *aum*, how it flowed here from all over the world, congregating here at the Poseideion, the greatest of the Seven Great Nodes that formed the many-chambered beating heart of the earth, beating not with blood, but with pure power. The very stones of the pyramid trembled with it, vibrating with *aum*, which flowed up the steps like water, filling her as she stood there. She gasped; unbidden the power entered her, climbing up her spine, opening the psychic centers of her body, expanding her consciousness, already far gone in trance.

The god seemed to stare at her, implacable, remote.

Is it true? she cried to the god with her mind and heart. Are the seas sickening? Are the deep leys unbalanced?

The only answer seemed to come from deep within herself: *Seek the source of power.*

With a shivering cry, she felt the *aum* leave her, draining out of her like spilled wine, spiraling down into the very stones of the temple, and down to the secret that lay buried at its heart.

She swooned, dizzy with the sudden emptiness. Strong arms caught her, held her up in a firm grasp. "My lady?"

It was the prince, Branek. She had all but forgotten him in that moment of icy ecstasy, of possession. Now he gazed at her with wonder and concern, holding her by the arms, his face still softened by awe. She trembled in his hands, shaken by the residue of power which still hummed in her bone and blood.

The power beckoned her from deep inside the pyramid.

"Attend me," she commanded him. Without questioning, he followed her as she went to the secret place behind the statue.

She searched for the hidden door, and found it where she knew it must be, a plate of plain oricalch its only lock.

She put her hand on the plate, and felt the current of power under the floor. With the touch of her hand, she completed the circuit and the door opened. This was the only test. Only a true adept of the empire could open the door to Poseidon's temple.

Inside was a tiny room of plain white metal. She entered. Branek hung back. "I cannot," he said. No outlander, none of the uninitiated had ever set foot here. It was forbidden.

"Attend me," Herata repeated, moved by what wisdom she knew not. But he would be needed, of that she was sure. She gestured, and reluctantly he stepped inside.

The door shut and the little room began to sink, falling in its shaft through the many levels of the temple and deeper yet, down into the hidden levels beneath the Plains of Gold. Here the truest work of the Poseideion was done.

The doors opened.

They stepped out onto a low balcony encircling a huge, vaulting room.

Below them at floor level, an array of massive crystals gleamed in their sockets. Adepts stood silently, or moved quietly to and fro, tending them. The stones pulsed steadily, moving energy in vast amounts to power the city and the ships of Atlantis.

This was the secret of the Sea Kings' power. This was the true heart of empire.

Silently, drawn by some compulsion she did not understand, Herata descended and approached the awesome crystals. Prince Branek made to follow her, but adepts surrounded him and held him back, for he was *inaum*, blind to the power, and his random, untrained energy could be fatal if it disturbed the crystals.

Down here, among the stones, the power was immense, a living thing. The hair on her head was lifted by it. The floor thrummed with the current. The sharp scent of ozone was thick in the air.

When they pulsed, it was almost too bright to look at.

Down below her, under the floor, were even more banks of crystals, massive batteries that stored the flow of power that was drawn in here from all over the world, and saved for the Sea Kings' pleasure. Several major ley lines converged here in this very chamber, at this very spot, the Great Node of Atlantis. Here there was *aum* to burn.

It was this accident of geography that had made the Atlantean race so responsive to *aum*; their ancestors had lived here, bathed in the flows of earthpower from all across the globe, since time beyond memory, since before the Great Ice had come and enrobed the northern continents, since before men had known fire and had lived in caves like rude animals. And it was this gift of power which had made the men of Atlantis lords of all other men, in whom the gift came only sometimes, and then weakly.

Pulled, entranced by the power, Herata kept walking, until she was in the middle, in the very vortex between the six giant crystals at the heart of empire – the Hexachon -- the center of the center, the holiest of holies.

Her body jerked and swayed as the power took hold of her. Without willing it, without even touching a crystal, she was swept out of her body and into the flows.

The power that had called her down now carried her up, up, out of the temple into empty space. The plains of Atlantis lay below. In a flash, she felt the power stretching out: east, west, in all directions, within and without. She could see the whole world at once. She *was* the world. On the day side, on the night side, she could sense the flows of *aum*, see the web of life spun out in a delicate lacy net like frost on a windowpane. In the sea, under the hearts of brooding mountains, the power flowed, everywhere one and the same, tying all life together into one unified whole. Water, fire, stone, flesh, and sea, it was all one, all part of the web.

But there were gaps in the web. Dark spots, tears, empty blank holes like the eyes of long-scoured skulls. She could see them – ah, she could *feel* them, like sores in her own body. For sores they were, in the living body of the earth.

There! The white city Ilethelme, a pustulent sore on the shores of the Ocean of Suns. The mountain plains of the southern continent: a dry, scaly scab on the virgin flesh of the Mother. And other places she had not guessed at, many places: deep in the body of the earth, on the tops of highest mountains, festering in the hearts of verdant jungles, bubbling in the bottom of the sea with sulfurous poisons. And there! Brooding under a mountain in the green waters of the Inner Sea, at the headwaters of a yellow river in the land of the Han: everywhere. They were everywhere. And they were growing, spreading, tearing the lacy web of life.

You see it, a voice said to her – six voices, speaking as one, resonating from everywhere and nowhere. *Yours is the vision. You must stop it.*

How? she cried into the web, feeling it shiver and run around the world.

You must stop the burning … you must…only you can stop the burning…

And then the power released her and she was falling, falling, falling back with a shock into her own body, which jerked and convulsed and collapsed onto the floor of the ley chamber.

As consciousness left her she heard her own heels drumming against the floor in seizure, and the chaos of shouts that surrounded her. Then it all went blessedly still.

Chapter Four

She awoke in a darkness shot by dim lights and soft sounds, murmurs just beyond understanding like the hum of the leys. Candles: a dark room lit by candles. And someone was talking quietly nearby.

"She's awake," a voice said, and a strong arm lifted her, setting something to her mouth. "Drink," the voice commanded, and she did, weakly, spluttering. It tasted warm and medicinal but she did not fight it.

"This should help with the dizziness," a familiar voice said.

"Lamike?" Herata asked bemusedly.

"You gave us all quite a scare, my lady," the old priestess said.

Herata remembered. "It wasn't me," she said. She struggled to rise, but her head felt like a granite monolith on the end of her neck, immobile on the pillow. Strong, gentle hands pushed her back down.

"I told you," Lamike said to someone behind her. "No, my lady, stay still. It is too early yet."

"They spoke to me," Herata said. "The Hexachon. The crystals in the heart of the temple; I heard them."

"We thought as much," Lamike said.

"Where am I?" Herata asked. It was so dark.

"In the Salmon Hall, in the Great City. We did not risk moving you far."

"How long …?"

"Three days."

"Three days?" Herata gasped. "No, that's too long." She pushed fitfully at the blankets covering her. "Let me up."

Hands held her down. "The draught!" Lamike said, and another cup was forced to her lips. She tried to pull away from it but was too slow. A good bit of it spilled but enough slipped down, and she could feel the heaviness spreading through her limbs.

"Why are you doing this?" she cried.

"If you get up now you will die," Lamike said flatly. "You are too weak. You almost did, you know."

"No!" Herata said doggedly, but her limbs would not obey her. "There isn't time."

"For gods' sakes, child, what did they say to you?" a deep voice spoke from the darkness.

"Father!" Herata cried. "Help me!"

"No, daughter, be easy," Herodian said. "What did they say?"

"Burning," she mumbled, as the darkness of a drugged sleep claimed her again. "The burning is coming…"

Branek, Prince of Lacaon, paced in the entrance hall of the House of the Salmon. Anxiety churned his guts, but he made no show of it as his retainers Nestor and Sokar watched him pace. He was not acting like himself, he knew, and that worried them. But after what he had seen and done in the White Temple, he was not the same man he had been five days before.

By now he barely noticed the fine furnishings of the House of the Salmon, the marble walls with oricalch and crystal sconces, the silk hangings, the rare art from the Nome's holdings across the world. The gorgeous chamber seemed like an antechamber of hell.

For four days he had attempted to see the Lady Herata, and for four days he had been refused. The Sea Priestess was gravely ill, the household staff said, near death. She could receive no visitors. He could not figure a way to tell them that he was no ordinary visitor. And so he waited, every day.

He had told no one of what he had felt in the Poseideion. Had he even really felt it? Branek was *inaum*, he could not sense the power that flowed through the earth and the crystals. He was beginning to wonder if he had imagined it all, or if he too had some strange manifestation of crystal sickness.

These thoughts chased around and around his head until he thought he might go mad. There was only one person who could tell him he was not. And so he waited.

"Prince Branek," said a slave, gliding up in that peculiarly soundless way that Atlantean servants had, "King Herodian is in attendance and is willing to receive you, if you will speak with him."

"Certainly I will speak with the Sea King," Branek said. Finally some progress! He had seen no one higher than the House steward since first he came, the day after it happened.

The slave led him back to a large, sunlit room on the canal side of the House; a library, the shelves lined with scrolls, tablets, and racks of memory crystals. Long tables of gleaming wood filled the center of the room. At one of them stood Herodian, the Salmon King of Atlantis.

They gripped wrists. "By the gods, it's good to see you, my boy," the King said.

"And you, Majesty," Branek replied. He studied the man's face. Herodian looked tired, shadows under his eyes. His thick black hair was tied back in a plain tail. It had obviously been a grim four days in the House of the Salmon.

"The Lady Herata, your daughter – how is she?" Branek asked, unable to help himself.

Herodian did not answer right away. "Will you drink with me?" he asked instead, indicating a fine glass and oricalch wine service on the table between them.

"Please," Branek said, feeling a little rebuked. The same slave who had conducted him in poured the wine. "Half watered," Branek said, for his. The truth was he had been drinking too much since the Poseideion. But it quieted the voices in his head – whether they were his own fears, or … something else.

They drank an uncomfortable moment in silence. Branek recognized the vintage as one from the Inner Sea. Once he had been proud that his people produced the finest wines in the empire; now it seemed irrelevant, even laughable.

"I understand I have you to thank for my daughter's safety," Herodian said at last.

Branek shrugged. He did not like to speak of it. "It was the least I could do," he said.

Herodian shook his head. "Not least! To go in among the root crystals, untrained – you could have been killed!"

"They let me," Branek said, remembering. "After she – fell, they powered down so I could reach Herata. I think they wanted me to help her."

"Nevertheless, a brave thing, to face the Six, untrained and ley-blind. Many – most – would not have dared."

Branek looked away. All the praise he had received over the last days only made him uncomfortable. Herata had been the brave one. But so helpless in the end there, used and cast aside by the powers of the Hexachon. He had acted without thinking.

"She says they spoke to her," Herodian said.

Branek ducked his head, trying to hide the flood of emotion that swept through him. Herata was awake! Or at least had been – awake, and her mind was intact. And she said the crystals had spoken to her! She at least would understand what had happened to him when he, too, had stood amongst the Hexachon.

When Herata collapsed, he had torn free of the restraining grip of the temple priests and run into the Hexachon's vortex to retrieve her where she lay convulsing on the floor.

As he breached their boundary, the Hexachon had dimmed themselves, relinquishing power, sinking down to a sullen bronze glow. Raw earthpower had still buffeted him, swarming over his skin like ants, but it had not burned out his nervous system in a flash, as he had been warned it could. He knelt beside Herata, and at his touch she stopped convulsing, but lay bonelessly, still as death. He lifted her into his arms. She was so light, as if all the life had been sucked out of her.

As he took her up, he had felt an echoing emptiness in his head, a sensation of vast distance and huge age, crushing him. He felt suddenly very tiny, as if he were looking down on himself from a godlike height. He felt, more than the heard, the thundering voice all around him, *within him*, refracted, sixfold, the voice of the Hexachon:

Defend her, they said.

"I will!" he answered, and he knew they heard it, and marked it.

Then the sensation was gone, and he clasped her body to him and ran out of that place.

Once clear, the temple adepts had whisked Herata away from him, and him to the healers, and he had not seen her from that instant, four days ago.

Branek started at a touch on his shoulder, pulling him from the memory. "I am moved to see that you care for my daughter's well-being," Herodian said.

"I am glad to hear she is recovering," Branek replied.

"And you," Herodian asked. "Are you well?"

"Yes," Branek said. "I am fine." He rolled his wineglass between his palms. He couldn't speak of it. He must have imagined it, in the shock and tension of the moment. The great crystals did not speak to those who were *inaum*, certainly not the Hexachon, most certainly not to colonials. "I thank you, yes," he said. "No harm done."

"I rejoice to hear it," Herodian said.

"May I see her?"

"Alas, no," Herodian said. "Most of the time she is kept sedated until her body's flows are stabilized."

Branek sighed.

"I promise you, my son, if I could let anyone see her right now, it would be you. But we dare not risk it. The smallest effort weakens her dangerously." Herodian's expression tightened; he was worried in spite of his reassuring words.

It put a sick feeling in the pit of Branek's stomach. Was Herodian lying to him? Was she dying? Wearily he rubbed his forehead. Why did he care, what had come over him? He barely knew her.

But what he had seen in the Poseideion was like something out of the romances of the bards. He had seen the powers call Herata, and she had responded unreservedly, at the risk of her own life. He had seldom seen such courage, even in battle. He had *felt* it.

Defend her.

"I pledge to you, Prince Branek," King Herodian said, "When my daughter is able to receive visitors, you will be the first we call."

Branek nodded, gathering his manners. He was being dismissed. It was a feeling he had grown accustomed to since coming to Atlantis. "Of course." He set the empty goblet down on the table. "Thank you for the wine."

"Do not mention it." Herodian walked Branek to the library door, his arm around the younger man's shoulders. "I know I do not need to ask you ..." he began.

"Not to discuss her condition, of course," Branek said. Gossip traveled faster than *aum* in the Great City.

"Good man." Herodian slapped him on the back. "I count myself fortunate indeed that you were with Herata that day."

Fortune, Branek wondered, or something else?

The slave reappeared and led him back to the foyer where Nestor and Sokar were irritably cooling their heels.

"My lord?" Nestor asked.

"She has recovered consciousness, but she is still very weak," Branek relayed.

"So can we go?" Sokar asked. Since boyhood he had always been shockingly insubordinate. He did not understand why his prince spent days moping after a strange woman. He had not accompanied Branek to the Poseideion that day.

Right then Branek did not have the will to rebuke him. "Lead on."

They returned to his father's townhouse in the Golden Circle. Branek said nothing as they walked, unsure if he should be reassured by the visit, or not.

He would send Laodice his sister a message by crystal. At the least, she should be made aware of what had happened. And she might have some words of counsel. He had always trusted her advice before.

But in the end, he said nothing about what he thought he had heard in the temple. Laodice was not the one he truly wished to speak with.

This time Herata's recovery was long in coming. She drifted for days in a listless, druggy sleep. In her brief periods of wakefulness she was so weak that trying to drink a cup of broth exhausted her. She was constantly attended by Hecuba, Amalthea, or Lamike, who had come from the temple to nurse her mistress. Sometimes even Herodian was at her bedside when she woke, a scroll unfurled on his lap, working while he watched over her.

Asleep, she dreamed, traveling the world in her dream-body, seeking out the holes, the tears in the web of life, searching restlessly. She dreamed often of trying to weave a tapestry that would not be woven, or untangling a massive, bunched skein of wool – dreams that drove her to wakefulness with tears of frustration in her eyes. Her dreams frightened her keepers, and they drugged her more so her sleep was black and insensate and debilitating.

She knew that her visitation in the temple had caused a furor in the corridors of power. The Council debated it; the leys hummed between the great temples with talk of the display. But she herself was too ill to speak of it. And this, too, made her weep with rage at her weakness. The crystals had spoken to her. Hers had been the vision. But her voice was not heard.

"Will you tell them?" she begged her father. "Will you show them?" And he said he would. But prisoner in her own sickness, she could not be sure that even he believed her. He would not tell her what went on in Council, fearing it would upset her too much and impede her recovery.

And so her convalescence dragged on for many weary days.

Eventually they allowed her to get up and walk. And then to go outside, to rest in the sun by the water gardens on the great canal. She was not allowed to go near a crystal. But still she could feel them, all around her, great and small, vibrating, and her bones seemed to resonate with them. She knew they would always be with her. They were watching her.

She began to practice again the exercises and disciplines that strengthened a ley-worker's body and mind. But her progress was frustratingly slow.

One morning she sat cross-legged on the water terrace, irritably trying to meditate. The hum and chatter of the household's crystals buzzed in her ears. She was learning to sense events at a distance, through the medium of the silent, ubiquitous crystals.

A commotion in the atrium caught her attention. She concentrated, opening herself to the flow of the crystals as she would do in the leys.

A sense of – alienness: a stranger in the house. That she got. Conflict, an argument: these were the emotions she felt radiating from whoever was in the room. But nothing specific; her sensitivity was still too raw.

Shortly Lamike arrived with tidings for her priestess.

"What is it?" Herata fretted.

Lamike looked grave. "A visitor has arrived for you, my lady."

"Who?"

"The Father of Stones, my lady – the Patriarch of the White Temple,"

Lamike said. She looked afraid now. "Your father tells him you are not well, yet he insists on seeing you."

At last! Someone from the temples, to whom she could speak, priest to priest. Someone who had not seen her in her weakest moments and so dismissed her visions as fever dreams. Someone who would *do* something!

"He is coming back now, in spite of what your father says," Lamike said.

Now? Here? "No," Herata said. She would not receive the Patriarch unwashed in a sweaty tunic. "Call the servants. I must bathe and dress."

"But the Patriarch will be kept waiting," Lamike worried.

"Then he will be kept waiting!" Herata said. "I have waited long enough, so can he." If he saw her disheveled and unkempt, he would never hear her words as anything but the maunderings of an invalid.

Herata got her way, and she received the Patriarch of the Poseideion in the water garden by the great canal. She wore a gown of fine pleated linen and a fillet of pearls on her freshly washed hair.

The old man, leader of the faith of Atlantis, master of the leys, was pacing angrily across the tiles. He stopped when he saw her.

"So," he said. "You are not on your deathbed after all."

"No, Grandfather," she said, using the term of familiar address for his station. She had spoken to this man, touched his spirit many times in the leys, but they had never met in person. He had not been Patriarch when she left the Great City for Nine Seas.

She sat down on a garden bench, offered him wine. He declined. He stared at her, his eyes probing, seeking out weakness. Demurely she cast her eyes down, carefully shrouding her mind. He was strong, she knew that. But she would reveal what she knew in her own time, not his.

"What did you do to my crystals?" he said abruptly.

"I visited them," she said carefully. "They … invited me."

His eyes narrowed. "They *spoke* to you?"

"They did."

He paced away again, agitated. He turned to face her, his long white robes swirling. "None – not one – of the Six has spoken in five generations. And now you say – they *all* spoke to you?"

"As one they spoke." Herata said. "With one voice."

The old man's hand rose up to clutch his curled white beard. His eyes bored into her. "What did they say?"

Herata put down her wine cup. "They say there is a great conflagration coming."

He frowned at her. "What does this mean?"

"I think you know," she said. "You've know for a long time, and yet you have done nothing."

"Nothing about what?" the old man blustered.

"The leys are out of balance. *Aum* is overdrawn. What have you done to correct it?"

He frowned. "There is no imbalance."

She told him what she had seen: the white city Ilethelme, burning like a funereal pyre night and day. The dead, blowing soil of the pampas in the Southern Continent. The dark places and the hot bright sores in the net of the leys.

"This is of no concern," the Patriarch said. "These are natural variations. The earth is not a static creature, but dynamic, alive. *Aum* moves. It has always been so."

"*Aum* moves to the rhythm of the Mother. Not to our rhythm! To make it so is blasphemy. It is folly! If we strain the system too much, it will correct itself – radically."

"No. There will be no conflagration. You have misunderstood."

"Do you think me a child, that I cannot comprehend what is before my eyes?" Herata said quietly. "I have struggled through the dying leys of the desert, I have burned in the cauldron of Ilethelme. I know what I see, and what I have been told. Now we must act!"

"What would you have us do?"

"Make the necessary changes. Reduce the taking of *aum*. Cities like Ilethelme and Kythera must be helped to see the danger of what they are doing. I pray that it is not too late." A shudder ran through her as she remembered what the stones had shown her.

The old man gave her a gimlet eye. "On your word, the whole web is to be restructured. Who are you, to say this?"

"I am Herata of Nine Seas, Priestess of Atlantis. And I am the interlocutor of the Six."

The significance of this could not be denied. None of the Six had spoken with their keepers in many generations. Never had they spoken with one accord before.

The Patriarch only stared at her, appalled or amazed she could not tell. "And yet, in the sanctum, the falling sickness took you."

"I fell back into myself. It was a long way to fall."

"I shall send you a physician from the temple of Kos, in the Inner Sea. Their gifts are great, and you have been sick for many days."

"I have already seen physicians," Herata said. "My health is not the issue. My vision is."

"How can you be sure it was not all a fever dream, the sick imaginings of a disordered mind?"

"If I were sickly, would the Six have chosen me to be their messenger?"

"Now your argument turns in upon itself. If you were ill, how do you know the Six spoke to you at all, and it was not but a phantasm?"

Herata gestured impatiently. "It is your temple; you were there. They spoke. You know it. You *felt* it."

He did not answer her, but she could see in his eyes that he had. The Hexachon had woken from their ancient sleep. They had spoken, and every mind in the web at the time had heard the echoes of that Voice.

"We must examine this matter further," the Patriarch said. "The elders shall convene."

Herata knew what that meant. "Meetings, ponderings? Endless talk! While the empire burns around you?"

His gaze upon her was flinty, distrustful. "Do nothing. You will be summoned to speak when the time is right."

"The time is now!" Herata cried. The sense of terrible urgency that had overwhelmed during her vision threatened to rise up and choke her. She had lain sick too long already; the time of the burning was coming closer. She could feel it.

"We cannot act rashly, not upon your word – no, nor even upon the Hexachon's. We must take care."

"Then take care you do not destroy the empire to save it."

He shook his head. "Return to Nine Seas. You will speak of this to no one, nor alter the flows from Nine Seas in any way."

There was a day, once, when she would have obeyed without question. But that was before.

"I am an elder of the faith and the keeper of a temple in my own right. You give no orders to me."

"Enough!" the old man barked. "Enough talk from an impertinent girl. You may hold the leadership of Nine Seas, but you do not command here – I do! I will say what is to be done or not done with the power of empire!"

Herata faced him down with incredulous anger. "Then say what must be done! Dim the lights of the temples, slow the flows of power in the empire. Heed the warnings before it is too late!"

"Be silent!"

It was too much for Herata. She had not expected to meet such resistance, and from the very Father of Stones himself.

The strength drained out of her; she slumped down onto a bench, her head spinning, exhausted. The hum of the crystals rose to a hectoring shriek in her mind, drowning out her own thoughts.

The Patriarch stared down at her, implacable.

"You are not well," he said, as if this explained all. "I see. You can hardly be responsible for the things you say in the grip of the falling sickness."

Herata shook her head, despairing. She did not have the falling sickness. But the powers in the Great City would use that fiction to dismiss the message she bore.

"Will you do nothing?" she asked.

"I came to visit you too soon," the Patriarch said. "We will speak again when you are well. I will send you the physician from Kos after all. In the name of the Mother, good day."

And with that he swept out, leaving her alone with her vision, and the sound of the agitated crystals in her head.

She had failed. Nothing would be done.

The screech of the crystals rose up to overwhelm her, and they had to carry her back to bed.

The disappointment impeded her recovery. She had exhausted herself contesting her energy against the Patriarch's. All the *aum* crystals had to be removed from her room; in her weakened state she became convinced that their silent hum bore words of reproach.

Her caretakers thought her mad, but did as she demanded. Only then could she sleep.

One morning she was sitting in the water garden, listening to the soothing play of the fountains, when Amalthea announced she had a visitor.

"No, no," she said fretfully. "No more bureaucrats. I have nothing more to say, until they *do something*."

"'Tis no bureaucrat, my lady," Amalthea said. "I think you might want to see him."

"Who?"

"The young prince, Branek."

A spark of interest lit the gray pallor of her despair. She had not heard word of the prince since the Poseideion. She sat up, pushing at her hair. "Bring him."

The prince arrived bearing gifts, a huge bouquet of wildflowers, fragrant with the scents of the Plains of Gold. But he did not offer them to her, standing there, staring at her with a strange intensity.

"At last they allow me to see you, my lady," he said.

"Have you been by before?" Herata asked. No one had mentioned it.

He shrugged a little, self-deprecatingly. "Almost every day."

She was touched. "I did not know, or I would have insisted you be received." She gestured him closer. He offered her the blooms as if he had forgotten them until now.

"How beautiful," Herata said, burying her face in the blossoms to hide her blush. She had thought he would be monitoring her for the Council, not making a personal visit.

"The starflowers are as blue as your eyes, my lady," the prince said.

"My eyes are green," Herata said peevishly.

"Well," Branek said, "I know. But there are no green flowers."

That startled a laugh out of her. "You are a funnyman!"

He smiled. "If it pleases my lady," he said.

"It does," Herata said. Amalthea took the flowers to put them in water.

"May I stay awhile?" Branek asked, looking down at her kindly. It was his eyes that were as blue as flowers, she thought.

"Please," Herata said. He pulled a stool up and sat down beside her.

They regarded each other a moment in silence. Goddess mother, but he was beautiful. She had forgotten.

"Are you well, my lady?" the prince asked gently.

"Herodian says I have you to thank for my safety," Herata said. "That you carried me out of the vortex yourself."

"It is my honor to serve," he said.

"That was very dangerous," Herata chided gently. "You are not trained."

He looked at her with that same intensity as before. "How could I leave you there defenseless?"

Herata looked away, confused. "You are too kind."

Amalthea arrived with wine, breaking the tension. Herata could only have hers ten times watered; Branek courteously took the same. He dismissed Amalthea and poured for them himself.

"How are things in the City?" Herata asked. "I have not left this house since... I don't know. I've lost track of the days."

"It is five days past the new moon of pressing," Branek said.

"That long," Herata sighed. Three weeks. She squeezed her eyes shut against a wave of frustration. She should not be sitting here, lounging in a garden and entertaining princes. She had work to do!

She was startled by a warm touch upon her hand. "You must take as long as you need, to be well," Branek said.

"Were I not so weak I would be about my work already!"

Branek took her hand in a strong grip. "You are not weak, my lady!" he said. "A lesser priestess would have died in the Poseideion!"

"How do you know?" Herata protested.

"I know what I saw with my own eyes," Branek said. "Like something from the old tales about the Golden Age. It was said at first that no one could survive that vortex. But I said, no, my lady Herata will survive, for she is a great priestess."

She regarded him. How much did he know about what had really transpired? Indeed, he had been there, but he was *inaum*. It might have meant nothing to him. Was her story being told?

"They spoke to me," she said. "The great crystals."

This seemed to move him greatly; he looked down, then back up again with a searching expression. "This ... has been rumored. But what did they say?"

"They showed me things," Herata said. "It is as I said, the first time you and I met. The earth is sick. Too much *aum* is being drawn."

The prince sighed. "If true, my lady, that is terrible news." He took a long pull on his watered wine, then set the cup on the ground, staring at it.

"Then will you say so?" Herata asked him intensely. "Will you bring it to the Council?"

He hesitated a moment. "If you wish it."

"There is sickness in the Inner Sea," Herata told him. "Fires in the earth are waking."

"I will send word at once," he said.

"Tell your sister to look to her crystals," she said. "And tell the Council!"

"I will tell them," he said, "if you will consider it a favor from a friend."

She looked at him, puzzled.

"I hope that you think of me as a friend," he said.

Herata felt an unbidden surge of warmth at his words. "Why are you so kind to me?" she wondered.

He hesitated a moment, watching her. He picked the wine cup back up again, twirling it in his strong fingers.

"May I speak freely?" he asked her.

"Please."

He cleared his throat a little, seeming nervous. "When I first came to the island home," he said, "I was advised that the King of Salmon Nome had a single daughter of marriageable age. I was told she was a priestess of the temple, never married, who had been sworn to the temple since childhood. I confess, when I was set to meet you the first time, my lady, I expected ..." He faltered.

"A dried-up old prune," Herata said, understanding. She was surprised to find that the thought amused her.

He blushed. "An older woman, of serious mien," he said. "One unaccustomed to the ways of the world."

"And?" Herata said, beginning to enjoy this.

"And instead, I found a woman of great beauty and spirit. A woman who captured my attention, with whom I could speak as an equal. Someone, I hoped, who could be a friend, instead of just an alliance." He looked at her earnestly.

"I see," Herata said, a little breathlessly. His eyes were so very blue, like crystals.

"May I call you friend, my lady?"

Now Herata blushed. "You may."

"And when you were called by the Six, and went in amongst them, alone and unarmored, and they cast you down, how could I not follow?" He shook his head, remembering. "I had to follow."

"You did not," Herata said. It had been extremely foolhardy. "But you were brave to do so."

"I could not leave you there defenseless," Branek repeated. He refilled their cups. He seemed to want to say more, but did not.

Herata laid her hand upon his arm, so warm, and hard with the muscles of a fighting man. "What is it?"

He hesitated. "Only this, my lady: may I see you again?"

Ah, he was asking to court her. She had not expected that.

Celibacy was not required of the temple priesthood, but it was expected. Crystal work burned up so much of the body's energy, there was little left for concupiscence anyway. She had grown up in the temple, walking the leys from a young age; she had given little thought to the pleasures of the flesh. Until now.

She studied him, this prince of the colonies, the bright outland glory of him, with his blond hair and bronze skin, the strong, square hands, the clear blue eyes. His mouth was strongly set, yet had a gentle line, as if it awaited a tender touch.

She remembered something her father had said the night of the feast, something about *more personal satisfactions*. And, by the gods, she needed some satisfaction in her life now.

"You may," she said.

"Ah," he said, "you have made me very happy, my lady."

Herata was happy too. She realized she had not felt that way for a long time. Since the dolphins had not come on summer solstice.

She turned her face to the sun, thankful, feeling a rush of sudden giddiness. If this could be happening, coming to her now, after all that had happened, surely things would be all right. She would grow strong again. The Sea Kings would listen to the wisdom of the crystals, and the sicknesses in the earth would be healed.

She sighed, a deep happy breath. She felt she had been holding her breath for weeks now.

Prince Branek mistook her exclamation for weariness. "Forgive me, my lady, I have tired you. I should not have stayed so long." He stood up.

"No, not at all," Herata began. She rose too, then tottered as a wave of dizziness swept over her. Branek caught her elbow and held her in a strong grip.

"Oh," Herata said, a little dazedly. "It must be the wine."

Branek slipped his arm around her waist, warm and strong. She leaned into it, glad of the support.

Branek looked down at her, oddly serious. "You are not yet strong, my lady. You must grow strong, for the Empire has need of you in the councils of power."

"The darkness is growing," Herata said, understanding. "Nothing is being done."

"With you in withdrawal, your words are not heard," Branek said.

"Do you believe me?" Herata asked again.

"I saw you in the vortex that day," Branek answered. "I believe that your concerns are valid."

She clung to him, frustrated anew at her weakness. "You must help me!"

"I will," the prince said.

His arms tightened around her waist; he pulled her close. She clung for strength to his broad shoulders. Her face tilted up to his, searching his lips, his eyes, breathing his breath. He bent his head to her, and their lips touched.

It was a single long, slow, searching kiss. Herata drew strength from it as from a healing crystal. Her eyes closed, her mind hummed like the song of the leys. She had never been kissed before.

When it was over, Branek swept her up into his arms and carried her into the house like a little child. Trustingly she laid her head on his shoulder.

"You must grow strong," Branek repeated. "I would grieve if you did not recover, my lady."

"Herata," she whispered.

He said her name as if it were the greatest of secrets: "Herata."

Chapter Five

After that, Branek went to visit the Sea Priestess almost every day. Quickly it became the high point of his long days politicking in the councils of the empire -- work which he detested, but which was required for the betterment of his island nation, a striving colony in the shoals of empire. This was why his father had sent him to Atlantis, to learn the ways of the Great City, and make friends there, long before it would be needed. Hekau his father was not old, but Branek was his only son, and would be King of Lacaon after him.

And the best friend he made was Herata. She taught him to play senet, and he taught her to play dice, which she was ridiculously good at, once she learned.

"It is not fair," he complained, "you have the sight, you can see the dice before they fall." He had long made the same complaint to Laodice his sister when they gamed, and Herata laughed at him, just as Laodice always had. "You are a sore loser, is all," she teased him, snatching the dice up for another throw. "The student has surpassed the master."

The fact that he still could not beat her at senet did not improve his mood on that score. But then she kissed him, and he would have forgiven her anything.

He could not explain why he was so drawn to her – except that she was intelligent, beautiful, high-spirited, a highborn Atlantean princess, and her courage in the face of her long illness impressed him. He could tell she was in pain much of the time, but she never complained. The discipline of the temples would not allow it. He knew a little of that, from seeing his aunt and sister at their work. It was a discipline more rigorous even than a warrior's in some ways – an armor of the spirit as well as the body.

And yet he did not tell her of what he had experienced in the White Temple. He had mostly come to believe he had imagined it, speaking with the Hexachon – it was ridiculous. *She* was the interlocutor of the Six, not him, a colonial princeling.

But still, he remembered it at night when he went to bed, alone now, which was not usual for him. *Defend her.* Even if it was an imagining, it was true enough – her words were disruptive of the balance of power in the empire and she made few friends by it.

Slowly she grew well, and Branek hoped his attentions had somewhat to do with that. It was a happy day when she felt well enough to visit him at his townhouse in the Golden Circle, instead of him coming to her at the House of the Salmon. She exclaimed over the decorations, which were done by the best artists from the Inner Sea – frescoes on the walls, blue faience tiles on the floor.

"It's amazing," she said of the frescoes in the main hall. She touched a dolphin, carefully rendered in gray paint on the white plaster. "These dolphins almost look like individuals, as if you could tell them apart by name."

"Well, I couldn't, but my Aunt Meara could. She speaks to them. She advised the artist, I'm told. That was a while ago, before I was born."

"And this is Lacaon?" she asked, turning to the mural on the opposite wall.

"Yes," Branek said, "That's home." The mural depicted the white palace on its height, the blue roofs of the town clustered beneath it, the dark volcanic beaches, thyme and tarragon green on the hills. He missed it, even though compared to Atlantis it was a dusty little backwater, and he knew it.

"It's beautiful," she said, slipping her arm around his waist as they looked at it.

This simple gesture filled him with an absurd happiness. He had let this woman capture his heart. So far he had done no more than kiss her, which was a hardship for him, but he was willing to bear it. She was a virgin of the temples, and a civilized man knew how to control himself around women, or he was no man. He would not push her or do anything to frighten her. She was worth the wait.

Branek sighed inwardly. He wasn't sure it was wise, although his father the King would be immensely pleased to see him win a princess of Atlantis. But she was not only a princess, she was priestess, too, and her crusade on behalf of the Hexachon was not received well in many quarters – including Lacaon.

Laodice had sent him a message by crystal. *You had best not meddle with things you don't understand, little brother. Leave the mysteries to the adepts, and try and get us better fishing rights in the Ocean of Storms for next spring.* But it was too late -- by stepping into the vortex of the Hexachon, he had already meddled, and somehow, he knew, Herata's destiny and his were forever intertwined.

"What is the matter?" Herata asked, sensing his unease even though it was unspoken. Her sight, he was finding, gave her an uncanny sensitivity to his moods. Not necessarily an asset, but it was undeniable.

"Homesick," he said, grasping at the most likely answer as they stood in front of the mural. "Will you come visit Lacaon with me someday?"

A fleeting look of dismay crossed her face.

"What is it?" he asked.

"It's just … it has been so long since I have been anywhere but Nine Seas," she said. "Even this trip to Great City felt like a huge adventure."

"You are the priestess of the Nine Seas, are you not? " he asked. "Maybe you should go see some of them."

Her face crumpled prettily in a frown of chagrin. "That is a good point. You are very logical."

He laughed. "Indeed, even us stupid natives can think a little. I studied rhetoric with the finest philosophers in the Inner Sea."

"Stop it," she said, smacking his chest lightly. "I think no less of you for coming from a colony, you must know that."

"I would hope not," he said, catching her hand and pulling her a little closer to him. "I hope that one day you will come to rule that colony with me."

"What?" She stared up at him, green eyes widening.

"Come to Lacaon with me," he heard himself say. "Marry me."

"You want me to be your queen?" Herata asked. "You can't mean it."

"I think I do," Branek said. Good gods, what had come over him?

"I think you don't!" Herata said. She laughed, but it was nervous laughter.

He slid his hand down to the small of her back, pulling her closer. "It is no accident that we met that day on the bridge," he said. "We belong together. The powers have decreed it."

"No," Herata agreed. "It was no accident." But she could not meet his eyes.

That did not deter him. "A-hah! See, I knew it! You must come to Lacaon with me. At least come and see it; it is lovely this time of year. We could leave tomorrow."

"I cannot." She pushed a little away from him, but he held her close. "I came to tell you; I have been granted an audience by the Five Kings at last. In three days' time."

"Ah, " he said. "I knew there had to be something serious to make you leave the House of the Salmon." He was disappointed, but also obscurely relieved. He couldn't believe that he had just proposed marriage to this girl, with no gifts, no ceremony. She was right to turn him down. Hekau his father would be livid if he knew, and probably Herodian too -- and rightly so. But it had felt so right, in the moment. It was truly no coincidence he had been with her at the Poseideion; he knew it. He was *sure* of it. Even Laodice would have to admit that.

"Will you come with me?" she asked him. "To the Palace? I could use a friend there." She looked worried.

He reached up to tuck an errant strand of hair behind her ear. "Of course," he said. "It would be my honor." He was touched. There had been many women in his life, but few enough that he could call friend.

Besides, Laodice and Meara would want a firsthand report of *that* meeting.

Three days hence, Branek dressed with care for the appearance before the Five Kings. "The sapphires, I think, my lord," Galen, his Atlantean body slave, suggested.

"All right," he said, and let Galen put the heavy gold bracelets set with blue gems upon him. With them went a blue tunic and gold sandals, and Galen braided his long hair back in a neat queue tied with a blue silk cord.

Branek irritably spun one of the bracelets around his wrist. He hated fussing like this, but it was necessary. He could not present a poor showing for Lacaon in the courts of Atlantis; it was the whole point of his being here.

Besides, he was going to see Herata.

At the palace of the High King, he loitered in the soaring white hall before the audience chamber, waiting for Herata, trading inane pleasantries with other courtiers from Nomes and colonies from half the world. That aspect of life in Atlantis had certainly been an education; he had never imagined there were so many different peoples, so many different customs and histories and gods in the world. In one land, it was a grave insult if a man did not offer you his wife to warm your bed upon visiting, and an even graver insult if you refused her; in another, even looking at that wife could start a genocidal war. It was the rule of the Sea Kings of Atlantis that kept these differences from chafing into open, perennial warfare; the *pax Atlantica*, no wise man could deny it. The lands of the Inner Sea had submitted to it generations ago.

It was just this lesson he had been sent to the Great City to learn, and he had learned it.

He finally saw Herata arrive in the hall. She was alone, except for the fluttery girl who always attended her. Herodian had gone well before her – he was one of the Five, after all. She wore the robes of a priestess and a fillet made of silver and pearls, worked in the shape of seashells. The hum of conversation lulled as she came in; they were here to see her after all, to see her speak before the Five.

Branek met her, pulled her a little aside from the staring crowd, behind a pillar. "You look very handsome," he said, taking her hand and kissing her cheek.

She touched the fillet in her hair. "I speak in my capacity as Keeper of Nine Seas," she said. "Not Herodian's daughter. People must see that."

"They will never doubt it," he said honestly. She had the carriage of a queen, but her eyes were deep with a wisdom beyond her years. "Are you ready?"

"I am nervous," she said.

He laughed. "You, who went into the Hexachon alone, are afraid of five old men?"

She smiled, her expression brightening somewhat. "They are the Sea Kings, after all," she said.

"True, but Six beats Five on any shore of the empire." His fingers twined with hers. "See, it is practically proverbial."

"I'm glad you're here," she told him honestly.

"I would not miss it," he said. "I will be in the first gallery. Good luck."

Branek waited in the gallery with a crowd of other courtiers, forcing himself not to fidget. There was business enough to conduct that morning; Herata's appearance was only one of many. Finally the great orichalc doors to the royal audience chamber opened, and the majordomo intoned all her names and titles: "Herata of Salmon Nome, daughter of Herodian, Salmon King of Atlantis, Mistress of the Radiant Stone ..."

He tuned them out. The only titles that mattered here were two; that she was High Priestess of Nine Seas, and the messenger of the Hexachon.

She walked forward into the crowded hall, and silence fell. Alone, she walked the length of the high-ceilinged room, and bowed before the Five Kings in their high seats of ebony and coral.

The royal thrones spread out in a shallow arc at the nape of the room. On both ends were the Kings of the Four Nomes of Atlantis: Salmon, Kraken, Orca, and Ammonite. In the middle sat the High King, first among equals and possessor of the tie-breaking vote in royal decisions. The banners of each Nome and the five-pointed star of Atlantis itself were hung high above the thrones, woven in brilliant colors and embroidered with threads of gold and orichalc.

This was the lesser audience chamber, not the formal Council Chamber of the Five Kings, where royal decrees were handed down and justice was dealt – but it was still impressive, big enough in itself almost to swallow Branek's whole palace back in Lacaon. Herata looked tiny, standing alone on the dazzling white floor, but when she spoke, her voice was strong.

"Majesties, may I address the Council of the Five?"

The High King said, "Speak, for so you have been summoned."

Their voices were audible in every corner of the room. Branek shook his head; how this trick was managed he could not fathom, but it certainly was some use of the crystals. Every day in Atlantis he discovered some feat of crystal science that had never been imagined in the Inner Sea. Not without reason were the Kings of Atlantis, Kings of all the earth.

Herata took a deep breath and began:

"I come before you today as Sea Priestess of Atlantis, Keeper of the Temple of Nine Seas, and I come before you also as she who has spoken with the root crystals of the empire, the Hexachon. In these roles, and also as a citizen of the empire, I bring you a warning."

"Proceed," said the High King.

"One month ago, when summer solstice came, I went to make the rites of summer with the dolphins of Orca Nome, as has been done at Nine Seas temple since the Silver Age of Atlantis. But no dolphins came. The rite I was forced to observe alone."

A murmur ran through the first and second galleries at this revelation. This had not been generally known. It was alarming. The faith of Earth, Sea and Stone was not observed as fervently in the Great City now as it had been in ages past, but it was still the backbone of empire, the repository of crystal science, and power source for the whole vast empire. When it was lacking, people noticed, and were dismayed.

"Did you know this?" one of Branek's neighbors asked him – Janus was his name, an ambassador from the Five Lands on the northern shore of the Inner Sea. The Five Lands were old allies of Lacaon, and Branek's association with the Sea Priestess was becoming known among the members of the court.

"Yes, " Branek admitted, never taking his eyes off Herata. She and he had discussed her experiences many times; what they could mean, what should be done.

Another courtier behind him said, "I am of Orca Nome. My cousin's last trading venture has not yet reported back. They are weeks overdue. If we have been abandoned by the dolphins, then small wonder. We must make sacrifice. Why has this not been reported until now?"

"Sh," Branek said. The Ammonite King was speaking.

"What reason did the sea folk give for abandoning our ancient agreement?"

Herata took another breath. "They say they have not abandoned it, but we have. The Sea Kings have neglected their duty to the Sea. The oceans are not well; the Sea Kings have sickened them. And so, the sea folk withdraw their cooperation from the fleets of Atlantis."

This brought a much louder response from the galleries. The doings of the cetacean races were often mysterious to men. That they explained themselves so clearly was unusual, and what they said, alarming.

Branek felt a shooting pain in his hand and realized he was gripping the stone balustrade of the gallery with painful tightness. He let go with an effort.

He had written to his father and his aunt about this very thing, and had received no useful reply. It was worrisome, but it was not crucial. The Inner Sea was fickle, and the help and guidance of the dolphins was welcome, but Branek's people had been sailing the wine-dark sea since before the Atlanteans had breached the Pillars of Hercules. They could make do without dolphin guidance, as they had before the rule of Atlantis descended over the Inner Sea.

"Can you explain this?" The Orca King asked.

"I can," Herata said, "for I have followed the leys deep under the waters, and I have seen what the dolphins see. The ley lines of the earth are being overstressed. Too much *aum* is being consumed by the cities and ships of the empire. The earth grows overstressed, and this sickens the waters. So say the sea folk, and so I have seen. It is true; the Sea Kings have stopped caring for the ocean."

This brought an uproar from the watching audience. For the dolphins to say this was no small thing, but for the Sea Priestess of Atlantis to confirm it was even worse yet.

The Orca King spoke up. "What then did you do?"

"I came straight to the Great City, to seek the counsel of my father and the Five," she said, inclining her head toward Herodian. "While awaiting audience I resolved to visit the White Temple to make sacrifice. Once there, I was … called. I was summoned to the presence of the Hexachon."

The galleries barely rustled, hanging on her words. Rumors of this visitation had been wild throughout the city. Now she spoke of it in open council. Branek felt a chill as he remembered the events of that day. *Defend her.* Indeed, that was why he had come today.

Herata continued, the barest tremor in her voice. "The Hexachon showed me things which I had already seen myself, but which I did not understand. The Nomes of the Sea Kings consume too much *aum* and return none back. The Mother Earth is strained; this strain cannot continue. A rebalancing is coming -- mark me, it is coming whether we aid it, or fight. The empire of Atlantis must correct its course, or dire things will befall us. There will be conflagration. There will be … burning."

This put the galleries in an uproar. Not since the dark days of the Twenty Kings had any Keeper or priest prophesied the doom of Atlantis.

Branek surveyed the courtiers in the galleries around him; some anxious, some angry. The thought of cutting back on power would not be popular, either with the people of the island home, or the outlying colonies. He could hardly imagine Hekau or Meara consenting to such a thing. The life of ease, warmth, and abundance brought by crystal science and the rule of Atlantis, once tasted, was a hard thing to give up. He of the Inner Sea knew that; Lacaon was small and poor compared to the island home, but even common farmers there lived like kings, compared to those in the outer lands who used no *aum* and were not part of the empire.

The Five let the tumult roll on for a while. Then the High King raised his hand. The roar died down. Into the charged silence, the High King spoke:

"And you, Herata of Nine Seas, and you alone, were given this wisdom by the Six."

"The vision was mine to take to the people," she said. She looked up for the first time at the galleries. "And so I have."

A voice called out from the stands, the voice of the Patriarch himself: "Lies! Untruths! She is a false prophet!"

"I am no prophet!" Herata cried. "What I say is simple fact. Enter the flows and see for yourself!"

"Do not instruct me in my anointed business, my lady," the Father of Stones replied. "I have done so, and what you claim to see is only the natural variations in the pattern over time. You might know this, had you walked the leys as long as I, my girl."

Herata flushed at the intimation that she was naïve or inexperienced. That jab hit home; she was young to be Keeper of a major temple, even though she had passed all the tests and initiations, and the oracles had named her Sea Priestess. But she kept her voice level. "Why would the Hexachon tell me what was not so?"

"How do we know they told you anything at all?" the Patriarch insinuated.

Herata's mouth opened in a little gasp of dismay, that he would accuse her of lying in open council. She looked from the patriarch to her father, but Herodian said nothing.

Branek was incensed. This sort of flagrant insult would be answered in the Inner Sea with the point of a knife, and a fight to first blood or worse.

"No!" he spoke up, pitching his voice to carry across the floor. "The lady does not lie."

Herata looked up at him, and he could see the surprise on her face.

"The Lady of Nine Seas is wise," he continued. "Her gifts are strong.

We must heed the message she brings."

The Patriarch waved his hand dismissively. "What can a provincial know of these matters?"

"I was there!" Branek said. "I watched when the Lady spoke with the Six. I saw it with my own eyes!"

"But you could not understand what you saw," the Patriarch replied. "You are no initiate. How then can you speak of it now?"

Branek leaned forward on the balustrade, looking at the Five Kings, trying to catch their eyes. "I can tell what I saw, and let the Sea Kings make up their own minds as to what it means."

"Speak, then," King Herodian said. "Tell us what you saw in the sanctum that day."

Branek took a steadying breath. He had not yet addressed the Five in open council, but he had trained for this sort of exchange his whole life. "The Hexachon are the heart of empire, the master crystals of the entire grid," he began. "So mighty are they, it is said, no adept since Prince Ralan Stonekeeper himself could touch the full flow of all their power combined, and survive.

"Yet that is just what the Lady of Nine Seas did. Alone she walked in among the Six, alone and unprotected. And they received her! Long did she stand in the center of their circle, surrounded, unmoving, communing with them.

"So great was the storm of power unleashed that we who watched could not even see her in that cauldron of light. Keepers of the temple tried to approach and could not; the power of the stones beat them back. But there my lady stood, alone, unmoved, listening.

"How could she have ever survived, unless what she heard was great enough, terrible enough, that the whole world must hear it?

"And who would they have picked, this Hexachon, whom would they have brought to the bosom of their power, except one whose vision was true! Whose heart was great enough to do the tasks that must be done? No one else could have survived this trial but the one strong enough to meet it. Herata walked into the vortex of the Hexachon, and walked out again. That alone demands that her words be heard!"

He finished on a ringing note, as he had been trained; the crystals picked it up and carried it echoing around the chamber, a vibrant note of affirmation and strength. *Ah, clever that,* he thought, glad of it, wishing they had such tricks in Lacaon to overawe the obstreperous petty chiefs of the smaller islands.

The galleries murmured in approval, and a smattering of applause began and grew in response to his words. The Five let it run its course. Branek stood back, pleased with his performance. On the floor, Herata pressed her hand to her heart and then opened it toward him: *Thank you.* He nodded; it had only been the truth, after all.

The Patriarch of the White Temple did not respond; a consummate politician, he certainly had no desire to invoke the enmity of the crowd by opposing such a popular performance.

"Well spoken, Lacaon," said Herodian. "We thank you for your insight." Branek bowed slightly to him and the rest of the Five. This could not have worked out more neatly if they had planned it.

"These are grave tidings you bring, Herata of Nine Seas," the High King said, raising his voice to still debate. "Words which may change the course of empire. We, the Five, must take counsel on these things. No such decision can be made lightly. Once we have spoken, our decision will be made known. This council is ended."

Conch shell trumpets blew, echoing around the chamber. The Five stood as one and left the dais, filing out by a door behind the thrones. Herodian paused a moment to speak to Herata. She nodded, then shook her head; Branek wondered what they were saying, but it was hardly his business. The noise in the galleries surged as a thousand separate conversations began.

Branek left the lower gallery and tried to make his way to the floor, to see Herata, but he was absolutely mobbed by well-wishers, by the concerned, and by the merely curious, all asking the same things: what had he seen, what did it mean? Could he tell it again? He inched his way toward the stairs, often carrying on three conversations at once, belatedly wondering if it had been wise to speak so forthrightly.

It was a good twenty minutes before he got to the floor, talking all the while. When he finally did Herata was still there, but she also was surrounded by a mob of courtiers, all engaging her in debate, even more strenuously than they had Branek.

He caught snatches of what she was saying – "Yes, it was the Prince of Waters with whom I spoke at Solstice ... no, the Hexachon said nothing of your drought, I am sorry..." -- a babel of conflicting conversations.

She looked tired. Branek set himself to wade through the throng. He was tall; over the heads of a group of Han merchants he caught her eye. She gave him a somewhat pleading look and started toward him through the crowd. But a man in the white robes of Ilethelme caught her arm, pulling her back. "My adepts tell me there is nothing wrong with the way we work power in the Northern Sister, what is your proof –"

Branek surged through the crowd and forcibly took the man's hand off her arm, forcing him back a step. "That is enough," he said. "The priestess has spoken. If you have any inquiries you may make them to the House of the Salmon -- in writing." With that he put an arm around Herata and drew her out of the circle of courtiers. This time, they fell back before him.

There was another huge crowd at the doors to the hall; he took her to a side exit below the galleries instead. They passed through into a hallway that was relatively quiet.

Herata let out a heavy sigh. "Thank you!" she said, leaning into his side where he had his arm around her. She rubbed her arm where the Ilethelmite had grabbed it.

Instead of releasing her, he tightened his arm around her a little. She felt good in his embrace, so slim and vibrant. "I would have come sooner, but I got the same up in the gallery. Everyone wants to know what happened that day; someone should compose a ballad."

She smiled. "It would save some time." She put a hand on his chest. "Oh, Branek," she said, "You were wonderful! Thank you for speaking up."

"It was no more than the truth, my lady."

Her gaze upon him was searching. "I've wondered how well you understood what transpired that day. Now I see that you do."

He reached up and brushed that errant curl of hair away from her cheek again. Now would be the time to tell her about the words he too had exchanged with the Hexachon. But he couldn't. It would seem --- self-serving somehow. He did not want her to think him self-serving.

"It seemed clear enough to me," he said instead. "They called. You answered. And you have done as they bid."

"I hope it will be enough," she said.

Privately, he wondered if it would be. He remembered that mocking note from Laodice, the dismissive things he had heard from other courtiers since the incident. The empire of Atlantis was so vast, so rich; it was hard to believe it might be in trouble. Had he not seen it himself, he was not sure he would have believed it.

But he said none of that to Herata. It would only discourage her.

He became aware that they were standing very close, almost embracing, in a public place, and stepped back a pace. Her hand lingered on his chest a second, then dropped.

"I thank you again," she said.

"I am at my lady's service," he said, "as always."

She blushed prettily. She was not used to being addressed as a great lady of the court; such flowery speech embarrassed her. But she was worthy of it.

"Let me see you home," he said. "I have a litter waiting in the water garden."

"I would like that," she answered.

So they left by a side entrance and made it back to the Hall of the Salmon unmolested. The thing now was to wait upon the pleasure of the Five Kings.

Chapter Six

Upon hearing word of his performance in Council during Herata's interrogation, Hekau, King of Lacon, called Branek back home. Branek was not sorry to go; the Great City, which once had seemed so glittering and joyous, felt empty to him now with Herata gone. She had returned to Nine Seas, and they had said their goodbyes then.

He knew that feeling was ridiculous, but he felt it nonetheless.

He went to the plaza and contemplated the White Temple before he left. The great pyramid towered above the plaza, dwarfing the people who bustled around its foot. The wind sang and sighed about its corners; the marble gleamed white as sea foam in the noonday sun.

He did not seek admittance, feeling sure he would be rebuffed after what happened the last time. Besides, he was a little afraid to look on the Hexachon again.

But he remembered their words. *Defend her.* Well, he had done that, hadn't he, speaking in her favor in the royal council. What else could a priestess of Atlantis need defending from – what could harm her in the island home?

Still, he left Atlantis and set sail for home with mixed feelings – glad to have seen the Great City, but glad also to escape its overwhelming embrace. Glad to be headed home, but regretting that he would no longer see the Sea Priestess.

Six days later, his galley made port in the harbor of Lacaon. He felt a strange twinge when the island first appeared on the horizon; it looked so much *smaller* than he remembered. Yet it was still beautiful – the white cliffs, the blue roofs of the town thickly clustered along the shore, the palace tall and gleaming on its height. He studied it eagerly as his ship dew closer across the wine-dark sea.

His family came out to welcome him home. He embraced his sister, clasped hands with his father the king on the dock.

"What did you bring me?" Laodice asked him teasingly.

"Han silk, and a singing crystal from Cloud City." He looked at her fondly. Laodice was a woman grown and matriarch of a temple, but she was not above playing the spoiled princess when it suited her. The deep blue silk he had brought her would go well with her blond hair and blue eyes, the same as his. She was older than him, but not by much, and they were of a height. People often assumed they were twins.

Laodice clapped her hands in exaggerated delight. "We wondered if that city would swallow you, little brother. The stories we heard!"

"It's good to be home," Branek said, and it was. The air, the sea; it smelled like home, not the thousand and one unknown scents of the Great City. He had a thirst suddenly for the dry wine of the island, and a craving for his own bed in his own chamber.

"You must report to me of this … incident at the White Temple," Hekau his father demanded. "Your written report I have read, but I want to hear it from your own lips."

"Oh, Father, let him unpack at least!" Laodice said. "You know what a letdown it is, coming home from the Great City. Give him some time to get used to little old Lacaon again."

"It's not a letdown," Branek said. Was it? He could walk the entire width of the island in half a day. The Great City could not be crossed from dawn to dawn. But he knew every nook, every cranny of Lacaon – the beaches, the hills; he had climbed them, plumbed them all since his boyhood. Atlantis would swallow a man from the Inner Sea – even a prince.

"I do wish to tell you," he told the king his father. "Everything. But I need to gather my thoughts."

Hekau smiled. "As you wish, son. It *is* an adjustment, coming from the island home to your home island. How well I remember."

His family walked along with him up the great stone way to the heights of the palace, a switchbacked path of cyclopean stone, built by hand, with vast labor, by his long-forgotten ancestors. Gulls perched on the rocks and screamed at them, or wheeled overhead. Branek contemplated the palace above them with a twinge of love and dismay in his heart. Once it had been the most magnificent place in his world, built of gleaming white stone, and painted with frescoes of powdered lapis, pearl, and malachite. But now, he knew, it was not even as fine as the guest quarters of the Hall of the Salmon in the Great City.

But still, it had its own rustic beauty, and beyond that, it was home. One day it would be his palace in truth; the marble throne in the great hall would be his to sit. The people of the town and the hills would be his to rule. Lacaon was his, and he was Lacaon's. One day soon, he hoped the show it to Herata, as he had promised. Thinking that, he felt unaccountably shy. What would a princess of the Nome think of such a salt-stained little backwater?

"You must tell me of the priestess of Nine Seas," Laodice said, interrupting his thoughts in that uncanny way she had. She had always been sensitive to his moods – their shared blood, or the sight, or both. Much like Herata had become, he realized.

He felt a warmth rise in his face that he prayed was not a blush. "She is like you," he said.

Laodice laughed. "Lucky you, then." She tossed her long hair back challengingly, fixing him with her sapphire gaze.

"No, truly," Branek said, thinking on it. "She is strong in the faith, devoted to her work. Learned, wise. Strong." He remembered her fortitude during her long illness after the Hexachon. Laodice would have suffered in silence too, just the same.

Laodice laughed again. "And beautiful."

He grinned, recognizing her game and refusing to be goaded. "She has the Atlantean looks, the old blood, but her eyes are green. Her mother was from the Misty Isles."

"Hm," Laodice said. The Misty Isles were a Great Node in the ley network, a center of power, as Atlantis was; the *aum* ran high there, the veil between the worlds was thin. The sight was strong in the folk of the Isles, stronger as a whole than in the Inner Sea.

"She bid me ask you about the work you do here in Lacaon," he said. "The earthquake protocols."

Laodice frowned. "You told her about that?"

"Yes." He shrugged. "I didn't know it was a secret, sister."

"It is no secret, Branek," she said. "But some things are our own. Our aunt and her mistress before her, and myself, have worked on those rites for generations. They are workings unknown to the priests of the island home, even after all these years, even though Atlantis also suffers the terror of the shaking earth. They are ours."

Branek felt confused. Laodice had always spoken so proudly of the earthquake bindings before. There was little enough any colony could do with crystal science, that the Sea Kings and their priests had not already done and forgotten, centuries before. "I am sorry, sister. I only meant to do you honor."

"I suppose you did, little brother," Laodice said. She gave him a sidelong look. "Well, what did she say, then, Herata of Nine Seas?"

"She sounded quite interested. As you know, she is much concerned with the uses of *aum* around the world. I told her you would be happy to speak with her."

Laodice sniffed. "Certainly if Nine Seas calls upon us, little White Mare must respond."

They had reached the top of the cliff, their father going ahead of them. His guards opened the carved cedar gates to the palace, and the family walked in under the huge stone lintel, a trilithon, the oldest thing on the island. Branek felt a chill as they passed under its shadow.

"Wait." He caught Laodice's arm, made her stop in the gate. "Is there something you've not told me?" Branek remembered Herata's impassioned speech in the royal Council, her fear when she spoke of the imbalance she found in the web. He barely understood ley science, being *inaum*, and trained for other things besides. He had always trusted his sister and aunt, the adepts of White Mare, with the burden of that knowledge, and never had cause to doubt them – until just now. "The earthquake protocols – are they dangerous?"

"No," Laodice said, laughing. She covered his hand on her arm with her own. "No, no. Well, no more so than any ley work is dangerous. And it can be, you know that – dangerous."

"Herata was very sick," Branek said. "After the Hexachon." He yearned suddenly to tell Laodice of his own experience. But something, some sense of unease, stopped him. He said nothing.

"Our workings are to protect Lacaon, and all the Inner Sea," Laodice said. "It is what White Mare has worked toward for generations. They are powerful, yes. They move much *aum*, and more besides. But it is only for the good. There is nothing to fear."

Not *nothing*, Branek thought. Like fire, like a blade, or any tool, ley tech could be used for both good and ill. But he trusted that Laodice knew her art, and that she followed the rules of the Faith.

"I will write Herata," he said. "She will be relieved."

"I am glad to hear it," Laodice said.

They came into the courtyard, and the royal household came out to welcome its prince home, and in the bustle Branek forgot about Atlantis and Herata for a good long while.

In the Great City, Herata knew, the problem of *aum* consumption was debated at length. Results were inconclusive; the Patriarch of the Poseideion did not agree with her assessment. He said he could find no imbalance in the ley lines.

In the end, nothing was done. All her exhortations were to no avail.

Back at Nine Seas, Herata tried to return to normal. But at night as she dreamed, her senses ranged out along the leys, searching out the weak spots, the gaps, the snarled vortices of overdrawn *aum* that set her teeth on edge, and caused her to wake many mornings with dull throbbing headaches.

And still she could hear the crystals, everywhere around her, singing and humming in the back of her mind, whispering to her at a level just below the threshold of understanding. Watching her. Waiting.

But she didn't know what to do. What could she do, one adept against the entire priesthood of the temples, against the Sea Kings themselves?

She put her temple on the most basic regime, drawing only enough *aum* to meet their own needs and those of the local area, the villagers and fishermen who depended on them. She sent no more *aum* north to the Great City, in spite of angry missives sent by crystal from the Poseideion. They could not command her; she was the Sea Priestess of Atlantis and could administer her own temple as she chose.

She spent many hours working the crystal in her ley-chamber, watching the web as the power ebbed and flowed around the world, moved by natural forces and channeled by Atlantean technology. The city of Ile-thelme continued its profligate orgy of *aum* burning. A missive from her to the city fathers had met only stony silence. Her reputation as a mad seer was preceding her.

The dead area on the Nazca Mountains was growing. She did what she could, routing what earthpower she could cadge from other sources into that region, but it was as a teardrop in a desert. How could she hope to correct what the earth itself could not naturally maintain?

The volcano in the Inner Sea was growing ever more restless. So much *aum* had been drawn from that area for so long, the bed of the sea was sinking, disrupting the delicate balance of forces deep in the earth, creating a tension that must someday be released. Someday soon – a century from now, or tomorrow.

She received a letter from Prince Branek, charmingly scribed on paper in the old-fashioned way. She was surprised at the girlish flush of pleasure she felt as she cracked the wax seal stamped with Branek's sigil, a running horse, the White Mare of Lacaon.

My dearest Lady of Nine Seas, he wrote,

I hope this letter finds you well. My return to Lacaon was uneventful. As of yet, here in Lacaon we have heard no news of decisions made by the High Council regarding aum *distribution. I can only hope that the old adage about "no news" applies here.*

I have spoken with my sister Laodice about your concerns, and she assures me that the ley network is stable in the Inner Sea. Indeed, it is her primary concern as keeper of White Mare Temple. The volcano at Thera is entering a phase of heightened activity, but nothing beyond what our adepts have recorded in generations past. The Inner Sea has always been volatile, as you certainly know. Laodice and her fellow adepts in the region monitor it regularly, and I know she would alert Atlantis if the leys here become strained or aberrant in any way.

I had hoped to bespeak you by crystal. It would be good to hear your voice. But Laodice bids me not to disturb you with routine messages while in the midst of your work, so I resort to these antique measures. I hope this letter gives you a moment of diversion, and confidence that matters are in hand in the Inner Sea.

Your loyal servant,
Branek, Prince of Lacaon

Smiling, Herata ran her fingers over his signature on the thick, creamy paper. The letter sounded just like him. She could almost hear his voice. She missed him, she realized suddenly. His good nature and steadfast friendship has made her time in the Great City so much easier to bear.

There was no one her own age with whom she could speak as an equal at Nine Seas, since she was made Sea Priestess. Everyone was her subordinate. She had not realized the lack, until she had traveled to the Great City and opened her eyes to the larger world.

As for his report on the Inner Sea, that was good news as far as it went, but she had seen. The island of Kythera was not far behind Ile-thelme in its profligate use of *aum*. She had touched the power there and felt the burning of the stressed currents. It was only a matter of time. She wondered if this sister of his, Laodice, was watching as well as he seemed to believe.

Day after day she stood in front of the crystal, watching, sending her thought out along the leys, until she ended each day cold and cramped and light-headed with fatigue, stumbling from the ley-chamber to pick at her supper and fall into bed for another night of restless dream-wracked sleep.

Even Lamike thought she was mad.

At last one morning the old priestess strode into the ley chamber, flanked by two burly young attendants. With a curt word she shut the crystal down, taking it out of the flows. Herata stumbled back from the suddenly cold stone, startled and bewildered.

"You will come out of here or you will be carried." Lamike said with deadly finality.

Looking at the embarrassed young men, reluctantly ready to man-handle her out of the room, Herata had a sudden blinding instant of clarity. She saw herself: haggard, unwashed, crouched over the crystal day and night, like a witch out of some ancient horror tale, raving about visions no one else could see.

"I'll come," she said.

Lamike had sent for a sumptuous luncheon to be spread for them on the terrace overlooking the beach.

"Sit," she commanded her priestess. "Eat!"

Herata sat, glad suddenly for a reprieve from her self-imposed vigil. There was sweet cheese and honeycakes, and fish baked in layer pastry, her favorite. She set to with genuine pleasure. Amalthea appeared and attended her silently, pouring her a mixture of sweet wine and juice.

Lamike watched her like a cat.

"You are trying to fatten me up," Herata said at last.

"And mustn't I?" the older priestess cried. "You are trying to kill yourself!"

"I'm not," Herata said, reaching for the dish of olive paste. "Truly, I'm not."

"Well, what would you call it?" Lamike said. "No food, little sleep, staying in crystal until your heart almost stops? You have hardly even recovered from last time!"

She leaned forward over the table. "Whatever you think you are trying to accomplish, you won't do it by dying."

Herata grew annoyed. "Well, what would you have me do? Nothing? Pretend it never happened?"

"You have done what you can. You must leave it to other hands now."

"Whose hands -- the Father of Stones? The Poseideion? What will they do? Nothing! They are fools."

"I would not say the King your father is a fool," Lamike said. "Trust in him."

Herata shook her head. "He thinks I am mad. They all do!"

"He does not think that. But he is worried for you. As are we all."

"I'm fine!" But as she picked up her knife, the blade shrieked and rattled raggedly across the plate. They both stared at her shaking hand, which trembled as with a palsy. Herata hurriedly put down the knife.

"He is right to be worried," Lamike said quietly.

Herata wearily sat back in her chair, acknowledging defeat.

"I have to do something," she said, like one lost. "I don't know what else to do."

"Of course," Lamike said, more gently. "But consider this: if you hope to be ready when the crisis comes, you must save your strength. You cannot hope to accomplish your goals if you are sick and unable to channel."

"But they said I could stop it," Herata murmured.

"Not by ruining yourself," Lamike said.

Herata put her face in her hands, weary and frustrated. What wicked god had sent her a vision no one believed?

"And consider this also," Lamike went on. "You cannot do this alone. If you hope to succeed, you need allies. Your father. Others. The young prince, for example."

"Branek?" Herata mused.

"He is a favorite of the Council. And there are so few left of the true old blood. Branek may be Sea King one day."

"What are you saying?" Herata asked.

Lamike raised a hand. "Only that he may speak for you in Council, if you can win his confidence."

She produced a scroll, handed it over. "The young prince has sent word. He is coming here, to see you. Tomorrow."

Herata could not entirely suppress a smile as she scanned the message. Suddenly she longed to see him. It had been a hard time these past weeks.

"Branek believes me," she said.

Lamike shook her head. "I am not so sure, my lady. He believes *in* you. But that is more a personal thing. He has not accepted the truth of the darkening. Not yet."

Herata frowned. "Why say you?" she said.

"He is from the Inner Sea," Lamike said. "The colonies there are old and proud. They would see themselves as a second Atlantis. They study hard to advance crystal science; they would be hard pressed to give it up. They would take many risks to aggrandize themselves in the eyes of the Sea Kings."

"Even their own destruction?" Herata asked.

"Perhaps even that."

"I can't believe that," Herata said, putting the letter from Branek on the table.

"Ask him," Lamike said. "He will tell you true. And then you must make him see.

"But to do that," Lamike continued, "you yourself must present a pleasing appearance. He is coming to see you, after all. Not a presentation on *aum* usage."

She clapped her hands; servants appeared and began to clear the table. Amalthea produced a soft, loose robe for her mistress.

"To the baths with you!" Lamike said. "Henna your hair and paint your eyes with malachite. Show the prince of Lacaon a vision such as he has never seen. And then you may speak of other, darker visions."

Laughing, Herata did as she was bid. Her heart lightened at the thought of a visit from her friend.

The Prince of Lacaon arrived in splendor early the next day, in a brightly painted trireme from his native islands. He brought many gifts to the temple: costly myrrh and spikenard resin from Asia; wine from the rugged lands north of the Inner Sea; silk cloth from the lands of the Han, to decorate the icons.

Herata received him on the water steps, decked out in full priestly regalia, hair braided with wires of oricalch and ribbons of cloth-of-gold, with a headdress and pectoral of tiny crystals, alive with humming *aum.* The women had scraped and oiled her skin smooth, plucked her eyebrows into shape and stained her lips red as pomegranates. Henna designs anointed the palms of her hands and the soles of her feet, and scents of Kheftiu graced her neck and wrists.

Branek bowed deeply at the foot of the stairs. He looked quite overwhelmed. "You do me too much honor, my lady."

He was not so regally dressed, attired for traveling in a plain linen kilt, with his hair braided back. But even so, Herata' breath caught at the sight of him. Gods below, she had almost forgotten how beautiful he was, golden and bronzed, tawny and lithe as a great cat of the veldt, eyes as blue as glacial ice.

Steadying herself, Herata smiled, reaching out and taking his hands in welcome. "It is you who honor us, my prince, with your presence. Be welcome in the temple of the Nine Seas."

They kissed chastely in the manner of long acquaintants, on the cheek. Herata breathed in the spicy, sun-warmed scent of him, and she felt a strange loosening within her chest, as if her heart was opening. She took a deep breath, slowing her pulse with her inner awareness, trying to remain calm.

"Allow me to make obeisance in this holy place," Branek asked formally. But it was her eyes into which he looked, not at the temple.

She took his arm to walk him into the sanctuary. "Of course."

Herata attended him herself as he visited the sanctuary and made burnt offerings to the Sealord. He prayed in the language of his people as the grains and blossoms withered in the flame of the offering bowl.

"Perhaps I am guilty of hubris," Branek said as they left the sanctum. "For my prayers have already been answered."

"What prayers?" Herata asked. Had he seen something of the dangers lying ahead?

"Why, to see you, my lady," he said.

Herata smiled. "Are you a prince or a poet?"

"Surely you must know, my lady, that every good prince is also a poet," he said. "He must plumb the hearts of men with understanding and sway their minds with pretty speeches."

"I wish I could do that," Herata said, remembering her fruitless appearance before the Council.

"If we were allied, my lady, then I could speak for you," the prince said.

Herata looked at him sharply. What sort of alliance was he proposing?

His eyes on her were intent. Flustered, she looked away. So he had meant it, what he asked her, before her Council audience. She had enjoyed their association so far, enjoyed it far more than she would have imagined only a few weeks hence. But to make it more, to leave the temple and go to Lacaon, into his house – she could not. She had work to do here.

"Can you not speak for me now?" she asked.

Some of the light went out of his eyes. "Of course, but only as a friend. Not with authority."

"Then it is as a friend you must speak. A friend of Nine Seas Temple."

"Of course," he said courteously, but the moment was gone.

Herata was not making much use of Lamike's plan, she realized.

"Let me show you the gardens," she said brightly, trying to lighten the mood.

"As you wish," Prince Branek said.

He relaxed as they wandered the winding paths, under flowering trees carefully cultivated and brought from all parts of the empire. Herata chatted lightly, pointing out rare specimens.

"And this moonflower was brought from Colchis."

"My mother was from Colchis," Branek said, touching one of the pale, white flowers.

"It is said to be a cutting from the tree under which Denatha sheltered while waiting for her lover Pyndaros, and under which they were buried after the tragedy."

It was one of the most romantic and tragic stories in all Atlantean literature. As she spoke of this tale of doomed, foredestined love, their eyes met, and their mysterious attraction sparked between them, a current of feeling deeper and older even than *aum* itself. Herata felt herself move, almost flow toward him, and he took her in his arms under the spreading tree of legend.

Herata thrilled to the feel of his body pressed against hers, the strength in his thighs and chest, cleaving to her own.

"You could have a thousand women," she said.

"But it is you I want." His lips traced the curve of her neck. His hands caressed her, down the curve of her waist, cupping her buttocks, lifting her into him. The scent of the moonflowers and the spice of his hair commingled in her senses, dizzying her.

She had never been touched in this way before. She had gone to the temple when only a child; the love of a man had not been part of her life, until now.

"Wait," she said.

But he did not wait, his lips finding hers with increasing urgency, his hands roaming more freely. Her crystal headdress slipped askew.

For a timeless moment she gave herself up to his kisses, her body hungering for sensations she had never known, straining against him in a trembling desire for a greater union. Her fleeting mind considered places in the garden, secret bowers with mossy banks –

She pushed him away. "Wait! Stop!"

For a split second he looked angry, a prince who had the world at his feet, thwarted in his desire. Then it was gone and he looked truly abashed.

"Forgive me, Herata. I forget myself." He stepped back, away from her, and despite her protests Herata had to clasp her hands together to keep from reaching out to him.

"It is not that," Herata began.

"No, you are right." He laughed shakily. "This is happening too fast."

"Is it?" Honestly, she had no idea. But she knew that when she saw him, she – wanted him, like a woman wants a man.

"Yes," he said. "Certainly it is. But, since the Poseideion … I cannot stop thinking about you."

"No one could go through what we did there and remain unchanged," Herata said.

"Do you say it?" He seemed intensely relieved. "I thought it was only me."

"It is not." She felt it too, an almost magnetic pull. He was so strong and beautiful, and kind and funny -- and he had risked his life to save her. She remembered suddenly, telling him to attend her in the White Temple. She would have need of him, she had seen it with the force of vision. This experience of power they had shared bound them together. She could not deny it.

"But there are things you must understand," she went on, "if we are to continue in this vein." In spite of herself she touched his cheek.

He turned his head; his lips brushed her hand. "What things?"

How to begin? "I cannot leave the temple now. As much as I might wish to."

"Do you wish it?" he asked huskily.

She moved her hand down to his chest, stroking lingeringly. "Perhaps, Branek. But I *cannot*. Not now. My work here is just beginning."

His hand brushed the line of her jaw; it seemed to leave a tingling in its wake. Her body cried out for him, but she kept her silence on it firmly.

"There is a temple in Lacaon," he said.

She smiled, trying to lighten the mood. "And displace your sister?

That would hardly be a kind gesture from a newcomer to your house."

"You outrank her," Branek said. "The temple would be yours if you wish it."

"This temple is mine," she said. "And here I stay."

The light went out of his eyes. "Then perhaps I should go. Elsewise this may be … too painful."

"No!" Herata said. "Please, stay. It's been so difficult. I've felt so alone." She stretched out her hand to him. "Stay with me for a while. Whatever comes, I promise I will always be a true friend to you."

After a moment he took her hand. He pulled her close and dropped another searching kiss on her mouth, as if setting the seal on it.

"I will be waiting," he said.

Hand in hand, they continued their walk though the garden.

Chapter Seven

Prince Branek stayed at Nine Seas for some days. Herata showed him the workings of the temple, the daily rhythms of prayer and work that ordered the life of the sanctuary. He joined the dedicants in their devotions and their work, net-fishing, tending the small orchard on temple land, cleaning and attending the sanctuary. The icons were dressed in the gift of silk which he had brought.

He was a man, Herata saw, unafraid of hard work. Nothing like the image of an eastern lord, lounging on a divan and serviced by slaves, his hands touching nothing harsher than silk and vellum.

He told her, "I worked harder than this in Lacaon as a boy! Spear-fishing, pressing olives, herding goats on the mountain. My island is lovely but not large. We provide for most of our needs ourselves."

They were walking on the beach at sunset, after a day counting jars of oil and beer sent by colonies as tribute to the temple. Herata smiled, remembering the mural in his house. "I would like to see your island, some day."

"Only say the word, my lady, and you shall. My ship can take us there straightaway." He looked at her with hope, and something more, a hint perhaps of triumph?

But she only smiled silently, and would not say.

They spent hours in the evenings beneath the moonflower tree, or down the beach on a hidden cove, a blanket spread on the cool sand, as Branek educated her in sensations previously unguessed at in her life of monkish devotion. She had never imagined that such feelings could ever come outside of the ecstasy of the ley lines. She felt that she went through her days with the scent of him on her, the feel of him under her hands tingling in her palms all day, and she could not wait till nightfall, when they could be alone. In the dark of night she dreamed new dreams, of him and only him, and of the culmination which awaited them.

But her maidenhead remained intact. She began to feel a little foolish that she did not give herself to him fully. She was a grown woman after all, not a trembling child bride from the barbarian lands. And he was a noble man, a prince, who in his life had his pick of women, not accustomed to being put off. But it was new to her, she was not yet ready. She knew that the energetic bond between a man and woman who had been true lovers was intense. She feared that if she gave him her virginity, she could not resist his pleas to come to Lacaon. She feared, also, that it might interfere with her work, sap the energy she needed to travel the leys and maintain the balance.

In the meantime he was patient, and a delighted teacher of the arts of love.

This night they were on the beach, hidden from prying eyes by a rocky headland, bathed in the light of the rising moon, just off the full. The moonlight seemed to stir the tides in her blood, and she reached for him with a new urgency, trembling with desire and longing.

When they were satisfied, they lay nestled together in the sand, shivering a little in the ocean wind, sticky with a sheen of sweat and other fluids.

"What a shame to spend my seed so, that could be giving you sons," Branek purred.

"I don't want any sons," Herata murmured, eyes half-closed.

He raised himself on one elbow to look at her. "But if you become my Queen, you will have them. Many sons, sons of Atlantis, with my strength and your wisdom. Perhaps it is our sons that will save the empire, Herata, if it needs saving."

"You really mean it, don't you?" Herata asked. "You want me to marry you."

"Yes, I really mean it, and I will bring whatever gifts and make whatever pledges you and your father require, when we return to the Great City. If I did not mean it, I would not say it. The rulership of my home is not something I take lightly."

A whirl of confused thoughts tumbled through her mind. Before meeting Branek, she had never even considered taking a husband; she had never doubted her life would be spent in the temples. But oh, it was sweet to be with a man, sweeter than the poets could sing. And the task the Hexachon had laid upon her was too large for one person.

"You said this was happening too fast," she said, stalling.

"Yes," he said. "Certainly. Far too fast. But so does the dawn, or the growth of a child, or the spring, or anything worth living for."

At a loss for words, she answered him with a kiss, pulling his head down to hers, and they kissed in the sand while his nimble fingers satisfied her again and again, until she begged for mercy.

"If you came to Lacaon," he whispered, "we could do this every night

– and more besides. I have not yet begun to show you what lies between a man and his wife."

"We're doing it now," Herata said, breathlessly.

He stroked the curve of her hip. "I cannot stay here forever. I must return to the Great City, and thence to Lacaon. I too have work to do."

"So soon?" she cried in dismay. She took his face in her hands. "Now that we are … lovers, will you leave me so soon?"

"It has been a quarter moon."

She lay back in the sand, defeated. Of course he could not stay. She had known that all along. Never did she think a week could go so fast.

"I will visit you in the Great City, whenever I can."

He took her into his arms, cradling her against his chest. "And Lacaon?"

She hesitated the tiniest fraction. "When I can."

"There is a temple in Lacaon, Herata," he said, as he had said before.

"My work is here," she answered, as she had answered before.

"Yes. In these last days, I have seen your work." He rolled over to look her in the eye, suddenly serious. "From what I have seen, there is nothing you do here at Nine Seas that you could not do at Lacaon."

She frowned, looking up at him. "What are you saying?"

"I am saying that is no longer an answer, Herata. I am saying, there are crystals at Lacaon, there are adepts enough at Lacaon, the rites are the same. You could continue your crusade, or whatever it is, in my home as well as you can here."

She pushed away from him a little and sat up, suddenly cold in the sand.

"Is that an ultimatum?" she asked.

"No!" he said. "I am just asking you to think about it. Come to Lacaon, visit the island and my temple. You will see that your place is at my side, and your life will not be diminished in any way. You will be giving nothing up."

"It is not my life that is at stake," Herata said, frustrated. "It is all our lives. And they said I can stop it -- they said only I can stop it. I have to find a way!"

"Were we man and wife we could speak with a unified voice in Council," Branek said. "My father would support us as well; he is accorded much respect among the lesser kings."

"The danger is here," Herata insisted. "Here, Atlantis! Here I must stay."

"But I cannot govern from Atlantis," Branek said. "I must go home to Lacaon; my people need me there. One day I will be king. I must have a queen."

"Why are you doing this?" Herata asked miserably. Her feelings of joy and drunken satiety had evaporated in the ocean breeze.

"Why?" He grasped her wrist suddenly, pulled her down across his broad chest. In the moonlight his eyes bored into her own. "Why? Because I must have a queen to rule my people and continue my line, and I would not have that queen be anyone but you. Don't make me ask you again. Leave me some dignity, I beg you."

"You're relentless!" She laid her head on his chest. "Oh, I don't know what to think."

He stroked her hair. "At least I have confused you. Divide and conquer."

And then there was silence again between them for a time, punctuated only by gasps and murmurs.

"Do you know what I think?" Branek said at last when it was done and they lay spent once more. "I think I need a bath. This sand is everywhere."

They cleansed themselves with a swim in the moonlit ocean, then walked quietly homeward for a late supper and sleep.

The next day Herata rose early and broke her fast alone. She wanted to spend some time monitoring the leys first thing, so she could spend time later with Branek.

In the ley chamber, she had set up a rack of smallish recording crystals, into which she had been inputting records of any events she encountered while ley-walking that were related to the imbalances. Things such as earthquakes, poison tides, strange light phenomena. In Olmec lands a low persistent buzzing noise had come out of the earth in one region, bad enough to drive the people from their homes. Herata had not felt it firsthand; no one could pass through the leys there, the disturbance was too great. A colleague had sent her a recording of the hum made at a distance. To listen to it made one feel as if one's teeth were shaking loose in their sockets.

She was in a state of light trance, hands on the central crystal, feeling for any disturbances rippling through the global net, when a chime sounded outside the room: the signal that something important had happened and she must disengage.

She took her hands off the crystal, returning to the here and now. "Enter!"

Amalthea tiptoed in. "It is the Prince, my lady. He must speak with you."

"Send him in." It must be urgent; Branek never disturbed her while in the ley chamber.

Branek came striding through the door. As he crossed the threshold into the sacred space, a sudden blinding pain assaulted Herata's senses. She stumbled back from the crystal, clutching her head. "Aahh!" It was if an axe had split it.

"What is it?" Branek cried, rushing toward her. Through tear-blinded eyes she saw him approach, held up a hand. "No! Stay back!"

He jumped back as if burned. "What is the matter?"

"Your weapon," Herata gasped. "It's disrupting ... the field." A trickle of blood crept from her nostril.

Branek was dressed for traveling. He was wearing a shortsword on a tooled belt; a good one, made of steel, not bronze.

"Gods!" He unbuckled his swordbelt, and slung it wholesale out the door. As soon as the metal passed the shielded frame of the door, the pain diminished. Herata sat gave a sigh of relief. "Thank you!"

Branek looked almost as white as she felt. "I didn't know! My sister doesn't like metal in her sanctuary either, but *that* –"

Herata shook her head. The pain was gone now. "It's alright. You couldn't know. Things have been different for me since ... since the Poseideion."

Branek wiped the blood from her nose with the hem of his cloak. "I thought you were going to have another fit."

"I feel them, all the time now," Herata explained. "The crystals. They are always with me ... watching me."

"The Hexachon?" he asked in a kind of wondering dread.

Herata glanced at her own crystal, glimmering faintly in its socket. "All the crystals. Wherever I go. All the time."

Branek looked around the ley-chamber, at the great circuit crystal in its nest, at the memory crystals in their racks, the crystal lights on the walls. "How terrible!"

"It is necessary," Herata said. "I need to know, to feel ... no, I can't explain. But it will be needed, before the crisis."

He put an arm around her, holding her close against his side. "I did not know."

Herata rested her head against his shoulder. "What were you going to tell me?"

He looked down at her, troubled. "It is nothing. Should I call for Meilikki?"

"No, I'll be alright. What was it?"

He shook his head. "I have been summoned back to Poseidonis. But I don't think I should leave you now."

"It was a passing thing," Herata insisted. "I am fine. Why were you summoned?"

"There is an issue before the council; my father wants me there, to represent Lacaon in the debates. A new temple site is being considered for the ley lines. He wants me to speak for the Inner Sea."

"No, no!" Herata pushed away from him. "That is a very bad idea."

"Why?"

"The Inner Sea is already strained enough! A new power tap there could be disastrous." A cold stab of terror hit her. "That could be the final straw!"

"Perhaps you should speak to my father."

"I will! Is he in the Great City?"

"No, he is at home. At Lacaon." He looked down at her. "Why don't you come there with me, speak to him? And visit my home? Take a rest. Leave this place." He looked around the ley chamber as if it were a prison.

"You think I'm mad," Herata chided.

"No," Branek said. "But I am concerned for you. Meilikki tells me you spend all your time in here, in the leys. You say the crystals are watching you. You need to take a step back, Herata. This ... this condition of yours, could consume you."

"Meilikki said that?" Herata asked, annoyed. Everyone thought she was unhinged! Why couldn't they *see*?

"If I could just show you," Herata said. "Show you the danger to the Inner Sea, you would see. You would know." She looked at him, her eyes lighting with a sudden idea. "Let me show you!"

He looked very dubious. "How?"

She nodded at the recording crystals on their racks. "By crystal."

"No," Branek said, shaking his head. "I am no adept."

"It's alright," Herata said. "These crystals are static recordings. They won't hurt you, if I am with you."

"I don't think so!" Branek said. He laughed uneasily. "You make them sound like wild beasts!"

"No," Herata said, intent now on showing him. "It will be fine. Come!"

"My sister told me never to touch a crystal, it could be deadly."

"And it could be, if you were alone. But I'll protect you. Or are you afraid?" she taunted him.

That got his blood up, as she had guessed it would. "All right then, damn it. Show me!"

"Here ... like this." She placed his hands on a record crystal, then slipped her own underneath them. "Nothing will happen while I am here with you," she reassured him. "Close your eyes."

With a brush of her own energy she woke the crystal up; it began to hum and glow under their joined hands. Branek flinched. "Easy, easy," she murmured, steadying him. The uninitiated's fear of the *aum* stones could be deep indeed, and with good reason. Herata made sure that any flow to Branek from this crystal was mediated through her. A crystal could burn out the nervous system of an untrained user, leave them blind or paralyzed or worse. This stone was hardly that powerful, but she would take no chances.

"Now, she said, "watch." And she called up the *eidolon* which she had stored in the crystal.

A wave of light surged out of the crystal, engulfing them. The light swirled, brightened, and then suddenly it was as if they were *inside* the crystal, the *eidolon* surrounding them, real as day.

They were in a small village in the Misty Isles, somewhere on the foggy plains of the midlands. Rolling countryside surrounded them in all directions, where there had been the temple walls only a moment before. Sheep grazed and the tang of woodsmoke came from the small cluster of huts that was the village, some distance away on the heath.

Beside her Branek stood blank-eyed and stiff with surprise.

"Fire!" he said. "I can smell it."

"It is only a recording," Herata reassured him. "But watch."

The recording progressed, the sun rising and falling overhead as days cycled by in moments.

The disturbances started innocently enough, with a few flickering lights on the heath on certain nights, when the moon was full or dark. Nothing of account, the will-o-the-wisp, a minor mystery. A story to spook children while they were safe in their beds.

But the lights got worse, bigger, night after night, huge glowing plasmatic blobs of sickly green and purple light, writhing and shivering like live things in the air above the nighttime fields.

"Hold," Herata said, and the recording slowed. Before them the strange lights bobbed and twisted soundlessly in the air above the heath, glowing eerily in the light of the gibbous moon. A sharp chemical smell filled the air, like lightning during a storm.

"What is it?" Branek whispered, caught up in the darkness and silence of the image.

"I am not sure. I think the air molecules are being excited by the ley underground. The *aum* is coursing too fast. But that is only a guess."

The recording continued.

Next, the noises began. First only with the phases of the moon, then every night, then all day, every day – a low subsonic rumble that made the guts churn and the bones ache, overlaid by a high-pitched shrilling that crawled on the skin like vermin.

"Hold!" Herata cried. The recording slowed and Branek grunted as the full sonic assault of the hum touched him.

"The ley is overstressed," Herata said. "When the earthblood is unbalanced, nothing else can survive."

"Let it go!" Branek said, grimacing from the pain of the unholy noise.

Herata let the *eidolon* spool on. Cattle ran mad. Wildlife fled the area. At last, the villagers left, driven away by the apparitions. Their chief could find no place to settle them. They wandered the countryside like beggars, centuries of history and tradition destroyed inside half a year.

"Look," Herata said, pointing down. Beneath their feet, the earth seemed to grow transparent, rock and soil fading and growing thin. Deep in the earth, the channel for the earthpower pulsed and throbbed, passing energy from north to south at a tremendous rate. It glowed a sullen crimson like the heart of an angry forge, vomiting forth *aum* at a spectacular volume.

This was a simulation, of course; you could not see *aum* with the eyes of the body. But Herata had made it so, hoping that when people gazed on the *eidolon*, they would see with their eyes what was impossible to explain in mere words.

The air crackled around them; the hair on their arms raised up from the power of the earthblood flowing under their feet.

Herata pointed, southwest across the fields of the misty midlands. "This ley crosses the ocean to Atlantis. It feeds the Poseideion itself."

The simulation continued. The lights generated by the disturbance blighted the grass. Trees dropped their leaves, starved of the *aum* they needed to live. The earth began to tremble from the strain of carrying so much power. The sun and moon cycled hectically above.

"Back!" Herata cried, and the recording zoomed out, away from the village to the edge of the plains, the ground seeming to unspool beneath them. From a distance they viewed the unhappy scene.

The ground began to shake under their feet – at first just a light trembling. Then harder, more, a genuine temblor, hard enough to make them clutch each other to stand upright. The earth bucked and heaved, protesting at the swollen power shuddering through it. With a tremendous, deafening roar, a gaping hole opened up in the middle of the plains, torn open by the violence of the *aum* stream, like a mouth shouting in protest. Unchanneled *aum* burst out of the hole, freed from its artificial constraints, a burning geyser howling skyward, lighting the sky and the ground for leagues around like the flames of a charnel fire. The village – what was left of it – was consumed, the rude huts and stone walls alike flashing into vapor in an instant. Had Branek and Herata really been standing there, they too would have disappeared in the ravening flash.

Branek covered his eyes, but Herata stood unmoved. She had watched this scene play out many times before, studied it. This *eidolon* served to concentrate her attention. She watched it often.

The burning geyser of unfettered *aum* towered skyward, scorching the clouds. A bitter rain began to fall. Herata let the *eidolon* run forward, and at last the column of flame sank and died, to become a burning, sullen glow in the glassy crater, a hellmouth in the middle of placid countryside.

And to this day the hole remained, a sucking wound in the body of the earth. Only with great effort and constant vigilance were the adepts of the Misty Isles able to reroute their leys to compensate for the ruined one. And still Atlantis demanded more power from the Isles, more energy, more life: an ever-gaping maw, always hungry, never satisfied.

The recording ended. With an eyeblink they were back, safe in the confines of Nine Seas temple.

"Mother of waters!" Branek jumped back from the crystal, shaking his hands as if they had been burned.

"You see," Herata said.

He shook his head, pulling loose hair back from his forehead. He breathed heavily; he was sweating as if he had stood before that fire in fact and not just in image. An *eidolon* was a powerful experience.

"That was real?" he asked.

"As real as this room you are standing in now," Herata said. "That was three months ago. The fire burns still."

"A tragedy," he said. "But surely, a singular one. A freak accident."

"I have many such recordings," Herata said.

"But are you sure – ?"

She interrupted him, burning with the need for him to hear, to understand. "The fires in the earth burn hot in the Inner Sea," she said. "You know that; they always have. Imagine what would happen if a hole like that opened up in Lacaon."

He shook his head; it was too terrible to contemplate.

"Or not even Lacaon," she pressed him, "somewhere else. Damonos, Kythera. The tidal wave would scour the islands clean as picked bones!"

"You really think -- ?"

"Ask your sister," Herata said. "Ask her what a new temple would mean to the Inner Sea."

Branek threw up his hands in surrender. "All right! I will ask her! And I will speak to my father."

"And to the Council?"

"Yes, yes! If you wish it." He shook his head. "No wonder you are making yourself sick."

At that moment Meilikki the healer bustled into the ley chamber.

"What is going on here? We heard screams!"

"Forgive, wise one," Branek said contritely. "I brought iron into the sanctuary."

Meilikki shrewdly studied Herata's still-pale face, Branek's disheveled appearance. "Iron? Then that is quite enough for you today, my lady."

She hustled them both out of the room. Herata was ordered to eat something. Branek made his preparations to leave for the Great City.

When he was ready, Herata walked with him to the water steps to see him off.

He bent to kiss her. His long hair, unbound from its tail, cascaded down around her face; she breathed in the warm spicy scent of it, of him.

"Be safe," he said to her. "Do not lose yourself in the leys, Herata; remember I am waiting for you."

"Tell them," Herata said. "Tell the Council what you saw."

He planted a gentle, almost fatherly kiss on her forehead. "As my lady wishes, I will."

Then he was gone. Herata watched his ship out of sight around the headland, hoping that she could trust him, that he would do what he said.

Chapter Eight

Herata tried to return to the life that she had known. It had only been seven days which Branek spent with her at Nine Seas temple. Seven days, and seven nights of passion and ecstasy under the stars. But as she went around her duties at the temple, she found herself wracked with a loneliness she had previously never imagined. Perhaps she should go to Lacaon after all. Perhaps she had been too hasty, to refuse. Such thoughts tormented her as she lay in her bed alone at night. But of course she could not leave Atlantis.

They heard little news out of the Great City. She wrote to her father, King Herodian, demanding information. He sent back a brief note that all options were being considered, including the option of opening no junction at all. Somehow she could tell from the phrasing that he was only saying this to placate her. Furiously she burned the letter in a lamp, and stamped the embers out on the floor.

Then she went out and sat on a headland of the beach for a long, long time. Maybe she was mad after all.

She sought certainty in the leys. Where they were good, where the power ran cleanly and in balance, she found ecstasy, a joy and pleasure as piercing and real as what she felt in her prince's arms.

And where they were not good, where the earthpower was overdrawn and the channels were dry and feeble, or where the far-flung outposts of the Sea Kings burned the land with hoarded flows of stolen power, she saw the truth of her vision. Darkness here, a sickly orgy of light some-place else, it was all connected.

And it was growing worse. Day by day, as the cities of the Atlantean empire burned *aum* night and day, the darkness was spreading.

Many times Herata circled the world in spirit, searching, always searching. Her collection of memory crystals grew.

She engaged in acts of small sabotage, routing trickles of power away from the great cities, out into the countryside, to places where it was needed. Reversing the flows in temples all over the world when no one was looking, sending the power back out into the net, where it would spread naturally, revivifying that which it touched.

She received many angry messages by crystal. She ignored them.

Inevitably, this led to consequences.

A week after Branek left she was traveling the web, monitoring the energy. She passed up the Trident, through Poseidonis, and onto the ley known as the Spear, which shot straight and true, northeast to the Misty Isles.

Here the leys split into many smaller channels, and merged again, a dense network of energy. The Misty Isles were a Great Node of the ley network, like Atlantis, a center of the energy body of the earth herself. It was one of the first places Atlantis had colonized during the Golden Age, millennia ago. There were many temples here and old, established colonies; *aum* usage was high.

She cruised along, slipping from ley to ley, temple to temple. She came to the Isle of Glass, the central temple of the Misty Isles, built over a spring at the foot of a great tor, a sacred mound of prehistoric times. It was a beautiful sanctuary, with a peaceful vibration, but as it was a Great Node she felt she could not be too careful, and visited often.

As she glided into the central ley-chamber, she suddenly felt herself grabbed by a harness of power, and delayed. Her mental cry of surprise vibrated down the Spear. She thrashed, trying to free herself, but before she knew it her consciousness was shunted off-ley and into a vacant crystal. It was a strange sensation; as if she had been tossed into a tiny room, tumbling across the floor, even through her body rested in trance hundreds of miles away. Behind her she felt a snap, as the crystal was removed from the flows. She was trapped.

So finally I catch you, someone said into the silence of the vacant crystal.

Release me at once! she demanded, climbing on her dignity as Sea Priestess of Atlantis. *What is the meaning of this?* She resisted the urge to batter around inside the crystal like a fly trapped in a jar; it would only weaken her, and besides, it was undignified.

Who are you? the strange adept demanded. For whoever it was, was a very gifted adept, to catch and pin her like a butterfly. Herata herself would have hesitated to try it.

There was no use in lying. She was his captive. It was a man, she could feel it now. Anyone skilled enough to do this could ream the truth out of her mind if he wished, and that would weaken her too. *I am Herata of Nine Seas.*

A-hah, the mad seeress of Atlantis! I suspected as much.

And who are you? Herata asked in return.

I am Taran, Keeper of the Isle of Glass. This is my Temple you have violated so willfully.

I am only passing through.

Twice a week for the last few moons? I think not. Why are you spying on us?

I am not spying, Herata said, wounded. *I am* observing.

An image resolved inside the crystal, a stone-pillared hall with a bubbling spring of water in its center, and high, arched windows filled with misty light. The sanctum of the Isle. Herata found herself possessed of her body again. Before her stood a middle-aged man with thick black hair shot with gray, and calm gray eyes. He wore a simple woolen robe and a fillet of silver in his hair.

Herata cleared her illusory throat. "Taran, I take it," she said. "An excellent simulation."

He inclined his head. "My Lady of Nine Seas. May I ask what you have observed?"

She thought a moment. It would be wise to be careful. Although he was a colonial, this man had received every initiation and passed every test that she had – and more, for he had walked the leys far longer than she. And more, he was the Keeper of a Great Node, so if he chose to make an issue of it, he could be said to outrank her. Not a good enemy to make.

"I have been looking for imbalances in the web," she said honestly.

"Here, at the Isle of Glass?" He sounded affronted.

"Forgive me," she said. "The Misty Isles are a Great Node. Trouble here could affect the whole world."

"Yes, I am quite aware of that, my lady," he said. "As it is my particular charge. If you were concerned, why did you not simply ask me?"

She sighed. It sounded like such a reasonable question.

"If you *had* asked me," Taran said, "I would have told you, look to Ilethelme. That also is a Great Node, and a profligate one."

"Ilethelme!" Herata said. "Yes! It is terrible – have you been there? I have warned them."

Taran shook his head. "I have no need to go there, that city draws straight from us, across the Ocean of Storms and the Northern Sister. I have had to step down the flows in that direction. Their thirst is boundless, it seems."

"It is a fire that will not be quenched." On this they were agreed. Now was the time to press her advantage. She could not stay trapped in this crystal for much longer; it would weaken her spirit's link with her body. Too long, and that link could break for good. "You must have heard about my … experience in the White Temple."

"All have heard," he said.

"So you understand what I am searching for. What I am trying to prevent."

He shrugged. "Ilethelme is unfortunate. But it is just one city." So he said, but his eyes were flat. Was he testing her?

"No. There are many more."

"What have you seen?" Taran asked. A furrow appeared between his brows; he was concerned too.

Truth, Herata thought. Only perfect truth could convince him of the rightness of her cause.

She stretched out her thoughts to him, opening her mind. A mad, risky thing with a stranger, but necessary now.

She felt his presence in her mind – age, calm, his thoughts cool and ordered like beads on an abacus. Amusement at her, but underlying it, a genuine concern.

See what I saw, she said, and she showed him – Ilethelme, Kythera, her possession by the Hexachon, all of it. Pain, terror, joy, she held nothing back.

I do see, he said, when it was done. It had taken only a moment, but Herata felt drained as if she had spent all day in the leys.

Then you'll help me?

How can I not? You speak for the Earth our Mother. It is true. He meant it wholeheartedly, she could feel it.

"Thank you!" Herata said, retreating into herself. At last another adept who believed her!

"What must I do?" Taran asked.

"Continue to squeeze Ilethelme," she said. "And the White Temple, too. They must be made to see the consequences of their actions. And speak to other temples, to the other Great Nodes. They will listen to you."

"It shall be as you say, my lady."

A wave of weariness washed over her. "I cannot stay in this crystal much longer," she said.

Of course. The simulation of the temple disappeared, along with Taran's image. There was a click, and she could feel that the crystal had been placed back into the flows. She was free to leave.

Thank you, Herata said again, mind to mind in the ley.

Call upon me when you have need, Herata of Nine Seas. Farewell.

In the days to come, Taran of the Isle of Glass proved himself to be a true friend to her, until the very end, and after.

Her meeting with Taran was one bright spot in many days of discouragement and increasing disarray. Sometimes she was surprised she had not been imprisoned yet, that the Five Kings had not sent armed men to drag her away from her crystal and throw her into some secret dungeon under the Great City. It was, she realized, because people were afraid of her. After all, the Six had spoken to her, as they had not in living memory. She had walked into the vortex of the Hexachon and survived.

Branek sent her a message by crystal, with a more candid account of the Council debates. Few actually believed in her vision, but it had thrown the Council into chaos nonetheless. Every little king and ambitious priest used the specter of her vision to advance his own agenda.

That disgusted her. These men were princes, wise men. Did they not understand their own teachings? Couldn't they see?

The damage she reported was explained away as bad management by the keepers of local temples and nexuses. Governors and elders were sometimes replaced. And still they did not touch her, for she was the mad seeress of Nine Seas and they were afraid.

Fools! They were afraid of the wrong things.

And so things continued for two long weeks, until one day near the dark of the Moon of Whitecaps.

Herata spent that morning in the ley chamber, monitoring the flows. Her former responsibilities, of channeling and managing power for the southern half of the island home, she left to Lamike and others to administer. She had more important objectives now.

Still and pale, her body knelt by the giant *aum* stone while her mind ranged free in the net. Today she was studying Olmec lands, whence Lamike came. A very old, settled region, long clients of the Sea Kings, wise in the use of power. Lamike's people were serious and honorable. She expected little trouble here.

And she found little. The Olmec flows were high but regular; the artisans and technicians of the middle lands used power often, but wisely. There were sinks, places where unused power was restored to the flows and sent back out into the world, and collectors, where power was harnessed in tiny trickles from sunlight and wind, and tumbling rivers, and channeled back into the earth.

This was the most ancient and sacred way of *aum*, the technique with which Atlantis had built its empire. Power taken must be given back. What was unused must be returned to the flow, giving while receiving. That was the way of all life on earth, and so that was the way of power. Olmec lands had a clean vibration; a high energy, but regular. This part of the web was whole.

Pleased, she passed on, out over the Ocean of Suns, toward the Islands of the Dawn.

The small, dark-eyed people of these Islands accepted the rule of the

Sea Kings only with difficulty, their faith in their own greatness shattered by the arrival of Atlantean longships a generation ago. But as with any subject folk, in their cold and humid islands they could not say no to Atlantean technology, to crystal power to heat their homes and help the rice to grow. Once they accepted the Sea Kings and made tribute, they applied themselves diligently to the study of crystal science, hoping to glorify themselves by surpassing the Sea Kings at their own craft.

To Herata's mind, this made them dangerous. The Islands of the Dawn lay on a subduction zone in the earth's crust, where one great plate of the world's crust was being sucked under another, in the ancient dance of continents. The stress was amazing; earthquakes and volcanoes were common. The lines of power in the earth were tangled and confused, twisted by the collision of the crust. The power did not flow cleanly here, blurting out in great gouts at times, strangled down to narrow squirts at others. It was perhaps a place better left unchanneled, but the Islanders, proud and independent, refused to buy their *aum* from some other country. They were determined to harness their own earthpower themselves. They had in fact made several advances in growing battery crystals, to catch the power when it flowed freely and store it for when it did not.

Herata spent a good part of her time cruising the leys around the Islands of the Dawn, watching the progress of the Islanders, spooking the other adepts she met in the nets, hoping to be ready if something dreadful happened.

And here she hovered now, watching, waiting.

When the explosion came that morning, it was from a quarter unexpected: behind her, in Olmec lands.

One moment everything was fine, the leys flowing, pulsing in their regular rhythms, pushed by the ancient tides of earth and sun. The next, there was a sudden shrieking behind her in the great ley across the Ocean of Suns, an unbalanced harmonic, an interference pattern in the flow of power that shook her in the ley like a rat in a dog's mouth, addling her thoughts and blinding her supernatural vision.

It lasted but a moment, and then, down the ley, across miles of ocean, she felt and heard it: some kind of explosion. A terrible concussion, a sudden, unregulated outflow of power, surging out in all directions across the net like a dam bursting – and with it, the screams of people dying, and the sight, taste, smell of burning and blood.

Herata had a split second to realize what had happened before the cresting wave of wild power raced down the ley and snatched her up like a twig in a flood. The unthinkable, the impossible: a crystal had exploded, releasing its hoard of stored power in a single orgiastic burst of destruction.

She screamed, her own tiny chord in the symphony of destruction. Others joined the chorus, all around her, far and near, other adepts in the net, shaken and ripped by the tsunami of *aum*. In that instant the whole world seemed to scream.

Tumbling, blinded by the burst of energy, Herata knew only that she must try to stay ahead of it, try to ride the shockwave and get back somehow to Nine Seas and her own crystal before it too was shattered by the blast. Get back and through and into flesh and out of the sanctuary, try to warn the others before the whole grid exploded and the temple itself came down.

The only way was over the pole. To go around the whole far circumference of the earth was too far. She could not go back; the net around Olmec lands was a burning inferno, a holocaust of wild power as all the leys which had fed into the exploded crystal spewed their *aum* out into the gap in the net, feeding the shockwave.

Feeling the ghostly sensation of burning, hearing the screams of Lamike's kin – *tasting* their screams in the synesthesia of the web – Herata by a supreme effort of will wrestled herself into a northerly channel, away from the Islands of the Dawn, shunting up toward the top of the world, over, through the cold thin channels that flowed in the ice there, then down, down past the volcanoes of the northern islands, down the great northern ley, down the Ocean of Storms, into and through the Great City on the Trident, south across the island home to Nine Seas Temple, at the very crest of the shockwave.

All this took a split second. Herata surged through her own crystal and back into form, blinking aware just in time to be hurled bodily across her own ley chamber by the force of the explosion, the swelling surge of power that engorged her own crystal as the shockwave of the Olmec explosion touched it. Thrown against the wall, blinded by the flash, she knew only that she had made it back. Somehow she found the presence of mind to shriek the command word that shut down the crystal and took it out of the flows – too late, perhaps too late.

Her head cracked against the marble wall. She sagged to the floor; she could not see. Shouts reached her from the rooms beyond as the floor of the temple trembled with the concussion.

The population of the temple crowded into the ley chamber, adepts and novices, crying out in confusion. Meilikki hovered over her; she could hear Amalthea sobbing somewhere behind the healer.

As always there was a moment of suffocating panic as the prison of flesh surrounded her spirit. But as full bodily awareness came to her, Herata screamed and convulsed in agony on the floor. It was as if she were still in the leys, as if some protective skin of her mind had been stripped off and she was naked to the burning. She could feel – *everything*.

The glowing, gutted crater where the Olmec temple had been. The ghostly fires of unfettered *aum* that raged in the Olmec city, spreading, consuming flesh and stone alike. The bodies of the dead in that city, tumbled like dolls, and burning.

The hideous bubbling cauldron in the middle of the ocean on the opposite side of the globe, at the antipodes of the Olmec disaster, where the shockwave raced around the whole world and came to a second, hideous culmination, *aum* spewing upward and outward, turning water to steam and air to fire.

She felt the suffering of her fellow adepts all around the world: blinded, paralyzed, hands burned off, eyes seared out by the burst of wild power. Catatonic, insane, dead, or just gone, consumed by the leys.

Even in her extremity the crystals, the Hexachon, were with her, watching her. They showed her these things, forced her to see, to know, to *feel*.

She felt it, and she screamed.

Only you can stop the burning. And she had not.

Meilikki cradled Herata's twisting head in her hands. Herata felt the healer's mind touch hers, felt Meilikki's hands press her eyes, her heart, her stomach, closing down her energy centers, blinding her inner senses. The horrifying visions retreated, the pain lessened.

"I saw it!" Herata sobbed. "I felt it!"

Lamike was there, radiating love and strength, a balm to the horror. "Yes, lady, we know. Thank the gods we did not lose you!"

"That you have survived at all is a miracle," Meilikki said. "Drink this."

It was milk of the poppy, which shut down the sight. Herata swallowed it eagerly.

She hid her face against Lamike's skirts, not wanting to feel, to think, waiting for the drug to kick in.

"I've failed," she whispered.

"You are alive," Lamike said. "That is victory enough."

The poppy claimed her thoughts, and Herata gave way gratefully to unconsciousness.

That same day, Branek was sitting in a stultifying trade meeting, listening to representatives from the Great City and the Great Land haggle over how many lumps of amber were worth how many tiger skins. It was hardly a debate worthy of the attention of the great men of Atlantis. Or anyone, for that matter.

Gods below, I could have hunted my own tiger skins by now, he thought.

Slouching in the back row of the conference chamber, he juggled two little glass-encased memory crystals, the kind used by the inaum, in one hand, a trick his old swordmaster had taught him, to encourage dexterity. He was just about to ask his secretary the absolute minimum time he had to stay before he could politely escape, when the crystal he was thoughtlessly tossing burned him as he caught it.

He squawked as a flash of searing pain rocketed across his palm, out of nowhere. He dropped the little crystal, but out of sheer habit he reached up to catch the other one out of the air with his left hand as it fell. As he touched it, he felt a different pain, a burning kind of coldness, and a confused babble of sensations like shouts in his ears in a crowded room: heat, screams, a kind of soundless concussion like his ears were popping.

He jumped to his feet, heart thumping. Something was wrong. People around him looked at him quizzically. Everything happened very fast. The crystal lights in the walls of the conference room buzzed, flickered and went out. In the dimness, those of the delegates who were *aumvre* moaned and shivered as some kind of soundless wave seemed to ripple through the room, not touching the *inaum*, but leaving an electric charge in the air as it passed that even the ley-blind could feel. Branek's little crystal glowed an eerie blue-green at its passage. The floor shook. Far away, across the city by the docks, a series of muffled explosions thudded into the morning air.

Something was very wrong indeed. Branek tossed the still-glowing crystal onto the table. It had known. The little crystals had warned him somehow.

"Let's go," he said to his people, and they made there way through the suddenly milling crowd of delegates. Guards at the door tried to keep them inside, but he just stared at them with such grim intensity that they were compelled to stand aside. Branek and his small retinue left the Kraken King's palace and went out into the city, where the crowds were larger but just as confused. Across the cityscape, clouds of rosy golden smoke were rising from somewhere by the docks. There was a massive bank of crystal batteries there, for the fleet, he remembered.

The conviction was growing in him that something very bad was happening. Something worse even than he could grasp. Maybe not here, now, but somewhere, and for some reason it had an intimate effect on him.

The walk back to the townhouse through the curving streets of the Golden Circle was nerve-wracking. Nothing he could put his finger on, but he found himself going faster and faster, almost jogging, feeling like he was running toward some kind of calamity, one which he had barely escaped, yet which still waited for him out there. But where?

Crowds of citizens milled on the streets, watching the smoke boiling up from the eastern quarter of the city, speculating on the cause. The streetlights were buzzing and flickering erratically the whole way home, in broad daylight, and there was a smell of ozone in the air.

When they got home there was already a message for him, from Lacaon. His sister wanted to speak with him. That, and also the main house crystal was not working correctly, buzzing and stuttering just like the street lights. What was going on?

Ardath, the novice ley-worker who served the household, dug up a smaller, older crystal that had been in storage and seemed to be working. "What's happened?" Branek asked her. She stared at him, eyes big, obviously frightened, but wouldn't or couldn't say. "You must speak with Lady Laodice," was all she said. She stood quietly, holding the backup crystal for a few moments, then it glowed with light and he heard his sister's voice.

"Branek, thank the gods. We feared the worst."

At the sound of her voice he became truly afraid for the first time. Her voice sounded thin and reedy and she was obviously terrified.

"What is it?" he demanded.

"We are not entirely sure. There has been -- a breach. In the web. Somewhere to the west, in the Two Sisters."

"A breach?" He had no idea what she was talking about.

He could hear her take a breath to steady herself. "A temple somewhere … has imploded. There was a backlash of power through the web. Other temples have been damaged. We feared at first, it was Atlantis."

"There was an explosion here, but not at the White Temple. And we felt – something. Even I felt it."

"The backlash." She said. "Yes, we felt it too, even here."

"Are you all right?"

"I … I…" she faltered.

"Sister! What is it?"

"Niobe, Niobe – is burned, but she is alive." Niobe was her acolyte.

"Gods," he said. "I'm sorry. Will she live?"

"I don't know, it's too soon. She was working in the ley chamber –" Laodice faltered again, obviously on the brink of tears.

He reached out to touch the crystal, trying to comfort her, but Ardath smacked his hand away, shaking her head violently. Startled, he took a step back. Of course he couldn't touch an active crystal, it could kill him.

"Father?" he asked. "Meara?"

"They are fine, they were nowhere near."

"I'm coming home," he said.

"No." Laodice took another steadying breath; he could hear it through the link. "I don't think you should, little brother. There might be – after-shocks? If you were stuck at sea with no power … I think you should stay there for now."

"But –"

"No, truly. We will manage. It-it could have been worse. It is worse, elsewhere. Many people are dead."

"I'm sorry about Niobe," he said again.

Laodice sighed. "I'd hoped you could tell us more, little brother," she said.

"I know nothing," he said.

"I hoped you had talked to that priestess friend of yours," Laodice said. "At Nine Seas."

The breath froze in his chest. Nine Seas. Oh gods. Herata!

Defend her.

Sweat gushed out of every pore in his body. He stumbled back and sank onto a bench against the wall. Now he knew why he had felt an increasing sense of sick dread as the strange events unfolded. Whatever had happened, whatever this was, Herata would be in the thick of it. Oh, goddess mother, was she even still alive?

"Branek?" Laodice asked, her voice small and tinny in the crystal.

"No," he managed. "I haven't spoken with her."

"Well, you should," Laodice said. "She might need your help."

"Yes," he said. "Help."

"I'll leave you to it, then," Laodice said after a moment. "Take care, little brother. We'll speak soon."

"All right," he said.

The crystal died, the connection cut off.

He put his head in his hands. *Gods oh gods oh gods.*

"Contact Nine Seas," he told Ardath.

She knelt beside him so she could look him in the face, the crystal tucked away. "I have already tried, my lord," she said. She put a hand on his knee. "There is no response."

Branek jumped up and ran out of the room.

Herata woke in her own chamber to the stillness of deepest night.

It was silent and pitch dark. Herata could feel an eerie quietness in the temple. The entire crystal array was offline -- some quiescent, others dead, burned out by the overload. Beyond that, she could feel the leys themselves, below the temple, thin and weak, the power slowed down to a mere trickle. Nine Seas had never felt so empty.

A shape moved beside her bed. "My lady, are you awake?" whispered a voice. Amalthea.

"Yes," Herata said, trying to rub the sleep out of her eyes. The lassitude of the poppy was still with her, but even under it she could feel the state of every crystal in the temple, alive or dead, awake or inactive. If anything, her sensitivity was greater that it had been just that morning.

"Rest a moment, my lady, I must get the healer," Amalthea said, and slipped quietly out of the room.

Meilikki arrived quickly, with Lamike alongside. The healer bid Herata sit up, then flashed a light into her eyes, took her pulse, scanned her with crystals and without.

"You seem to have escaped without major injury, my lady," Meilikki said at last. "We are fortunate you were not ley-walking at the time of the blast."

Herata stared owlishly at her. "But I was."

Meilikki's eyes widened. Lamike gasped.

"You were out of body?" Meilikki demanded. "You were in the flow?"

"I was near the Islands of the Dawn," Herata said. "I barely got back."

Her keepers stared at each other, looked back down at her with astonishment and dread. "How is this possible?" Meilikki murmured.

"What are you saying?" Herata asked.

Lamike took her hand gently, stroking it. Meilikki sat down beside her on the bed.

"We thought you had been only monitoring," she said carefully. "We thought you shut the crystal down when you felt the blast in Tiotiwakan."

"But what does it matter?" Herata sniveled, trying to fend off the truth.

"Our crystal is ruptured," Lamike said gently. "As far as we can tell Tiotiwakan is …" She closed her eyes, struggled to go on. "Tiotiwakan is gone. From what we have heard so far, no one who was in the leys at the time of the blast has survived."

Herata whimpered. "Are you sure?"

Meilikki nodded; he face looked grave, sunken. "Except, it seems, for you."

Herata twisted away from them, curled on her side. She covered her face, hearing a guttural moan issue from her own throat, too horrified even to weep.

"I do not see how this is possible," Meilikki said.

It was true, then, what she had felt from the Hexachon, their grim intent.

Herata knew she was a competent crystal worker, but not a gifted one. There were many adepts who had walked the leys far longer than she, many whose sight was more penetrating, whose sensitivity was higher. There was no reason why she alone should have survived. No way she could have achieved such a special destiny.

Except one. She had been spared for bigger things. This had not been the burning yet foretold; another, greater conflagration was to come.

One of Meilikki's acolytes brought her a posset; she dashed it away. "No more drugs!"

The cup rolled and tumbled on the stone floor. Amalthea scooped it up, ran for a cleaning rag.

Meilikki hesitated. "As you wish."

"You need rest, my lady," Lamike said.

"No!" Herata said grimly. "I've rested enough." Still weak from the poppy, she climbed to her feet. Lamike clutched her arm, steadying her.

"You should not," the old priestess said, concerned. "You are not well."

"I have not been well since the summer solstice and the dolphins did not come," Herata said. "It is no longer of account."

Chapter Nine

All the rest of that night Herata sat in council and heard reports of the disaster at Tiotiwakan. Before the end, Lamike broke down, tears streaming down her cheeks.

"I must go," she said.

Herata tenderly embraced the older woman, touching the tears on her cheeks. "Of course. At once you must go."

Herata sent her, and a cadre of experienced adepts, to help with emergency relief. It hurt her heart to see the older woman so grief-stricken. But no one at the Pyramid of the Moon had survived. How could they? And Lamike had been initiated at that temple, decades ago.

An *aum* stone had not overloaded and destroyed itself in a thousand years. It was unthinkable. Impossible – especially at a well-run nexus like the Pyramid of the Moon in Olmec Tiotiwakan.

Herata examined her own crystal. She had not been entirely successful in taking it offline; it was cracked, riven almost in two by the backlash of wild power. But in many other temples around the world, the crystals had exploded outright, compounding the shock-wave, sending more burning wildpower around the world. A near-chain reaction: the worst-case scenario of the ley line network. A true cascade could have brought the entire world to darkness and silence. Only the heroic actions of a few adepts, sacrificing their lives to take their own crystals out of the flows at key junctions, had stopped the powerstorm from consuming the network.

The crystal was useless, dead. They would need to grow a new one.

Herata shivered, looking at the cracked, blackened thing. If this was not the burning of her vision … what was? What could be worse than this?

The Hexachon had shut themselves down, a split second *before* the explosion. They had never done that before, never in all the history of the island home. But if they knew what had gone wrong, they declined to say. They remained silent.

It was the worst *aum* disaster since crystal madness had infected the ley-walkers in the time of Queen Elissa. Or no, the worst ever – an established crystal at a major juncture had never immolated itself before. Crystal explosions were usually the result of a flawed, poorly grown crystal, or one poorly placed at a new juncture, improperly harmonized. The juncture at the Temple of the Moon had been in operation for centuries.

Wearily Herata tossed down a handful of message crystals like dice -- reports from temples all around the world, cataloging the disaster. Tintagel: three dead. Uxmal: two crystals shattered, two dead. Nebes: one dead, one injured, one missing in the leys.

So far, over a thousand adepts around the world were believed dead or crippled. Thirty-five crystals had been destroyed – not counting the Olmec ones. In Tiotiwakan the destruction was so great they would never get an accurate count of the dead. Around the site of the temple the ghostfires still raged.

She rubbed her eyes, exhausted. Among the messages were many queries from Poseidonis and other places about the state of Nine Seas temple. Herata answered them cagily, saying only that the crystal had been damaged and the high priestess, injured. She couldn't imagine what might happen if anyone guessed that she had been walking the leys, and survived.

When that became known, there would be many questions. Herata had no idea how to answer them.

An attendant appeared at the door to her office. "My lady, you have a visitor."

"What?" Herata said. "Now?"

Before the young priest could answer, he was pushed aside. It was Branek.

The look on his face wen he saw her was indescribable – terror, relief, joy, all of it at once, and more, something she couldn't place.

"I thought you were in Lacaon!" she said.

With three huge strides he was across the room. She rose to meet him. He picked her up, crushing her to him, burying his face in her hair.

"Thank the gods," he chanted, "thank the gods." He kissed her again and again, mostly getting hair and the side of her cheek, but undeterred.

She clung to him for a moment, but he was so much taller than her that her feet were dangling right off the ground. She kicked them uselessly. "Branek! I'm all right. Put me down."

He did, but he didn't let go of her, his hands cradling the sides of her head. His eyes searched her face, and the yearning intensity in his expression was almost painful to see.

"Your aunt?" she cried, guessing at the reason for his distraught state. "Your sister?"

"No, thank Poseidon. I spoke to Laodice," he said. "They are safe. But Laodice's acolyte was injured."

White Mare Temple had gotten off lightly, then, but she wasn't about to say that. "I am sorry. But I am glad your sister was spared."

"You're all right?" he asked. "You're really all right?"

What could she say?

"Well," she said, leaning back against her desk, "yes."

He pounced on her imprecision like a cat. "What aren't you telling me?"

How could she even begin to describe it? "It was a near-run thing," she said.

He folded her in his arms again. "They told me –" he started, then broke off.

"Who told you? Told you what?"

"We tried to contact you," he said, "but you didn't answer."

"Oh." She looked at the pile of message crystals on her desk. It must have gotten lost in the jumble. "I'm sorry, Branek, I would have answered you if I'd known. How did you get here?"

"Overland," he said. "I rode. All night."

Indeed, he smelled of sweat and horse. Now that she had gotten over her surprise a little, she could see how exhausted he looked. What had gotten into him?

Come," she said, "sit down." She led him over to the couch across from her desk. "But why are you here?"

"I had to see you!" he said. "I knew – whatever had happened, you would be in the middle of it."

That was closer to the truth than she liked to admit. A wave of exhaustion passed through her. She dropped her head into her hands. Gods, she had slept for hours, but she was still so tired …

"What is it?" Branek asked. "Are you hurt?"

"Not – not hurt, exactly."

"Herata!" He slid down off the divan, knelt in front of her, looking imploringly into her eyes. "When I heard what happened, I thought the worst. And I know something is wrong, I can *feel* it. Please, just tell me."

So she did. She just told him. The implosion, the taste of screams, the sound of blood. All the dead, all the lost. Lamike's terrible grief. And how she had survived, she alone of all the web. By the time she was done, she was sobbing, as she had not been able to before.

"Oh, Herata. My poor girl." He pulled her into his arms again where he knelt before her. "I'm so sorry." She slid into his lap, like a little child, and he held her while she wept for all the death she had felt, and for the death that was sure to come.

At last she cried herself out, and she sat back a little, drying her cheeks with the palms of her hands. The look on his face as he regarded her was excruciatingly tender. She reached up, brushed his hair back from his face. Why did he love her so much? It would probably only lead to sorrow.

But she kissed him anyway.

As she did, the kiss changed in her from something kind and sweet to something dark and hungry. At the scent of him, musky with sweat and horse, at the feel of his mouth under hers, some gate seemed to open deep within her soul, and she gasped as a flood of desire swept through her. She had walked so close to death, rode the crest of death across the burning leys, that the life force suddenly swelled up in her – threatened, too long denied, demanding release. Her breath caught and shivered in her breast.

"You're trembling," Branek said, arms still locked about her. "What is the matter?"

"Nothing," Herata gasped, "nothing's the matter." She kissed him again, and again, more and more urgently, and he began to catch and answer her excitement, his breath quickening. She could feel his pulse leaping under her hand on his throat. His hands ran up under her gown across her thighs; she whimpered with desire, her heart fluttering in her breast like a caged bird, desperate to take flight.

Fingers trembling, she slipped open the front of her gown, exposing her firm virgin's breasts. She saw the sudden smolder of lust in his eyes as he cradled them in his hands, bent to taste.

Shockwaves of pleasure raced through her body at the feel of his mouth on her. She arched backwards spasmodically, grasping his shoulders, riding his mouth on her breast as she had ridden the crest of the leys. His hands slipped down to her buttocks, curving around, slipping under. He was excited, too, touching her wetness, his breath ragged in her ear. She could feel him growing hard beneath her, where she sat in his lap. She rubbed against him, hearing her own voice moaning, wanting -- needing -- to open herself to him to fully as possible, to be filled by him, to give herself to him completely. The desperate, burning life in her would settle for nothing less.

She cradled his face in her hands. "Take me, my love."

He started, surprised. "What?"

"Please," she begged. "I need you. I want you, now. Make love to me, Branek."

For a moment he almost did, the flame of lust burning higher in his eyes, his hands tightening on her waist. She pressed herself against him, thrilled at the thought that he would soon pierce her maidenhead. She had waited for this …

"No," he said.

"What?" Her pulse throbbed with desperate disbelief. "But … I'm ready. I want you, I want to give myself to you – now!"

He lifted her and sat her back on the sofa, putting her away from him. "I cannot," he said; she could feel that he was trembling with the need to control himself. "You are in no condition."

"But I want you," Herata said, desire and despair commingling in her breast. "Why, why do you torment me?"

"No more than you torment me," he whispered, one hand trailing down her body, leaving a line of fire in its wake. "But I won't risk it. I cannot take you now. From what you just told me, you almost died, woman! You are too weak; Meilikki told me."

"Meilikki!" Herata spat. "That hag – she hates me!"

"No," Branek said. He kissed her bruisingly; she tasted the bitter salt of her own tears. "If I were to get you with child it could be deadly! You would never survive a pregnancy now."

"With child?" Herata cried. "Don't you take the juice of the golden-flower?" It was the usual contraceptive; men and women both used it.

"I cannot." Passionately he kissed her neck and the tops of her breasts. Her hands reached up and fisted into his hair as if she could force him to mount her. "I am the only prince of my line; I must get sons. The effects of the juice are sometimes irreversible. So I cannot. I am forbidden."

"If it's sons you want, sons I can give you," Herata vowed. In that moment she would have said anything, done anything, to feel him inside her. She was as the fallow field waiting for the plow, the anvil awaiting the hammer. Her hand slipped down his waist, over his kilt, *under* it –

He grabbed her wrist, forcing her hand away. A madness flared in his eyes; for a second he almost lost control. "I say again, no!" He pushed her back a little. "Do you take the juice?"

She could only shake her head, tears of frustration choking her. She had never had the need, until he had come. His refusal only made her crazy with desire, not less so. She thought she might go mad if this ache in her deepest center was not satisfied.

"I will not risk it," Branek said, through his teeth, striving for hard-fought control.

Herata began to weep hysterically, completely undone by this reversal. "Love me," she begged him. "Love me!"

He cradled her face in his hands. "Do you think this is easy for me, woman? Look at you! You are like Cleito before Poseidon, the very mother of Atlantis, the beloved of the god. I assure you, Herata, no man has wanted a woman as much as I want you now, since the world began."

She kissed him, desperate with something more than simple desire. They both drank her tears. "Love me, Branek," she begged him.

"I will," he said.

And so he did, as an honorable man in his position was bound to do. With hands and lips he pleasured her, as he had done before, on the beach and in the groves.

No! It wasn't enough, it would never be enough. "No, Branek," she sobbed, imploring him, even as icy shivers of pleasure raced along her nerves. Her very essence cried out for more, for the ultimate. "Please, no."

But soon enough it was done, of course; her body was too aroused not to respond. It was a release of more than sexual tension, a release of the grip of death on her, and the triumph of returning life.

She collapsed on the couch, sobbing again, spent in a more than physical sense. Branek sat on the sofa, held her against him as she wept, dazed and overwhelmed. "Hush," he murmured like a father comforting his child. "There, now, I know. Hush."

He held her there until she cried herself out again and her sobs quieted to weary hiccups.

"I don't understand," she said at last, miserably. "I thought you … wanted me, I thought you loved me."

Tenderly he dried her tears. "Of course. It is because I love you that I did this. When you give me your virginity it will be in our wedding bed, when this crisis is past and you are whole again. Not on the floor in your office," he said.

Despite everything Herata had to laugh at that. "I don't know what came over me," she said.

"I do," Branek said. "It is like that sometimes. The blood rises; it cannot be denied. Men feel it after battle, after facing death. Be glad; it is a holy thing."

Herata laid her head on his shoulder, unable to think, emotionally exhausted. "Now what?"

"Sleep," Branek said firmly. "The sun is almost up; the new day is almost begun. But it can wait, for a few more hours."

Chapter Ten

Herata jerked awake, an abrupt passage from unconsciousness to full wakefulness. She sat up. She was in her own bedroom in her apartments. The light slanting through the curtained windows told her it was about noon. She had only slept a few hours, but they were heavy ones.

The events of the past twenty-four hours tumbled through her mind in a crazed rush – the implosion, her escape, Branek's arrival, and –

She hid her face in her hands even though no one could see. Gods below, she had asked him to deflower her right on the floor of her office. What had gotten into her? She was mortified.

She sat on the edge of the bed, trying to understand everything that had happened. The implosion. How could that have happened at the Pyramid of the Moon, of all places? Her escape. No – if she thought about that too much, she would suffocate in fear and regret. So many had died and she yet lived. Branek – the snarl of her emotions confused her. Thinking of him even now sent a flush of desire through her body. She had wanted him so badly, and he had *refused* her. Why had he come to Nine Seas anyway? What did he want?

She stroked the message crystal beside her bed and after a moment Amalthea appeared, peering around the frame of the door.

"Is the Prince of Lacaon still here?" Herata asked.

"Yes, my lady, he said he waits upon your pleasure," Amalthea answered.

"Hm," Herata answered. He had not been overmuch concerned with her pleasure the night before. No, that was an unworthy thought. He had done what was right, she had been out of her head. Hadn't she?

She took a long hot bath, eschewing any attendants, scrubbing at her skin, trying to scrub away thoughts, memories, events. Once dressed, she lingered in her bedroom, afraid to face the world outside, the chaos, the destruction. Afraid to face Branek.

She forced herself to the outer door of her apartments. Was she Sea Priestess or wasn't she? She had been called to these events.

She should go to her office, but -- no. Not there. As she walked down the cool marble hallways of her temple, her stomach growled loudly. Gods, she was hungry. How long had it been since she had eaten? She couldn't even remember.

She gestured to Amalthea, silently attending her as always. "Food."

Bek, her secretary, was waiting for her in the airy dining room off the terrace, a rack of reports in his hands. "Smart man," Herata said, unsure whether to be annoyed or pleased at his intuition.

"You need to eat something, my lady," he said, "after -- "

"I know, I know," she said irritably. "I'm here, am I not?"

Amalthea announced the Prince of Lacaon. Bek raised his eyebrows at her, put the rack of crystals down on the table, and left without saying anything.

Gods below, did the whole temple know what had transpired last night?

Branek was dressed simply in a plain tunic, and his hair was tied back in an unadorned braid. He came to her as if to embrace her, but without even thinking she raised a hand, forestalling him, and he stopped.

"Have you eaten?" she asked him.

He shook his head. They sat at the table.

There was a supremely awkward silence.

"Well," Herata finally said.

"How do you feel?" Branek asked.

"Fine," she said. Actually, she did feel fine. Excellent, in fact. It made her angry. Hundreds, probably thousands were dead, and she could have circled the world twenty times in twenty seconds, and climbed to the top of Mount Atlas afterward. It wasn't fair. To anyone.

"I am very glad, " Branek said.

Food was served, fish and eggs and cheese, heavy for lunch but Herata welcomed it. Too much food shut the sight down as effectively as any drug.

They ate for a while in silence. Mother of waters, this was the most uncomfortable meal she had had since she first went back to Poseidonis to visit her father at the age of twelve, after he had sent her to the temple. That meal had been silent too; she had been furious at him for sending her away, and Herodian simply hadn't known what to say.

"About last night – " Branek finally said.

"Gods below," Herata blurted, "let's not talk about that, please."

"I think we should," he said. "Obviously you are upset."

Herata banged her cup down on the table. "Why are you here?"

He gave her a wounded look. "I came here because I thought you were *dead*. I am sorry if that is not a good enough reason, my lady."

"Who told you that?"

"No one told me. But we felt the backlash, or whatever you call it, in the Great City." He tapped his chest. "Even people like me felt it. So I knew you would be in trouble. And when you didn't answer, when we called, I feared the worst. So I came. Is that so strange?"

It *was* strange. He had been out of his mind with worry when he arrived at Nine Seas in the dead of night.

"There is something you're not telling me," she said.

He shook his head. "No."

"Yes. When you arrived, you said, someone told you something. Something that brought you here unannounced in the middle of the night. Who was it?"

"No one told me anything." But he didn't meet her eyes.

She grabbed his wrist. "You know, I could ream the answer out of your mind like a seed out of a grape, if I wanted to. Even if you are *in-aum*."

His eyes went hard and flat. "My sister is an adept like you, and she taught me a thing or two. I'd like to see you try."

"Did the White Temple send you to check on me?"

He banged his fist on the table. "Lest you forget, I am a prince of the Inner Sea, and no one *sends me* anywhere! I come and go as I please." He pointed at her. "You are trying to pick a fight, instead of discussing what is really bothering you, which is what happened last night, or did not happen, as the case may be."

Herata gaped like a fish at his audacity. She rubbed her face with her hands, trying to compose herself. This was absurd. The whole world was burning down around her, and she was squabbling with her lover about the state of their affair.

"Do not try to change the subject. You know something, about the Hexachon. About the White Temple. Something you are not telling me. Don't *lie* to me, Branek, I can *feel* it!"

They stared at each other. The charge between them was electric – not just anger, nor even eros, nor yet *aum*, all of that and more. It was true. Their time before the Hexachon had bound them. He could feel that she had almost died yesterday, it had brought him all the way from Poseidonis. Just as she could feel that he was withholding a truth from her now.

At last he dropped his eyes, sat back from the table. "Yes," he said. "There is something."

"So just tell me. Please."

"The debates in Council," he said. "The opening of a new nexus."

She was puzzled. "Surely they can't think to go through with that now."

He shook his head. "On the contrary, the idea of opening a new nexus will be more popular than ever."

"Madness!" Herata said.

"That is not all," he said. "The thought now will be that the new nexus should not be in the colonies, that we cannot be trusted to manage power, after Tiotiwakan."

"Well, then, it will not be in the Inner Sea," Herata said, relieved at that.

Branek sighed. "You don't understand, Herata."

"What?"

"They don't trust the colonies. The Five Kings wish to open a new nexus in Atlantis itself."

Herata frowned. "All the junctions in Atlantis are in use, they have been for millennia."

"Yes. So they seek to create one."

Herata shook her head, confused. "Create one? What do you mean?"

"A faction in the Council wants to move the leys, to bring them to a new nexus in the island home."

Herata stared at him as if he were mad. "Move the leys? That's impossible. You can't move the leys, they are natural features."

"No." He would not look at her. "It can be done."

"I don't believe it."

"I have seen the reports." He ran a hand distractedly through his hair. "Indeed, I should not be telling you this -- it would be called treason by my father, and yours. But a cadre of adepts at the Poseideion has perfected a technique. They have been working on it for many years. Given enough power to feed in, the earthblood can be rechanneled. Like damming a river."

"They would do this?" Herata whispered, shocked to her core. "This – blasphemy?"

"Right now, only the Five and the elders of the Poseideion know about this. Most of the lesser kings and the faithful do not know." He looked at her over his wine cup, his eyes dark with secrets.

"So how do you know?" she whispered.

He shrugged. "Let us just say I lucked into this information," he said.

Treason. "Why would you not tell me this?" she asked.

He gave her a sidelong look. "Do you have to ask? Because you, in particular, they do not want to know."

The mad seeress of Nine Seas. Of course not. "Damn them!" she whispered. "Could they be so mad?"

She squeezed her eyes shut against the horrible image. The power ripped up from the living body of the earth, wrenched by brute force across the landscape, stolen from those that needed it, forced to serve the greed of the Kings of Atlantis. Was such a thing even possible? Try to make the wind blow backwards or the river run uphill.

If they had done this, if the priests of the Poseideion could rape the earthpower and bend it to their will, they had abandoned any belief they still held in the Mother Earth. If they could do this, they were capable of anything.

"Damn them!" she said again.

Only you can stop the burning.

The vision rose up like a fever and took hold of her. Her goblet dropped from her nerveless hand. She could see it. This was what the Hexachon had warned her about.

It would not work. They would try to drag the veins of the Mother out of the living earth, and the Mother would rebel, and punish them. The destruction of Tiotiwakan would be as nothing in comparison.

Before her inner sight the Great City fell, in flames, swallowed by a furious open throat of molten magma. Power, unchanneled, howled across the Plains of Gold, burning everything in its path. The foundations of the island home shook, and cracked, the ancient brooding fires in the heart of the island unleashed in an instant. Power, warped and distorted by the assault, raced through the web, shattering crystals everywhere, scorching the earth, boiling the oceans. Shrieking feedback shattered crystal after crystal, all down the line, setting more wild *aum* free to rage across the landscape, vaporizing earth and flesh, turning forests into funereal pyres and cities into crematories. A howling fire raced across the world, unstoppable. And in its wake, darkness, endless darkness, lit only by smoldering embers.

Somewhere someone was shouting, shouting her name, shaking her. She opened her eyes.

"Herata! Herata!" It was Branek, clutching her shoulders. "Stop it!"

She covered her mouth with her hands, and collapsed back into her seat. He stared at her, horrified.

"Oh," she sobbed brokenly, "Branek – the burning! I saw it, I saw it!"

"You were screaming," he said. "You wouldn't stop!"

She clutched at him. "Oh, Branek, you can't let them do it! It's terrible, so terrible! You've got to stop them!"

"Get Meilikki!" Branek shouted to the appalled novice who had appeared at the door. He swept Herata up into his arms.

"Stop it, please, you must stop it!" she begged him. Some distant bemused corner of her mind knew she was hysterical, but she could not stop crying. She could still feel the fires burning down the leys, the pain of the violated earth.

Branek carried her to her rooms. She sobbed on his shoulder with a thin wail that sounded hideous even to her own ears. The shriek of the dismembered leys still howled in her ears; the burning, foundering Great City lay wrecked and smoking before her eyes.

Meilikki forced another potion down her throat, and gradually her sobs quieted as a drowsy numbness spread through her limbs. Branek sat beside her on the bed, stroking her hair. Even in her drugged state she was grateful for his strength.

Meilikki gestured to him; with a final caress he left Herata and went with the healer.

They spoke quietly in the next room, in whispers, but Herata could hear them. Meilikki was holding a diagnostic instrument, a healing crystal; Herata could hear them through it. All the crystals were open to her now; she saw through them all with the eyes of prophecy.

"What happened?" Meilikki asked in a kind of dull amazement. She was growing used to her mistress's fits, but this …

Branek shook his head. "She had a vision. I think it is a foretelling."

"Of what?"

Branek hesitated.

"I must know, so I can treat her, " Meilikki said.

"It is restricted information," Branek said.

"Not if she is envisioning it," Meilikki pointed out.

Branek, Herata could tell, felt outmaneuvered. But it was true. Now that she knew, she could never keep silent.

"My lady had a vision of what would happen if the leys were moved to form a new junction in the Great City," he said.

Meilikki gasped; the crystal in her hand thrummed. Even the smallest crystal would not hear of it, Herata saw.

"Is that even possible?" Meilikki asked in amazement.

"Theoretically, yes," Branek said. "The Poseideion has developed a technique."

Meilikki shook her head in wonder. "And what did she see?"

"Burning," Branek said. "She could not tell me all of it, she was too … frenzied. But burning."

"Like Tiotiwakan?"

"You saw her!" Branek said. "Worse, I think. Much worse."

Herata was slipping farther down to sleep, the drug stealing over her. Their voices slipped into her mind now like a dream.

Meilikki sat down, turning the healing crystal over and over in her hands. "And will this come to pass?"

Branek paced about the room. He wanted to be with Herata. But he was afraid, too, afraid of her visions.

"It is being discussed," he said. "It was not thought possible, until recently."

"Madness!"

"So Herata said. But many on the Council do not think so. Even some of the Five Kings. The disaster in Olmec lands will only make their case more reasonable: colonies cannot administer power, the Great City must do it."

"The Poseideion allows this talk? This – blasphemy?"

"They are behind it! They have seen their power diminish since times of old, as colonies grow all around the Nine Seas. Their counsel does no hold the sway it once did. With a stranglehold on the flows of earthpower, it would once again. Or so they believe."

Meilikki looked at him shrewdly. "And you, Prince of Lacaon? What do you believe?"

Branek was silent a long moment, silently pacing. Herata, dreaming, strained to hear his voice. What he said now he had not said even to her face, even in the secrets of love.

"I saw Herata enter the vortex of the Hexachon and live. I believe in her vision. But I know also that the colonies, the empire, need more power to live. You know the earthquakes of the Inner Sea, how dangerous they are. In my great-grandfather's time the earth shook and there came a killing wave; twenty thousand died. Whole towns destroyed, fleets smashed. The isle of Keftiu ceased to govern the islands, destroyed by a mere shrug of the earth. In Lacaon our adepts work night and day to keep the fires of the deep earth banked, to keep the ground from shaking. This takes much *aum*. Vast amounts of earthpower, just to preserve our lives."

No, Herata thought. This she had not known; he had kept it from her, this dangerous work of his sister's. It was madness, hubris. No force in nature could keep the ground from shaking when the great plates moved in the deep earth. Not all the *aum* in the world.

"Perhaps," he continued in the other room, "if this technique is successful, the leys at Lacaon could be moved, and the earth would quiet. Then, *aum* would be saved, instead of wasted on a stopgap effort."

No, Branek, Herata whispered in her mind. That's not the way.

But he could not hear her. She was asleep.

And that night, and every night thereafter, until the end, her dreams were filled with burning.

Chapter Eleven

Branek spent that night at Nine Seas temple also, but he got little sleep. He spent most of it pacing around the spare but roomy guest quarters he had been assigned. Pacing, and drinking, trying to quiet the incessant chatter of his own thoughts in his head. Branek was not a man given to questioning or second-guessing himself. When it did happen, he hated it.

Sokar his swordmate, who had ridden with him from Poseidonis, watched him pace from a stool in the corner of the sitting room. "You need to calm down, boss," he said.

Branek shook his head. "I can't."

"Things seem well enough here," Sokar said. "We should go back to the city."

No!" Branek said. He stopped pacing long enough to point an angry finger at his swordsman. "Do not say that again."

Part of him was afraid to let Herata out of his sight even for a moment. He closed his eyes, remembering the cold, abject terror he had felt when he realized she might already be dead or mortally wounded. It was not just the compulsion that the Hexachon may or may not have put upon him. He loved her, he could not stand the thought of losing her, by estrangement or death, or anything else.

He had loved women before -- or thought he had, but not like this. A flush of heat went through him as he remembered the night before. Gods below, he could have had her last night, truly and fully, in the way he wanted so badly, the way that kept him up at night now, shivering with desire, remembering, imagining. He had been honored to wait for her, but a man could only wait so long. Only the barest thread of sanity had kept them apart – and on his part, not hers. He laughed.

Herata was reckless, he could see that now. She had done crazy things, and would continue to do crazy things in the service of her visions, of the principles that moved her. She needed watching.

But another part of him heard Sokar, and thought it sounded good.

That part of him wanted to mount his horse and ride back to the Great City and never, ever come back. She was too much for him, this slip of a girl. She had outmaneuvered him and he had spilled his guts like a maudlin drunk in a tavern.

He threw the goblet across the room. It fell and clanged melodiously into the brightly painted hearth. "Damnit!"

"Whatever it is, boss, it cannot be that bad," Sokar said.

Branek gave a bark of humorless laughter. "Oh yes it can."

He had made a major error. Hekau and Laodice would be incensed. The White Temple as well. Moving the leys, the darkest secret of the Empire -- and he had told Herata of Nine Seas, sure to be its chief opponent, all about it.

What in Poseidon's name had he been thinking? In service of a small, personal secret – the words he traded with the Hexachon -- he had given up a major, strategic one of imperial import. He was a loyal subject of the empire; so he had been raised and so his people had been for generations. And Herata might be the Keeper of a major temple, but she was no friend of the Poseideion's, at all. *Treason.* It was not too strong a word.

And yet, and yet, a third part of him was relieved. He had told her willingly in the end, and the telling had felt like an absolution. She had needed to know, she deserved to know. Surely the Hexachon wanted her to know. Was that why they had chosen him, to be her protector, that day at the White Temple?

He had no idea. He was *inaum.* He was a simple colonial. He had been raised to sail and to fish, to herd and to fight, to render tribute to Atlantis, and to rule his tiny island when the time came. These matters of world-wide import were beyond him.

He stood for a moment at the open balcony doors, watching the waves on the shore as they tumbled, silver in the moonlight. That was something he missed in the Great City, the sound of waves on the shore. All his life in Lacaon the surf had never been out of earshot. But Poseidonis was too far inshore.

"I wish we could go home," he said impulsively.

"Why can't we?" Sokar asked, coming up behind him. "What's keeping us?" -- although he knew the answer perfectly well.

Branek said it anyway. "She is."

"The priestess seems well enough for the moment," Sokar said. "And Lady Laodice will surely want to see you."

Branek whirled on him. "Do not presume to lecture me on *Lady* Laodice, or women, or priestesses, or anything else. Just shut up, Sokar!"

Branek knew perfectly well that Sokar was his sister's lover, and had been for some years. Laodice's status as Keeper of White Mare Temple had never overawed him; to Sokar, she was still and always the girl whose braids he had pulled when they played on the shore as children. Branek did not begrudge either of them their companionship. He credited them with enough sense to use the goldenflower and spawn no bastards to complicate the family line.

But Sokar's mention of Laodice infuriated him. He longed to speak to his sister, take her counsel – she was a priestess as well, she would know of these things. But if he spoke to her at all, he would have to tell her everything, and if Hekau heard that his son could not be trusted to keep the family secrets, he would be recalled from Atlantis back to Lacaon, in disgrace, and doubtless for good.

Sokar raised his hands in surrender. "As my prince commands, I obey," he said.

To hear such obeisance from the usually insubordinate Sokar was ludicrous and Branek gave another snort of disgusted laughter.

He could not leave now. He needed to stay with Herata. And he wanted to. She had seen things, more terrible even than the immolation of Tiotiwakan. This burning she kept speaking of. What did it mean? Was it a true vision?

He did not know. He was a simple man. It was beyond him. If he could talk to Laodice … but that was impossible.

And so the whole cycle of tormented thoughts would begin again, round and round til the wineskin was empty and dawn was still hours off.

Finally Sokar, who had matched him cup for cup, and who had no guilty conscience to keep him awake, managed to push him toward bed and sleep. "Think on it again in the morning, Bran," he said, using his prince's childhood nickname. "Things will seem clearer in the morning."

Branek doubted it but in the end he ran out of reasons to refuse. When his head finally did hit the pillow, he was surprised at how quickly sleep claimed him.

Herata awoke before dawn. She sat quietly, crosslegged in her bed in the pre-dawn darkness, stretching out, feeling with her sight for the people and crystals in the temple. Not many were awake, of either kind. The silence of the temple's psychic space gave her room to think.

She was getting damned tired of ending up flat on her back with another one of Meilikki's drugs forced down her throat. She felt a strange combination of lassitude from the drug and a buzzing energy from having slept so much over the past two days. A horrid suspicion bloomed in her mind; was Meilikki trying to keep her quiet, keep her inert, with all these drugs? What if she worked for the White Temple?

Herata dug her heels of her hands into her eyes, trying to clear her thoughts. No, that was paranoia. A residue of the drug. Meilikki had been at Nine Seas longer than Herata herself, and had sworn oaths, on the temple's great crystal itself, oaths of healing and doing no harm. Herata would trust her until the healer gave her a concrete reason not to. If she could not trust her own people, the oathbound initiates of her own temple, she was already undone.

But she summoned the healer to her with a touch of the message crystal.

Meilikki came at once, with her healer's kit. More drugs.

"Are you well, my lady? Did you sleep well?" She kindled a dim light, looked in Herata's eyes, felt her pulse.

"I dreamed of burning," Herata said.

Meilikki reached for her bag. Herata put a hand on hers, stopping her.

"No more drugs, Meilikki. Not another drop, not another grain. I mean it."

Meilikki snapped her bag shut. No healer liked to have her orders questioned. "Should that not be my decision, lady? I am responsible for your health. For your care."

"No. I need my mind clear. No matter what happens."

"And if you strain yourself too much, and burn out your sight – if you become *inaum*, my lady, what becomes of us all then?"

It could happen; it had happened to many who had been injured by Tiotiwakan, and to countless hapless or unlucky adepts over the centuries. It was what the *aumvre* feared most, to be blinded, cast out of the flows. But:

"No." Herata closed her eyes for a minute. Clasping her hands together, closing the circuit of her body's energy, she searched within herself, searched the leys of her own body, searched the threads of consequence that she had seen in her terrible vision. "No, I will not burn out. I don't think I could, now."

"You have done what has not been done in centuries, survived what no one else could survive," Meilikki said. "How can we know what else may be to come?"

Enough arguing. Herata invoked her authority as Sea Priestess. "Do not challenge me on this, or I shall have to ask another to take over my care. I need to know I can trust you, whatever happens."

Even in the dimness, Herata could see Meilikki's expression hardening. It would be a grave insult to make her step down as chief healer of the temple. "As my Priestess commands, I obey," Meilikki said stiffly. "Call upon me if you have need," she added, then picked up her bag and left.

Herata regretted her displeasure, but it was necessary.

In the dim light of the single crystal Meilikki had kindled, she summoned food, bathed, dressed, ate alone in her rooms. Dawn was breaking as she went to the ley chamber, where an array of smaller, secondary crystals was couched, taking the place of the shattered master stone, until a new one could be grown.

With some trepidation she considered them. A shudder went over her at the thought of stepping back into the leys, where she had lately run for her life and almost been consumed. If it happened again, when the burning came, would she be able to escape a second time?

The crystals swelled with light at her approach, humming a silent note of approval. They knew her; they welcomed her. She was one of theirs now. She placed her hand upon one, then another. They opened to receive her; she was in no danger. They would guard her.

There was much work to be done. Many holes in the web to be rewoven since the immolation of Tiotiwakan. Composing her body for trance, she let her mind sink into the ley, and began.

Hours later, when she stepped out of the flows and regained her form, she was told that Branek was awaiting an audience.

She stretched, rubbed her arms, her flesh chilled from long hours in trance. She was not sure she wanted to see him. The last time he had seen her, she had been hysterical and drugged. And before that, they had argued. And before *that* –

She sighed. No, they probably needed to talk.

"Ask him to meet me down on the beach," she told Bek.

A walk in the sun and sea breeze would do her good. After long work in the other realms, it was good to connect with the things of this realm. And the last vestiges of summer still lay upon the island home. She should appreciate them before the cold winter of the Ocean of Storms descended. She had not spent enough time with the sea or the island this season, and it was from these things that she drew her strength, from which all Atlanteans drew it.

Branek came to her where she waited on the shore – right where this had all began, when she had gone to call the dolphins at summer solstice. The buildings of the temple were indistinct in the summer haze. The sun on the sea was as bright as a mirror of finest glass.

"I wasn't sure you would see me," he said. "After – everything."

"I was not sure either," Herata said. "But here you are. Walk with me."

They did walk along the strand, the waves tumbling around their feet. Gulls wheeled and shouted in the air above them. The ocean breeze was stiff and chill with the first touch of autumn.

"It's good to feel the surf," Branek said. "I miss it in the Great City. In Lacaon you can always hear it, feel the wind. The canals in Poseidonis are not the same."

"Why didn't you tell me about the leys in Lacaon?" she asked him. "The earthquake prevention?"

"I did," he said, surprised.

"But not the full extent," she said. "Not how much *aum* is drawn, how risky it is. It is wrong, Branek. No one can stop the earth from shaking when she wishes. It is folly to try."

He turned her to face him, frowning. "Is that another prophecy?"

"If you like. Your sister plays with fire; mind she is not burned."

He looked disgruntled. "I thought you were concerned with the new nexus."

She looked up at him, disbelieving. After everything that had happened, did he still not understand?

"The nexus. The earthquakes in Lacaon. The ziggurat in Ilethelme. It's all connected. The balance has tipped too far; the pendulum must swing back the other way. Soon."

"Now you are a mystic as well as a visionary," Branek scoffed.

She turned away, faced the sea. "I thought you believed in my visions. Did you not tell Meilikki so?"

He sighed, as if he was having to explain something over and over again to a child. "I believe your concerns are valid. But I don't believe yours is the only way."

"What other way is there?" she asked him.

"I am no adept, I do not know. There could be many other ways! The Sea Kings have tapped the flows for centuries, why suddenly would it all fall to pieces?"

"Maybe that is why: the Sea Kings have tapped the flows for centuries."

Branek turned her back around to face him again. "I don't believe that and neither do you! There are wise and safe ways to use the earthpower, we just have to figure out what they are now."

"No." It was all so clear to her now. "They may open this nexus, or not. They may move the leys, or not. But one day they will do something, and that will be it. The balance will fall the other way, and the burning will come."

"No," Branek said. "You cannot think that! If you see the consequences so clearly, then you are the one who must find another way. So find it!"

"There is no other way."

"You sound like you want this burning of yours to come."

"No!" Herata cried, moved to anger. "Never! But – I don't know what to do. They said I could stop the burning, but I don't know how…"

A storm of weeping muffled her. Her hands raised to dash the hot tears away from her cheeks. She cried so easily these days.

Branek put his arm around her, holding her tight against his side, warm and strong. "Stop, stop! You don't have to do it alone. Others will help."

"Will you?"

"Of course."

But somehow she detected a hollowness in his words. He cared for her, he respected her opinions, but on some level he was not convinced.

She slid out from under his arm, as much as she wanted to cling to him for comfort. "Who sent you here to check on me?" she asked him. "The Patriarch? Herodian?"

He looked at her askance. "No one sent me. How often do I have to say it?"

"I don't believe you," she said. She wanted to, more than anything. But she didn't.

"Gods below, Herata," he said, "how can you say that to me?"

"You did not tell me about what the White Temple is planning. What else haven't you told me?"

"I did tell you!"

"Under duress. What else is there? How can I know you are telling the truth?"

"Now you are just being insulting. What have I done to deserve this?"

"You – you—" She pressed a hand to her mouth. Conflicting emotions overwhelmed her. She wanted to believe him, but none of his actions since he arrived the night of Tiotiwakan made any sense to her. How could he come to her in such agitation, and yet keep secrets about the Poseideion from her? How could he pledge his love, and then refuse her when she offered herself to him freely? Was he manipulating her? She had no experience with men. How could she even know if he was?

Branek took a step back, folded his arms. "This is about the other night." It was not a question.

"No."

"You are angry at me. You are trying to punish me."

"No!"

"Well, it's working. You might as well just kick me in the stones, finish it off. It would be more honest."

"I want to believe you, but how can I when you are working for the White Temple?" she cried, at her wit's end.

"How dare you accuse me of that, when I have told you flat out that I am not!" he said with flinty anger. He reached out and grabbed her wrist, dragging her close to him. He towered above her; usually she loved that but now it made her a little afraid. His eyes were blazing with anger. "Go on, then – what did you say? 'Ream my mind out like a grape.' You'll see I'm not lying to you. Come on, do it!"

He meant it. And she did try, touching his temple with her fingers, attempting to match the leys of her own body and mind with his, use that harmony to touch his mind, share his thoughts. But the buzzing cloud of her anger, and his, made it impossible.

"I cannot," she said. "You are closed to me."

"So." He dropped her wrist. "It seems you will just have to trust me, my lady."

Herata closed her eyes. "I can't."

He was quiet a moment. "I see," he said at last. "Then there is nothing more to say. I have told you I love you, and I have asked you to be my wife. And instead you accuse me of plotting against you."

The tears started again. "I'm sorry!" And she was. "But I just can't take the chance."

All of a sudden Branek grabbed her and pulled her to him. He kissed her, long and hard. Confused, despairing, she yielded to it, kissing him back, clinging to him, and it went on until he left her breathless. Then he let her go.

"I will leave you now," he said. "Coming here was a mistake. I hope you can find it in yourself to trust me again. If you come to your senses I will be in the Great City for another moon."

And he left her on the beach, and she wept, and her tears were as bitter and salty as the ocean.

Chapter Twelve

One week later Herata was summoned to speak before the Council of Kings, at the festival of the Equinox. By now her deeds were infamous; her name was bandied about in wineshops with that of the blackest sorcerers in legend. It was used to frighten children when they would not go to bed: *Lady Herata will come and get you and feed you to the Hexachon!*

Amalthea pulled her from the ley chamber, where she was lost in the flows, and brought her to the temple docks. A black longship warped in under crystal power. On its black sail was the five-pointed star of the Sea Kings.

From it descended men armed in black scale, marines of the Sea Kings' navy. They surrounded Herata and her small party – Amalthea, Bek, a junior priest – on the stone jetty. Their captain addressed the Sea Priestess.

"Herata of Salmon Nome, Keeper of Nine Seas Temple, your testimony is compelled by the Council of Kings at the Feast of the Autumnal Equinox. Your involvement in the disaster at the colony of Tiotiwakan will be examined." He handed her a crystal case; inside was a message stone which carried the same missive in plain text, but embedded with the Star of Atlantis, the royal seal.

Herata knew this man, the captain. He was a cousin of hers, who had also been raised in the Hall of the Salmon in Poseidonis. She had not seen him in a decade or more; he was a man now, not a boy, but his pale gold eyes and the thuggish set of his jaw were still the same.

"I have no involvement in that disaster, Darir, except that I warned against it," Herata said.

"That remains to be seen," Darir said. "Your attendance is required."

"I will take my own ship," Herata said. She would not go as a prisoner; she had the dignity of Nine Seas to uphold and the temple had ships and to spare.

"We will sail with you," Darir said. "We are charged with … attending you."

Arresting you, was what Herata heard in his voice. She decided to push it.

"We will leave on the morrow," she said. "I must prepare."

"We will leave now," Darir said, his voice strained. "You are commanded."

"If my lord the Prince of Lacaon were here, he would not stand for this, my lady," Amalthea said quietly into Herata's ear, moved to speak by loyalty, even though she was trembling at the sight of so many armed men.

Herata frowned at her. "I need no sword-girt colonial oaf to defend me, girl," she said quietly. "Indeed, I need no defending at all, do I, Cousin?" she said more loudly, goading Darir.

"My sister was at our estates in the Great Land," Darir said in answer. "She administered the temple there."

Oh dear. Herata caught Bek's eye, flicked her gaze back to the temple. This was about to take a turn for the worse. *Go pack,* she mouthed. *Hurry.*

"I hope Dariti is well," she said to Darir. The cousins were twins, one *inaum,* one *aumvre,* as often seemed to be the case.

Bek tried to slip between two of the soldiers and leave the jetty; they loomed over him for a moment, menacingly, then parted and let him pass.

"She was at the crystal when … when it happened," Darir went on.

"I am sorry." And she was.

"She is blind now, she was made *inaum.*"

"I grieve with you, cousin."

"She may not survive," Darir went on. He stepped close to her, hulking over her. This close she could see his eyes were bright with unshed tears, but the feeling she got from him, through the crystals in his gear and hers, was unalloyed rage. "So, I pray you, Herata, defy me. Give me reason…" He gripped the hilt of the shortsword at his belt.

Herata put her hand on his chest, projecting strength and sympathy. Dariti was her cousin as well, after all. And she did grieve, more than he who was *inaum* could ever know.

"Nothing could make me keep you from attending your sister in her time of need. We will leave at once, cousin. In *my* galley."

In this, as in most small things these days, though not the large, she got her way, and the marines and Herata's retinue left Nine Seas for the Great City in her own green-painted galley before the sun had set.

The galley sailed all night, and dawn was just breaking as they entered the Grand Canal. The pale light of dawn sketched the carvings in the walls of the canal in stark chiaroscuro. Herata studied them, the great Kings and Queens of Atlantis, wondering what they would do in her place.

***

Two days before the Feast of the Equinox Branek rose at dawn, rousted Nestor and Sokar out of bed as well, and forced them to fight him in the courtyard of his townhouse with wooden swords.

They groaned and shuffled, as unused as he to hard living anymore. "Some food, lord, please," Sokar whined. "Beer, tea, something!" He was a very demon in an actual fight, but in peacetime he tended to outright indolence.

"No, no, lazybones," Branek said, whipping the practice sword around in front of him. "Defend yourself!"

He attacked and Sokar fell back, clumsily blocking his thrusts. Branek pressed him harder, backing him around the courtyard.

He felt weirdly agitated. He hadn't been able to sleep. And he would have to get back into fighting trim if he was going home to Lacaon. Too much rich food, too many parties, too much sitting around jawing and shuffling papers had softened him. No one even carried a weapon in the streets of Atlantis. It wasn't like that in the Inner Sea. Late autumn left plenty of time for pirates to stage a raid or two before winter made the wine-dark sea too turbulent to cross without benefit of crystal power.

He wanted to fight. Fighting made sense: the edge, the point, thrust and parry, live or die. It was simple. It was clean. No shades of gray, no hidden meanings. No secrets; you could tell where a man would strike next by his eyes, the set of his shoulders. No secrets.

Gods, he was sick of the capital. It was time to go home. So he battered poor Nestor and Sokar around the courtyard, using his blade to say what he couldn't in words.

Ardath, the temple novice who served the house, coming in for her day's work, stopped in the courtyard to watch them. She seemed rather fascinated by the sight of them, their half-naked bodies, sweating in the cool morning air. Branek found himself watching her watching them, wondering what she thought. She was sworn to the temple, still a novice, doubtless virgin yet.

Nestor used this moment of distraction to hook his blade behind Branek's knee and yank up, jerking the prince's leg out from under him. Branek fell hard on the hard stones of the courtyard instead of the soft sands of the practice grounds at home.

He just lay there for a moment, huffing uselessly, immobilized, the breath knocked clean out of him. "Hah!" Nestor crowed, "That's worth a bite or two I wager!" Sokar hooted in agreement and they went to kitchen door at the back of the courtyard to pester the cooks for some breakfast.

"My lord, are you alright?" Ardath asked, standing over him, looking anxious.

He nodded, still unable to speak. She was biting prettily at a fingertip at the sight of him on the ground. From where he lay he could see right up the slit in her skirt to the sweet curve of her hip. She had the old Atlantean looks, copper of skin and black of hair, with huge amber eyes. Not unlike Herata. Gods, but it had been a long time. He wondered if she was amenable. He preferred free women to slaves, always had.

Ardath reached out a hand to help the prince to his feet. He took it and levered himself up. Still holding her hand, he ran his thumb caressingly along the back of it.

She didn't seem to notice. "I heard something strange in the market just now," she said.

"And what -- might -- that be?" he asked, still breathless.

"The Lady Herata has been arrested," Ardath said. "She is being brought before the Five Kings."

"What?" he said stupidly.

"She will be tried at the Feast of the Equinox. Her galley is in the outer gates of the harbor right now, or so they say." The look on Ardath's face was apologetic, concerned.

Branek leaned over, hands on knees, sucking in air, trying to get his lungs to work properly. Suddenly the floating anxiety he had felt all last night, all morning, made perfect sense.

Defend her.

"Her own galley?" he asked. "You're sure?"

Ardath spread her hands. "It was just talk of the market, my lord. I don't know."

"Yes," he said. "Contact Nine Seas. Try to find out. Right now!"

Catching his anxiety, Ardath nodded and ran into the house.

His shirt was lying on a bench. He yanked it on and followed her.

Part of the cloakroom was a small armory; Inner Sea habits died hard even on the island home. He racked the practice sword, took his own steel shortsword from the rack, belted it on, chose two more for Nestor and Sokar.

Back in the courtyard he whistled. They shuffled toward him. He tossed the swords to them.

"Come on!" he said.

They gaped at him in surprise.

"Herata has been arrested," he said. "Come on, come on!"

The two of them buckled on the swordbelts and followed him out the front gate.

Halfway down the street he heard a call behind him. Ardath.

"Her galley," she called after them from the gate. "They usually dock at the Street of the Albatross."

He raised a hand in thanks, his earlier intentions completely forgotten, and the three of them ran down the street, toward the outer circles, and the docks.

Herata's galley passed through the outer harbor and into the inner canals of the city. The Great City was a-bustle for the festival of Equinox. It was a less sacred festival in the temples, less keyed to the flows of the earthpower, but it was popular with the common folk and the merchant class. Folk came from near and far to visit the Great City, before the close of winter made traveling difficult. In the spirit of the balance between light and dark that occurred on the Equinox, gifts were exchanged between friend and foe alike, symbolizing restoration of order and new beginnings.

The city streets were crowded and the canals choked with longships and gondolas. Lights were strung everywhere, candle and crystal and ordinary electric – from the eaves of houses and the prows of gondolas, upon the gleaming walls of the city circuits. Bonfires were lit in the crossroads. They symbolized faith in the cycles of life on the earth, faith that in the gathering dark of the year that the light would return.

Shops were overflowing with the expensive, beautiful and meaningless gifts that were traditional on this holiday: *aum*-lit jewelry, singing crystals, eternal flame lamps that tapped into the flows. Herata shivered to feel so many crystals everywhere, all around her, put to such trivial uses. They were unhappy. They did not like to see their potential squandered so blatantly. They blamed her.

Or perhaps, Herata mused, she really was stark raving mad after all.

She shook her head and the feeling passed. She remembered the joy she had taken as a child in the Great City bejeweled for the Equinox. Amalthea beside her was gaping around with wonderment, in spite of the direness of their situation.

Off *aum* power in the inner circles of the city, Herata's galley glided along the central canal, sweeps plowing majestically. Crowds gathered at the sides of the canal, pointing and exclaiming: *The lady of Nine Seas! The mad seeress!*

Something landed with a splat on the deck beside her; Herata jumped and screamed, startled. It was a rotten egg. She stepped back; but following it immediately, a flower landed on the deck beside the stinking, runny mass. A starflower, the sacred blossom of Atlantis. People were throwing things to her galley, to *her*, and at her. Gifts and poison both. She stared at the things on the deck, amazed. People were hearing her words after all.

Darir pulled her back into the shelter of the awning. "Your reputation precedes you, cousin," he noted with spiteful pleasure.

Herata picked up a blossom that landed at her feet, showed it to him, its stem curled with a twist of ribbon tied in the Mother's Knot, a symbol of protection and good fortune. *Maybe it's not too late after all,* she thought. She slid the flower into her hair, above her ear.

Darir spoke to the captain of the galley. They traded words; Darir gestured threateningly. The galley left the Grand Canal and glided to a stop at a quay in the Silver Circle, sweeps up, nowhere near either the House of the Salmon or the sacred precincts.

"What is the meaning of this?" Herata asked the both of them.

"His orders, lady," her captain said. "Or – he'll arrest us too…" He looked miserable, but he had stopped the galley.

Herata put a hand on his where it lay on the tiller, comforting him. "It is alright, Lir, do not concern yourself." She would not allow Darir to torment or humiliate her people.

The gangway slid out. A crowd was already massing on the quay.

There was no carriage on the quay, no gondola awaiting her in the water, and they still had a ways to go, wherever they were going.

"No transport?" she asked Darir.

"No." His eyes were hard. "We walk."

She eyed the crowd gathering on the quay. So. A gauntlet. In ancient times the kings of Atlantis had run them in truth, and those who could not run fast enough or fight back hard enough had not made it to the end alive, and a new king was crowned. It was an ancient rite, and an effective chastisement. Whether Darir had been given these orders, or it was his own spite, she did not know. She was fairly sure no one would actually hurt her, but the scorn of the common crowd, their disapprobation, would be hard to bear.

Fairly sure. Why then was she so afraid?

"No, no," Bek was saying, arguing with Darir. "This is unacceptable!"

Herata raised a hand, silencing him. She would not make a scene. It was what Darir wanted.

She took a deep breath. "Let us go then."

Marines marched down the gangway. Darir gestured to her. She went.

On the quay, the marines fanned out, pressing the crowd back – but not too far, out of weapon's length, but not out of shouting distance. The shouts of the crowd washed over her; curses, blessings, questions. She had wanted people to hear her words; now she was hearing theirs.

The marines formed a rectangle for march, Darir at its end, behind her. She could feel his gloating eyes on her back. Within the square of soldiers her people moved to surround her, Bek in front, Meilikki and Amalthea behind. It was a small retinue but she was grateful for their support. The sense of Darir's malignant gaze on her lessened.

The lead marine looked back, at her, at his captain. She nodded. They began.

The streets of the Silver Circle were wide, but they were crowded this morning -- for the festival, and it seemed word of her passage was quickly getting around. The crowd grew and grew all the time as they walked, seething around the square of marines, then pushing on it, jostling the soldiers, yelling, arms flailing. The soldiers pushed back with the shafts of their spears, and sometimes the points.

Herata spoke to Darir over her shoulder. "The Five won't thank you if I end up trampled out here."

His face was grim. "Just keep walking."

A flash of shadow alerted her and she ducked; something exploded at her feet – an overripe melon, spraying seeds and guts around the street. Herata pulled her skirts aside and stepped over it, just glad it was not something worse. Her heart was hammering, but she was still reasonably certain that no one would really try to harm her – or at least that Darir's marines would be able to stop them before they did.

Cries of "betrayer" and "sorceress" rang from the crowd. And she was, she was those things, but only in the service of a higher purpose. She hoped people could come to see that. Behind her, even across the distance between them, she could feel Amalthea trembling. The girl had been called to a service harsher than she could have ever imagined when she first pledged to the temple. Herata groped back with one hand and took Amalthea's, squeezing it. "Be strong. No one will harm us." After a moment Amalthea squeezed back.

The marine to Herata's left stumbled, pushed by an especially hard surge of the crowd, and into the momentary gap in the line a figure darted, straight toward Herata. The marine on the other side raised his spear, but Herata cried out," Stop!" putting a hand out to forestall him.

The whole line of march lurched to a stop.

"It's only a child," Herata said. Although a child could carry a knife as well as any adult.

It was a girl, about ten years old, perhaps, dressed in a good but plain gown, a garland of ears of grain in her hair, for the Equinox festival. She came up to Herata, and raised something in her hands.

In spite of herself Herata flinched back. But it was not a weapon: instead it was a necklace, links of copper holding a thin crescent of copper set with colored crystals, that softly shifted through the spectrum in a repeating pattern, glowing brightly even in the morning light. *Aum* stones.

The girl held it out to Herata, who took it, wondering.

"It is my Equinox gift," the girl said. "From my father. I give it to you, Lady Herata. It is wasteful of *aum*, as you have said. I do not want the empire to fall. So I renounce it."

The restive crowd grew silent, watching. Herata ran her fingers over the little crystals on the necklace. Such a little thing, such a tiny use of *aum*, but multiplied a thousandfold, a millionfold… such a gesture could make a difference.

Herata cupped the girl's cheek in her hand. "What is your name, child?"

"Ayesha, lady."

"I thank you, Ayesha. I will see this *aum* is returned to the earth."

The girl curtseyed, then darted away again, past the marines and through the crowd. There was a murmur through the watching crowd at the scene they had just witnessed.

At a harsh word from Darir the procession started up again.

The crowd started up again as well, yells and shoving and insults, but now here and there amongst them, were also people who brought forth their tools of *aum* to be renounced, and gave them to Herata – jewelry, toys, memory crystals, crystals keyed to locks, crystals for heating cold food, all the little trinkets that made life in the island home pleasant and easy. So many that Herata could not carry them all, and handed them off to her people, and then to the marines around her. Sneaking a look behind her, she could tell Darir was incensed, but she would not stop taking them. In this small way people were trying to help her. She would not ignore them.

Someone in the crowd brought forth a basket, and she took it on her arm and received ever more of these reverse Equinox gifts, not given to promote harmony, but given up. In spite of the dread of her arrest, and her upcoming tribunal, joy filled her heart. All her work, her struggle, her quest was not in vain. Her message was being heard.

Branek and his men ran along the street at the quayside on the outer canal of the Silver Circle, darting between the crowds. It was a long way to the outer harbor, to the docks, but you could get most places in the inner circles as fast on foot as you could in any conveyance, given the twisting, circular nature of the streets and the many canals to cross.

Branek had no real idea what he would do when he found her. He just knew Herata was in the hands of her enemies and he had to be at her side. Whether it was a compulsion the Hexachon had laid on him or it was the urging of his own heart did not matter. The hard words they had traded on the beach were set aside. He only knew he had failed her before, disastrously, during the destruction of Tiotiwakan, simply by failing to be there, and he would not fail again.

"My lord, Bran, wait! Look!" Nestor caught his arm, pulling him to a stop, and pointed across the canal, at a galley that was docked across the way and down, on the outer side. Its sail was down, displaying no sigil, but its lines were familiar.

Branek snapped his fingers, pointed. "That's it, that's her ship!" The *Queen Elissa*. What was it doing docked in the Silver Circle, away from anywhere in particular? That made no sense. "Come on," he said.

They ran back down the street to the next bridge, doubled back to the quay where the galley was docked. Figures moved about on the deck, securing it for what looked like a long stay, lashing the sail about the yard-arm, coiling ropes.

Branek pounded up the gangplank.

"Prince Branek!" said Lir, the captain, completely astonished.

Branek gasped for a minute, his still-bruised lungs trying to drag in air. "Is your mistress on board?" he finally managed.

"No," Lir said. "We sailed with a company of marines. They took her."

"Where?"

Lir pointed northwest, around the curve of the canal. "Landward, into the inner circles. There was a crowd; they followed." He looked worried.

"On foot?" Branek asked incredulously.

He nodded.

"Why?"

Lir's mouth hardened. "To humiliate her."

Or worse, Branek thought with a chill. The anxiety he had felt sharpened into real fear.

"If they're on foot, that means we can catch them, boss," Sokar said.

"Right," Branek said.

Lir looked confused. "What can you do against twenty men? In the middle of the city?"

"We'll think of something," Branek said.

"There's something else," the captain said. "The marine captain; the lady knows him, but he is no friend of hers. He threatened her."

Gods below, what's going on here? Branek thought. "Let's go," he said to his men, and off they went, westward along the canal, pushing through the crowded street, looking for a bridge to cross without having to double back.

The marine procession crossed a bridge into the Golden Circle, where the streets were wider, and the crowd grew correspondingly as thick. Even through the streets were wider, the sense of crowding did not diminish, as the buildings were higher here, white and black stone townhouses, cutting off the morning sun.

Here the tenor of the crowd changed. Less people came to surrender their toys of *aum*, more insults were thrown: "Witch!" and "Traitor!" Herata could sense the many crystal devices in use in the houses and shops around her as they passed – locks, lights, books, weapons, all sorts of things. The people of the more affluent inner circles were less receptive to her message, for if *aum* must be renounced, they had more to lose. She realized that with a new appreciation now, as she felt the presence of their crystal-based way of life all around her, as she never had before; felt it in her body.

The crowd grew uglier and more physical. The marines had to use the butts and even the points of their spears more often to keep the crowd back. Had Darir known, had he planned the line of march this way? She did not quite credit him with the wit to do that; when she'd known him as a child he had never been the brightest stone in the array. But someone had, perhaps. Where were they going, anyway? It was frightening, not knowing.

She turned back to face him. "Where are we going?" she asked.

"Just keep walking!" he said.

"I demand to know!"

The marine beside her took her arm, trying to drag her along, but she threw him off.

"You are in no position to demand anything," Darir said. "Now move!" He stepped up between Meilikki and Amalthea and gave her a hard shove.

She was unprepared for it and she stumbled. This seemed to incite the latent bloodlust of the crowd; the noise level surged up, and Bek shouted with dismay as a stone bounced off his arm, thrown from somewhere in the crowd. The marines tightened up their formation, crowding Herata and her people, but the surrounding mob pushed in as well, jostling the square of marines, blurring their formation.

The crowd turned on itself, the fewer members who were Herata's supporters pushing back against the many who were not, those who feared her message or even wished to see her blood spilt, her supporters trying to give her party room to move, to get out. Darir yelled orders at his men over the din of the crowd, and they stepped in tighter, closing formation, shifting their spears to their outer sides, held level alongside their bodies, a barrier against the crowd.

Except for two. The marine who had caught Herata's arm turned not to the outside, but to the inside, facing her, and swept up the point of his spear. At the same time the marine on her right, his opposite number, fell inside the formation too, back to back with the first, and raised his spear toward the other marines, holding them off.

Before Herata could even scream the first marine swung his spear in a low slashing arc toward her, the point huge and long and glittering steel in the morning light. That swing was meant to terrorize her, not kill, and terrorize it did; she jumped back, the point whistled bare inches from her belly, and she stumbled and fell hard on the flagstones of the street.

The marine raised his spear for a killing thrust. Everything seemed to slow down; she could see the edge of the spear point gleaming in the sunlight, hear Amalthea's screams behind her, smell the brackish water of the canal just beyond them, feel the pounding of her own heart. She was going to die. She had failed. She hitched in her breath for a scream, her death-scream. The spear thrust forward.

And then someone else darted in from the side, through the gap in the marines' line, and slammed into the spearman, carrying him away from her and out through the gap in the other side of the line, into the press of the crowd. People shrieked as the two bodies went flailing down. Blood spurted as this newcomer buried his shortsword in the marine's belly. The street was bedlam – shouts, screams, the clash of arms.

The second marine who had been holding off his compatriots, whirled around and saw his fellow assassin gutted, and Herata lying defenseless on the ground. He tossed his spear lightly into the air, caught it in an overhand grip, and drew back to throw it and pin Herata to the ground through the belly like a fish. She scrabbled back, pushing with her hands and feet, but there was no way she could get away.

And then the point of a sword exploded out through the man's chest, shattering the links of his mail shirt. Herata finally did scream as blood burst from his chest and sprayed her. His mouth opened in a huge gaping hole. His spear clattered to the ground.

He sank to his knees, already dead, and behind him, holding the sword that pierced his chest, she saw Branek. He was looking right at her.

The prince had to put a foot up against the shoulder of the dead man to wrench free his sword. The dead marine pitched forward and collapsed bonelessly onto the street. Branek flicked the blood off his sword with a whirling cut in the air, and strode toward her.

The blood on him, on his skin and clothes, and the still-bloody sword, came toward her. His blue eyes blazed into hers.

He stood above her. Utterly helpless, she looked up at him.

He offered her his free hand to help her up, and she took it, and he pulled her to her feet.

Relief exploded within her. If he was really working for the White Temple, there was no way he would let her live through this carnage; even if his directive had not been to kill her, it was too convenient an outcome for the Poseideion's plans. He hadn't lied. He wasn't her enemy.

She fell into his embrace like a comet falling into the sun.

He caught her up with his free arm, crushing her to him, kissed the top of her head, pressed his cheek against it. "Thank the gods, we came in time."

"How did you know?" Herata asked him.

He shrugged. "I felt it."

Just like before, after Tiotiwakan. It was true, the Hexachon had set him to be her protector. The Six were wise, they had chosen well.

Time and sound seemed to crash in on her again: Amalthea's wails, the din of the crowd around them, the coppery stench of blood in the air.

A sudden thought made her spin around; who was responsible for this?

Her eyes fell on Darir, still standing at the back of the ragged formation. When her gaze fell on him, his eyes widened in alarm and he backed away, as if making to dart into the crowd and disappear.

"Hold him!" she cried, pointing. She started toward him.

One of Branek's men, Nestor by name, and a man from the crowd took Darir by the arms and held him, struggling, as Herata approached. Herata stepped up to him and grabbed his face in her hand.

This time her anger gave her strength, focus, and she shaped it into a weapon, a probe, and she did indeed split Darir's mind open like a soft fruit, rummaging through his thoughts for knowledge of his orders.

She sensed first of all sorrow at his sister's fate, and fear for her, crippling fear that his twin might die and leave him alone. And then anger, terrible anger at what had happened, and at her, Herata, his childhood playmate, whom he imagined responsible for the disaster. And then finally a cruel pleasure at the thought of her fear, running the gauntlet through the streets of the city. He had received orders to do that, yes – but no more. There was no scent or taste of murder in him; he had been as surprised as she at the attack. He had not commanded it. He hadn't known.

It only took a moment, but by the time she was done he was screaming like a banshee at the pain of her mind pillaging his. The crowd had grown completely silent, staring in horror.

She released him, and he sagged helplessly in his captor's grip.

"It was not him," she said. "He didn't know."

The two assassins were dead, bled out on the street. Only the gods could question them now.

Herata looked around, wiping the spearman's blood off her cheek. "Anyone else?" she asked.

"My lady," said Darir's adjutant, his face sickly pale, "We were only given orders to conduct you to the High King's palace, and in safety. We knew nothing of this, on Poseidon's name, I swear it."

The other marines followed suit, swearing also that they had no orders to harm her: "No, lady, we swear it." "By the goddess mother, we swear." She believed them. They looked too scared to lie.

"Where to, my lady?" Branek asked, his sword still held ready.

"The House of the Salmon," she said.

"But these are soldiers of the royal navy," Branek said, kicking one of the bodies. "King's men."

"If my own father has raised his hand against me, better I know it now," Herata said. "And I know the wards set upon that house, once there I can protect myself."

"As you command," he said.

She raked her gaze over the crowd around her – her people, Bek supporting a fainting Amalthea; Branek's men, the blood-soaked Sokar, who had killed the first spearman; the marines, shuffling uncomfortably; the gaping crowd beyond.

"Your captain is indisposed," she said to the marines, "and, whatever my legal status, I am the ranking member of this – this assemblage, and until we reach the hall of my father *you will follow my orders!*" By the end she was shouting; rage filled her, but right now rage was better than fear.

"By your command, lady," the adjutant said.

"Then we march!"

Crowds followed them all the way into the Oricalch Circle and the very steps of the Salmon Hall, but no one moved against them. After all, Branek still had a bloody sword in his grip, and Herata had made a man scream like he was dying with just the touch of her hands. And word of that traveled even faster than they could march.

Chapter Thirteen

The appearance of an armed and bloodied party at its doors created a furor in the House of the Salmon. At first the door guards would not let them in, until Herata spoke the code word that unlocked the crystal locks on the doors and made them swing open. Then the marines, eager to redeem themselves it seemed, crowded in, making way for Herata and the others.

A servant passing through the front hall yelped in fear and dropped a vase of flowers she was carrying at the sight of the three of them, Herata, Branek and Sokar, disheveled and covered with blood.

"Get Hecuba," Herata told her, and the slave girl ran back into the depths of the house, only too glad to get away from the awful scene.

"The wards," Herata said, a bit frantically, "we must set the wards."

"But if your father-" Branek said, trailing off. It was a terrible prospect to contemplate.

"If no one can get out, then no one can get in either," Herata said. "No reinforcements." She ran to an array of fist-sized crystals set in the wall, and pressed several of them in a complex sequence. They hummed and glowed redly at her touch.

Branek couldn't see or feel them, but he knew that lines of radiant energy had been drawn around the perimeter of the house, lines that would deliver a painful, incapacitating shock to anyone who tried to breach the walls. They would not stop a determined assault, especially a force that had the *aumvre* with it, but they would hold off a few men, for a while. Long enough for the truth of things to be known, perhaps.

"There," Herata said. The task accomplished, she sagged in sudden reaction against the wall, covering her face. "Oh, gods!" she cried. Her shoulders shook; fear radiated off her in waves.

Branek went to her but she flinched away, and he realized he was still holding his bloody shortsword in his hand. He cast it down on the floor, but his hands, too, were still covered in blood. He didn't want to touch her like that. Herata breathed in whooping gasps, trying to get control of herself, and failing.

"What has happened?" a voice cried from the stairs at the end of the hall. It was Hecuba, the house steward.

"Herata was almost just murdered in the street!" Branek said, glad to have someone to vent his emotions on. He had fought and killed men before, but in pitched battle, pirates at sea or nighttime raids against his home. Never one on one, in broad daylight, in front of a street full of staring civilians. Never someone who had a weapon drawn on someone he loved. His hands were shaking. He still felt like he couldn't catch his breath.

Is that what I have to do to make you love me? he thought, looking at Herata. Kill a man?

Herata shot him a dark, anguished look, as if she could read his thoughts. A sob broke past her hands clamped over her mouth.

"My gods!" Hecuba said. She hastened down the stairs toward the priestess, but Herata flinched away from her too.

"My lady," Amalthea said, coming up to her mistress. "Let me." Her face was ghost white and wet with tears, but she took Herata's hands and held them firmly, looking into Herata's eyes.

A strange stillness came over both of them, still but charged with some unnamable tension. Amalthea was doing something, some thing only the *aumvre* could do, to help and calm her mistress, seeing into her body, slowing her heart, her respiration, regulating the flow of *aum* through her body. Laodice had told Branek of such things, but he couldn't really imagine it. He watched with a complex mixture of jealousy and relief; he could never share that intimacy with Herata, whom he loved, but after what he'd seen in the street, he wasn't sure he wanted even her to touch his mind.

Hecuba crossed over to him. "My lord, let us help you," she said. She took his elbow, guided him to a seat on the stairs. Slaves appeared with bowls of warm water and cloths to clean the blood off his hands and face. He let them, but he couldn't relax. Nothing was really resolved.

"Is the King in residence?" he asked Hecuba.

"No, he is at the high palace, in council," she answered. "But I shall send word to him at once."

"No!" Branek grabbed her hand with his still-damp one, dragging her closer. "What do you know of this?"

"Nothing!" Hecuba said. "Why, how can you ask it?"

He gestured to the marines that still milled about the hallway. "The men who attacked us were marines of the Kings' navy. Under whose orders, if not one of the Five?"

Hecuba jerked her hand out of his grasp, took a step back. "By the gods, if I were a man, I would kill you for that insinuation. For that dishonor to my House! You shame yourself with such talk, Prince."

Branek rubbed a hand across his face. "Herodian does not tell you everything."

"What kind of man do you think he is?" Hecuba said, outraged. "She is his *daughter!* His only child!"

Her rage seemed genuine, but how could he know? He could read no one's mind. He remembered how hurt and angry he had been when Herata had made similar accusations against him, only a week ago. It was a hard thing. But so was murder.

"I will send word to the Salmon King at once, and you will regret those words, Prince of Lacaon," Hecuba said with icy dignity.

A servant returned his sword to him, cleaned of gore. He stood up and slid it into its scabbard with a menacing click.

"I devoutly hope so," he told her. "But we shall see."

He looked to Herata. She and Amalthea were apart now, no longer bonded in psychic trance. Herata seemed calmer. She embraced Amalthea, kissed her forehead.

"Thank you," she said. "Well done, child."

"Thank you, my lady," Amalthea said shyly. She seemed calmer as well.

Branek went to them. He gathered Herata into his arms, and then on impulse, Amalthea, too – it had shown unusual strength of character for her to overcome her own terror and tend to her mistress. He kissed the top of her curly dark head. "Good girl," he said.

She leaned into him with a little sigh, and they all stood there for a moment, arms around each other, taking comfort in that simple contact.

"Is my father--?" Herata asked, her voice muffled in his shirt. She did not finish. She was still afraid.

"Herodian is at the high palace, but Hecuba will send word," Branek said. "She denies any knowledge of this. She seems sincere, but – I don't know."

Herata peeked at the house guards who had appeared in the hall, armed like the marines with long spears, taking up positions at the corners, but otherwise seeming calm. "It seems if they meant us harm they would have done it by now," she said.

Branek could only shake his head. He just did not know. Plots and schemes in the Great City had always been as thick as smoke, and they could not know who their enemies might be, even in the House of their own Nome. He wished they were in Lacaon, all safe in faraway Lacaon. By the gods, things were simpler in the Inner Sea; your enemy did not plot and scheme against you, but stormed your gates with fire and sword. At least that way, you know who and where they were!

Hecuba approached them. "My lady, let us tend to you," she said, gesturing to the many servants waiting in the hall. "You cannot see the king your father like this." She indicated Herata's blood-spattered gown. She looked at Branek; her eyes were flat. "My lord, you should go," she said.

"Not likely!" he said angrily.

"Then may we attend you and your men in the guest quarters?" Hecuba said icily. She indicated the west wing of the house, away from the family apartments.

"No," Branek said. His arms tightened about both girls.

"It's alright," Herata said. "I am not afraid." She whispered in his ear, "You will know if I need you."

He would, he knew it. Suddenly he was very tired. By the gods, the sun was barely up and already he had killed a man today. That man's blood was still on him, on his clothes, in his hair. He suddenly wanted a drink and a bath, very badly.

Herata had a flower tucked in her hair, a starflower. In it was a spatter of blood, thickly clotting. Disgusted, he plucked it out and threw it on the floor.

"If you have need of me, I will be there on the instant," he vowed.

Herata nodded. Reluctantly, he released her.

The marine captain seemed to have recovered somewhat. He sat slumped on the stairs where Branek had been a moment before. Herata went to him, bent down to look him in the face.

"Believe it or not, I do grieve with you, cousin. I pray Dariti recovers."

He couldn't meet her eyes; Branek couldn't blame him. "Will she-?"

"No," Herata said gently. "She will never recover her sight."

A sob wrung from him. Herata touched his arm; he flinched away.

"I am sorry," Herata said. "I would have stopped it if I could. I did try, you know."

The man just wept, head bowed on drawn-up knees.

Herata addressed the marines, who were still expectantly waiting. "You are dismissed."

They gathered their captain up, and left the House of the Salmon.

"My lord?" a servant said beckoning Branek to the guest quarters. Sokar and Nestor were waiting for him, still bloody, looking as drawn as he felt.

He looked over his shoulder. Herata was going to the east wing, the family quarters. Out of his sight, but yes, he would know if she needed him. He could feel it, like a wire drawn tight between them.

He let the slaves lead him away.

***

Herata and Amalthea bathed together; neither of them wanted to be alone, and Herata could not bear the thought of strangers' hands on her, even trusted slaves of the Nome. Having cleansed herself, she soaked for a while in the hot water, trying to ease her tight muscles, clenched in horror at what had happened.

She tried to push it away, tried not to think about it, afraid she would slide down into a maelstrom of panic. She had almost died! If Branek had not been there ...

She refused to think about the thought she had heard from him, in the front hall... *kill a man*... no, she would not think it! She would have to think of it at one point, and soon, all of it, murder, terror, the feel of the dead soldier's blood spattering her face – but no, no, not now. Tomorrow she would be brought before the Five Kings in Council and tried for a crime she did not commit. She had to save her strength for that.

"Come," she said to Amalthea, climbing out of the bath. It was not helping. She was too keyed up.

They dressed, and Herata paced around her mother's old apartments, waiting for her father to appear, wondering if she had run willingly into a deadly trap.

At last they received word that Herodian had returned. Herata met Branek in the hall before the king's audience chamber.

At the sight of him she went into his arms, pressing her face into his shoulder. He held her tightly, stroking her hair. She owed him her life twice over now. The feel of his arms around her was the feel of life itself.

"I should never have doubted you," she said. "Forgive me."

"Always, my princess," he said.

She turned in the circle of his arms and apprehensively eyed the large double doors to the royal audience chamber, set with steel and oricalch. Two house soldiers guarded them, their long spears upright, watching the couple dispassionately.

"Are you ready?" Branek asked.

Ready to face her father and ask him if he plotted to have her killed? "Yes," she said.

Branek started forward, his arm still around her.

"Wait," Herata said. "I must do this alone."

A look of alarm came over his face. "No," he said, "I could never allow that."

"Herodian is a subtle man," Herata said. "Even if he wants me dead he will never draw the knife himself. The gods curse those who spill their own blood. He would never do anything so – crude."

He put his hand to her cheek. "I can't let you go in there alone!" He made the audience chamber sound like the pits of hell instead of a royal abode.

"I need to. I have to show him I'm strong enough, myself. If you're there he'll think I'm weak, that I can't face him."

"But-"

"Don't make me command you, my prince," she said gently. "Remember I am of the royal blood of the Nome, and you are just a simple colonial." She smiled to take the sting out of it, but she would do it if she had to.

He shook his head, knowing he was beaten. "I will be right out here," he said.

She nodded to the guards, and they opened the doors. Alone she walked into the audience chamber.

Herodian, the King her father, was waiting for her.

The king sat on a low but richly carved chair; not quite a throne, but close enough. He wore regalia of his office; the purple robe and oricalch crown of a Sea King. This was no simple family visit.

But at the sight of her, the stern look on his face completely melted, and he jumped up, rushed to her and clasped her in a crushing embrace, lifting her off the ground.

"Herata, my child!" he said brokenly, "Thank the gods!"

Caught off guard, her arms went around him and she clung to him as she had not since she was a little, little girl and was frightened by nightmares. "Father!" she gulped, her throat swelling.

"I swear, minnow, I swear by Poseidon's name, that I will find who did this. A thousand deaths will not be enough for them! Ah, my daughter!" he said raggedly.

Who did this. The phrase filled her mind with cold clarity. Herata slipped away from him, fighting for composure, dashing away tears.

"Father," she said, "Open your thoughts to me."

His face crumpled; tears actually came to his eyes. "No," he said brokenly, "you cannot ask it. How can you ask it?"

"It was King's men who attacked me. Royal soldiers. Who else could command them?"

He went and slumped down in his royal seat, shaking his great head. "I know things have not been well between us since you went to Nine Seas, but how could you think that of me? Gods below!"

Since you sent me to Nine Seas, Herata thought. Which was not the same at all.

"I cannot rest in this house until I know I am truly safe. Don't make me force you," she said, coming up to his chair. "I'll do it if I have to."

With him sitting, their eyes were on a level, and he glared at her. "We do not compel testimony in this empire. Ours is a government of laws. Even tomorrow, your testament will not be forced from you with stones. How can you ask it now?"

"I ask as your daughter, not your subject," she said. "Father, please, let me know I can trust you!"

He bowed his head, his face grieved. "As you wish."

He did not resist her as she aligned her thoughts with his. It was distasteful, an intimacy no parent and child should share as she sifted through his thoughts of the last few days: sex with a bedslave before dawn / breakfast alone with Hecuba, who also occasionally shared his bed, but she was not his wife, she was no equal, no confidant / loneliness / exercising in the gymnasium, his breath far shorter than it used to be, ought to be / he was old / meetings meetings meetings, Stone and Sea, so boring, the same idiotic arguments again and again / entrenched dislike for Bortas, the Kraken King, an unimaginative boor who thought himself far cleverer than he was / under it all dread and horror of the disaster at Tiotiwakan, shame, he was a King, he was supposed to care for the land not burn it, how could this happen / damn the priests they were not doing their job / annoyance at herself, Herata, what madness was she up to now, why did she not keep her place / grief, loneliness, why had he sent her away, his minnow, all those years, gone utterly gone, all grown now, a woman, a woman who hated him / her hearing, a spectacle / he would have to judge his own child / then word, a message in a meeting, Herata had been attacked in the street FEAR fear fear fear oh gods his baby no –

"Ah!" With a wrench she pulled away, stumbling back from him, clutching her head. Blinding pain! It had not hurt like this when she had read Darir in the street: the closer the relationship, the more gruesome the intimacy. Telepathy was a terrible thing.

Tears ran down his face, and she felt the same tears on her own. That fear had been too real, too overwhelming, there was no guilt in it. Herodian did not plot against her, she would stake her life on it now.

She stood for a moment, doubled over, hands on knees, gasping from the effort.

"I don't hate you, Father," she said at last. "But you are right, those years are gone."

He wiped his face, looked at her with an unfathomable expression. It went both ways, after all – what had he seen in her mind, while she saw his?

"Are you satisfied?" he asked.

She nodded. "That you did not order the attack, yes."

He made a disgusted sound, waved a hand in a warding-off gesture. "Is that all?'

She hesitated. What did he want? "And that I am safe here, for now."

"Then will you bide quietly here until Council meets tomorrow?"

"Do I have a choice?" she asked. "I am under arrest!"

"You are!" he said. "And rightly so. The guards were supposed to be for your protection."

"And how well that went!"

"I said I would get to the bottom of that, child, and I will. No one attacks the blood of the Salmon and lives to brag of it, I swear it to you! But are you surprised? The news of your coming has swept the city. The people are in an uproar."

"I saw," she said tensely.

Herodian sat back and sighed. At some unseen signal, servants came in, bearing food and wine. Herata's gorge rose at the very sight of it.

A servant poured wine, offered a cup to the King, and then to her. She took the cup, then hesitated and shoved it back at the man.

"Taste it!" she ordered him.

"Herata!" her father snapped, exasperated.

Rage rose up in her again, and she slapped the cup out of the man's hand, spraying wine across the room. "I was almost just killed in the street! Can you blame me?"

Herodian gestured, and the servant poured again. Herodian took the cup and drank of it himself. "There! Are you satisfied?"

She nodded, and took it.

"You dishonor yourself, to act so in your own Hall," Herodian said. Anger darkened his face. He rose and paced in front of his fine chair.

"Do I?" she asked. "I come to this Hall as, at best, a witness. At worst a suspect. And clearly there are those who wish my testimony to go unheard."

"Did you cause the deathwave in Tiotiwakan?" he asked baldly.

She gaped at him. "You just shared my thoughts as I shared yours. What do *you* think?"

He gave her an opaque look. "I hardly know what to think. You have changed since last we met, my daughter," he said.

She thought, how would you know how I have changed? You sent me away when I was a child!

"Much has changed since last we met, Majesty," was all she said.

"Bah! You sound like the Patriarch, with his oily platitudes!" Herodian threw himself down in his fine ebony chair. "Enough!"

She bit her lip, unsure. "What would you have me say?" she asked him.

He studied her a long moment, his eyes thoughtful. "Sit," he said at last, kicking over a stool towards her.

She hesitated.

"Sit!" he bellowed.

She sat.

The attendant topped off her cup. She smelled it: fortified wine. Sailor's courage, they called it. She drank some, hoping to still the shaking in her hands, take the edge off the fear that still howled inside her.

"Now," Herodian said, leaning forward, "tell me."

"Tell you what?" she asked, confused.

"Everything!" he scowled. "Since you left here this summer. I ask as your King, as well as your father."

So she did. Herata told her father all that she had seen and done since she left his House in the Moon of Pressing.

She told him of the gaps and tears she had found in the net: dying rivers, shriveling forests, empty and abandoned towns. And of the crystals, how she could sense them now always, wherever she was, and how they showed her things. She surprised him by identifying all the crystals in the audience chamber, those visible and those concealed; the lights, the heaters, the listening devices, even the disguised jewelry he wore, defensive devices.

She told him of the fires burning deep under the Inner Sea, and of White Mare Temple's experiments to control it, doomed to failure.

Of what it had felt like to run the leys before the crest of the death-wave from Tiotiwakan, feeling the deaths of her comrades as she ran, and of the fires and the utter destruction in the Olmec city.

And lastly, she told him of her visions, of the burning that must soon come. She told him of the death of the island home and of the great darkness falling. And she told him, though he needed no reminding, of what the Hexachon had said to her:

"*'Only you can stop the burning.'* That is why I have done what I have done. And why I will do what I must do, even as you try to stop me."

Herodian sighed, leaning back in his chair and rubbing his eyes wearily. Herata took a thirsty gulp of wine. It had been a long talk indeed.

"Herata," he started, "how shall I say it? You need some perspective. You have not been well, my daughter, not for a long time. We understand that."

"If I am not well," Herata said angrily, "it is because of the evil that has been done in the leys! If I am sick it is because we are sickening the whole world!"

Herodian sighed. "You need to take a step back."

"Branek said that," Herata remembered.

"The young prince?" A gleam came into Herodian's eye.

"He fought for me this morning," Herata said. "I owe him my life."

"He is quite taken with you, child. Did you know that?"

Herata blushed. Herodian laughed. "Ah, I see that you do!"

"He is a noble man," Herata managed, choked with embarrassment, not understanding the way the conversation was turning.

Herodian lounged back in his chair, eyeing her speculatively. "He has asked for my blessing upon his proposal of marriage," he said.

Herata could only look at the floor, her face flaming. What did this have to do with anything?

"Has he not discussed it with you?" Herodian asked.

"Well, yes," Herata said, flustered, "but not to the point of a formal proposal. Not – as such."

"I see." Herodian said. "Have you lain with him yet?"

Herata coughed on her wine. "Father!" She remembered the intimate images she had seen in his mind, covered her eyes, aghast. What had *he* seen?

"Come, come," Herodian said. "We are both adults here. So?"

Herata could only look into her wine cup and shrug, too embarrassed to speak.

"Yes, I see. Not quite. Well, it is good sometimes not to rush these things."

Herata had no idea her father the king was so crafty in the ways of the world. It was as if he could see right through her, as with crystal vision. She wished the floor might just crack open and swallow her, she was so mortified.

"Does he please you?" Herodian asked.

Herata nodded despite herself, feeling a tide of warmth sweep over her at the memories.

"That is well," Herodian said. He sounded genuinely pleased.

Herata only looked at him, confused. "I don't understand this line of questioning."

Herodian held out his hand to her. "Come here, daughter."

After a moment she went over and took his hand, wondering what he was after.

"I cannot deny it pleases me to see in you such a maidenly bearing, my daughter," the king said. "But that is of no real account. You are a grown woman and a priestess. Your choices are your own.

"But if you were to ask your father's advice, I would say, marry the young prince. Go to Lacaon and be happy."

"You would have me forget my vows?" Herata said.

"They are not forgotten. Say instead that they are fulfilled."

"I can't leave the temple now!"

"Perhaps you can," Herodian said. "Think of it: you have given a lifetime of service to the temple, to the empire, from the time you were a little child. You have seen the danger to the leys, and you have lived to speak of it here in Council – at the risk of your life! Is that not enough? Give your testimony, and then be done with it. Stay in the Great City and make plans for your wedding. You have done enough for the temples, child. Now it is time to do something for yourself. Marry your prince; he loves you, you know. Go to the islands and be his queen. You will be happy there, I am sure of it."

"Happy?" Herata said, disbelieving. "What is happy when the whole world is going up in flames? How could I be happy knowing I have failed in my charge?" She yanked her hand out of Herodian's grasp. "You would send me away to the colonies, and have me be so addled with sex and babies that I would forget my vision! And let the whole world go to ruin while I disport myself in Branek's bed? No!"

Herodian sighed, the sigh of a man who knows he has been defeated. "That's not it at all."

"Are you ordering me to abandon the temple and marry Branek?" Herata asked icily. "Is that the judgment you will level against me?"

Herodian just shook his head sadly. "You make it sound like a punishment. I thought you cared for him? But you know perfectly well I have no power as father to order you anywhere. And you always were as stubborn as a cat, even when you were a little child. I only wish you would consider that there might be other options in your life. And that, were you well and happy, these vision of yours might not seem so overwhelming."

In other words, exactly what he had just denied. Go have the prince's babies and be his wife and stop all this nonsense about the end of the world. Herata stared at him with utter contempt.

"I have nothing more to say," she said. "If this interview is over, may I be excused?"

"Go," Herodian said. "But think on what I have said."

Herata left by the back way, too confused and upset to think of seeing Branek. How could she explain the conversation she had just had? She sent word that she was well, and had retired, and the single message, *It wasn't him.*

Back in her mother's old apartments, she ate doggedly at the meal which was provided, simply to keep up her strength, finding little pleasure in the rich food of the king's kitchen. Conflicting thoughts buzzed in her head.

Was Herodian right? Was she simply exhausted and deranged from a life spent servicing the crystals?

No, she thought, that couldn't be. If she were a weak vessel the

Hexachon would never have chosen her to carry their message. She could never have survived all that she had seen since the summer solstice.

Picking at her food, she was suddenly terribly lonely, sitting in the rooms abandoned by her unstable mother years ago. The Inner Sea frescoes on the walls reminded her piercingly of Branek. She wanted to see him, be with him now. But she would not. It would hardly help her case with Herodian to go running to her lover the first time she was challenged on her motives.

But she was lonely; she knew now that she had been terribly lonely for years, so long that she had forgotten what it was and simply thought it the normal tenor of life. Seeing the loneliness in Herodian's mind had reminded her with a shocking clarity. The friendship and shared work of the temples could substitute for real love for many people: but not, she knew now, for her.

And what, she thought, if the burning did not come? If by some chance it was averted, or if she was successful in her quest to prevent it, if she convinced the Five Kings to limit their expansion? The chances had seemed so remote and the danger so immediate that she had never considered it, but now she did. What if her goal was accomplished? What then?

She realized it for the first time; one way or another, either through defeat or disaster or her own free choice, she would be leaving Nine Seas temple.

If so, why not leave now? Could she be Branek's wife and serve her vision as well? What would life be like in Lacaon?

Did she love Branek? Or did she only love his hands, his lips? How could she know, with the charged aura of lust and danger that had colored their interactions until now?

A crystal lamp sat on the table before her; she studied its subtly shifting golden light -- wordless, enigmatic. "What would you do?" she asked it.

"My lady?"

Herata started. She had not realized Amalthea was at her shoulder, clearing dishes. "What would I do?" Amalthea asked. "If I were you?"

She was staring at her mistress, anxious but intrigued. Herata was not about to admit that she had been talking to the crystal.

"Tell me what you think. The prince has asked for my hand in marriage," she said.

Amalthea flushed in girlish pleasure. "Oh, my lady, if it were me I would marry the prince! He is so handsome. And he obviously loves you."

"Does he?" Herata mused. She had led such a sheltered life, she realized. She did not know what love was.

"Why, certainly, lady! How can you doubt it?"

Is that what I have to do to make you love me? Kill a man? No, no, she flinched away from the horrible memory. Doubt it? Branek doubted her love for him! The thought made her feel sick with regret. She owed him everything. Herata bowed her head, ashamed. "You are right, child. I forget myself."

"If you marry the Prince, my lady, he could protect you, if anything else happens," Amalthea said.

"What else could happen?" Herata asked. What could be worse than murder?

Amalthea looked troubled. "Hecuba told me. People are afraid. There have been – incidents. Trouble in the outer rings."

"They think I am dangerous."

"Some people think you caused the Tiotiwakan disaster, to make your point."

That dismayed her, but she could see how people could think that. Frightened people believed what would make them feel better.

"It might be better if you left Atlantis for a while, my lady. Lacaon is distant. There have been few troubles there. Or so they say, in the streets."

"After I testify, I might do that," Herata mused. "I might just do that."

"And after you testify, sooner rather than later. Your news is not happy, lady. The City will not be pleased."

Herata looked at her. "Do you believe my vision?"

Amalthea nodded, wide-eyed. She was too afraid not to, Herata saw.

"Then you see I cannot abandon it."

"Wedding the prince is not abandoning your vision, lady. How do you know it is not destined to be?"

But it was not. That she knew; she had seen it. No wedding would be theirs; it was foolish to pretend otherwise.

"Prepare my bed," she told Amalthea. "I am tired." She had not slept all night as she sailed to the Great City.

A flicker of disappointment crossed the novice's face. Her mistress seldom confided in her, and this rare moment of candor was clearly done. Silently, she bowed and withdrew.

Chapter Fourteen

It was at the Hour of the Dragon the very next day that Herata was commanded to appear before the Council of Kings. Herodian had already gone ahead, to make ready for Council with his fellow rulers. He did not speak with his daughter before leaving; today he judged her as her king, not her parent.

Herata carefully prepared herself for the audience, dressing herself in the full regalia of a High Priestess of Atlantis. The Council should not be allowed to forget who and what she was. She donned heavy robes of silk brocade, and a collar of jewels and *aum* stones. On her brow she wore the wave-crested crown of Nine Seas Temple, which Queen Elissa had worn before her, in the days before she assumed the throne of Kraken Nome in the Silver Age of Atlantis.

She surveyed herself in her mother's mirror. She looked very fine. But that could not still the fluttering beat of her heart, or calm the fear that rose in her at the thought of facing the Five Kings.

She had done what she had done, spreading dissent, sabotaging foreign temples, because of what she believed. She was quite innocent of the Tiotiwakan disaster, even if she had been the only survivor of the death-wave. She was the mistress of her own temple, and in its affairs accountable to no one, except the Mother Earth and the gods.

But all of that would be as nothing, if the Five Kings wished it. Theirs was the ultimate authority, the final judgment in the empire. If they found her to be guilty of treason or heresy, things could go very hard for her indeed. Herodian's parentage of her would mean little if the rest of the Five were arrayed against her.

They could strip her of her priesthood, exile her from all territories of the empire, even have her executed. Or worse – and she hardly dared think it – they could order the operation performed that would blunt her sensitivity to the earthpower, and leave her as mind-blind as the most primitive outlander, and take her out of the leys forever.

No, she would not think it, the thought terrified her. She would die if they burned out her sight. They may as well execute her outright.

A servant of the Hall came to the door of her quarters. "A visitor, my lady," he announced. "Prince Branek of Lacaon."

Herata shut her eyes, overwhelmed by a wave of gratitude. "Send him in."

Branek strode into her sitting room. Herata caught her breath at the sight of him, he looked so magnificent, dressed in all the finery of an outland king. His hair was loose and curled into the majestic spirals of a Keftian lord. He wore a robe of purest white wool and a broad collar of beaten gold. A fillet of gold set with a single huge blue stone capped his gleaming locks. The stone caught the color of his eyes and made them look kingly and piercing.

"Do you not look fine!" she said admiringly, pure pleasure loosening the hard knot of apprehension in her chest.

He came to her, took her outstretched hands.

"My lady, you look as lovely as the first day I came to you at Nine Seas. No, more so. You are a goddess!"

Herata smiled at the memory. "That seems so long ago now."

He touched her cheek, careful not to smudge the paint. "It is as yesterday to me."

His kindness disarmed her. "Oh, Branek," she gasped. "I'm afraid, I am so afraid!"

"Do not be. You are strong, Herata," he said. "You have survived trials that would have destroyed a lesser person. Wherever they send you, you will triumph."

He folded her into his arms. She clung to him. "They could mind-blind me, Branek, take me out of the flows!"

"I do not think so," he said. "I doubt the Hexachon would allow it."

She had not considered that. He might be right! The thought both dismayed and relieved her.

"They are doing good things with battery crystals in the Islands of the Dawn," she said.

He laughed. "See, I said you would be fine." He stood back, regarding her. "I have spoken with your father, King Herodian," he began.

"So I heard," she said rather dryly, remembering her remarkable conversation of the day before.

"He has agreed, that if you are sent down from Nine Seas, or – exiled, that you should come to Lacaon with me."

"That would not be so bad a fate," she admitted, smiling.

But he still looked troubled. "It may not be possible. Public opinion is against you. The things that are being said about you..."

"I know," she said. "That I caused the deathwave."

"And worse things," he said. "Terrible things. Those of us who know you speak out against them, of course, but foolish people believe the worst things they hear."

She nodded; she knew this.

"So I must ask you, Herata, my lady –"

"No, Branek," she interrupted, knowing what he would say, "do not!"

"I must!" he persisted. "You should at least consider – recanting some of the things you have said. Disavowing some of the things you have done."

"No!" she said angrily. "How can you ask it of me?"

He took her hand, pressed it to his chest; she could feel his heart thumping heavily. "Only because I am afraid for you, love. Only that."

"Is it so bad, then?" she whispered.

"Your father and I will do everything we can to protect you. But he is only one of Five. And I am only one of a hundred lesser kings and princes."

She took her hand away from his chest. "If you love me at all, you cannot ask it. If you know me at all, then you know it cannot be."

Sadness suffused his face, sadness and understanding. "So be it, then." He kissed the palm of her hand, a passionate, lingering kiss. She fisted her hand over it, to keep it.

"Then I must go," he said. "You will come before the Council alone."

"I know. I am ready."

"May the gods be with you, my lady." He bowed to her, very deeply, as a subject king to a Lady of Atlantis, and was gone.

A soldier of the house guard arrived at her door to escort her from the Hall of the Salmon. She went alone, with no attendants, as it was decreed.

She was taken by palanquin over the vast, winding paths of the central round of the City, the sacred precinct. Across the canal, crowds lined the bank for as far as she could see, stretching away on both sides. The whole city awaited her testimony.

Her palanquin, flanked by soldiers in the silver scale armor of the Hall of the Salmon, swayed up the great processional way to the High King's palace, at the very heart of empire. Her bearers climbed the flights of marble steps, rising to the gleaming marble bulk of the palace, a vast pyramid, ornamented in gold and oricalch and decorated with hanging gardens and crystal waterfalls.

Herata saw little of the beautiful, geometric gardens and plazas that surrounded the palace as her entourage went along, so lost was she in her own thoughts, her own fears. The majesty of empire meant little to her now; in her mind's eye she saw it blasted, ruined, burning, dead. It was all already dead to her.

In the very heart of the pyramid, buried under tons of rock yet by cunning craft made open to the sky, lay the grand chamber of the Council of Kings, where the rulers of empire met and dispensed their laws and wisdom unto their subjects and their tributary kings.

At last they had penetrated to the center of the palace. Her phalanx of guards had fallen off; there met her now only a trio of priests, sworn to the service of the Council and the High King. A shaven-headed acolyte handed her down from the palanquin.

They stood in a cool, bare marble hall in the lowest levels of the pyramid-palace. The hall itself was empty and silent, but from the great carved doors at its end could be heard a murmuring rush, like the sound of waves in a seashell: the Hall of the Council, crowded full of the powerful and greedy of empire, waiting to see her judgment.

Herata tried to remember who and what she was, but it was difficult, with that sound coming at her, like the restless mutterings of a caged and hungry beast, eager for diversion, and for a meal to fill its empty belly.

A senior priest of the High King held a crystal out toward her; she spoke her name and rank, that her appearance would be recorded in the annals of the Council. She stretched toward the crystal, seeking something, some consolation, but it was silent.

After she spoke, the priest, a gray-haired elder with the smooth un-lined face of one who had spent many years in the leys, regarded her for a moment, quizzically. Then he stroked the crystal, and darkened it, turning it off.

"I would have a word with you, Lady Herata," he said quietly. His acolytes stared unseeingly into the middle distance, silent, unobservant, practiced in not hearing what should not be said.

Herata nodded, hardly daring to trust her voice.

"Not everyone who has heard your words or felt your presence in the net thinks you mad. There are those who feel the wisdom in your way."

"Then why do they not speak?"

The priest shook his head, regretfully. "Surely anyone who felt the Ti-otiwakan deathwave would speak in your behalf. But sadly, most of them will never speak again."

"That is why *I* must," Herata said. "Even more must I speak, for those who cannot."

"Perhaps, but is it necessary to do so in this way? So harshly?"

Herata was confused. "It is the Council who summoned me here; I must testify. I cannot disobey."

"No. But perhaps you can – dissemble."

"If you have seen what I have seen, you would know that there can be no varnishing of that truth."

"Varnishing, no. But sweetening, perhaps. Anyone who has felt your passage in the flows would have a good idea of what you will say today and how you will say it. Not the words themselves, but the feelings behind them. Nor can we fault you for those feelings, we who have not suffered as you have.

"But perhaps today is not the day. Sometimes the greater part of wisdom is silence."

"You would have me recant?" Herata asked angrily. When Branek had asked her she had been afraid, now she was simply disgusted. Branek knew her, his thoughts carried weight. This man was a stranger; he did not know whereof he spoke.

"Recant, no, my lady. Never that! But … speak softly. Do not bring the temple down around their ears, and their wrath down on your head. Be mild. Live to speak another day."

His words made a dangerous sense. How could she save the empire were she mind-blinded and exiled to the southern islands? Or a virtual prisoner in Lacaon, under Branek's dominion?

But no. "There is no other day but today," she said. "After this I may never be able to speak again."

The old priest shook his head, regretfully. "So be it, then. My name is Innu, lady. If you should see the sunset of this day, call upon me at need. Even now you are not without friends."

Herata nodded, tightly. It was a very big *if*. He and his acolytes bowed, and stepped aside. Her way to the Council was clear.

She walked those last steps alone, as she had raced the deathwave alone along the limb of the world. These last few steps were more frightening than those many desperate miles.

The tall double doors, carved with the five-point sigil of the Sea Kings, were so finely hung that they swung open at the slightest touch. Before her lay the chamber of the Council.

It was a great bowl shape below her, a mighty amphitheater carved from the bedrock of the Plains of Gold in ancient times. The whole bulk of the pyramid palace lay above it, yet cunning channels in the body of the stone, lined with mirrors and crystals, brought the light and air of day into the subterranean space. Cool breezes played around her, sweet with the perfumes of the island home. The roof of the chamber seemed to go up infinitely, filled with golden light, blue as the sky of springtime. It was as if the chamber were under the open sky of the Plains of Gold, naked to the sun above, caressed by the ocean breeze.

This was the Sea King's craft. Few who were not adepts, who could not feel the presence of the crystals that lined the hidden, domed roof, could ever guess at the secret of the chamber. Barbarian tributaries who were brought here were awestruck, thinking they had been magicked from the palace to some secret grotto in the mountains, and so they learned and were made afraid of the Sea Kings' might.

But it was not magic, only craft. A craft of which she too was mistress. Herata reminded herself of that, as she descended the marble steps to the floor of the chamber, her naked feet soundless on the stones.

Around and above her, the seats of the amphitheater were filled with the wise and powerful of the empire, kings and adepts from across the nine seas. Warrior lords from the Islands of the Dawn, hardy mystics from the frozen southern continent, grieving survivors of the Pyramid of the Moon. Her coming here had long been known. All the world had joined to witness her judgment before the Sea Kings.

Where was Branek? She couldn't find him in the sea of faces. But if she closed her eyes, she could feel it, the bond between them, drawn tight like a wire of oricalchum. There! He was in the lowest gallery; opening her eyes, she found him, looking down at her intently. It was a relief just to know where he was. He pressed his right fist to his shoulder, a warrior's salute. She nodded, hoping he would see, too nervous to make a larger gesture.

As she entered, the chamber fell silent. Not a word was spoken as she descended to the floor before the Kings. The only sounds were the whisper of the wind, a snatch of birdsong brought in on a channeled breeze, the haunting rush of hundreds breathing.

At last she achieved the floor, bare white marble devoid of all ornament. Only Truth was to decorate the Chamber of Atlantis when the Kings met in Council.

Before her, above her, sat the Five Kings on a dais of pure oricalch. The Four Kings of the Nomes of Atlantis: Salmon, Kraken, Orca and Ammonite. And between and above them all, on a throne grown from a single crystal, the High King of Atlantis, descendant of Poseidon Himself, their leader and lord.

She looked at Herodian. His face was as impassive as a stone idol's. Here she was not Herata his beloved only child, but Herata the heretic, the mad seer and saboteur.

Into the awesome silence the High King addressed her: "Speak."

Struggling to keep her voice steady, she said loudly, "I am Herata of Nine Seas, and I come as summoned to face the Council of the Five."

Targeted crystals picked up her voice and broadcast it to every corner of the chamber. A murmur ran like water over the crowd in the stands, as the watchers speculated on every nuance of her bearing.

"Herata of Nine Seas," said the King of Orca Nome, "you are summoned here to answer charges brought against you; charges so extreme that their like has never been encountered in the annals of Atlantean law. Their existence strains credulity, but these charges are grave and they must be addressed."

"I did not destroy Tiotiwakan," Herata said strongly. "I did not cause the deathwave."

The crowd shifted and muttered at that. Calls of "Liar!" and "Witch!" echoed around the chamber.

"Silence!" the Orca King called. He stared down at Herata; in him she saw no trace of the man she had known since childhood, whose children she had played with when she was little. "The witness shall answer only when addressed."

"I must be allowed to speak!" Herata cried. Was this a kangaroo court? Had the verdict already been reached?

"You will have your opportunity, once our questions have been answered," Herodian said. "Until then, you shall submit."

His eyes were hooded, dark. Was it a warning?

"Yes, Majesty," she said, bowing to the inevitable.

"Herata of Nine Seas, answer these charges: Did you visit and speak with the Hexachon of the Poseideion, as has not been done in living memory?"

"I did."

"And do you claim to have a revelation of the future given to you by those Stones?"

If she were to dissemble, to retreat, it would be now.

Looking up at the ranks of spectators, she spied the priest, Innu. He gave her the barest of nods, a mere tilt of the head, urging her. His eyes were intense.

"I do have such a revelation," she said.

A mutter of comment went around the cavernous room. The Five continued to gaze down at her, masked, impassive.

"Then speak it," the High King said.

Herata lifted her head and spoke proudly, though her heart was hammering in her chest.

"I have addressed this Council before, and I have spoken of what I have seen in the web, and of the warning which the dolphins brought at summer solstice. The changes which were required to address these warnings have not been made. I can only repeat what the Hexachon told me: a rebalancing is coming -- mark me, it is coming whether we aid it, or fight. Before it the destruction of Tiotiwakan will seem as dust before the wind. There will be burning. There will be conflagration!"

The muttering changed to a roar by the time she was done. The crowd was on their feet, some shouting in anger, some with fear. The crystals picked it up and amplified it, echoing around the chamber, ricocheting from the ceiling and the walls, feeding back into a howl of white noise, a roar of wordless rage.

Herata endured it, standing alone on the vast empty floor, keeping her hands from covering her ears by sheer force of will. For that sound terrified her; it was the very sound of imbalance, of the Sea Kings' prideful lust for power and luxury. It was the sound of the burning given voice.

The High King touched a crystalline stud on the arm of his crystal throne. "Silence!" he called, and the crystals caught his voice and carried it outward, drowning all the others, booming like the voice of Poseidon himself, shaking the bones in one's very flesh: *Silence!*

The crowd was silent.

"There are those, Herata of Nine Seas, who say you have created these supposed imbalances yourself," the High King said.

She bit her lip, struggling for control. What she said now could mean life or death for her – or worse, the blinding rites.

"I have studied much the ebb and flow of the earthblood these past months," she began. "I have sought to understand the things which the Hexachon showed me.

"I have seen lands that were burned where the *aum* flowed too strong, and parched where it flowed too little. The web can no longer regulate itself. There are – thin places, rents. Tears in the web of life." It was so hard to explain to those who were not adepts, who had not felt the earthblood flow in and through them.

She took a deep breath. "It is true that I have altered the flow of *aum* in the temples – "

The crowd roared again.

" – but only to repair what had already been damaged!"

The crowd erupted in rage, calling for judgment, calling for her blood. A phalanx of soldiers, the Kings' Guard, filed into the chamber from the Kings' Door and took up positions on the perimeter of the chamber, ready to maintain order with the butts of their spears – or the points if necessary. Herata breathed deeply to quell the terror she felt at the sight of them. Further compatriots to her failed assassins might be among them.

The High King roared the crowd to silence again.

"What say you of this?" the Ammonite King asked the Patriarch.

The old man stabbed an accusing finger at her. "She is a false priestess! It is true – she has stolen *aum* from distant temples to feed her own. Nor has she given up that store of earthblood which is the rightful tithe of every temple to the Poseideion. It is she who hoards power, storing it up for her own unspoken purposes!"

"No!" Herata said. "I do not hoard power. I cycle it back to the earth, as we all must to prevent the conflagration! Giving, we receive. That is the most ancient way of *aum*. The best way!"

The crowd continued to shout. Herata's fear rose at the sound. How could she explain the mysteries of earthpower to legions of frightened, angry commoners, who knew little of the intricacies of the *aum* disciplines, and who knew only that their life of ease and plenty was in jeopardy? People would do anything to protect that, their riches and comforts. Everything except what *must* be done.

A small stooped figure in black approached the edge of the viewing balcony. "Majesties," the old woman called, straining to be heard in the din. "May I speak?"

The High King gestured, and the crystals in the ceiling suddenly stopped reflecting back sounds, and instead drew them in, swallowing them, until the chamber was filled with a resonant hush, as quiet as the roar had been loud only moments before.

"Proceed," he said.

"I am Lamike of Nine Seas temple," she said, "and I speak for my mistress. Herata is no false priestess. She does not hoard power, but tenders it back to the Mother Earth, as she must. As we all must."

"But you would say that anyway, to defend your mistress," someone else from the crowd said into the great silence.

Lamike gripped the edge of the balcony railing. "I am Olmec," she said. "I was initiated in the Pyramid of the Moon. I do not defend despoilers of the earth!"

A murmur ran through the crowd at that.

"But she caused the deathwave!" someone cried.

"No!" Lamike's voice rang out strongly in the vast chamber. "My lady has fought to prevent just such a tragedy since these visions first came to her! If I thought," she continued, "that Herata had aught to do with the destruction of my city, I would have killed her myself!"

There was silence and a soft whispering at that: her passion had impressed the crowd. They believed her, for the moment.

Lamike sagged at the railing, her outburst seeming to have exhausted her limited strength. Branek came up and drew her away, his arm around her, supporting her.

The King of Ammonite Nome spoke up now. "But it is said that Herata of Nine Seas was the only adept to survive the deathwave intact." His hands clenched on the wide arms of his throne. His eyes bored into her: dark, burning, terrible. "My own son, my heir, was in the flows that day. He did not survive. How could you?"

Herata could not meet his gaze; tears stung her own eyes. Not an hour had gone by that she had not considered that, her freakish survival. Hers alone.

"My King, I do not know. But I can only think – fear – that I have been spared because my purpose is not yet done."

"Enough!" called a richly dressed man from Olmec lands. He came to the railing. His regalia identified him as an adept of that people.

"Admit it!" he said contemptuously down to her. "You are a flawed prophet. You saw the deathwave in your vision, but failed to prevent it. Failed! Now admit your weakness, and end this! My people's suffering has gone on long enough."

Herata stared wonderingly up at him, into the cauldron of his rage and grief.

"If I could stop the burning of Tiotiwakan, I would have, with my life. But no one can turn the tide of wild *aum* when it is unleashed. If the sins of the Sea Kings continue, there shall never be any stopping it! No: Tiotiwakan was only the small burning, before the greater."

Cries of dismay and outrage filled the chamber. The Olmec adept barked a hoarse shout of rage, and spat upon Herata where she stood alone on the floor. She wiped the spittle off her cheek with one hand. Let him vent his fury. He had more than earned it.

"Enough!" the High King bellowed. The mob quieted.

"Majesties, may I speak?" asked another voice from the stands. A familiar one, Herata realized: Taran, High Priest of the Isle of Glass.

"You may," Herodian the Salmon King assented.

Taran took his turn at the railing of the balcony. Herata allowed herself to feel a glimmer of hope; since the day he had trapped her in his crystal, Taran had been solidly behind her. He shared her fears.

"I am Taran, Keeper of the Isle of Glass in the Misty Isles. As Keeper of a Great Node, monitoring the flows is my particular task. I can offer some insight into this, if I may."

"Proceed," Herodian said.

"I was not in the flows at the time of the deathwave. But when I went in, later, to help contain the damage, the nature of the accident was very clear. The resonance, the echoes of the accident were strong. The deathwave clearly originated in Tiotiwakan itself."

"Of this there is no doubt," the Ammonite King said.

Taran bowed his head respectfully. "Indeed, no. But the nature of the detonation was so violent, so complete its destruction, that there could be no doubt the catastrophe was an instantaneous event. The crystals of the Moon Pyramid overloaded all at once, and simultaneously. What else could cause such destruction?" His face was a mask of sorrow as he remembered.

"What are you getting at?" the Kraken King asked.

"Such an event could not be triggered from far away, or even from another crystal nexus close by. Even a small lag in the flows would have failed to trip the stones in concert, and overload the temple. I believe I can safely say that Lady Herata could not have caused the deathwave, either by accident or intent. She was nowhere near the Pyramid of the Moon, either in spirit or in the flesh. And she would have had to be, to do this dreadful thing. No: if she had, she would have never survived."

He spoke evenly, without rancor or pride. It was clear he spoke the truth. Herata nodded to him in quiet gratitude. Few could have explained the nature of the tragedy to laymen in such clear and simple terms.

Behind the frozen golden mask, Herata imagined the High King looked subtly relieved. "We accept your testimony." The four lesser kings nodded in agreement.

The chamber hummed as the crowd discussed this among themselves. Taran bowed low and retired.

Herata let out a breath she had not known she was holding.

"I am innocent of the destruction of Tiotiwakan," she stated, once and for all.

The High King bowed his head in assent. "So shall it be recorded, in the annals of this Council."

Cheers and shouts of anger intermingled in the council chamber. Herata tried to catch her father' eyes, but they were closed – in relief?

The Patriarch of the Poseideion arose again. "So! She may not be a murderer. But there is still the question of her heresies to confront."

"And what of your heresies, Patriarch?" Herata countered, raising her voice to be heard by all.

"Caution!" the High King said. "You speak to the High Priest of Our Father, Poseidon!"

"The very man to whom I brought my vision," Herata said. "And he did nothing!"

"The ravings of a damaged priestess, mad with crystal fever?" the Patriarch scoffed. "Of course I did nothing!"

"My vision is not madness!" Herata cried. "I have walked the leys, day after day, from the roof of the world to the depths of the ocean. I have seen the sickness myself.

"You all know it!" she cried to every lord and adept in the chamber. "You cannot deny it! You have seen it, and done nothing. You are guilty!"

She scanned the ranks of faces above her, looking for those she had noted, those whose thirst for power ran unchecked.

"You!" A clutch of men in the white woolen robes of the northern continent. "Ilethelme! I have been there, I felt my nerves almost burned out by the *aum* you glut your city upon!" She pointed accusingly at them; one of them stepped back as if her very attention was deadly. "You use more energy than any five cities combined – and what for? Fountains and light shows!"

She stalked around the chamber, staring up at her accusers. There were others. At last she let the fear and anger of the last few days out to rage unchecked. "Kythera! I have watched you in the nets, long have I watched you. Would you open *another* nexus in the cauldron of the Inner Sea? Can you not feel the very earth burning under your feet? How much more do you think your islands can take?"

No one was spared her anger, not even the City of Clouds, oldest and most sacred of Atlantean colonies, site of a Great Node in the vast Serpent Mountains. "While you dream your noble dreams of peace and wisdom, the pampas lies dying only leagues away! What good are dreams when life itself is drying up and blowing away in the desert wind?" The keeper of the Cloud Temple only looked down at her, shaking her head in puzzlement before turning away.

It enraged her. She, Herata, had suffered, she had struggled, she had lost herself in the leys for days, weeks on end, and still the Sea Kings refused to see what must be seen. The finest adepts in the empire dulled themselves to the wrongness that bled through their crystals bit by bit, more everyday, because they were too afraid to face the truth.

"It is you who are guilty!" she cried. "All of you!"

"Enough!" Again the voice of the High King boomed through the chamber, drowning out all other sound. The echoes rolled around, until all was silence.

"She *is* mad," someone said into the echoing quiet.

"But can what she says be true?" the High King asked.

"It is not so very much that we ask," Herata said in answer, "the stones and I. Some wisdom, a little restraint. Some thought as to the way we weave the web of empire. A little more frugality and a little less display – that might be enough to tip the balance!" She raised her hands to the lords and commoners in the galleries alike. "Surely that is not too much to ask for the Mother Earth."

A ripple of sound across the galleries; a few cheers, cries of her name. She turned to the Five Kings, seated above her. "All I have done, I have done in service to the empire and the island home," she declared. "Judge me if you will, but judge also my intent, for I wish only to serve as the earth and the gods command me!"

Shouts of approbation from the galleries now. Above her Branek clenched his fist on the balustrade, confident of victory.

The High King spoke. "You may well speak truth, Lady Herata, that more thought must be made as to how we 'weave the web of empire.' Indeed, you are not the first devotee to have this insight. It may be that the adepts of the Great City have come up with just the solution you seek."

Herata watched with a sudden feeling of sinking dread as he nodded to a clutch of white-robed Poseideion priests nearby in the gallery.

A spare priest with iron-gray hair came forward at the king's summons.

"Since well before the Tiotiwakan disaster, adepts of the White Temple have considered the place the empire takes in the web of life," he said. "It has long been clear that the needs of the empire for *aum* will soon outstrip our capacity to harvest it. For power the empire may one day need to depend on cruder methods to supplement: the burning of combustibles, or the splitting of the atom. But such practices are dirty and dangerous, terribly so. Far better to maximize our use of the earthblood as we have always known it: clean as water, safe for all, the harmonious energy of life itself. Since ancient days have the Sea Kings lit their way with the glow of *aum*: it would be folly to turn our backs on what has served us so well."

So far Herata could argue with nothing he had said. Yet her fear was growing.

The scholarly priest continued. "The problem then, is to find some way to maximize our use of the earthpower as we use it now. But this is easier said than done. Temples already exist at every major node and many minor ones, all across the face of the earth. Those nodes left untapped have been those traditionally considered too unstable too tap, or too meager.

"To tap these nodes seemed the only future solution. But it was always unpopular. Many of the nodes in the Inner Sea or down in the Icelands were left fallow since ancient times, for good reason. It seemed reckless to defy the wisdom of our ancestors and try to gather what they had wisely left alone.

"So the thought was had: what if we could create new nodes?"

"No!" Herata cried, her worst fears confirmed. "Do not speak of it!"

The grizzled priest stared down at her as if she were an interesting specimen for his studies. "But it is the perfect solution. Instead of going to dangerous places where the power is unstable, bring the power to us, where it can be monitored and controlled."

"It is blasphemy!"

"It is science," the old priest said, unperturbed.

Herata turned her back on him, whirled to face the audience. "Do you understand what he is saying?" she asked them. "What madness, what evil? He is talking about *moving the leys!*"

Astonished shouts and cries burst from the watching crowd. One might as well talk about turning the sun back in its course. The vast, mysterious flow of the earthblood was the mystic heartbeat upon which the empire had built its life for centuries.

A vortex of emotions swirled around the chamber. In her excited state Herata could feel them, as if the sound crystals were picking them up and sending them to her: the terror of the Olmecs; the superstitious wonder of the cityfolk themselves; the sudden, naked greed of the Ilethelmites and the Islanders of the Dawn. Hope and fear, wonder and terror, all commingled in a babel in her head.

"No!" she cried. Stretching, she reached out to the crystals, and they picked up her voice and carried it above all others, "Do not think it. Heed them not! To move the leys, to cut and splice the very threads of life itself – that way lies our destruction! I have foreseen it."

"But, lady, this technique may be the very thing that saves us, if it works," called the elderly priest into the chaos.

"Sorcery!" cried some of the watchers.

But, "Show us!" cried others.

Herata threw her arms out, and the crystals responded to her wish, and damped all sound in the chamber.

"It will not work," she said heavily into the silence.

"Can such a thing even be done?" Taran of the Misty Isles, asked, wonder in his voice.

"They would do it -- force it -- with their will and for their pride's sake." Herata answered him, pointing at the delegation from the White Temple. "They would twist the magic of nature to suit their own ends, and count not the cost. Even if that cost is another deathwave!"

"No," said her adversary, the scholarly priest. "Our methods are safe, we have made sure of that."

"You can *never* be sure," Herata insisted. "You meddle with things beyond your understanding."

"My lady," he said, offended, "I have walked the leys more than half my life. I do not think the web is beyond my understanding."

"Is it not? Do you count yourself the equal of the Mother Earth?"

"Everything we have done has been in service of the earth, and of the empire," he said.

"If you warp the very fabric of life on this world, you will destroy the empire to save it."

"No, you are wrong. It is our nature, human nature, the Sea Kings' nature to sift the stuff of life, to seek out that which is better and more perfect, more useful for all. Does the physician not seek to destroy disease? Does the herdsman not seek to improve his flock, breed out the weak and the sick? Does the astronomer not study the heavens, charting the course of the stars, seeking to divine their secrets? Once in primitive times that would have been thought black magic, seeking to divine the will of the gods themselves. But now we know, and our ships cross the nine seas more swiftly and surely than any other nation's, for in plumbing the mystery of the stars we have also come to understand the earth –"

"Enough!" cried Herata. "It is our charge to steward this Mother Earth, not bend her to our will."

"You cannot say that anything I have said is untrue. It is the Atlantean way to struggle to improve ourselves and our situation."

"Perhaps one day," Herata said, struggling for control of her self and of the black flames of prophecy that licked at the corners of her vision. "But not here. Not now. You move too fast, you do not comprehend the powers you would unleash. Your work, priest, will unleash the burning. If you try this, you will destroy us all. I know it. I have *seen* it!"

"But if you could see our work, the nature of our weavings, I think you would be reassured, my lady. That is why we have arranged a demon-stration."

"Here?" Herata said, aghast. "Now?"

"Indeed. We have brought the equipment."

At his words, a crew of men came through the Kings' Door, carrying a mid-size crystal in an elaborate metal frame. They set it down in the center of the council chamber, in front of the kings.

Directly atop the flow of the Trident ley, which ran under the holy pyramid -- and under this very chamber.

"If your Majesties will allow," the elder said, "we will demonstrate our techniques by moving the Trident beneath us three minor degrees of diffraction west, and then back again. It is perfectly safe, I assure you," he said, louder for the benefit of the crowd, who was shouting and hanging over the gallery, staring at the strange crystal, and hollering for the Kings to proceed – or not.

"No!" Herata said, backing away from the crystal, horrified to the core of her soul. "Do not!" When Branek had told her about this terrible secret, she had no idea it was so close to completion.

Fear engulfed her. She was suddenly fully conscious of the Trident, running beneath her very feet, an invisible swift-flowing river of life and magic. It bisected Atlantis, running from the rocky shores of the north clean through the Great City, beneath this very temple where they all stood now, beneath *this very floor,* flowing beneath the Plains of Gold south to her own temple, Nine Seas, and beyond, plunging into the ocean, girding the world and coming back to Atlantis again in an endless circle of light and life. It was the very girdle of the mother earth, here beneath her feet, flowing hot and bright as she had never felt it before. It had never seemed so precious.

And they would tamper with this? Unknot the Lady's girdle, on a whim, as a show of their power to the uninitiated?

Her heart thundered in her ears with her terror. Was this it, then, was this when it was all fated to begin? Was this the first spark of the burning?

"You can't!" she cried. "You mustn't. Do not do this!"

"Lady Herata!" the High King commanded as she cowered at the foot of the dais. "Contain yourself. A demonstration would be most useful. We have been most curious about this new discipline. Be still and watch; you may learn something."

"No, the risk is too great." She ran up the dais to Herodian's side. "Father, my King – you mustn't let them!"

He covered her hand with his own. "Calm yourself. It has all been arranged. It is only a small demonstration. If we thought there was any danger we would not allow it."

The scholarly priest and his associates descended from the galleries. They clustered around the crystal, stroking it, adjusting the tensions on the metal springs which held it in its cradle. The crystal flickered uneasily in a way Herata had never seen before. It filled her with dread, like some demon's eye from an ancient fairy tale.

At last the cadre of priests filed away from the stone, back to the galleries above. She should do something, Herata thought, she should charge that crystal, wrench it from its stand, shatter it on the marble floor.

But she was too afraid. She had never guessed the black art was this close to fruition. She slumped to the dais, shaking in terror of the burning.

"Perhaps you should go," Herodian said.

"Go?" she stared at him, wild-eyed. "Go where? I'll never outrun another deathwave."

He just shook his head, considering it another of her sick spells.

She turned her tear-filled eyes up to the stands, looking for a familiar blue-eyed face in the throng. Branek! There he was, across the way with a cluster of her folk and his, looking grave. He at least heeded her warnings.

The High King gestured for silence, and the crystal priests began their working. Softly at first, then louder, they began a chant, the specially coded sequences of sound that awakened and programmed a leystone. They used a cadence Herata had never heard before. The flickering lights inside the crystal began to grow and steady. A resonant humming arose in counterpoint to the chant.

Herata rolled aside and vomited on the golden steps of the Kings' Seat.

Herodian, disgusted, gestured for a guardsman to take her away. A soldier came and pulled her none too gently to her feet. He dragged her across the floor to the Supplicant's Stair, right past the glowing, humming crystal.

She cringed away, her skin crawling at the closeness of the alien stone. Her fear seemed to roll out and fill the entire chamber, leaving an echoing emptiness in her head.

The priests deepened their chant, calling up the power in their ill-wrought crystal – power enough to warp the very ley beneath it. It beat on Herata's skin like a black sun.

Under it, she felt a terrible pressure rising in her vacant, terror-struck mind. Her vision blurred; suddenly it was as if she saw herself from outside, from a great distance, a tiny dancing flame of spirit cloaked in a skein of flesh, so strange: so fragile yet so powerful.

That vision rushed in; the pressure in her mind built, began to fill her senses utterly, chasing out the necromantic moaning of the crystal priests, and the discordant humming of the diffraction crystal.

It was the Six, the Hexachon. Their linked, stony consciousness filled her, squeezing her own thoughts to the margins. They were angry, with the cold, static anger of a stone. Had they not spoken?

Herata's mouth opened. "Do not do this," it croaked.

No one heard. The chant continued.

Herata felt her body rise, standing tall before the diffraction crystal, arms spread wide. The Six wore her flesh now, she was but a passenger in her own frame. Their power filled her, kindling along the leys of her own body, lending her their ancient strength.

She cried out, her own throat booming with the sixfold lithic voice of the Hexachon:

"DO NOT DO THIS!"

It filled the chamber, rattled the crystals in the ceiling, blasted into the mind of everyone present. The crystal priests faltered in their chant. Watchers gasped and shivered in the galleries, overcome by the touch of that ancient stony intelligence. Such a thing had never occurred since the earliest days of the Sea Kings, when the gods still walked with men on the Plains of Gold.

Herata trembled, caught in the grasp of the stones' power like a fish in a net. The diffraction stone before her took on a cast of evil yellowish light. It looked alien to her, a stranger. It was malformed, it had been badly grown, badly taught. The Six did not know it. They rejected it.

The light in the stone flickered and died as the priests faltered in their spell. They too had heard the voice of the Hexachon.

But over the rolling echoes of that cry, the Patriarch said one word:

"Continue!"

The scholarly priest and his cohorts looked up at him in confusion. Dare they?

The High King gestured assent. Slowly at first, then with strength, the adepts resumed their chant.

The stone awakened and throbbed with light while Herata stood before it, transfixed with anger, hers and the Hexachon's. She saw with the clarity of crystal vision the flaw in the strange stone's heart.

The stone began to pulse, the light it generated shifting from side to side within its heart, west to east, east to west. The shifting quickened and the stone pulsed more rapidly, synching itself to the frequency of the ley upon which it squatted, an interloper.

But as Herata watched with the eyes of the Hexachon, she could see that it could not catch up. The stone was flawed; it had been grown in haste. It could not synch. The pulsing light fluttered wildly as the stone lost its rhythm. A squeal of feedback ripped through the air. The diffraction crystal strobed wildly. It could not even entrain, far less alter the flow of the Trident. It was being overwhelmed by the ley.

It was going to overload!

From deep in the earth beneath the Council Chamber came a low snarling rumble as the Trident was disrupted by the alien crystal feeding off its flow.

The crystal coughed an ominous burst of light.

The ground began to shake.

The Chamber erupted in screams and shouts, which were picked up, amplified, refracted a thousand times by the crystals in the ceiling, until the Chamber of Atlantis trembled as much from fear as from the violence of the accident.

Released by the Hexachon, Herata collapsed to the floor, the marble under her piercingly cold after the warmth of possession. She struggled to gain her feet, the floor pitching and rocking beneath her like the deck of a storm-tossed ship.

The crystal in the middle of the Chamber flared with actinic light, its tone rising to an outraged shriek as it built up to detonation. She threw up her hands to block the sight from burning her eyes out of their sockets. Behind it, she sensed more than saw the Five Kings being whisked out of the Chamber by their men-at-arms.

She stumbled backwards as the floor tilted and shrugged under her. Pandemonium reigned in the Chamber; the crowd of onlookers struggled and screamed like mad things as they stumbled toward the exits. But there could be little movement, little progress of simple human strength against the remorseless shaking of the earth itself. People were knocked off the railing above to tumble shrieking to the floor below. Some few struggled to the doorways and freedom.

Knocked clean off her feet, Herata crawled, dragging herself along the tilting, shuddering floor toward the shrieking crystal. She must try to shut it down! If it overloaded it would destroy the whole Chamber, perhaps even bring down the Pyramid itself.

The Patriarch was nowhere to be seen.

A crack opened in the floor directly in front of her; from it poured a gaseous exhalation, foul as the breath of hell itself. Coughing, choking, she covered her mouth, trying to press forward. The crack was not so very big; if the very ground were not leaping like a maenad she could step right across it. But with the floor tilting first one way, then the next, it was impossible. Great gouts of foul smoke and gas choked her, making her eyes water.

The crystals in the ceiling began to pick up the harmonic from the overloading ley-stone; they sang with a deadly humming keen, louder and louder above the screams of the trapped. She screamed every shutoff code she knew at the shivering, howling crystal. But her voice could not cut through the bedlam.

Someone stumbled into her, bowling her over. She clutched at him helplessly; they both tumbled headlong across the bucking floor. They did not stop until they fetched up against the steps at the edge of the chamber floor. Even amidst all the chaos she could feel the warmth of the bond that joined them, renewed by her visitation by the Hexachon.

She opened her eyes to find herself looking up into two blazing blue eyes. It was Branek, just as she had known.

His arms went around her waist, his gaze locked with hers with a deadly intensity as the whole world seemed to tilt and slide under them. There could be no escaping now. "Hold on!" he cried.

The dying crystal belched out a new, blinding surge of almost pure *aum*. Branek shouted with the pain of it, burning his skin, his eyes.

But Herata felt it pass over her, through her, like a warm wave of the ocean. It seemed to carry her out of herself, her consciousness spreading to fill the chamber. She looked down from the singing, dying crystals of the roof, out through the thousand terrified eyes of the struggling victims.

Looking down, she saw the Trident, the great north-south ley that ran through the chamber and the city itself. She could actually see it, pulsing golden clear under the floor, as she had never seen it before: the precise wavelengths of it, the pulse of life itself. So clear, so obvious, as if she could measure it with her fingers.

Somehow she saw herself clamber to her feet, pulling Branek with her. "Hang onto me!" she cried to him, mind to mind in the howling golden light. "Hang on tight!"

Branek behind her, her body faced the crystal, opening her arms to the storm of power.

It exploded -- light, sound, *aum* filling the chamber, blinding her bodiless vision, sweeping outward in a wave of destruction.

It struck them –

Chapter Fifteen

-- and they fell, shouting with surprise and landing sprawled on the hard ground beneath.

They were on the causeway that bridged the innermost canal from the sacred precinct. The bulk of the city lay before them. Behind them, they heard a terrible, grumbling roar.

They turned to look. It was the pyramid of the High King's palace, where they had been only a second before. Searing golden light spilled from every door and window.

As they watched, the light flashed in a final paroxysm of fury and the façade of the pyramid split and cracked all down the front as if riven open by some mighty weapon of the gods. The crack belched forth a final gout of power and flame, and then all was darkness and silence.

Behind them, chaos reigned in the city; people ran in terror as fires raged and buildings fell under the onslaught of the earthquake.

Herata dragged herself to her feet. The causeway quivered under them; the ground was still shaking.

"Aftershocks," she said. "We must get somewhere safe."

Branek, still sitting on the ground, stared up at her, his eyes glassy and vacant. He looked at her, at the ruined pyramid in front of them, at the canal below them, at her again. "How is it we are not dead?" he asked.

It was shock, Herata realized. He was going into shock, and she concentrated on that instead of his question, which she could not contemplate without descending into gibbering hysteria.

"Never mind!" she barked. "On your feet! We have to find shelter."

A bridge over open water was no place to ride out the last vestiges of the Mother's wrath. She snatched up his hands and tried to drag him to his feet, but his dead weight was too heavy. "Get up, Branek!" she cried, starting to panic. The hair on the back of her neck was rising; her breath came fast and shallow. Another temblor was coming any minute; she could feel it. She could feel everything now.

"Get up!" she cried again.

At last he staggered to his feet. "We should go," he said stupidly.

That glassy look was still in his eyes, but it took no seer to recognize that this bridge was a dangerous place to be. Dust sifted down into the water as the bridge trembled under the effects of the explosion.

Herata pulled him off the bridge and into the city, still unable to believe they were alive.

What had happened? How had they escaped? She had felt the power – reached out and grasped it –

No! her mind screamed. *That's impossible!* Yet here they were.

They stumbled down off the bridge into the Orichalc Circle, the innermost ring of the city. It was a shambles. The streets were littered with debris from shattered marble pediments of the fine houses. Fires licked up from the ruins. People ran here and there, wailing and shouting, some trying to douse the fires, some looking for lost loved ones, others simply hysterical. The crystal streetlights strobed and sputtered spasmodically though it was full daylight. They hummed like angry bees in Herata's mind. The city's power grid had been smashed.

Poseidonis had not suffered so since the Wars of the Five Kings.

"Oh gods!" Herata moaned. "I warned them!"

"Hush!" Branek said, putting an arm around her. "Not now!" A little light of sense came back into his eyes.

People were staring at them. Branek hustled Herata along into a side street.

"Don't talk like that!" he said to her. "People know you – they might think –"

"That I did this?" Herata cried. It was like a spear thrust into her heart. "No! I warned them!"

"Quiet!" He gave her a little shake. "What *did* you do, Herata? How are we here? Why are we still alive?"

She shook her head wildly, a bubble of panic rising in her throat. She would not speak of it!

The bubble popped. "It's coming!" she screamed.

The ground shook again as an aftershock seized the city. Falling to their knees, they clutched each other as the angry hands of the gods shook the debris around them. With a roaring crack, another marble panel tore itself away from the building beside them. Blocks of stone rained down around them. Branek pushed Herata down and covered her body with his own.

By sheer chance they escaped having their brains dashed out. At last it was over. Branek arose and pulled Herata to her knees.

"Will there be others?" he asked.

She searched for the knowledge inside herself, feeling out the leys.

"Yes. Many more."

She broke down, sobbing on his shoulder. Now it was her turn to give in to shock and fear. *O Mother, I tried to stop them!*

"Where is it safe to go, Herata?" Branek asked. He caught her chin in his hand, forcing her to look at him, pushing tear-sodden hair out of her face. "Herata! Where can we go?"

He did not know the city as well as she. She wiped her nose on the back of her hand, trying to think.

"South," she said. "Beyond the harbor, onto the plains."

He frowned. "That's a long way." Halfway across the city.

"Once the palace had shelters but – not anymore …" The palace had nothing anymore. Only corpses. She whimpered, fear clawing at her throat. She could feel the violence of the disrupted earthlines like a slow burning in her belly. It was not over yet, not by half.

"The plains then." Branek hauled her to her feet and they started walking.

The going was slow; they had to detour often past streets that were choked with rubble or still aflame. Herata wanted to stay and help, to put out the fires, but Branek would not let her. The whole city knew the Council had questioned her that morning. The people had no reason to think she had not destroyed the palace to save herself. They received many horrified looks, but the citizens were terrified and no one dared approach them.

Once they had to detour around a giant, shattered leystone in an intersection, part of a sculpture that had once graced the street. It had been ruptured by the disharmony in the Trident. It buzzed and flickered erratically. Herata shied away from it in terror. It was not lifeless yet; she could feel its pain, impossible to describe and slow as honey dripping. Branek dragged her back the way they had come until they could find another path.

It almost overwhelmed her. She felt as open to the earth energies as the Plains of Gold to the skies: outspread, naked, vulnerable. The angry keening of outraged leystones everywhere around her filled her mind. She imagined she could hear the groaning of the stressed, fractured stones deep in the earth, where the earthquakes started. They ground together, disturbed, their energy building until it would explode outward in a sudden shock that made stone flow like water. They made their way very close to the path of the Trident, straight south. It was still quivering with erratic harmonics, trembling like a plucked bowstring from the indignities of the disastrous experiment. She could feel its disharmony like ants on her skin, tingling, burning. She longed to scream, but bit down on it. There was enough screaming in the streets of the Great City today.

She needed to concentrate; they were in the Silver Circle now, still a long way from safety. Others were also streaming that way, out of the rings of the city onto the open plains beyond. Branek held her close and shouldered his way through the crowds of dazed, bleeding people.

They came to the fourth great canal that circled the city, the first in from the harbor. The only bridge over followed the path of the Trident. Herata stepped onto the arc of the bridge as gingerly as onto broken glass, cringing at the touch of the outraged leyline.

"Quickly," Branek said. Another shock could send any of these bridges tumbling down.

Hurrying across, Herata caught a glimpse of the water below. It was shallow and turgid-looking. The walls of the canal were slick with moisture far above the level of the water. The canal was half empty.

"No," she said, "Oh, no, no!"

Searching, she sent her landsense out, east to the ocean, seeking, feeling along the threads of earthblood, out into the open sea, farther –

There! Far to the northeast, deep on the bed of the ocean, the torment of the Trident had shifted a long-buried fault line as the earth sought new equilibrium. A wave of geologic force was rolling out from the center – and above it, in the sea, the corresponding deadly wave of water, racing across the surface of the ocean, sucking all the water before it into a killing pile, very close now: the dreaded spawn of the earthquake, the tidal wave.

"The canal!" she cried, snapping back into mortal consciousness. "Look at the water!"

Branek looked, and he saw. He lived in the Inner Sea, he knew.

"How far will it get?" he asked. "Into the canals?"

"All the way!"

"The canal! Look to the canal! Tsunami!" he shouted, his voice ringing out across both sides of the canal. "Take cover!"

But there was no cover to take. If the wave breached the canals there would be no place to hide.

In the distance, stadia away, Herata felt more than heard the great wave come crashing ashore, smashing into the port of Atlantis and raging up the Grand Canal. The water in the canal beneath them sank lower, draining away to feed the deadly wave.

The bridge trembled under the distant impact.

"Oh gods. It's too late!" she cried.

The Trident beneath shivered at the assault of the groundwave that accompanied the tsunami. Disrupted power sang down the ley. She felt it, hitting her like a gust of hot wind, filling her –

She snatched at it, and the world was swallowed in golden light. She opened her mouth to scream, but her mouth was gone, *she* was gone –

Then she was back.

They stood in green grass, somewhere on the open plains. Rolling green land flowed away from them in every direction. Around them stood a ragged circle of standing stones, an ancient node of natural power. It was to this she had been drawn.

They had left the city. They had translated again.

"Oh gods!" Herata staggered to a standing stone, clutched it for strength. She felt the earthquake, boiling along the ley. "It comes!"

Branek stumbled up behind her and grabbed the menhir, pressing her against it. They held on for all they were worth as the shockwave hit and the earth beneath them bucked and leaped.

It was worse this time, bigger; the quaking seemed to go on forever. Herata bit her lips to stifle her screams; in her ear she heard Branek praying desperately.

At last it was over. Herata painfully released her hold on the standing stone. Branek's head was bowed on her shoulder. Wearily he lifted it, looked around.

In a curiously flat voice, he asked, "Where are we?"

"The Plains of Gold. South of the City."

She squirmed around to face him; he leaned back a little, giving her room. She looked up into his face, framed by tangled sweaty hair, blue eyes dull with shock.

He seemed to struggle with it. "So we are alive, then. Not dead?"

She reached up and brushed away the hair from his brow. "No. Not dead."

He repeated it: "We are alive."

She felt the earth under her feet, the rough surface of the menhir at her back. The sun on her face, shining as it would always shine, earthquakes or no, whether princes and priestesses lived or died.

She breathed, felt the air pumping in and out of her lungs, felt the pulse beating in her neck. Alive, yes -- they lived yet, they breathed, they sensed. Many had perished; she felt it. But *they* had not.

He was still holding her close against the menhir; she felt the length of his body against her, the hard strength of his chest and limbs pressing her into the stone. She could feel every inch of him against her; the warmth of his skin, the strength of his muscles, skin to skin, flesh to flesh, the most exquisite sensation she had ever known, even in the leys. The feel of him against her seemed to light a fire in her; of a sudden she wanted nothing more than to pull him even closer, meld his living flesh with hers as close as she might.

"Alive," she gasped, "Yes."

A wave of pure lust rolled up from deep within her soul. She cried out and clutched him, trembling with frantic need. A pulse beat at the base of Branek's throat, his breath was ragged; he felt it too. In his eyes she could see the same crazy longing that had possessed her. She could feel his manhood rising, stiff against her thigh.

She twined her arms around his neck and they kissed with a maddened intensity, fueled by the terror of death and its aftermath. She snarled her fingers in his hair, pulling him closer as if she could drink him in. He grunted at the pain, lifted her by the hips and pressed her harder against the stone. Her legs twined around his lean waist. She moaned as desire filled her like *aum* filling the magic stones of the circle.

Far away across the plain, the city was still burning, she could feel it if she tried. But no! She beat it back, wanting only this, here, now. Him. Branek!

She pulled out the fibula of her gown, cast it into the grass. Her garment slipped away. Branek buried his head in her bosom; she yelped as his mouth found a nipple and seized on it. Pleasure raced from her breast to her loins and back again, a circuit closing, sped by the power of the circle that contained them. She convulsed with pleasure, her nails gouging his back.

"Ah!" he hissed. His breath was harsh in her ear. "Harder!"

She fumbled with the complex knot that held the shoulder of his robe, until he reached up himself and ripped it away. One-handed he held her against the menhir. She arched her back; he bit her other nipple. She slipped her tongue into the hollow of his ear. Goosepimples chased over his flesh. He groaned.

Stiff-armed, he braced them both against the stone, looking deep into her eyes. His mouth was distorted with pleasure. Her legs remained locked around his waist, cleaving her to him. She caressed his face with her fingertips, pulled him close again. She slid her tongue into his mouth, slipping it in and out, slowly, pulsingly. The question was asked and answered.

Easily he swung her into his arms and carried her into the center of the circle. Before the ancient stone altar, the ground dipped in a mossy hollow. Tenderly he lay her down. She exulted in the way he loomed over her, blond as the sungod, his weight pressing her into the bosom of the earth.

He filled her sight. No there was no burning, no terror, just she and Branek and the thing that they made together. Her limbs trembled in anticipation and desire.

He covered her. Their legs twined together. His breath caught as his manhood touched the wetness there, between her legs; she was ready for him, so ready, aching for him. With a little cry she spread her legs.

But with a twist and heave he rolled her over, and now she was on top of him, straddling him as he lay underneath her, his blond hair spread out upon the grass.

"Better this way," he whispered, "for you."

She caressed his chest and shoulders, delighting in the strength there. His hands stroked her thighs, cupped her breasts. His eyes never left her own.

Leaning forward to kiss him brought her nether lips against his member. A shock of pleasure raced through her at that touch, the feel of his hardness against her tender warmth. She was overcome by the aching need to have him enter her, fill her. Her womb cried out to be breached. Gasping, she lifted her hips.

Skillfully he took her by the waist and guided her onto his erect manhood. There was pressure, a flash of pain, but she bore down and then he was *in her*, his phallus filling what had seemed a bottomless ache. She called out as he pierced her, touching her as she had never been touched.

Branek gave a long shuddering cry as she took him in, her wetness surrounding him, enfolding him in their long-delayed culmination. He grasped her hips and began to rock her back and forth, up and down his shaft.

Little yelps of pleasure burst from her as the sensation of him inside her diminished and increased with each thrust. Her hands caressed her own breasts, her throat. His hips bucked under her.

"Herata, my goddess," he sighed. His hands ran up her body, clasped her breasts. Catching the rhythm, she rocked herself against his hips. A sweet ache began to build inside her, an ache that would shortly be satisfied.

"Oh ... Branek! Branek!"

Their rhythm increased. She clasped his hands, leveraging herself against his strength, stroking, stroking. The leaping of his hips between her legs grew more frenzied.

A final stroke, and the balance was tipped. She arched her neck and keened as overwhelming pleasure cascaded through her. This was a lifewave, greater than she had ever experienced. She felt that light and life was pouring out of her, filling the little stone circle, filling the world.

Branek grasped her hips, grinding her down into him, until he too cried and convulsed beneath her. His hot seed spurted inside her. She felt it touch the lips of her womb, and gasped anew at the tingling warmth that spread from that contact, as if some cosmic circuit had been completed. Head thrown back, she stared unseeing into the blue heavens, transfixed, as if the world turned on the axis of her awakened womb.

Then it was over. Released, she collapsed forward onto Branek's broad chest. It heaved under her as he gasped with exertion and release. His hands ran everywhere over her back, her hips, her arms, as if he would encompass all of her at once.

"Oh," he said, "Oh gods, Herata. I love you so!"

Only then did her tears come.

She wept for the burned city, for the dead, for the folly of men. Branek tried to console her at first, whispering, cajoling, words she couldn't understand in the extremity of her despair. In the end he simply held her, giving her the comfort of his strength as she grieved in bitter sorrow for her ruined home.

At last, her tears ran dry and she was spent. But she could still feel the burning city, a glow in the back of her mind. Back there, the warriors of the army and the adepts of the temples struggled to control the blazes, to shore up the weakened buildings. The long work of rebuilding had already begun.

"We have to go back," Herata said wearily, lifting her head from Branek's chest.

"Of course," he said. "But there is one thing I do not understand. Please – you must tell me: how did we get – here?"

There was nothing else but to say it. "I took us out of there. Along the ley. First to the bridge – then here. We teleported."

"In the leys?" he whispered, amazed.

Herata nodded. She looked down at her hands, rubbed them together, touched her face.

It was supposed to be impossible. To merge so fully with a leyline, with the *aum*, subsume yourself into the flow body and spirit, and then reclaim yourself at the end, every cell intact: matter to energy, then back again. The ultimate act of mastery. Unattainable.

And she had done it not once, but twice. And brought Branek through as well, safe and unharmed. Impossible.

"How?" Branek asked.

She shook her head. That, there were no words for. "I just did it – it was so simple ..."

"You really are a sorceress."

She looked at him, unsure. "I couldn't do it now." Like a millipede walking – if thought about, it became truly impossible. The power eluded her.

Branek gazed at her, his eyes troubled. "You are as dangerous as the White Temple says."

"Do you fear me, Branek? Then well you should. Look." She pointed, to where the dull glare of the burning city glowed on the horizon. "Behold what my enemies would do. To prevent that, I will bring down the White Temple if need be. I would tear down Nine Seas itself, if it would stop the greater burning."

"I do fear you," Branek said, "and love you, as a sailor fears and loves the sea."

She covered his lips with her hand. "I am not some queen out of legend," she said, the tears starting in her eyes once again. "Just a woman, a young woman who wants to lie with her lover on the beach and watch the moon rise."

He smiled sadly at the memory of their first nights together. "Could we not do that?"

She looked at him, looked at the burning glow on the horizon. The smell of burning was coming to them now on the wind. "You know we can't."

He bowed his head, accepting defeat. Herata stood, and gathered her things. Branek silently followed suit.

She could not find her fibula; it was lost in the grass. Branek showed her how to tie up her gown in his people's fashion.

The ground quivered with another aftershock. When it was over, they began the long walk back to the city.

Chapter Sixteen

For three days the aftershocks of the Chamber catastrophe rocked the city of the Sea Kings. The ancient fires that slumbered uneasily in the heart of the island home had been stirred to sullen life; long would it be before they quieted again. That had always been the Sea Kings' curse as well as blessing. The ancient fires in the earth made the *aum* run hot and strong – until the fires woke, and the earth shook once again.

To Branek those days were a blur of grief and horror, as they worked alongside priests and soldiers, commoners and princes, to rescue those still living and recover the dead. Buildings had collapsed all over the city, and the high palace – the high palace, where the explosion had occurred, was a charnel house.

Amalthea was dead, crushed by a piece of falling masonry in the collapsing council chamber. Neither Branek nor Herata had known she was there; Branek had managed to get his and Herata's people out before the flawed crystal detonated, but he hadn't known to look for Amalthea. She had slipped out of the House of the Salmon and come to the Council on her own. When her body was brought forth, Herata's grief and rage were terrible to behold.

They burned her on a pyre in the burning grounds on the northern arc of the harbor – a mass pyre; no one had the luxury of a private funeral then. Herata lit the blaze herself, dressed in white, the color of death, of nothingness, of endings. She stood there and watched it burn, too close, embers scorching her gown and hair, her face wet with tears that burned off in the heat of the flames. But behind the tears, Branek saw a fire in her eyes, burning hot and steady like the fires of the earth herself.

When it was done and the fire was burned out, and the grave attendants were sweeping up the ashes, they returned home, to Branek's townhouse. He did not feel safe at the House of the Salmon; he only felt at ease when she was within arm's reach of him, and his own trusted men guarded them.

Once alone there, Herata threw herself at him with a furious intensity, seeking oblivion in his arms, an oblivion he could not provide no matter how resolutely he tried. And try he did, night after night. Their days assumed that pattern: long days of heartbreaking work, short nights of passion as the consummation they had long awaited devoured them like the fires devoured the earth. Indeed, the one fed the other; Herata seemed on fire with the swelling anger of the earth, and Branek, drunk with her, dazed, could not but respond in kind.

In all phases of the recovery *aum* was in constant use: lifting stones, lighting worksites long into the night, stabilizing weakened buildings, healing, warming, lighting fires to burn the dead. Branek could tell it made Herata furious, furious and desperate, but what could she say against work to rescue the injured and restore life to the shattered city? Until finally she could keep silent no more, and went to visit the Salmon King her father, where the Five held council in the ruined temple of a minor god. Branek attended her, as he attended her everywhere now, afraid to let her out of his sight.

"I would speak with you," Herata said to Herodian.

The others saw the look in her eyes and let them be. The gods were upon her: better to be out of her way, before she broke like the tsunami, burst like the thunderstorm.

"I know what you would say, so save your breath," Herodian said before she could speak. "The work will continue. The new nexus shall be opened."

"You shall not do this," the priestess said.

Herodian gestured around at the ruined chamber in which they stood. "Yet we must. We must rebuild. How shall we look before the subject kings, if we cannot rebuild our own city? They will turn on us; they will fall upon us like the pack of wolves on the old leader. The reign of the Sea Kings would be over."

"If you do this, there shall be no more Sea Kings. I have seen it."

"We need *aum*. The nexus will be opened. It will be done."

"It is folly," Herata said.

He hardly had the will to argue with her. He spoke as one resigned to his fate. "To do nothing would be death."

"I will stop you," Herata said, implacable as the tide.

"We both do what we must," the Salmon King said. What must be done must be done, and the gods would have their way of them, no matter whether they struggled against their fate or not.

"So be it," Herata said. "I return to Nine Seas."

"Go then," her father said. "I do not think we will meet again, my daughter."

"Only in death," Herata said, and so left him.

Not until they were home did she break down with wretched tears of sorrow and despair. Branek moved to comfort her, and things went they way they always went now when they were alone, the only comfort they had in this nightmare of death and destruction.

"You are leaving?" Branek asked afterward, as they lay together in the rumpled sheets, the breeze blowing over them from the garden. She had said nothing of this to him.

Herata sat up, retrieving her discarded robe from the floor. "I must return to Nine Seas."

"So soon?" he asked, trying to keep his voice even. The thought gutted him. How could she leave him now? How could he let her?

Herata reached over and trailed a hand down his chest, a touch that made him shiver and ache with pleasure, though they had just spent themselves utterly.

"Yes," she said. "At once."

"When were you going to tell me?" he asked, struggling not to sound as wretched as he felt.

"Don't be angry," she said. "You know I need to do this."

He knew no such thing. How could she leave him? How could she expect *him* to leave her unguarded, after everything that happened?

"Leave, yes. But I had hoped you would come with me to Lacaon." Far away from Atlantis, from the Great City and the White Temple. Lacaon was safe. He had to believe that. Laodice was a wise and skilled adept; no matter what came, she would keep Lacaon safe. And Herata would help her.

She turned to face him on the bed. "Nothing would please me more. But I cannot."

"I want you to meet Laodice," Branek continued doggedly. "She will be your sister. And it is she who will marry us."

"Will we be married?" Herata asked him quizzically.

"Of course!" he said. "I have said it – were we lawfully wed I could protect you from the Council as a sovereign prince. Only say the word and we will sail for Lacaon on the instant." They could leave this place of death and start a new life.

Heart looked away, her gaze distant, frowning. "In my vision I saw no marriage in our future. I was sure it was not to be. But now … I don't know."

"What has changed?" Branek asked, wondering what could possibly be the answer.

She glanced at him, looked away again. Her gaze turned inward, as if she were listening to something with her inner hearing. "Everything." Her gesture indicated their newly intimate relationship, the ruination of the

Great City, things unseen and unsaid in her vision.

"I have spoken with Laodice," Branek continued, forging ahead, unwilling to discuss her vision. "She is eager to meet you, a sister of the leys. There are few adepts in Lacaon, only her and my aunt and a few acolytes. She looks forward to discussing the craft with you."

Herata regarded him quizzically. "Does a man always want his lover to like his sister so?"

Branek shrugged. "Our mother died when we were children. There were always just the two of us; our father left our raising to the household. In a way we raised each other. And she is the Lady of our House – at least until you and I are wed. Her opinion matters."

With unspeakable relief Branek saw that Herata was actually considering it, the little frown line he found so endearing growing between her brows as she puzzled over it. He knew, he prayed, that if he could just get her to Lacaon, she would stay and never leave, and they would be safe, far away from whatever doom awaited Atlantis. He knew it was an unworthy thought, but he could not help it. Laodice knew what she was doing; he had to believe that. Her work would protect them if the worst came. She had promised him.

"Should I be worried?" Herata asked. "I mean, I am the mad seeress, the destroyer of temples, after all."

"She is very curious to meet you," he said. "And I think you would like to meet her, too. She is very gifted; she could show you many things that have been done in Lacaon."

"The earthquake protocols," Herata said, less than pleased.

"And other things. We are far away from the island home; we have had to figure out how to do some things for ourselves." Branek ran his hand softly along her bare shoulder; it made her sigh and shiver with delight. But even so, she took his hand and removed it from her arm.

"Soon," Herata said. "But not now."

"And what of me?" he asked.

She lifted his hand and kissed it. "You should go back to Lacaon, my love," she said. "It isn't safe here. Physically, spiritually, it isn't safe at all."

"How can I leave you undefended?" he asked angrily, hurt that he would even have to say it after everything that had happened. "How can you ask that of me?"

"I swear to you, Branek, no one can harm me in my own temple," she said. "I set the wards, and I control the crystals. The very stones of the walls would move to protect me if I were attacked. I could be no place safer than Nine Seas."

"How can you leave me?" he asked before he could stop himself.

Her face softened; her lip suddenly trembling. She slid across the bed, curled into his side, looking deep into his eyes. "You know I will always be with you," she said. "In spirit. But right now my body must be at Nine Seas."

Catching her in his arms, he rolled her over, pinning her down. His body exulted to feel the length of her under him, feel her quivering as he caressed her. He was angry, but that did not stop him from wanting her; if anything it made him want her more. He stripped the dress from her form, which she had only just donned. If she would send him away, he could at least make her regret it.

"Right now?" he asked. "This very minute?"

"Well," she said breathily, "perhaps not just yet."

But in the end, Herata returned to her temple, and Branek returned to his home in the Inner Sea. It grieved Herata to part from him, but she needed her full attention for her task. Her work, she knew now, was only just beginning.

Upon getting home to Nine Seas she walked alone down to the shore. She could feel the Trident, stretching away out before her, down south into the sea. With voice and mind, she sent her call along it.

Sleek and fast, racing from the south came a single finned shape. The dolphin leaped from the water, and raced to meet her in the shallows.

"I greet you, Herata, Lady of the Nine Seas, daughter of the Salmon King," it whistled.

She knew this dolphin. "I greet you, Thalassa, lady of waters, daughter of Akasha," she answered. "What news from the deep seas?"

"No change. The flows stutter; the power is stolen. The waters are sluggish; the fish die. When will the thirst of the Sea Kings be slaked?"

"It will never be slaked," Herata said. "Never while men walk the shores of Atlantis."

"What then can dolphins do?" Thalassa whistled. "Why do you call us?"

"Go," Herata said. "Stop the longships of the Sea Kings in their tracks. Lead them astray with your songs. Cut the fish from the nets, open the weirs, let not the swimmers on the white beaches enjoy the waters in peace. Set up a hue and cry around the water steps of every king's palace and temple in the Nine Seas. Never sleep; sing the songs night and day; make the waters churn with your wrath. There is much that dolphins can do."

"Is it war then?" Thalassa whistled, a long, mourning call.

"It shall be war," Herata said. "Go now, and tell the others. The Mother Earth calls you to service; fail Her not!"

"It shall be done," Thalassa vowed, and was gone. Herata returned alone to the temple.

***

In the days that followed Herata continued her program of resistance, which she had begun in the days after her first contact with the Hexachon. Hours she spent in the leys, searching, watching, mending what she saw that was hurt. Shamelessly she stole power from other temples and sent it abroad, channeling it down the Trident and the Golden Dragon, out to the open sea and to the wide world beyond.

Other adepts set wards on their crystals and temples, trying to keep her out, as had not been done in the temples of the Faith since the days of Solon the Black, the King in the Gates, when Sea King fought Sea King for control of the empire. But Herata found that these wards were no barriers to her; she could defeat them easily. They were as transparent to her as a child's twice-told riddles. Nothing in the crystals was beyond her now. She could have shut them all down if she wished – forever.

The Sea Kings were right to be afraid, she realized, hanging effortlessly in the flows for hours on end, seeing all, feeling it all. She could send a deathwave around the flows that would snuff the lights of every temple in the wide world, if she wished it.

But she did not. Such thoughts were anathema to her. She still held out hope that a middle way would be reached.

And so she continued to hope, until she received a visitor she never expected.

It was late afternoon, almost evening. She had been in the flows for hours and hours, almost all day, monitoring, observing, correcting the flows where she could. Messages passed her by on the ley, sounds and scents and words from around the world. The Sea Kings had few secrets from her anymore. Those they wished to keep they did not transmit by ley. She heard with approval complaints to the Poseideion about disruptions in shipping; the dolphins did their work well.

At last, exhausted, lightheaded, she drifted home along the Golden Dragon ley, back to her cramped, cold body sitting in trance by the new leystone.

As she approached Atlantis she became aware of a drain on the ley, an external node tapping the ley's energy. Dredging up a new surge of strength, she sharpened her sensitivity to examine it, pushing her sight outward.

It was a ship, a large one, following the ley across the ocean from the west, to Atlantis. To the southern tip of the island home, to Nine Seas. It could be going no place else; the southern coast was isolated, only small fishing villages, none of which would warrant a visit from a vessel such as this. Her senses noted its configuration from its turbulence in the water and the ley – high-prowed, sharp-keeled but with a low draft, a ship that could travel both open seas and far inland along rivers. It was a ship of the River People of the Southern Sister continent, the cities hidden in the mighty jungle along the banks of the Great Mother River. They were clients of the Sea Kings, and ships from the Mother River came often to Atlantis.

But this ship was different. She knew it by the vibration of the great crystal mounted in its prow, which powered its engine. That crystal had been programmed in the City of Clouds.

Almost before she knew it, she was along the ley, back into Nine Seas, and moving out through the leystone, back into flesh. As always, the first agonizing breath drawn into a body long neglected, and the rush of bodily sensation – light, cold, sound, thirst, a full bladder.

She chaffed her cold arms, unwound herself from the yogic posture that kept a trance-locked body still.

"Amal –" she started, then stopped, remembering. She cleared her throat. She did not remember the name of the new young acolyte who attended her.

"Food," she said to him, "and Lamike. And I am setting the wards. We have visitors."

Two hours later the ship arrived at their dock, its sail bearing the enigmatic glyph that was the sigil of the City of Clouds. Herata and Lamike watched from the temple peristyle as it disengaged its engine and drew into the dock under sweeps.

"What do they want?" Lamike wondered.

"I have no idea," Herata said. She had received no message.

"If they mean to attack us, I don't think they'd be doing it under sweeps," Nestor said from beside them. Branek had insisted on sending him, and a handpicked detachment of his own men, with Herata to Nine Seas for her protection.

"No," Herata said, "The folk of Cloud City are no warriors. Whatever it is, it isn't that. Let them dock."

Nestor gestured to his men, who drew back from the quayside.

The ship silently docked. A single figure disembarked from it, walked toward them. As she walked up the steps of the temple, she put back the hood of her cloak, and Herata recognized her – pale skin, blonde hair going gray, green eyes.

Herata felt the world tilt under her; she sagged, Nestor caught her arm.

"Aglaia," Herata said. "*Mother!*"

Aglaia bowed, as initiate to High Priestess. "My Lady of Nine Seas," she said. "Herata, my daughter."

Herata was at a loss for words; all that came out of her mouth was a little mew, like that of a lost kitten. She had never expected to see her mother again in this life. Lamike took over for her, seeing her distress.

"My queen-" she began.

"That title is no longer my own," Aglaia said. "I am only a sister like yourself."

"You have traveled a very long way," Lamike continued smoothly. "You must be exhausted. We will have rooms prepared for you and your party. Will you take a meal?"

"Gladly," Aglaia said. "But I must speak with my daughter first."

Still wordless, Herata gestured her forward, out of the atrium into a small side chapel. Nestor looked anxious, knowing how suspicious Branek would be of any strangers. Herata raised a reassuring hand to him, forestalling him from following them. Whatever on earth had prompted Aglaia to come to Nine Seas – Herata could not imagine – she did not mean her daughter harm. Herata knew that beyond doubt. But as she let her hand fall she could feel it shaking.

They stood in the chapel in silence, staring at each other. They were of a height now. Aglaia looked remarkably young, her face unlined, her hair streaked with gray only at the temples. She still possessed much of the beauty that had been the toast of the Great City and won a Sea King's heart. Life in the temples clearly agreed with her.

Aglaia was the first to speak. "Are you well, my daughter?"

"You have broken your vows," Herata said.

She must have, to be there at all. Aglaia had joined a cloistered order of priestesses in Cloud City after her marriage with Herodian had dissolved. Upon taking her final vows, she had closed herself off from the world forever. Her very presence here was a shattering of those vows.

On the way to the City of Clouds, she had stopped at Nine Seas to visit her eleven-year-old daughter. Herata had known it would be the last time she would ever see her mother in this life.

"Yes," Aglaia said, "I have. But it was necessary."

"Necessary? Why?"

Aglaia stepped closer to her daughter, touched her cheek. "Herata," she said, "my darling."

Herata smelled the incense that Aglaia had always burned in their home when Herata was small, a sweet mustiness that lingered on her robes. A flood of memories rushed through her.

"Mother," she whispered brokenly. Aglaia opened her arms to her, and before she even knew it, Herata was weeping in her mother's arms.

"There," Aglaia said, "my sweet girl. There, there."

"Mother," she sobbed; it seemed to be all she could say. *You left me.*

I've been so alone.

Leaning on Aglaia's shoulder, Herata felt Aglaia open her mind to her. Herata flinched away, mentally and physically, but Aglaia followed her, her thoughts bleeding into Herata's own. Herata remembered things she had not thought of, or allowed herself to think of, for many years – playing in the garden at her mother's feet while Aglaia meditated with crystals, bathing with her mother in the water gardens of the Hall of the Salmon, Aglaia singing her to sleep at night --

--It's all right, my daughter, I know why you don't want to share with me, why you've avoided the City of Clouds all these years …

--You left me! Herata's thoughts flashed against her mother's. I was nine years old and you sent me away and you left and never came back!

--And the gods will judge the rightness of that choice, Aglaia answered her. I had my gifts, and you had yours. And Herodian was inaum; he could never understand your skills, or your burdens. I did what I thought was right.

"And events have borne out the wisdom of that choice," Aglaia said aloud, holding Herata at arm's length and looking into her eyes, green eyes into green.

Herata looked away, still afraid of the emotions her mother's appearance brought forth.

"You never foresaw this," she said. She was certain of that.

"No," Aglaia agreed. "Unlike you, I am no seer. But I knew you had your path, your part to play in the service of Stone and Sea."

"Why are you here?" Herata asked, baffled. She could not imagine what could have brought her pious mother to break her vows and leave Cloud City forever.

Aglaia smiled. "Had you been wiling in your ley-walking to visit my City on occasion, you would know."

So it's my fault, Herata thought with resentment.

"No. I do not fault you," Aglaia said. "I understand your reasons. I left the City of Clouds of my own free will. But it's true that if you had come, much time could have been saved. I bring a message from the Bride of the Sun."

The master crystal of the Temple of the Clouds, a stone almost as old and wise as the Hexachon. Herata had regretted not consulting it in her endless travels along the leys, her restoration work. But the thought of stumbling upon Aglaia's mind in the leys of Cloud City had been too painful.

"Why did the Bride not bespeak me?" Herata wondered. The distance was no barrier to a stone so old and powerful.

"This message could not be transmitted by ley," Aglaia said. "She charged me to speak it to you in words of the flesh. I do not know what it means, but the message is simple."

"What is it?"

"She bid me say, 'Tomorrow it begins.'"

Herata blanched, closed her eyes. Yes, it was true; stretching out her inner senses, she could feel it, the ring of truth, the certainty. She had felt it in the leys that day, without understanding what it was: a tension, a breathless waiting. The priests of the White Temple were ready; their dread work would now begin.

"Do you understand?" Aglaia asked.

"I do," Herata breathed. "Yes, I understand."

"Good. Then I must go."

Herata was surprised. "But you should rest, eat." She would leave, just that quickly?

"I can rest on the ship. I must go. My coming here was – not authorized. Agents of the White Temple may be looking for me."

Herata was amazed. Her mother, the most slavish devotee of the temples she knew, had defied the Poseideion. Aglaia was on her side.

"Mother," Herata whispered, "I am so sorry." Aglaia had given up everything to help her daughter.

"Do not be," Aglaia said. She touched Herata's hair. "My dearest wish was always to serve the Earth our Mother, and so I have. I made this choice gladly. It will be good to see my childhood home. As it was to see you, my beautiful daughter."

With that, the tears came again, and Herata clasped her mother to her and sobbed, fear and sorrow awash in her, but tempered with something she had long sought, without knowing it – peace, solace in a mother's love.

Chapter Seventeen

Aglaia left that very afternoon; her ship's crew took on fresh water and then they were gone, sailing for the Misty Isles.

Herata watched the longship until it slipped hull-down and disappeared over the horizon. It was as if Aglaia had never come to Nine Seas at all.

But the Bride of the Sun's word was good. The troubles began that very night.

Pain woke her, pain and terror and the sound of screams in the night.

She had been sleeping heavily, one of her rare periods of dreamless sleep between the horrible visions. But even in her black senselessness something tugged at her, some sense of wrongness, some terror as yet unguessed. It followed her down and dragged her back up to awareness.

Pain assaulted her, shooting off bright clouds of color behind her eyes; the pain of a gross imbalance in the temple's field. Others felt it too; calls and shouts echoed through the cloisters.

She staggered up, pulled herself through the pain into the hallway.

The very air seemed to vibrate and hum with a dreadful tension, a knife on raw, bleeding nerves. The *aum* lights in the hallways suddenly died, then glowed a sickly pale green. The vibration, the sound, scaled up to a terrible wavering shriek, trembling in the walls, the floor, the very air in one's lungs. Even the dullest novice was wracked by a stabbing, ghostly pain, in the ears, behind the eyes.

She sped to the ley chamber in the green-shot darkness. In the chamber, the new gleaming crystal pulsed a deadly, sickening yellow-green. The life was being sucked out of it, in a way never seen before.

The outraged field battered at her ears, her mind. Blood splattered to the floor at her feet. Her nose bled from the strain.

She tried to reach the crystal, to shut it down, but the awfulness of the sensations stopped her, the pain and the bloodcurdling shriek, unlike anything she had heard. It was beyond her now, beyond even her.

The crystal groaned, like a timber about to break.

And then she felt it, sudden and overwhelming, worse than she had ever imagined: a sudden sensation of pulling or drawing, a hideous tension like a giant bowstring being stretched, stretched past its breaking point; a horrible sucking; the confused sensation of something inestimably precious being stolen from her by a thief far, far away. Her eyes felt as if they would pop from her sockets as the evil phenomenon grabbed her and pulled, seeking to pull her as it pulled everything in the temple -- everything that sat on, was one with, partook of the Golden Dragon ley. She screamed as her soul was ripped from her body.

And then it snapped back, the bowstring released. Herata was thrown back across the ley chamber by the force of it, as the distant power that had seized the Golden Dragon and tried to pull it north of its true course was suddenly, painfully released. The lights came back on, the violated crystal rang like a bell. It was over.

The great work of moving the ley lines had begun.

As it was midnight for Herata, a quarter turn of the world away, it was morning for Branek, when he learned just how compromised he was.

He was supervising the unloading of a ship just in from Kythera, bearing wines and spices from the Five Lands to the north of the Inner Sea. It was heavy work, wrestling huge tuns of wine and giant amphorae of dry goods out of the narrow hold of the ship. Men shouted and sang, children shrieked and ran underfoot, climbing over barrels and bales, hoping for a treat from the homecoming sailors. Gleaming darkly on the dock sat a brace of battery crystals in a padded wooden rack, the ship's outgoing cargo, bound for the colony of Enkomi in the eastern isles. Laodice's work improving the flows of White Mare temple had recently netted a dividend of excess *aum*, that could be stored in crystal, and sold or traded dearly to towns and islands that did not sit too close to the leys, and the fires of the Inner Sea. But loading and securing the crystals in the ship was a bloody delicate business, one that always made him sweat. Laodice swore they were stable – but what if they cracked one? He hoped never to find out.

It was a chaotic scene, so it was a while before he noticed that the edge of the ship was sinking even lower next to the dock, the gangway growing flatter and flatter.

Seeing it suddenly, his heart stopped for a moment in his chest. The tide was not due to turn for another five hours.

The water leaving the bay was the true sign of a tsunami, just as had wrecked the Great City only weeks before. Somewhere out to sea, an earthquake had occurred, and the shock wave was traveling along the bed of the sea, and in the water above it as the killing tidal wave.

His nutsack shriveled up from fear and tried to tuck back into his body. Not again, not here! Lacaon was supposed to be safe! For months he had been telling himself that tale, now exposed for the fantasy it was.

He leaped for the galley's mooring rope and frantically unwound it from the capstan. "Cast off!" he screamed to the crew. "Cast off!" Ships at dock snapped like matchsticks when hit by a tsunami – the ship's only chance was to back off and make for deeper water, ride out the wave before it crested.

The crew gaped at him, but then the captain looked around and saw the water sucking away from the bay, exposing beslimed rocks and the ruins of ancient docks at the shoreline. He bellowed orders and his crew leapt into action, securing the hold and starting the crystal engine.

Branek swiveled around, looked at the dock behind him. Sailors and citizens were staring at him quizzically, unaware as yet of the danger.

"Look!" he shouted. "The bay! Get to higher ground!"

And with that they looked, and they saw. Just at that moment a horn blew from the heights of the citadel, a long wailing tone, the general alarm. Every islander had been trained to that sound since birth – *danger from the sea. Flee to the heights.* And so the folk of Lacaon screamed and fled.

"Up the causeway!" Branek cried. "Get to the palace!" The king's house was the highest point on the island; it had withstood earthquakes before, and the highest waves recorded in memory had never reached it.

People on the docks and in the streets dropped what they were doing and crowded up the great paved stone way, yelling in terror. The sun blazed down, shockingly bright and cheerful for such a dire moment. With a shudder, the galley pulled free of the dock and made for the open sea. Branek picked up a wailing baby that had sat down on the dock, its little legs unable to hold it while it sobbed, and thrust it into its mother's arms, pushing her down the quay, toward the causeway that debouched on the harbor.

There would not be enough time, or space, for everyone to make it into the palace, but some of the people would survive.

Ever fiber of his being screamed at him to run, make for the causeway and never stop. The islander's ancestral terror of the wave swamped him, but by force of iron will he clamped down on it, focusing on his task, and herding more townsfolk up the path to the palace. They were his people. It was his responsibility to protect them.

The bay was half emptied now, the slimy seabed exposed, stinking and black in the sun, beached fish flopping all along its length. Small dhows and catamarans lay careened in the mud, sails flapping uselessly, crews wailing; they had not been fast enough to outpace the rush of the receding tide. He heard it now, a rushing, rumbling roar – the wave was cresting just outside the bay. He saw it, towering outside the mole of the harbor – dirty brown water with a frothed white crown, plunging inward, unstoppable. The narrow mouth of the harbor would channel it, amplifying the destructive force, shooting the killing wave forward like an arrow from a bow.

His nerve finally broke, and Branek ran for his life up the stone causeway, knowing he wouldn't make it, praying to pitiless Poseidon, the Earthshaker, that he would.

But as the wave surged through the mouth of the harbor, a weird humming filled the air, keening like the world's hugest nest of angry wasps. The ground trembled, but not with the force of the wave – something faster, more regular, almost mechanical like the striking of a vast hammer in the gods' forge.

A sudden light blinded him. Covering his eyes, he saw it came from the temple, White Mare Temple, perched on its rocky outcrop halfway up the cliff, between the town and the palace.

Lines of light flowed out of the temple, bursting from every door and window, blindingly bright like lightning crawling over the earth. They flowed down the rocks of the cliff, out into the bay, covering its emptied floor, a net of light to catch the tidal wave.

And they did. The lines of light touched the foot of the wave as it crashed into the harbor, releasing an explosion of steam. They crawled over the rocks of the mole, holding them fast, then reached out, stitching back and forth across the mouth of the harbor, over the very surface of the wave. The frothed, churning face of the tsunami trembled, caught in the web, then sagged and crumpled, the seismic energy that had fueled the wave drawn off and away by the lines of – *aum*, Brancke supposed it must be, though he had never seen it before with his own eyes. *Aum* was invisible to the unsighted. Well, no longer, it seemed. The lines of force across the bay and the water blazed more brightly than ever before, fed by the energy of the wave, lines of harrowing blue-white light, like cracks in the very universe.

In a smooth rush the water flowed back into the bay, a glassy hump instead of the killing wave that had been there seconds before. The stranded boats were lifted smoothly instead of being smashed to flinders. The leading edge of the waters swept up over the docks, along the edge of the harbor, lapped at the foot of the inns and warehouses on the harbor front -- but then slipped back, no more damaging than a spring tide under a summer storm. The water sloshed in the bay like in a shaken jug, restless but no longer deadly. For a moment the waters glowed a glassy green color, lit from below by the web of *aum* stitched across the floor of the bay. Then the lines of force faded, and all was utter stillness and silence. The air was heavy with the briny smell of the superheated steam that filled the harbor.

Branek turned, and saw the folk of Lacaon standing, rooted still on the causeway, staring in an amazement no greater than he felt. By some miracle of crystal science they had all just escaped certain death.

Above them, all the apertures of White Mare Temple still glowed with actinic blue-white light. As he watched, the light faded and went out. A final shudder shook the earth, and then all was still.

Laodice! Branek suddenly thought. Was this her doing? Was she safe? Shouldering past the dazed people on the roadway, he ran up the cyclopean stone road, to the temple.

White Mare Temple stood by itself on a smooth shelf of stone carved from the side of the cliff in ages past by ley work, perched above the town, but below the palace on the heights. Smooth-walled, circular, and white in the Atlantean style, it proclaimed to all who came to Lacaon the island's allegiance to the empire of the Sea Kings.

An acrid scent greeted him as he approached the temple, the smell of high energy ley work, splitting and recombining the very molecules of the air. Up here, on the temple height, he could feel a trembling in the ground beneath his feet, as if the energies the temple had released were not yet fully contained.

The main doors of the sanctuary stood open wide, inviting ingress to the shadowed interior. Cautiously he looked in, putting a hand on the jamb.

Ah! The very stone of the lintel was hot to the touch. He jerked his hand away. What had transpired here? Frightened, but also maybe a little outraged, he strode inside.

Priests and acolytes bustled about the shadowed interior, carrying glowing crystals and smoking censers of incense. The air was one of urgency but not panic, as if important work was being done, but not work that was out of the ordinary. Many of them paused as his form filled the doorway, but then proceeded without comment on with their work.

An acolyte, one whom Branek recognized but could not name, approached him. "My prince," he said, "we are in the midst of a working, as surely you must know. Now is not the time for visitors –"

"Where is your lady?" Branek interrupted him. Something unprecedented had happened here. He had no time for priestly obfuscations.

"She is in the sanctuary," the priest replied. "But –"

Remembering his earlier experience with Herata, Branek stripped off the gold armband and the bronze beltknife he wore, and tossed them to the priest. "See that we are not disturbed."

Then he entered the ley chamber of the temple.

In the center of the circular chamber, the leystone still glowed with a brilliant white light, fading down to red, then shifting to green and pulsing back up to white in a regular rhythm, but one which Branek found strangely disquieting. It made him feel tired, as if it were beating in exact counterpoint to his own heartbeat, pulling his own body's rhythms along behind it, and draining him of energy.

Around the perimeter of the room, junior priests and acolytes circled, carrying smaller stones that glowed like the heartstone in a counterpoint rhythm, green when the heartstone was white. His impression was that they were drawing energy off the heartstone, bleeding it off and storing the *aum* the great stone expelled. The air vibrated with tension and free energy. The smell of ozone was sharper here than it had been outside; it made his eyes water.

At the center of the chamber, standing over the heartstone, arms spread, was Laodice, completely naked. The light from the stone threw her breasts and the planes of her face into sharp relief. She was chanting in some language Branek did not know, Old Atlantean maybe, a rapid chant that went up and down with the pulsing of the stone, faster and slower as the light brightened and dimmed. Was she controlling the stone, or was her chant trying to contain it? Branek had no idea.

Seeing all this, Branek came to a stop, staring. He recognized the sudden rank, coppery taste in his mouth as that of fear. The acolyte had been right. He had trespassed into things he did not understand. He dare not interrupt Laodice now. Who knew what might result if her concentration was broken?

But Laodice saw him; her eyes widened across the stone. She called out a single sharp word in that strange language, and everything in the room came to a stop. The light in the crystal faded and died. Everyone stared at him.

Their eyes bored into him like beams from crystals. The room was electric with a different sort of tension. Branek tried to speak, cleared a dry throat, and tried again.

"Laodice," he said, "what happened here?"

His sister's face split with a huge grin -- the very last thing he had expected. "Branek," she said, "we did it!"

"Did what?"

She came around the leystone toward him, still naked. He looked away. An acolyte brought her a robe; she shrugged into it, hardly noticing. To his amazement she came up to him and embraced him as excitedly as she had on her naming day when they were small children. "Stabilized the ley, of course! Stopped the wave."

Instinctively he put his arms around her, returning her embrace. She was vibrating herself like a struck crystal, with excitement and something more.

"The earthquake protocols," Branek remembered. Laodice's great work, what she had devoted her priestesshood toward. She had spoken of it countless times, but he had never imagined it would look like … that.

"More than that, so much more!" Laodice said. She stepped away from him, spread her arms wide, spun around like a giddy schoolgirl. She seemed manic, bursting with hectic enthusiasm for something he could barely comprehend. "Look around, Branek! Remember this moment – we are at the dawn of a new age!"

"I don't understand," he said. He took her shoulders in his hands, trying to calm her down, get her to focus. "Laodice, are we safe?"

"Yes, Branek, yes, safer than we've ever been! We will no longer be at the mercy of the tides and humors of the earth – we will be able to control then now, reconfigure the grid onto a stable matrix based around the tectonic gradients at the plate boundaries, and quartered on the ancient continental shield zones –"

"Stop, stop!" he said, glancing at the other priests in the room, wondering if they understood her babbling. They were all watching their high priestess, rapt, and evidently understanding her perfectly well.

He put his hands on her shoulders, trying to calm her. "Words of one syllable," he said. Her excitement concerned him; what had happened was far more than some common earthquake, it seemed.

Laodice took a breath, clearly trying to slow her racing thoughts down to the level of a neophyte, an *inaum* one at that. "The earthquake protocols work by shifting large amounts of *aum* away from the fault lines very quickly, to ease the stress," she said. "And then applying equally large amounts of *aum* in precise patterns to the fault once the moment has come, a fault has slipped, to stabilize it and minimize tremors and damage at the surface."

Branek nodded; that much at least he understood. The movement of the *aum*, away from the fault and then back, would, she had told him, have to be done faster than a blink of an eye, faster even than the most gifted adept could move. It required pre-programmed crystals at points across the ley network near a fault, and stored caches of free *aum*, ready to be tapped by the crystals and moved at a moment's notice. Automated, in other words.

"We have learned," Laodice continued, "that with the programmed crystals, we can move much larger amounts of *aum* than we expected. *Far* larger. And keep it moving as well. Continually. Wherever we want." She grinned again, that huge, almost manic grin, like she had uncovered the biggest surprise in the universe.

Branek just shook his head. He did not get what she was driving at.

"Branek!" she said, almost chiding him, as if he were exceptionally stupid. "We can move the leys now."

Move the leys. So it was true.

"Is – is that what this was?"

"An initial attempt." One of her priests brought her a crystal; she scanned it a moment, handed it back with a silent nod. "Unsuccessful so far, but promising."

"But – the tsunami." Branek felt like he was struggling to catch up. The tsunami, the panicked flight up to the palace, the *aum* display in the bay, Laodice's manic demeanor – it was all too much. Happening too fast.

"Yes, well, there will be side effects no doubt," Laodice said.

"Side effects! That was a *tidal wave!*" he blurted, pointing out at the bay. "This is your home! People could have been killed!"

"But they weren't, were they?" Laodice said. "I protected them. With my protocols. Just as intended."

Branek's mind was whirling. "That doesn't make it all right. Does our father know of this?"

Laodice frowned at him. "Of course."

"And he approves?"

"It is he who brought my work to the attention of the White Temple." Laodice put her hand on Branek's arm, tried to steer him out of the sanctuary.

"We still have much work to do, brother, so if you could allow us --?"

Branek shook her hand off, refused to move. He was working through the implications of what she had said.

"Your work is part of the White Temple's project to move the leys."

Laodice preened, tossing back her hair; it was as if she couldn't help herself. "The transjunction project is based in part on my protocols. Yes."

"Herata says that work will lead to the destruction of Atlantis."

Laodice looked annoyed. "She is mistaken. My protocols are solid."

"I don't think so," Branek said, "after what I just saw."

"My *aum* net protected the city, defused the wave, didn't it? Just as intended? We have planned for every contingency."

"Like Tiotiwakan?" Branek asked. "Did you plan for that?"

Laodice's frown deepened to a scowl, the look that had once had him quaking in his boots, when they were children and he had lived in dread of her anger. "That was an accident. An unforeseen occurrence."

"And what about the next *unforeseen occurrence?*" Branek shook his head. "Herata is right; you people have no idea what you are playing with."

"You people?" Laodice exclaimed. "I am your sister!"

"The sister I know would not endanger her entire island in the pursuit of power. What's happened to you, Laodice?"

Now she was angry; her blue eyes blazed with disdain. "What's happened to you, Branek? Has that girl you've been diddling addled your brain?" She poked him in the chest, driving him back a step. The other priests milled around them, anxious at their mistress's distress. "My work has brought Lacaon to the attention of the Great City, the Poseideoin itself! Our father is at the center of the councils of power in the empire now. Lacaon will be first among the colonies. Why, we could move a major nexus right here, to White Mare Temple!"

Branek gaped at her. "In the middle of the Inner Sea? Are you mad? Didn't you see what just happened?"

"My protocols will make us rich, Branek," Laodice said relentlessly.

"Not if there's no Lacaon to enjoy it! You could destroy us all!"

Laodice gasped; the look on her face changed abruptly from anger to hurt. "Branek! How can you say that? Don't you trust me? Don't you trust my skills?"

That brought him up short. He tried to collect his thoughts, closing his eyes, breathing hard.

Didn't he trust Laodice? Hadn't he always? His sister, almost a mother after their real mother died. And a powerful priestess, he had always known that.

"See?" Laodice said. "I would never do anything to hurt you, or anyone on Lacaon." She stepped closer to him, put her hand on his chest. "I've done all this for you, for father. For us all," she said softly.

"I need to speak to Herata," Branek said. He needed her clarity on this issue.

"I wouldn't do that," Laodice said, taking her hand away, her voice flat.

"If she knows your earthquake protocols are part of the ley-moving project, it will help her understand it better. If there's a flaw, maybe she can find it."

"There is no flaw," Laodice snapped.

"She needs to know," Branek insisted. He was out of his depth with this issue, and he knew it – but Herata would know what to do, how to speak to Laodice, make her see the danger.

"And if she does," Laodice asked, "what will she do?"

"She'll –" That brought him up short. Gods, what would Herata do?

"Go off half cocked, like she always does," Laodice said. "Try to sabotage the project without understanding it, without even talking to me. Won't she?"

"She —" Branek hesitated.

"Yes, she would. She is reckless, Branek."

"Yes," he admitted. "Herata is reckless."

"That could be worse than any accident, you must realize that."

Being *inaum*, he could hardly imagine what could go wrong. But he could imagine the destruction, the death. He had seen it.

"Don't tell Herata yet," Laodice repeated.

"I can't keep this secret," Branek said, shaking his head, falling back from Laodice, trying to find a way out of this impasse.

"You can," Laodice said, following him, backing him up against the sanctuary wall. "It's for her own good."

"What?" Branek said, surprised by that.

"If she learns the specifics of the transjunction project, she could do anything," Laodice said. "You know she could, Branek. Even attack the Poseideion."

"No, Herata would never –"

"Of course she would. You just admitted she was reckless." Laodice pressed him. "And she would fail, and they would drag her away in chains, imprison her for good. Maybe even ley-blind her."

Not that! Herata would rather die, he knew that. The leys were her very life.

"That would be worse than death, for her," Laodice said, echoing his thoughts. "For any of us.

"Branek, let me handle it," she continued. "Let me speak with Herata when the time is right. She will take it better from a fellow adept."

"I can't lie to her," Branek whispered.

"Of course not," Laodice said, her voice warm, soothing. "So don't lie. Just keep silent. For a little while."

"How long?" he asked miserably.

Laodice smiled. "Not long. The work has already begun. Long enough that she cannot interfere."

"You'll speak to her?" Branek pleaded. "You'll explain everything?"

"I promise," Laodice purred.

"I don't know." Branek shuddered at the thought of how Herata would react if she knew his people, his House, were involved in the Poseideion's unholy work. How could he possibly keep this from her?

"Just a little while, Branek," Laodice said again. She reached up to cup his cheek comfortingly. "Trust me on this, little brother. Everything is under control."

She reached out to him; he felt the feather-brush of her mind on his, her consciousness riffling through his thoughts, seeking his agreement.

"No!" he said, throwing up the mental image of a siege wall that she herself had taught him to guard his thoughts. "Not – that. I have had enough of that lately."

Laodice let her hand drop. "All right. But if I trust you on this, you must trust *me* to tell Herata, and in my own time."

"All right," Branek said, defeated.

"Swear to me, brother."

"I swear." She was his sister, his kin. He had to trust her.

"More, Branek," Laodice said, relentless.

He sagged against the wall, feeling trapped, desperate to get away, leave the sanctuary, escape into the clean sea air. "I swear on the name of our House that I will not tell Herata about your part in the White Temple's project."

Laodice smiled. She reached up and patted his cheek. "It really is the better way, little brother."

Branek hoped to the gods below that was true. He turned his back on his sister and fled the temple without looking back.

Chapter Eighteen

The disturbances were terrible. It was so much worse than she had ever imagined; she didn't know what to do. Earthquakes rocked the island home; tsunami raced around the world hundreds of miles distant, the sea pulled from its bed by the terrible suction of the moving leys, the very earthpower being yanked up and dragged out of the earth to an alien place.

Freakish phenomena abounded; violent weather, frightening visitations that were emanations of disturbed energy. Rivers flowed backwards. And Herata saw things, things in the leys that would never be made public, they were so terrible. A whole town consumed by ghostly fire. The entire staff of a distant temple killed in an instant; their flesh flipped inside out like old gloves, wrenched open by the dreadful suction of the ley in their temple being dragged out of true from halfway around the earth.

When the leys were in motion, being repositioned by their distant masters in the Great City, she could do nothing, even she; the torrent of outraged power was so terrible, so destructive. She could not even enter the ley chamber, the feeling was so agonizing; none of them could. They could only writhe on the floor, screaming, wracked by pain, waiting for the flesh to be ripped from their bones by the wrongness.

And it was not working. That much she knew; she could feel it, in the ache in her bones, the ringing in her ears, afterwards. The leys would not be moved. Again and again the earthpower was drawn off, and again and again it snapped back to the place where it had been before, the channel in which it was supposed to be, where it had run since the continents had assumed their current shape. When it snapped back, the destruction was terrible, as the damaged ley sought a new equilibrium.

She set wards on her own temple, her crystal, trying to keep the rogue priests in the Great City from gleaning any information they could from her resources. But she could not set any wards on the leys themselves; they were natural phenomena, controlled by no man. They were sacred, or had been, until now.

She could do nothing. Not at Nine Seas, not alone. Returning to the temple had been a mistake.

"I must go to the Great City," she said to Lamike as she packed her memory crystals in cases for travel – her evidence, for whoever might listen. "I am useless here; I can do nothing."

"They will arrest you," Lamike said reedily. "You will be disappeared as surely as if you had been consumed by a ghostfire." She sat in a chair, rocking uneasily. She looked ghastly, eyes vacant, skin papery. The carnage of Tiotiwakan had left its mark on her soul forevermore. But she had returned to Nine Seas, returned to assist her priestess in her quest.

Herata looked at her with concern. The older priestess was not long for this world, she could see it. Her spirit was broken. As she had many times in the past days, she wondered again what else she could have done, to prevent the deathwave.

"I may as well be disappeared already, for the all the good I do here," she said. "The criminals are in the Great City, I must confront them there."

"What will you do?" Lamike asked.

Herata paused in the packing of a crystal. "I don't know," she admitted. What really could she do against the might of empire? "I will consult the Hexachon."

"Another possession might destroy you," Meilikki said flatly, from the doorway. It was simply a statement of fact; Herata no longer took the healer's advice on any matters. Her health was no longer Meilikki's concern; it was, if anyone's, the Hexachon's, Herata supposed.

"No," she said. "They cannot hurt me anymore; in fact I would welcome it. Then perhaps I could accomplish something."

"What will you do?" Lamike whispered.

Herata held up a crystal, looked into its depths. This one kept the record of the murdered priests of Green Jade temple, in the Land of the Han, flayed alive by the force of the experiment. In its reflections she saw things she dared not say to anyone. Not yet.

"What I have to," she said. "You must keep the temple dark while I am gone. Whatever happens, Lamike, you must keep it off-ley."

Things were very bad in the Great City. The Council – what was left of it – remained locked in endless, futile debate about the problem of *aum*, while the transfer project went on from the heart of the Poseideion, unchallenged.

The mood of the City was ugly, as angry and hateful as people had ever seen it. Small quakes continued to shake the city on a weekly basis. Crime rose: violence against women, against outlanders, against property.

People were afraid. They lashed out, flailing against a threat they could not combat and could barely understand.

Herata had to travel about the city hidden in a plain, unadorned gondola. If anyone spotted her, there was a good chance she would be dragged out and drowned right in the canal.

It did not even frighten her. The things she contemplated in her own mind were a thousand times worse.

She visited every surviving member of the Council that would see her. Most were afraid not to. She showed them the memory crystals from Green Jade, from Tiotiwakan. They did not want to know, but with her will she made them look. When she walked into a room, the crystals in place wailed and sparked under her influence. The Hall of the Salmon had to convert to ordinary electric power. If she wished, the crystals around her displayed any image she chose to show, or else sputtered and died, sacrificing themselves at her silent order. This display terrified everyone who saw it. She had almost ceased to notice.

She no longer felt entirely human. She felt like something elemental and implacable: a tide, a desert wind blowing. A force of nature that could not be denied. She felt like a walking ley-stone: glassy, impenetrable, swollen with power.

She visited the Hexachon. The priests of the Patriarch could not keep her out of the temple; the wards fell, the gates opened before her with little effort on her part. She walked into the vortex at the center of the six mighty stones, unhurt, her hair and clothes burning with an unconsuming fire. The Hexachon said nothing to her, they did not speak. Yet she registered their silent acceptance. Her thoughts met with their approval.

Like a crystal, she existed now only to serve the flows, to keep the lifeforce running through the great body of mother earth. She and the crystals understood each other.

Only one thing could keep her attached to this life now. Well, two things, but only one was certain. And he was not here.

Her enemies were crafty. So they sent for him.

She was absorbed in communion with her record crystals when Hecuba announced a visitor.

"If it is not the High King's legate, I will not see him," Herata said. She had requested – no, demanded! -- an audience, and she would hear no words from lesser kings in the meantime. Such was the fear she invoked now that Kings of Atlantis answered to her call.

"My lady," Hecuba said. "It is Prince Branek of Lacaon."

Branek? A trill of surprised laughter bubbled up from her lips; it was a strange sensation. So mundane. "But he is in the islands!" she said.

"He bid me say that he has come to the Great City to see you, my lady," Hecuba said.

Herata sprang up like a maiden on her bridal day and flung open the doors to her study. There he stood, golden and gleaming and alive.

"Branek!" she cried, happy as a child with a surprise birthday gift.

"Herata," he answered, bringing her hands to his lips, so warm and tender.

Hecuba left them, and Herata was too unexpectedly happy to see the troubled shadow in her eyes.

Herata led him in, rang for wine. "But I thought you were in Lacaon," she said. She caressed his strong, square hand as she spoke; it felt so wonderfully warm, so real. Actually quite remarkable.

"I had to come and see you, my lady. Lacaon seems like a prison without you by my side."

"How sweet," Herata said. "You are a very poet, my love – did I ever tell you that?"

"And you, Herata?" he asked. "Are you well?"

"I am very well," she said idly. It was rather hard to explain how she was now. People tended to look at her as if she were mad. Well, if she were, sanity was a sadly limited thing.

"What?" Branek asked. "What did you say?"

"Oh, did I say that out loud?" Herata asked, bemused. "About sanity?"

"You did," Branek said, frowning.

"It's hard to tell sometimes. My crystals reflect things back at me, my thoughts. I do get confused."

"*Your* crystals?"

She shook her head; it was so hard to explain. "Or you might say I am the crystals'. It is much the same. But do tell me why you came."

He tipped her chin up to look at him. His blue eyes were clouded with worry. "I came because I missed you and I had to see you. Herata, are you feeling all right?"

"Why, I'm fine," she said.

His hand went to her cheek, pulled away, then touched her forehead, her bare arm. "You are fevered! You're burning up!"

"No, no, I am fine," she said. "It is just the *aum*." She touched his cheek in turn. The feel of his skin under her fingers fixed her attention like nothing had outside of a crystal in quite some time – smooth skin, rough stubble, such a fascinating contrast. She ran her hand down his jaw, across his shoulder. "How I have missed you, my love," she murmured, and it was true.

Branek removed her hand from his arm, held it prisoned in his own as if her touch disturbed him. "No, Herata, you are not fine. We must summon the physician. You are not well!"

She shook her head. "Don't bother. No physician can treat me any-more. Meilikki is afraid to look me in the face."

Branek frowned, and Herata was so attuned to him in that moment that she heard his thoughts as clearly as if he had spoken them aloud. *So it is true. Just as they said.*

"What is true?" she said indignantly. "Just as who said?"

Branek started and looked at her in genuine alarm. His gaze swept the office, cluttered with ley-stones of all sizes perched on tabletops and stacks of parchments. With a rough grasp he took her by the arm and hustled her out the terrace doors, into the garden and the fresh air and light.

"Stop it!" she cried, but he would not. He swung her around to face him. Then he gasped. "Gods below, Herata!" he cried. "Your eyes!"

She put a hand to her cheek. "It is the *aum*," she said. "It bleaches things out after long use." She had noticed in the mirror that her eyes were growing paler and paler green; they were almost gray now.

"You are not a thing, Herata!" he shouted. "What is happening to you?"

"I am being made ready," she said.

"Ready? For *what*??"

Ah, better not to say. She shook her head, trying to clear it. His anger was bringing her farther out of the crystal ecstasy than she had been in many days. She sorted through the sense of what he said.

"Who sent you, Branek? Have you come to spy on me?"

"Spy?" he yelled. "They tell me you are sick, dying, I come to your side, and you accuse me of spying?"

Now she was truly angry. "Who told you?" she demanded. "On whose bidding are you here?"

"Everyone's!" he shouted. "Meilikki. Your father begged me to come here, to speak to you. And look at you!" He ran a hand through her hair. "It's worse than he could even say. Your hair – it's turning white!"

"It is fine." She pushed his hand away. "It is just the *aum*."

"The *aum*? You are not a crystal, Herata!"

Now, that was a thought. "Perhaps I am."

"No!" He grabbed her by the shoulders, shook her. "Stop it!"

"Why are you here, Branek?" she asked again.

"I am here," he said between gritted teeth, "because my intended wife is destroying herself with sorcery, and I refuse to let it happen. Stop this, Herata! Stop it now."

"I cannot stop it," Herata said. "I am not doing it."

"I won't let this happen, do you hear me?" He dragged her close to him, his blue eyes seared into hers. "I won't lose you!"

"Branek," she said, wonderingly. "Poor thing – you are afraid."

"Yes!" he cried. "Yes, woman, I am afraid!" He crushed her to him in a desperate embrace. "I won't let them take you, the damn crystals! I'll tie you up in a sack and take you to the Land of Burning Ice if I have to. I won't lose you now. I love you!"

His lips found hers in a desperate, searing kiss. She swooned, swept up by sudden ecstasy, as if in the grip of a mighty leyline. Her arms slid around his neck; her nipples hardened, rubbing against his chest. Yes, yes, let it be: life rose in her, undeniable. She was a servant of life now, in all its guises. The crystals poked at her mind, displeased by her distraction, but she pushed them away, giving herself up to pure sensation.

"Yes, my prince," she sighed, delighting in the sweaty, bruising feel of him against her. "My darling. Love me! Love me, Branek …"

"I will!" he growled, his mouth against her neck, her hair. "I'll love you back to life, I swear it!"

He swept her up into his arms. Crossing the garden he kicked open the doors to her bedchamber. Herata shivered with pleasure at his strength, his anger and need.

Once inside, she gave herself utterly to his caresses. The crystals, the danger, her terrible purpose, were all for a time forgotten.

Afterwards, they lay still in the afternoon shadows, breathing, hardly moving. They did not speak for a long time, resting there intertwined.

At last Branek spoke. "Herata," he said.

"Mm?" She knew what was coming, did not care to speak of it, but it could hardly go unremarked.

"Herata, when we – when you – I think I saw … "

"Yes. I saw it too. The light. It is as I told you. It is the *aum*."

"Your skin … I could almost see through it."

"*Aum* is the stuff of life. Everyone has some; we would be dead without it. I have more now."

He looked at her, anguish in his eyes. "Are you dying?"

He had made love to her like a man possessed, almost hurting her, as if he must consume her before she disappeared like smoke.

"No," she said, trying to console him. "Not dying, no. I am changing."

"Into what?"

Even she was not entirely sure. "I am being made ready. For the burning, when it comes."

He pulled her close to him, cradling her as he had done that night on the beach, so many days ago. "I should never have gone back to Lacaon. Never have left you here alone."

"I am never alone now. Not anymore."

"All the more reason I should have been here."

She leaned up on one elbow. "Why did you come back, Branek?"

He looked at her a long moment, his eyes troubled, brushing back the tousled hair from her face, frowning over the white hairs now mingled with the black.

"Ah, Herata. I find I cannot lie to you, although I should. I feel you would know anyway, no matter what I said."

She nodded; she saw with more than mortal eyes now. More than that, she knew him, Branek, as a woman knows the man who covers her in the night.

"The Five Kings called me back to the Great City. They want me to … distract you. Silence you. They want me to take you away."

"So you are going to tie me up in a sack, are you?"

"I told them you would be unmoved," he said sadly.

She touched his lips with a fingertip, as she had wanted to do the first day he came courting her. She trailed her finger down his chin, across his chest, farther down. He sighed, such a sad sound, the sigh of a man doomed by love.

Her heart swelled with a tender and fragile love. Him, of all of them, she wished, prayed, could remain untouched in the coming madness. Her golden boy. How she wished he had stayed in Lacaon! Even as her body longed to hold him, to possess him again and again, still she wished it.

"My prince," she said. "I am not unmoved. But even in that my way lies clear. I have my duty as you have yours."

"I would that my only duty was to you and to my city!" Branek said fervently. "To me they are almost one and the same. I can no longer imagine being King in Lacaon without you by my side. This separation has been torture to me! How I pray that I get you with child, here, this very day. Then you would have to leave the leys. And I could take you to Lacaon, where you would be safe. Where we could all be safe!"

This admission filled her with an ineffable sadness. "Get me with child, this afternoon? Is that why you came here?"

"No!" he said angrily. "I swear to you, I came because I heard the reports of your behavior and I was afraid for you. And rightly so!"

She lay back down beside him. What should she tell him? "You cannot get me with child now, Branek," she said. "It is no longer possible."

Devastation filled his face. "Because of the crystals!"

Let him think that. "Not today, not any day."

He raised himself above her, looking searchingly into her eyes. "Come away with me, Herata," he said. "Come to Lacaon, or anywhere you want. Leave all this behind; let me protect you, I beg of you. This course you are on will destroy you!"

She slid her hand up the back of his neck and pulled him down for a kiss. No one could protect anyone, not anymore. All they had was this moment.

A crystal by the side of the bed chimed, signaling a message from without.

"Yes?" Herata inquired of it, her eyes not leaving Branek's face.

"My lady," Hecuba's voice said, "you are summoned for an audience by the High King."

She sat up, pushing Branek gently away. "I must go."

He just shook his head, miserable. "He will not hear you."

"One way or another, he will."

Chapter Nineteen

In the days that followed, Herata continued to entertain Branek's affections on a daily basis. Even as her heart and her body sang with the pleasure that he brought her, and she felt herself falling ever deeper in love with his passion and goodness, she was plagued by guilt. For she was using him shamelessly, as heartlessly as the Five Kings would use him, giving the appearance of being besotted with his love, so that her enemies might think her weak and distracted. Yet all the while she watched them through crystal eyes, and continued to plan.

"You should go back to Lacaon," she told him, time and again, even as they lay, limbs entwined, in her bed or his. The Great City was not safe. Earthquakes continued to rock the city on occasion, the aftereffects of the botched display in the Council Chamber. Even though his being here served her purpose, she wished indeed that he were safe.

"Not without you," he would say, and that would be that.

Until one night shortly after the ides of hunter's moon.

They had stayed up late talking, until they finally drifted to bed well after midnight. They made slow love, warmed by the wine they had consumed, and Herata fell into a black, besotted sleep.

She dreamed, of herself and Branek in Lacaon, as he had described it to her, the white sand, the thyme and heather purple on the hillsides. They ruled together as king and queen, as he had promised, and all was well.

In the dream, she went to White Mare temple, and suddenly all was not well. The crystal there gleamed redly, swollen with unhealthy power; it cast shadows like blood on the walls of the sanctum. A tall woman stood over it, blond and commanding. Herata knew her: Laodice, sister to Branek and mistress of the temple.

In the dream, Laodice raised her arms, commanding power out of the crystal, and it responded with power unheard of, virulent red and green, coming not from the leyline but much farther down, straight up from the molten heart of the earth. It was too much; the temple began to shake.

She was in the streets of Lacaon the City; the streets were shaking, the earth was aroused. The tormented fires in the heart of the Inner Sea were rising, wakening from their angry slumber, as she had always feared. Buildings crumbled around her; people and animals ran mad in the streets, terrified.

She was over the city, looking down. On the edge of town she could see a pale and flickering light, growing, spreading, moving from the temple district outward, pallid yet terrible, consuming all it touched. Ghostfire! Perverted *aum* set free from the leys to rage unchecked.

Something was coming toward her, flitting unevenly down the street, something pale and terrible and screaming, something human, yet almost gone, consumed by the pale fire: a woman, running, screaming, on fire. Laodice.

Behind her, a sudden blinding blast of light, an explosion, the temple of the White Mare, consumed by its own energy. And the ghost fire raced outwards in all directions, leaping across the shaking, quaking earth.

Herata awoke screaming.

Beside her Branek was instantly awake. "What is it, love? Hush, it's alright." His strong arms cradled her in the darkness. She clung to him, horrified.

"What is it, then?" he crooned. "A bad dream?"

And even as he said it the crystal by his bedside chimed and would not stop chiming. An emergency summons.

"Go," she said to him, terrified, "Oh, go!"

Fear leapt into his eyes at her tone. Throwing aside the bedclothes, he snatched up a robe and was gone.

Herata curled for a moment in the bed, sickened by what she had seen: the city crumbling, the people in flames. She had no doubt of why Branek was being called.

She got up and dressed, dreading to hear what she already knew. Branek would need her now, as he never had before.

As she made her way downstairs, she heard it, an anguished shout; Branek, calling out in unimaginable grief.

She ran to the audience chamber. Before she reached it he burst out, almost staggering. He saw her and stopped, eyes wild with grief.

She held out her arms to him, her golden boy, and with an anguished moan he came to her, falling to his knees, burying his head in her breast. His sobs rent the silence of the night. She bent over him, her arms circling his shoulders, wishing above all things that she could have kept this nightmare away from him. The people of his house hovered around, terrified, confused.

"Oh, gods!" he sobbed brokenly, in her arms, "It's gone, Herata, it's all gone. Laodice – my father! My city! The King is dead!"

"Long live the King," Herata said to the man in her arms, and the people of his house repeated it: "Long live the King."

He looked at them wildly as if they were talking craziness, looked up at her.

"You knew, didn't you?" he said. "You saw it. Didn't you, Herata?" His hands gripped her arms, squeezing painfully, but she did not complain. "You saw it. Oh, gods, why didn't you stop it?"

She would never let him know how those words pierced her to the quick. He was beside himself. He did not know what he was saying.

She wiped the tears from his cheeks with the palms of her hands. "My darling, I would have given everything I am if I could have kept this grief from you. I swear it by Poseidon himself." She would have surrendered her crystal vision, she would have blinded herself to the leys themselves, if it could have stopped such a tragedy from occurring. But it was not to be. This was only another of the many small burnings leading to the final conflagration.

His arms wrapped around her waist like a drowning man's clinging to life. He hid his face from the truth in her eyes. She bent her head to whisper in his ear.

"Not now, my love. You must wait for that. Your grief must come later. Your people need you, Majesty." He looked up at her, amazed, uncomprehending.

"You are their King, now," she said softly.

As he felt the truth of it, the light seemed to go out of his eyes. His own agony dulled to a weary sorrow as the mantle of power smothered it. There was no time for personal indulgences now. In such times, the king of all became the servant of all. There was work, terrible work to be done.

Unaided he rose. Though he held Herata close to his side and she could feel him trembling, he spoke strongly to the steward of the house: "Bring all the people together in the audience chamber; they must be told. And send word round to all our countrymen in the City, that they are summoned here. This news should not be heard in isolation, but together."

The steward bowed deeply and went to do as he was told. Herata conducted Branek back to his chambers, where she would help him bathe and dress more properly to address his people, not as prince but as King.

In the terrible days that followed the destruction of Lacaon, Herata was always at Branek's side, aiding him, supporting him as he had supported her for so long. When she spoke in Council about the needs of his ruined island, the awe and fear in which she was held gave her words extra weight. If the kings and representatives of neighboring regions would not cooperate, sending relief or money, she chastised them, and made their houses and halls go dark, as their crystal systems obeyed her wishes. When the city of Tharsis would not ramp down power in one of its leys which it shared with Lacaon, Herata went to their hall in Poseidonis and made them all see the burning, the city and the people consumed, in every crystal in the hall, until they agreed to stop. In fact one of their representatives had been injured in a duel in his youth and had an artificial eye with a tiny crystal in it to act as the lens. Even when he closed his eyes he could still see the burning, and Herata showed him no pity, though he wept and begged, until he swore to shut down the offending ley in Tharsis.

By day Herata felt again like a crystal, obdurate and humming with power. But at night, when she and Branek retired and were alone, she felt her humanity return, as she ached with sorrow at her prince's profound loss. As he had long sat with her in her illnesses, she sat with him as he lay on his bed, prostrate with grief. Like a mother she held him as he sobbed, night after night, consumed by guilt and sorrow.

"I should have been there," he said over and over again. "I could have done something."

She was sure that was not the case, but she would not torment him with second-guesses. What was done was done. She only held and rocked him, offering what comfort she could.

It was on her behalf that he had left Lacaon. Sometimes she was afraid it would poison his heart against her, and she held him closer, her own tears dampening his golden hair. She knew now that she needed Branek, needed him wildly; his love was the only thing that kept her from being consumed by her purpose, from her heart turning as glassy and pale as a ley-stone. In his eyes she saw the agony of all those who would be destroyed if her vision reached fulfillment.

Was she glad he had escaped the destruction in Lacaon? Of course, although she felt he was hardly safer here in Poseidonis. Could he have done something to save his family and people in Lacaon? She doubted it. If he had been killed, nothing would have remained to keep her from embracing the burning.

She kept these dark thoughts to herself. He had enough sorrow to bear.

Soon enough the day came when he had done all he could in the Great City, made all the plans, secured all the help he could. It was time to go back to Lacaon – what was left of it. Time to bury the dead and try to pick up the pieces. The city was in ruins, but the island yet remained. His people needed a leader.

He would be crowned King at the swelling of the full moon.

And so came the conversation Herata had been dreading.

They were in his chambers in his townhouse, now his royal palace in exile. She was packing his things for travel herself, a small act of love, one small thing she could do for him, as she could not do the larger.

"You are packing nothing of yours," he said dully, sitting in a chair and watching her.

She looked at him sadly as she folded one of his robes. The last thing she wanted was to hurt him now.

"Come with me," he said. "I am begging you, Herata. You must come with me to Lacaon."

She cringed inside. She wanted to, oh, how she wanted to. But she would not.

"I need you," Branek said. "I cannot face this alone."

She knew it was true. She felt a monster. She said nothing.

A loud, rumbling crackle rolled through the morning air, in through the open window. They both turned to it, listening. It rolled across the cityscape, growing in intensity, then died off to a low, grumbling mutter like distant thunder.

"You see," Herata said. "I must stay."

It was the fire mountain north of the city, Mount Atlas, which bordered the Plains of Gold. The disturbances of the earth brought about by the ley-moving accident had awakened it again from its uneasy slumber. All the City prayed its wakefulness would be brief, that it would not rain down fire and destruction as it had in the days of old. Adepts of the temples worked night and day to monitor it, hoping to give the city warning if its wrath overspilt, and to turn it aside if possible.

Herata had offered to take her turn at the crystals, like any adept. Her offer had been refused.

"The fires of Lacaon are awakened as well," Branek said.

She only looked at him uncertainly, sad, confused. Her human heart cried out to go with him, to aid him in his time of terrible need. But her crystal heart told her without doubt that she would be needed most here in the Great City, soon. Very soon -- within days.

"I will be made King," Branek said. "I must have my Queen."

"Don't," Herata said, her heart breaking. "Oh, please, don't."

Branek came to her and took the pleated kilt she had been ineffectually folding, throwing it on the bed. He took her hands in his.

"I am asking you now not only on a personal level," he said. "I am asking as a colonial ruler asking an adept of Atlantis. My aunt and sister are dead. The temple is destroyed. Lacaon has no adepts. I need you to help me rebuild. I need you to come and work the leys in Lacaon."

She blinked up at him, amazed. "You cannot be serious."

"But of course I am. Who else can work the leys for me but you?"

"You cannot mean to re-open the temple!" she cried.

"But I must. We must rebuild."

"But the leys there are unstable. It would be folly."

Branek paced away from her, she could see the line of tension tight in his shoulders.

"I know now that Laodice was reckless," he said. "She went too far with her researches. I curse her name for what she did.

"But that does not change the fact that power is needed now. My people need healing, they need food and light. They need to rebuild their homes. All of that takes power, *aum*. It must be had. And so I need an adept to work the leys. A responsible one, who will not abuse her power. You, Herata. Who can I trust but you?"

Herata shook her head. It was madness. "If you need power, buy it in crystal from other cities. Buy it from the Islands of the Dawn – they have it to spare, and their storage crystals are excellent!"

He shook his head in turn, still pacing. "No, no, I cannot. My city is devastated. It would bankrupt us to buy power. We must use what we have. We must re-open the temple."

"You cannot reactivate the leys under Lacaon. It would be suicide. Why do you think I tortured that poor man from Tharsis? To stop him from drawing too much power from under Lacaon itself! The earthpower in that region has been too much disturbed. It will take centuries to recover."

"I do not have centuries!" Branek said. "If we do not use *aum* to rebuild, then we cannot, and it will all come to ruins. Lacaon will cease to exist. And I cannot – I *cannot* let that happen. Don't you see?"

"I see that after all the time we have spent together, that still you have heard nothing of what I have said," Herata said. "You are no different from Herodian or any of the Council. You have learned nothing from my suffering – or indeed your own!"

"That is not true!" Branek said. "But things are different now. I am king. I must consider more than my own will. More than my own well-being."

"If you value your people's well-being, you will grow no crystals in Lacaon and leave the leys to lie fallow."

"No. My people are part of the empire now, they will not live like goatherds again, squatting in huts by the light of reed lamps! Nor would I ask it of them!"

Herata stared at him with anger and amazement. The crystal lamps in the ceiling flared up redly and commenced a resonant humming. Branek flinched; the way the crystals, all crystals, were tuned to Herata now scared even him.

"Don't you see?" he said in a gentler tone. "That is why I need you. Only you can I trust to use the power wisely, for the benefit of all."

Herata shook her head. "No, Branek. If you do this, you must do it alone. I will have no part of it."

"Then you leave me no choice. I must contract with the Poseideion for a replacement adept."

He would consort with her enemies rather than heed her advice.

"As you will," she said faintly. She looked at the rest of his things, spread out on the bed and chairs. The slaves could finish packing.

"We take ship at noon," Branek said. "From the outer circle."

"I cannot come," she lied. "I have a meeting."

He stooped to kiss her as she drifted toward the door. She let him, but her mouth lay still under his, not responding.

"I will come back for you," he said. "Soon."

"As you wish," she said.

"Don't be angry with me, Herata," he said. "I do only what I must."

"As do I," Herata said, and so she left him and his house, and returned to the crystals and her work.

Chapter Twenty

On the day of his coronation, Branek arose before dawn. He had slept but little that night, and there was no use lying abed alone. This day, a day he had prepared for his entire life, which should be a day of celebration, brought him nothing but grief and sorrow.

He summoned no servants, and dressed himself in homespun tunic and cloak. It was early spring on the Inner Sea, still almost winter, and the air was chilly and damp.

There was no mirror. His chamber was simple and unadorned – temporary quarters in the eastern, unburned wing of the palace, all that stood since the disaster. Since Laodice's folly.

Laodice! Thought of her brought a wave of rage and sorrow. He snapped a sandal tie while winding it. Cursing, he rethreaded it carefully, concentrating, trying to keep his thoughts off his dead sister, whom he had trusted implicitly. Who had done this.

Herata had been right all along.

Best not to think her name either. He all but fled the palace, trying to outrun the specters of his womenfolk.

He went to the stables, which were still standing, having escaped the conflagration. A small mercy of the White Mare. She had given few enough of them the night Lacaon burned.

That he had been half a world away that night, had survived to look upon the ruination of his home – he could not say if that was a mercy or a curse.

The cold sea wind blew across the heights of the island, bringing the stench of burned wood and plaster from the town below. It would be the work of many months just to clear the ruins of the town, before they could even begin to rebuild.

It was important that today's ritual be a success. The people needed a glimmer of hope, some sense of renewal. He must play the part of the righteous king, and let no one know that his heart was not in it, that the very thought of it sickened him.

He had thought he knew grief when his mother died in his boyhood. But he had still had his father, his sister, his people. He had known nothing.

He did not wake the grooms, and saddled his favorite horse, Triton, himself. The gelding huffed and stamped in the dark stall, sensing Branek's uneasiness. Branek slapped him on the neck with false heartiness. "It's alright, boy. A good run is what we need."

Once out of the stables, they took the back trail down to the beach, Triton picking carefully though the rocks and artemisia. Earliest dawn was a faint blue line on the eastern horizon. In the west, the light of the full moon, half set, silvered the waves. On the beach, Branek gave the horse his head and they pounded north on the hard wet sand of the tideline, away from the ruined town and its ghosts.

He needed some time, a few moments to himself, before he gave himself over to the preparations and rituals of the coronation. Once it began there would be no room for Branek the man, broken and grieving, in the figure of Branek the King, rightful ruler of Lacaon, who could make things right with his word alone. He would only a symbol, a prop in the ancient drama of kingship. He dreaded it, dreaded the thing his entire life had been pointing towards.

Triton ran, and Branek concentrated on keeping his seat, on the feel of the horse's muscles bunching under him, the briny wind in his face, the thud of hoofbeats on the sand. The shoreline curved and the half-burned palace fell away behind them. Sea birds wheeled above them, calling, disturbed by their passage. From this point, you could never tell anything had happened to poor burned Lacaon.

Branek let the horse run himself out, and they stopped at last on a small rocky promontory that jutted north, into the Inner Sea.

The wind sang, the waves crashed ceaselessly onto the rocks below. The dawn grew brighter, the thin bright rind of the sun peeking over the rim of the earth. The day of his coronation had truly begun.

Here, as he had known they would, his thoughts caught up with him and he was overwhelmed with grief and anger.

It was never supposed to be like this, a hurried crowning in a wrecked town. He had always known that one day his father would die and he, Branek, would succeed him. That was as it should be, as it had always been. But Hekau his father should have had a pyre of myrrh and sandalwood, attended by the kings of the neighboring islands, not the burning timbers of his own palace falling around him. And Laodice, his sister, should have stood beside him to light it, not been utterly consumed by ghostfires, no body left even to mourn.

And Herata. He had dreamed of her as well, standing beside him as his queen as he took the crown of Lacaon. He had always assumed it would be many years off, and he had not thought it too vain a hope.

Now Hekau and Laodice were gone in one night of burning, and Herata had turned her back on him.

Gods below, how he needed her! His father and sister were gone beyond recall; Herata was still here, but she had spurned him. His arms ached to hold her when he fell exhausted into his bed at night. Her face and voice haunted his dreams. Was she really calling to him across the leagues, or was it only his tortured imaginings? No, by day there was no message for him, by crystal or courier.

If it were only him, if he were a free man with only himself to care for, he would go crawling to Herata and beg her to take him back. In a heartbeat he would do it. *I should never have doubted you*, he would say. *Forgive me.* But he was not free. He was tied to this island by ancient bonds of blood and sovereignty, and his people needed him.

Branek stretched out across Triton's neck and buried his face in the gelding's mane. Tears burned behind his closed eyelids. He had wept countless times since Lacaon's destruction. But no, he was a man and a King, and this day he would not weep.

Triton shifted restlessly under him as his fingers dug into the horse's neck. Branek sat up, his face flushed but his eyes still dry.

He did not deserve Herata's forgiveness. She had warned him, after all. And he had not listened.

There came a rustling in the brush behind him. "My lord?" a voice said. He turned. It was Rakan, his body slave.

"How did you know where to find me?" Branek asked.

The Atlantean slave smiled. "Where have you always come when you were troubled, since you were a little boy?" He gestured at the promontory upon which they stood.

That was true. His earliest memory was of this place, feeding the gulls with his mother and Rakan, waiting for his father's galley to return from a trading mission.

But no one could have walked behind him from the palace so quickly. "Have you been waiting for me?" Branek asked.

Rakan nodded. Branek sighed. "Either I am too predictable, or you know me too well for a slave, Rakan."

"Never the former, I assure you," the slave said. "And for the latter, have I not tended you since you were that very boy?" Rakan came up beside Triton, put his thin, veined hand on the horse's neck. "My king, is there aught I can do for you?"

"Is there any message from Atlantis?" Branek asked. It was out of his mouth before he even realized what he was saying.

Rakan shook his head, his expression carefully neutral. "From Nine Seas, nothing. From the great houses, only the usual congratulations."

Stop being a wistful fool, Branek thought, irritated with himself. She said she would not come, and she is not.

It was no more than his lot. In the crux, he had listened to the wrong woman, his sister, not his lover. Now the sister was dead, the lover was gone, and he was left with an empty bed, an empty house, and a ruined home he could never fully rebuild.

"My king, it is time," Rakan said gently.

The kingship. The one thing he had left – the last thing he wanted.

"Yes," he said. He gave Rakan his arm, pulled him up to sit behind him on Triton, and turned the horse back to town.

This time they went up the front way, through the gates, and the women of the palace came out to meet him and took him away, to bathe and dress him for the coronation.

He gave himself up to it, passive under their ministering hands. If he followed the script, submitted to the ancient ritual, maybe he wouldn't have to think any longer.

The full moon came and went. It grieved Herata to be absent from Branek's coronation; it seemed so heartless of her. But she could not condone what he would do with the power in Lacaon.

The Poseideion was suspiciously quiet. No word came from them about their schemes. The aftershock and the rumbling of the fire mountain seemed to have stopped for the while. A chilly autumnal stillness hung over the Great City.

Herata hoped for some rest, some reprieve. She found none. She did not sleep well; the burning filled her dreams and the emptiness of her bed without Branek beside her broke her heart. The stillness she felt was as that before a storm.

A few nights later she woke with a start. A fleeting dream image hovered in her mind; she tried to snatch it but it evaporated like smoke, leaving only half-glimpsed impressions; figures moving a chamber, a crystal gleaming darkly, an echo like a scream.

Something terrible had happened. She was sure of it.

A light appeared at her door, a soft voice calling. "My lady?" It was Hecuba.

"Come in," Herata said.

"My lady, there is a visitor from the Palace. He insists he must speak to you."

"Who is it?" Herata asked, her heart quickening.

"The priest Innu, my lady."

The old priest who had spoken with her before the disaster in the Council Chamber. Herata took a deep breath, her heart suddenly racing.

Somehow she knew. This was it. It was beginning.

"Send him to my study," Herata said.

Quickly she dressed and went downstairs.

The old man was waiting for her, pacing anxiously around the lamp-lit library. There could be no crystals in here now; she was too agitated, she would only have set them off.

Innu bowed as she came in. "My lady."

"Tell me!" Herata said.

He looked startled. "Methinks you already know, my lady," he said, taken aback.

"It's begun," Herata agreed. "But when, where?"

"My lady is truly blessed with the sight," Innu said.

"Blessed or cursed. I can no longer judge. Speak!"

"We at the Palace have received word from the Poseideion. The Patriarch and his adepts believe they have at last perfected a technique for shifting the ley-lines. They plan to enact it at the first opportunity. Here, in the Great City, at a secret location."

"Where?"

Innu produced a paper from within the folds of his robe, a map with notes scrawled on it. "Here." He pointed. "The Hall of Mariners." In the outermost ring of the city.

Sailors should know better than to tempt the fate of the gods. "Damn them!" Herata said. The paper rattled; her hands were shaking.

"Is it so bad, my lady?" Innu asked.

"It cannot work. It will be worse than last time. They will destroy us all."

She crumpled the map in her hands. "I thank you," she told the old priest. "And so I tell you this: leave the Great City. Leave Atlantis – now."

The old priest looked frightened. "But my lady, you will save us, will you not?"

"I will do what I can. But who will perish and who may be saved, I cannot say. If you value your life, take ship and leave the island home tonight."

With a troubled mien, Innu bowed and withdrew.

Herata spread the parchment on the table, scanning it. It was a terse document, the Poseideion informing the palace as a bare courtesy of what it was about. It was marked as secret; for Innu to bring it forth from the palace amounted to treason, by the letter of the law. How he had acquired it, she did not know, and it did not matter.

When? When would they do this madness? She read the paper, looking for dates, times. It did not say.

At the bottom it was affixed with the seals of several houses and guilds, party to the project. Herata studied them, looking for clues.

One of them leapt out at her. A stylized horse, running, stamped in reverse, white horse on a black ground.

A whimper escaped her. No, it could not be true. No.

She knew that sign. Branek bore it, tattooed on his shoulder. The White Mare.

It was the seal of the House of Lacaon.

Afterwards, she had only the vaguest memory of her journey, which only made sense, for if she had been in her right mind she could never have made it.

She remembered running to the ley chamber of the Hall of the Salmon. She must have done some work with the crystals there, as they had all been taken offline when her abilities manifested themselves, but she had no memory of it. The ley-stone flared with light.

Then she was in the ley chamber of Nine Seas, her own temple; how she came there, she never knew nor cared. A novice was there; she gave a shrill, astonished scream at her mistress's appearance, then the crystal surged again. Herata remembered a rushing sensation, like she had felt once before.

And then she was outside, in a cold wind off the sea. It was near dawn; she could feel it in the air. Before her stood a shiny new ley-crystal; it trembled with power, humming weirdly at her presence. Around her stood a circle of crude stone menhirs, the minimum required to contain the power.

Another lacuna, and then she was in a richly decorated chamber painted in the style of the Inner Sea, with dolphins and gaily colored boats. Blue faience tiles covered the floor, a single smallish crystal rested in an ebony stand.

From his description, she recognized it as the ley-chamber of Branek's palace in Lacaon.

The letter from the Poseideion was still clutched in her hand.

She strode out into the corridors of the palace.

Servants, the only ones up at this hour, gasped in astonishment at her appearance. She came upon Euboleus, Branek's steward, giving the staff their daily assignments.

"My lady Herata!" he exclaimed in astonishment at her appearance. "You are well come! But how do you come here?"

She only stared at him. "Get him."

"Let me show you to the morning room –"

"*Get him!*" she screamed, voice cracking.

He went, running, and she followed him.

As she reached the outer rooms of the royal chambers, Branek came hurrying out, dressed only in a plain tunic, hair unbound. His face lit up like the dawn at the sight of her. "You came!"

Before she could protest, he had swept her up in a bear hug, lifting her up off the floor. But when he made to kiss her she drove him back, hammering her fists into his chest, sending him staggering. He gaped at her in surprise. "Herata!"

She slammed the letter down on the table. Pointed at the seal of the White Mare.

"When, Branek?" she shouted. "When is it?"

He stared down at the manuscript, and the color drained out of his face.

"So you know," he said.

Herata groaned. She staggered back from the table, covering her face with her hands. Even with the evidence before her eyes, she hadn't wanted to believe.

"Oh, gods," she moaned. "What a fool I am!"

"No, Herata!" Branek said quickly. "It isn't like that!"

"Isn't like *what*?" she cried. "Isn't like you lied to me? Isn't like you deceived me?" She turned away, sobbing, hiding her face against a pillar. Her hot tears watered the cold marble.

"Think what you will," Branek said, his voice deathly quiet. "But I never intended to hurt you. Nor to deceive you. All this was begun long before I met you."

"You knew?" Herata cried. "All along you knew?"

"I've known for a long time. Laodice was part of the project. Her earthquake protocols are part of the design."

He came up behind her, tried to take her in his arms. "No!" she cried, shoving him away. His face was desolate, but Herata felt as if she would go mad at the mere sight of him. "Don't touch me!"

He went and sat in a chair, sagged into it really, as if the air was going out of him. He put his head in his hands.

"Tell me what you want me to do, to prove that I truly love you, Herata, and I'll do it," he said. "Anything."

"Love?" she cried, aghast. "Love? You've lied to me from the beginning!"

"No! I never lied to you! I just … kept some things to myself."

"Oh, gods," Herata whispered. "I don't know you at all."

He looked up at her from behind his hands. "Yes you do. One day you'll realize it. And I'll still be waiting."

She laughed again; it had the high tilt of hysteria. A crystal lamp on a stand in the corner overloaded in a shower of fat gold sparks.

"One day!" she said, laughing. "Don't you get it? Your friends will activate their program and there won't *be* any more days!"

"It might not happen like that. Laodice thought the program was sound."

"Look what happened to her!"

He winced; there was no escaping that fact. "It's too late to do anything now. The program will be run."

A cold fury joined the sorrow and hurt that were raging in her breast. "No! Not while I have breath in my body."

She stalked to the table, brandished the paper under his nose. "When is it, Branek? The ceremony – when is it?"

He shook his head. "I do not know."

She stared at him, pale eyes blazing madly, focusing all of her will on him – her will and her wretched, betrayed love. "When?"

His blue eyes were dark and huge with shock and sorrow; she could not read them. "I am not an adept," he said wearily. "I do not know."

A final sob jerked out of her; ruthlessly she clamped down on it. Biting her lip till it bled, she turned and fled the chamber.

Branek shouted after her, ordering his men to catch her, stop her. She sped before them to the ley chamber.

His men caught her right at the ley stone, and held her until he came. Sobs wracked her and she was unable to stop them and did not care. What did it matter who saw her humiliation now?

"But where are you going?' Branek asked, sadness and confusion in his eyes. "I can't let you damage this crystal. You must see that."

She turned her face away, unable to look at him. Tears blinded her vision. Behind her the leystone hummed and sparked to life.

He gestured to his men to bring her out of the chamber. "You are just upset right now. Once you have some time to get used to it, everything will seem better. You'll see."

"No!" she cried. Twisting in the grip of the swordsmen, she lunged for the ley-crystal. Her hand touched it, the power flared up, and with Branek's despairing shout the ley took her and she was gone. West and south, back to Atlantis.

Many adepts wondered about the wailing entity that passed through their leys that morning, causing their crystals to surge and crackle. But none of them guessed the truth.

Chapter Twenty-One

Herata materialized back in the ley chamber of the Hall of the Salmon. She stared around for a moment, wondering at the power that had carried her halfway across the world and back.

But then the anguish rose up to swamp her and she collapsed, sobbing, to the floor.

Hecuba came running to attend her, but Herata without thinking flung up the force field at the door to the chamber, keeping her out. She wanted no comfort as she writhed on the ground, consumed by misery and despair. There could be no comfort for this desolation. Of all the forces arrayed against her, of all the people in her world, friend and foe, the one she had never dreamed would betray her was Branek.

Herodian arrived and spoke to her, first cajoling, then commanding, but she would not hear him. He too had known, and he had said nothing. Damn him too.

He could not reach her, so he left her alone. And still she mourned.

At length she cried herself out, spent from sorrow. Her face was sticky and flushed, her hair knotted and wet with tears. She lay there dully on the cold stone floor, hardly thinking. If her enemies had planned it out from the start, they could never have hoped to bring her so low.

It was that realization that made her get up. This was what they had planned. What they wanted. They had used Branek, his lips, his soft words, his lies, to make her weak. If she let them, if she gave way to grief, there would be no one to stop them while they unmade the world.

She felt her heart close over and seal within her, turning clear and hard. There was nothing to hold her back now. No human heart left in her now. Only crystal heart.

They would do it. It had been written; it would be done. And she did not know when.

But she could find out.

Like a ghost she drifted to the library, silent and cold. The people of Salmon Hall hovered, following her, wondering at her, but she paid them no mind.

From the shelves she pulled down star charts and atlases. She could calculate the time. The astronomical alignments would have to be precise, the cast of the stars exactly correct, or the terrible thing could not be done. They could not move the leys at just any time, only when the sky was right, and the earth receptive. She began to cast the horoscope.

Hecuba came to the door, inquiring. "Get out!" Herata yelled, throwing the ruler at her head. The old woman ducked away, scurrying back down the corridor.

At last she had it. The time of convergence, when the power surged high, unstable and plastic, dangerous to mortal men. She should have guessed straight off, now that she knew. The last night of the eight month, the darkest dark between the equinox and the solstice, the secret hinge of the year, when the power flowed high and the veil between worlds was thin. It was the dark of the moon, too, a rare convergence. That clinched it. Such black work could only be done when the friend of the earth hid her silver face. That had to be the day.

Summer's End. Three days from now.

She made her preparations. She went to Herodian and told him she was leaving his house.

He looked at her in consternation. "Herata, your hair! It's white!"

She fisted up a handful of her own hair, looked at it in dull interest. So it was, pure white where it had once been darkest black, bleached by her passage through the leys. White, the color of grieving. It suited her.

"Never mind," she said. "It will soon no longer matter."

"Do you mean to hurt yourself?" Herodian asked. "Tell me – what has happened? There have been many messages from Lacaon this morning, from Prince Branek."

Herata flinched. "Speak not that name to me! Never again!"

"Is it because of him that you must leave? Please, child, tell me what troubles you so!"

She only stared at him, amazed. Could he be so blind?

"The transjunction," he guessed.

So, he did know. Herata felt her world shriveling around her.

"Damn you," she whispered. "You should have told me."

"If I did not, you can see why. Look at how you are just at the mention of it. No, I am your father and I have a responsibility for you. I cannot let you destroy yourself this way, to no purpose."

"I am not crazy," Herata said. "And I know what I know."

"So you say. You are the great seeress and can do no wrong. But what if your vision does not come to pass? Have you ever considered that?"

"Everything has happened exactly as I foresaw," Herata said. "What more do you want?"

"Some wisdom! You have not been well, you are unbalanced. You cannot even touch a crystal without it shrieking like a banshee! Such a thing has never been seen in all the history of Atlantis! Have you considered, that is not a good thing? Perhaps it is you who are unbalancing the leys! How can we know?

"Well, we cannot. Even *you* cannot. Not knowing that, how can we allow you anywhere near the transjunction? It could be disastrous.

"You tell us to fix things, to restore balance in the flows. The transjunction will do just that. You will not be allowed to interfere."

"You will destroy us all."

Herodian shook his head. "Greater adepts than you have said it is not so. The transjunction will go forward.

"If it disturbs you so, then perhaps you should leave the City until after it is over. You could go to our estates in Olmec lands or the Misty Isles, somewhere far away, where you will be safe and it will not trouble you so."

Olmec lands? Was he mad? Did he understand nothing of the child he had raised?

"Perhaps I will leave the City," Herata said. "But not to idle at your estates while the empire crumbles. And you call yourself a King!"

"I am only concerned for your welfare," Herodian said.

Her glassy heart was unmoved. If he was truly concerned he would never have set that devil's pawn Branek to ensnare her and weaken her when she needed her strength the most.

"And I am concerned for yours," Herata said. "You are my father after all. So let me say this to you, Herodian: leave Atlantis. The transjunction will fail. If you hope to see another year in your life, then leave. Now."

"You are speaking foolishness. Listen to your father. Go to the Misty Isles. I have already arranged a ship."

"No."

"It is for your own good."

"Never!"

Armed men appeared in the doorway behind the King. "I had hoped it would not come to this, daughter." The King said, implacable. "But you will not be allowed to interfere."

"You cannot stop me!" Herata said, furiously, but with certainty. She breathed; she could feel the power rising at her call. Her hair rose and crackled with energy. Her skin began to glow.

The king's warriors fell back a step, unsure. "Seize her!" Herodian ordered, gesturing.

Herata turned and darted out into the hall. She ran down the corridor, sprinting for the atrium. It was there that she would find the power. The guards chased her. They could not hurt her, she knew that now, but if they caught her, held her, everything would suffer.

Bursting down the stairs, she ran for the great front hall of the House of the Salmon. More soldiers swarmed out of the side doors below; she skidded to a stop on the stairs, almost falling. She was surrounded.

But there, beneath the floor at the very foot of the stairs, in the ground, she could feel it: the Trident. She could see it, hidden golden clear in the heart of the earth. It ran right through the center of the Great City, under the Hall of the Salmon.

"Don't do this, Herata!" Herodian said, coming up behind her. "It is over. Accept it! No one wants to hurt you if you will just be still." He held out a hand to her. "Come to me."

She backed down the stairs, down toward the soldiers, closer now. "Liar! That is what Branek said."

"You should have listened to him," Herodian said. "He has your best interests at heart. As do I."

"No!" Just a few more steps now.

Herodian sighed. "Child, you cannot escape. Do not make a scene. Just come with me."

The soldiers closed in, surrounding her. She stepped off the last step, onto the floor. She could feel it, the Trident, under her feet.

"Where do you think you will go?" Herodian asked.

They were blind, so blind. They had no idea what she could do now. "Anywhere I want," she said.

She did not need the crystals anymore. She *was* a crystal.

She touched the Trident, let herself flow into it, and was gone.

Chapter Twenty-Two

South she went, under the rings of the city, onto the Plains of Gold.
She materialized in the ancient stone circle where she had gone with
Branek on the Night of Fires.

It was still dark, full night; dawn in this part of the world was still
hours off. A chill wind whistled across the plains, but Herata hardly felt it;
the supercharged *aum* flowing through her veins kept her warm. A faint
light fell on the standing stones of the circle; it came from her. From her
skin. Everything she saw was tinged with a blush of gold. Nor did it fade
as the dizziness of the ley transit left her.

She stood for a long moment looking at the distant lights of the city,
the glowing rings of Poseidonis on the Plains of Gold. Once it had been
her home; she had fallen in love there, then lost it; she had lost her mother there, and now her father too. Once her whole life had been there,
and now: nothing. The only time she would see it again would be to see it
destroyed.

Blinded by tears, by *aum*, she turned away. But here instead was the
stone circle where she had given herself to Branek for the first time. There
was the mossy hollow within which her maiden's blood had been spilt.
There were the ancient glyphs upon which they had pledged their love.

Despite herself, she reached out, touched the carvings. She remembered how, that day, she had felt she could touch, feel Branek's love there
– a warmth, an energy in the stones.

The stones were cold now, icy cold in the autumn wind.

What a fool she had been: a naïve, girlish little fool.

She could feel his arms about her even now, hear his voice in her ear,
whispering, cajoling.

Branek! How could you lie to me that way? How could you use me?

Her strength left her and she collapsed weeping on the ancient stones.
What she had felt here had never existed.

When there were no more tears left that night she slept, huddled alone at the foot of a standing stone. She was in no danger; the *aum* warmed her. But it could not thaw the glassy frozen thing that was her heart.

Herata remained in the stone circle for the three days until the ritual. As she had expected, the lords of the city never thought to look for her there. If they had turned their attention that way, she could have hidden herself, merging her essence into the leys, matching their vibrations exactly so as to become invisible to searching minds in the web. But they never did.

At the ancient natural crystal altar she listened to the messages being passed along the Trident as they looked for her. They were concerned. Questions were raised. She hoped Branek had to answer them, a lot of them; she hoped he was made to squirm by his masters, for losing her. She hoped he suffered, as she had.

They had no idea what she might do.

Neither did she. But when the time came, she would be ready; she trusted the power that moved her now to move her then.

Much of the time passed as in a dream, as she meditated, resting her mind in the leys, gathering herself. She did not eat; she had no need. Sometimes she wept, for everything she had lost, and everything still to disappear. She slept, woke, dreamed, all in the energy of the Trident that surrounded her, contained and amplified by the ancient stone circle, the first crude beginnings of Atlantean technology. Crude, but effective. She was being made ready.

Until at last, sunset of the third day arrived. As the light faded out of the western sky, she knew the time had come.

She rode the ley back into the city. She did it without thinking now, as easily as breathing. In a small park she reappeared, in the outermost ring of the city, under a spreading moonflower tree.

She stood there for a moment, gathering herself, breathing. The Trident was running high and fast under her, like a swollen river in springtime; they were drawing much *aum* tonight, too much.

She was afraid; the part of her that was still human was afraid. But even that could not turn aside the imperative of her glassy heart.

Around her the evening life of the Great City went on, oblivious to the danger in its midst: couples strolled the golden streets, vendors hawked the riches of the wide world, music and light spilled out of taverns and theatres alike. And all of it soon to be destroyed, gone forever. The last night of Poseidonis. The crystal palaces, the gleaming pyramids of oricalch, the great museums and libraries containing the accumulated wisdom of man, lost. The great ladies of the courts, the men of wisdom in the academies, the little black-eyed children playing in the streets: all dead. They were all already dead and they did not even know it.

Through it all, Herata walked, unnoticed, her light just one light among many, in the glittering city of the Sea Kings. Unmolested she came to Mariner's Hall, a long, low building with a dragon-shaped prow like an Atlantean longship, on the edge of the outermost canal, the great harbor of Atlantis.

The Hall was dark; no sign did it give of the monstrous act about to take place inside. But she could feel it, deep inside, underground; power gathering, a dull vibration that shrieked to her ears like nails on slate, though it would be soundless to anyone else, anyone not changed by the crystals, anyone who had not received the burning kiss of the Hexachon.

She turned her mind back, north to the sacred precinct at the heart of the city. There! She could feel them, those enigmatic stones, bathed in the flow of the Trident, watching, waiting. They too were ready.

There was nothing now in the world but to go forward.

The doors of the Hall were locked by iron locks – clever of them not to rely on crystal power. But even iron now was no barrier to her purpose.

There were two crystal lamps above the doors, dark now, quiescent. But with a thought she woke them to life and they began to hum, creating a resonance, louder and louder, feeding back one on the other, the hum scaling up to a wailing shriek, horrible to hear, that rattled the giant doors in their frames and finally burst the lock asunder just as the crystals themselves gave a final squeal and cracked into pieces, overloaded.

The doors swung drunkenly open on their loosened hinges. The way before her was clear.

She stepped in, then stopped, overcame by a wave of emotion. Would it be so easy, then? Was that all there was to annihilation? She was afraid, so afraid.

The power had her now, the earthforce, perhaps even the earth herself; she was its tool, its willing vessel. But power unchecked had a way of consuming that which would contain it. To her searching vision there lay before her only chaos and destruction. Even if she stopped them now, tonight, the destruction would be great. There could be no other way.

The awesomeness, the terribleness of it almost drove her to her knees. How had things come to this terrible pass? How had the Sea Kings, masters of the wide world, so lost their way?

That was not for her to answer. It was only for her to do, to act out the pitiless imperative of power with which she had been so horribly gifted.

She walked on down the hallway into the darkened Hall.

It seemed empty. The transjunction, the terrible deed, was taking place far below, in secret chambers carved out of the bedrock deep below the Hall. She could feel the power, below her, bunching and coiling as it was gathered to unholy purpose. She could have found it even if they had gouged out her eyes.

But they hadn't. They had lost her, they had left her free, and so here she was. And they did not even bother to guard their doors against her coming. So little did they understand the power which they sought to control.

She went on, alone in the darkness, yet not alone. She could see clearly; her own flesh lit her way, glowing with the *aum* which inhabited it now. She came to a stair, went down it, through another corridor to another stair, ever downward.

The crystals of Mariner's Hall marked her progress as she went: the mighty power crystals that drove the longships of the Sea Kings across the nine seas; the great navigation crystals, carefully tended for generations, that contained the charts of sea and sky. They were in accord with her purpose. It was all one now.

And now at last, guards, at the final doors, beyond which lay the secret way to the underground chambers. Soldiers of the Sea Kings, doing their duty. But their duty would not spare them.

They saw her approach, glowing in the darkness, like an apparition from the olden times when gods walked among men.

"Who are you?" they cried, frightened, brandishing their weapons. But mere iron could not stop her now, nor even crystal.

"I am Herata of Nine Seas," she said.

"Milady," said the senior one, voice trembling, "We have orders not to let you pass."

"Do you think you can stop me?" She raised her hands; all the crystals in the hallway – the lights, the door locks, the artworks – came to humming, burning life. But the crystals in their hand weapons stuttered and died, responding to Herata's silent will. "Do you?"

They were terrified; some distant part of her pitied them, who would soon fall victim to her purpose through no fault of their own. But her crystal heart was unmoved. It had all been foreseen.

The older soldier drew his sword. "Yet we must, lady." He said, voice wavering but defiant. "It is a matter of imperial security."

"There can be no security when the empire is run by madmen," Herata said. "Now stand aside." The crystals in the corridor hummed and sang and glowed ever brighter, mimicking her will.

They did not retreat. The younger one made a move toward her.

"Do not touch me!" she warned, holding up a glowing hand.

But he made a lunge for her, and the other followed suit, relying on force of muscle when their weapons were useless. She tried to duck aside – she had no desire to harm them – but they were strong and fast, young men, warriors in the prime of life. They grabbed her arms, one the right and the other the left.

As they touched her they burst into flame, as the supercharged *aum* that coursed through her flesh enveloped them and consumed them. They staggered away, and were dead in an instant, flashburned, unable even to scream. They could not have put the fire out had they even had time to try, for it was a thing of the spirit as much as the flesh, burning along the leys of their own bodies, in the spaces between their molecules.

Herata could not have saved them. She had been prepared. They had not.

She looked at their black, smoking bodies, burned ruined things that a second before had been young men in the fullness of life. Tears welled in her eyes, but she did not turn back. They were only the first of many.

She passed on through the door they had guarded, and deeper into the darkened Hall.

This corridor was bare and unornamented, cut from the living rock of the Plains of Gold. No side passages branched off; the way before her was clear, sloping steeply down.

Beneath her feet she could feel a throbbing, as of huge machines. It was the gathering of power for the transjunction. She felt it; the *aum* in her bones resonated with it, the light that came from her flesh peaking and ebbing in cycle with the throbbing. She was being attuned. There was pain, but most of her was beyond that now.

At last the corridor came to an end at a fork, curving off left and right. Light spilled down the corridors from both sides, golden light pulsing in time to the throbbing. On an impulse she took the left-hand fork.

The tunnel curved around sharply; it would meet the other fork and join in a perfect circle. The golden pulsing light came from windows, cut into the rock and overlooking a cavern below.

Herata looked down, into the unholy of unholies, the chamber of the transjunction.

Rock-hewn steps swept down from a door at the back of the circle. The great arching walls of the chamber were incised with glyphs and signs, sigils of power and control, to capture the power and contain it. On the floor, far below, white-clad priests of the Poseideion moved about, tending to the arcane business of the transjunction. In the middle of the floor, a dozen giant, gleaming crystals were linked in sequence inside a huge metal frame, spiraling in a complex helix pattern from smallest to largest, a titanic stone at the center of the array, glowing like the heart of a god. The crystals were an uncanny crimson red; she had never seen their like before. She tried to touch them with her mind; they did not respond. They were opaque to her. She had never encountered this before. What had been done to these stones? They had been warped somehow, she was sure of it.

The crystals throbbed with *aum*; it was they who cast forth the pulsing, golden light.

This was what she had felt from far above, the captured earthpower shaking through the ground.

Before the crystals lay a long flat slab of cultured *aum*-stone, like a medical crystal. She could not guess what that was for. Ruby beams of coherent light connected it to the greater array.

In ranks of seats around the walls of the room sat the great and holy of empire, kings and sealords, merchant princes and wise men of the temples, awaiting the terrible deed.

Herata watched, fascinated and appalled. Her bones throbbed to the pulse of the crystal array; her heart beat to its rhythm. She was being entrained. Before she could disrupt that dreadful rhythm, she must become one with it.

More priests and acolytes filed in from doors below the stairs; priests with glowing crystal standards, acolytes with smoking braziers of incense. Flutes and pipes wailed from a hidden alcove; drums throbbed with the pulse of the crystals.

Herata's breath caught in her chest. Her heart, her loins, throbbed to the beat of the drums. She could feel the power of the music, the chanting, the symbols graven on the walls. It was a very great ritual; it had to be. Only the numinous power of ritual could focus the adepts' minds enough to complete the dreadful work.

The rhythm of the drums changed; the ruby crystals in the great array began to pulse in sequence; first one, then the next, and the next, all the way to the great bloodred stone in the center, then over again; light circling in, a pulsing spiral of light.

The hair on Herata's neck stood up. She could feel it; the crystals were drawing power, from all directions, through the very air, ambiently. She could feel power flowing past her, through her, into the array on the floor below. She was amazed. Power had never been drawn in this way before. The skill and greed of her enemies was unprecedented.

And worse, behind her, some distance to the east, she could feel the clear strong current of the Trident, the great Atlantean ley, shiver and slacken, and begin to move, drawn by sorcery toward the crystal array. She could feel it, the drawing, the hideous tension that she had suffered that night at Nine Seas, that had stripped the staff of Green Jade from their own skins like fruit. The force of it pulled her flat against the thick glass window, as she too was drawn to the array by the *aum* in her blood.

The transjunction had begun.

Herata struggled away from the window, *aum* fighting against *aum*, her own cache of power in her bones and blood fighting to maintain its integrity against the whirlpool sorcery of the transjunction. Gasping, she stepped back from the window, and the pull of the bloody crystals lessened a tiny bit.

And yet the transjunction was not working. She could feel it; the Trident was sliding back to its original bed in the earth, the force of its own age-long current too much for the witchery of the sanguinary crystals. The awful drawing sensation eased as the natural flows were restored.

This was what they had tried before, unsuccessfully. Herata was sure of it. The sensations were exactly the same. It had not worked before, why would they think it would work now?

Or had they some new devilry to add?

The drums fell to a low, anticipatory muttering. The cycling of the crystal helix slowed, whirling hypnotically, waiting.

Out from one of the hidden doors a train of priests led a single other person, a young woman, clad in a white robe. Her eyes were dark and glassy; Herata thought she had been drugged.

The priests led her to the flat slab of *aum*-stone in front of the crystal array. They stripped off her robes and laid her down on the slab. The drums developed a new urgency; the whirling of the array sped up again. The watchers in the galleries leaned forward, muttering.

From within his robes the head priest drew forth something gleaming. He raised it on high.

It was a knife.

And as the drums reached a smashing crescendo, he yanked back the naked girl's hair, exposing her throat, and slit it wide open.

Her body convulsed; blood sprayed out, soaking the *aum*-stone. Her life energy fled in a billowing wave, only to be caught and trapped by the suddenly glowing slab of blood-stained crystal. The blood seeped into the crystal, along with the energy; the stone drank greedily of the girl's life, glowing obscenely. The ruby lights linking the sacrificial slab with the helical array increased in intensity; the whirling of the crystals increased, their light growing a deeper red.

Swollen, obscene power filled the chamber, burgeoned outwards, driven by the young woman's stolen life. The crystals whirled like a madman's dance. Away across the City, the Trident began to move.

Herata staggered away from the window, hands clasped over her mouth to stifle her own scream. The frantic power of the stolen life flowed around her, tugging at her mind, at the *aum* she carried within her. All the hairs on her body rose in outraged horror. She could feel the girl's blood and pain and terror, washing over her, covering her. Whimpering, she scrubbed futilely at her own skin, trying to rub it off somehow, but she could not. She had seen it, it was a part of her now.

Sobs wracked her. Blasphemy! This was worse even than she had foreseen. The actions of the tainted crystals were hidden from her oracular vision, they were so far beyond the pale of the earthpower that she knew. Crystals were meant to give life, never take it! It was unthinkable! Even in her most hysterical imaginings she had never predicted this.

And still the Trident was moving, trembling through the ground toward the deadly crystals, to be fixed by necromancy for all time in the wrong channel, warping the life of the earth, distorting it. She could feel it; the power unleashed by ritual murder was enough to change the very fabric of the world.

No! Then the Sea Kings would have unlimited power, and nothing could stop the burning! The earth would die by fire and blood, consumed by the insatiable greed of Atlantis.

Below, in the chamber, the priests dragged the lifeless body of the maiden off the crystal slab. The drums increased their rhythm. A new rank of priests came out of the secret doors – leading a new maiden, white-robed and drugged.

"No!" Not while she still had life in her body. She raced to the apex of the circle, and with a blast of power, burst open the great stone doors.

"*Stop!*" she cried, and that cry seemed to shiver the very stones of the walls. The crimson crystals shuddered in their racks. *Aum* flared and rose about her form, a fiery cloak. The music faltered to a stop.

The Patriarch came forward from the ranks of red-clad priests. "Herata of Nine Seas," he said. "At last you arrive."

Herata descended the stairs. The *aum* around her faded and withdrew, retreating into her flesh so that she glowed like a lamp. The crowd watched her, silent.

"Not while I live will you do this," she said, and *aum* carried her voice all through the chamber. "It is blasphemy."

"It is no concern of yours," the Patriarch said. "You should have remained in Lacaon when you had the chance."

"You make it my concern," Herata said, "when you use the power that I serve for murder and rapine! This cannot stand!" she cried, looking at the lords and princes in the galleries above. "I will not permit it! *She* will not!"

"There is no She," the Patriarch sneered. "The earth is only an empty vessel, useful for our purposes. The nation that uses it best rules the world."

"The nation that abuses it will soon leave the world," Herata said. "End this and you may yet save yourselves."

She continued to descend the steps. She bent her attention to the bloody crystals, trying to reach them, touch them with her power. But they remained impervious to her, unapproachable. They were twisted, warped things, abominations.

And yet they pulled at her, greedily drawn to the *aum* in her. These crystals were not one with the flows. Instead of riding the earthpower like a river, they consumed it, giving nothing in return. Instead of giving life they took it, drinking blood like the vampires of legend, to serve their master's unclean will.

They thirsted for her, for the *aum* in her blood. They were calling her.

She took a step toward them. Another. They were calling.

"You see," the Patriarch said. "Even you cannot resist."

Herata stumbled to a stop on the lower stairs. With a wrench she jerked her attention away from the deadly stones.

"But I can," she said. "And I will!"

She stretched out her power again to the crystals, her mind fueled by the *aum* within her, battering at them with her will, trying to unseat them, to burn them out and smash them down as she could with any crystal of the Sea Kings' power. Surely that was what the power she had incubated was meant for, to smash these bloody crystals and wreck them for all time.

Her will beat at them, the power flaring around her like a cloak. The regular crystal lamps in the chamber whined and sparked. The glyphs of power on the walls writhed like snakes. The evil stones trembled in their metal braces under the assault. But they remained untouched. They were impervious, blind to her will, deaf to her power. They did not resonate to her energy, but waited only to consume it. All her power, which she had mysteriously incubated for so long, was useless against them.

At last she stopped, confused and disheartened. The Patriarch laughed, in gloating triumph.

"You see! Your witchery is useless here against this new science of power! Our will shall be done; a new age is dawning for Atlantis, and no one may gainsay it! At last true power shall come home to roost, in the hands of the Sea Kings, where it should be! None shall resist us, nothing shall stand in our way!

"You would have been better served staying at your temple, chanting your spells and performing your empty rites. Or better yet, little fool, should you have stayed in the home of your lover and kept his hearth as a woman should. Then he might have been able to protect you. But now, you have no protection. And we have use of you."

He gestured, and soldiers swarmed up from the sides of the chamber, up the steps to take her. Herata fell back several steps. "Do not touch me," she cried, "or it will be your death!"

They hesitated. "Lies!" said the Patriarch. "Believe not her empty threats. Take her!"

The soldiers pushed forward again. Herata stood still to meet them, sorrowing, but ready for the conflagration. The loss of any single life could not stay her purpose now.

They surrounded her and seized her. They did not burn. The *aum* in her remained sheathed within her flesh, did not burst forth to consume them. A cry of confused dismay left her lips as they dragged her down the stairs.

What was happening? How could the power she had so long harbored abandon her now?

The soldiers hustled her before the Patriarch. "And so your reign of terror comes to an end," he said.

"I will never serve you!" Herata cried.

"Indeed, no," he said. "As you did not serve in life, you will serve in death. And be the more useful thereby, and rid us of the thorny problem of your discontent. Lay her on the slab!"

"No!" Not that, anything but that! She struggled wildly. But the guards were too strong for her. They dragged her across the floor to the bloodied slab of crystal.

A priest came up with a bowl of some dark, foul-smelling liquid, and tried to force it down her throat: the narcotic that kept the victims from struggling. Herata twisted her head wildly, fighting to avoid it, but they held her head and made her drink. She coughed violently, choking, but a gulp of the drug went down, and she began to feel a deadly heaviness in her limbs.

The music began again. The crowd in the galleries shifted and muttered, displeased. A succession of drugged, anonymous victims was one thing to see, but a lady of the temples fighting for her life was something else entirely.

They slung her on the altar stone. She struggled weakly to rise, her limbs betraying her. They held her down. The crystal array towered over her, humming menacingly. She could feel it in her bones now, she was so close. The incarnadined crystals gloated on her, on the *aum* housed within her flesh.

Why? she cried within her mind. Why had all her trials, all her suffering, come to this? She screamed.

And her cry was echoed by another voice, high in the galleries of the chamber: "No!!!"

A commotion high up in the galleries, as someone fought his way to ground level. "Stop!"

Even dazed and drugged, she knew that voice. Branek! Arching her neck back, she could see him, in the galleries above the crystal array. Like a hero out of legend he came racing down the stairs, his blond hair flying behind him. A wedge of his own men followed him, and a naked sword was in his hand.

He leaped the last ten feet from the edge of the gallery to the floor, and he and his men began to hew a path through the soldiers of the Sea Kings. He bellowed in wrath like the bull of heaven, and no man could stand before his fury.

He was facing many men, not just one, many warriors with wicked steel swords, and more coming in all the time. He and his men were outnumbered. But slowly they began to carve a path through the ranks of troops toward the altar.

Pinned on the wicked stone, Herata watched, amazed. Branek! He was coming to her! The drug licked at the edges of her vision, giving everything a hazy aura of golden *aum*-light. The ring of swords and the cries of men echoed weirdly in the vaulted hall, giving the whole scene an unreal aura like an opium dream. Was it real, she wondered? Or had she conjured this vision out of her fear and the drug?

Across the floor, through the fray, his eyes caught hers. Their gazes locked. Like a current of earthpower she felt it, his presence. The touch of his mind on hers jolted her back on the slab. She could feel him, his anger and fear, his wild need to get to her, no matter the cost, no matter if she fled from him in fear afterwards. His love, beating around her like great wings, filling the temple.

He felt it too, her presence in his mind, her terror and confusion amid the chaos, the weakness of the drug and the wild hope that leaped in her breast at the sight of him. He stumbled, hesitated.

His enemies struck. A sword bit deep, slicing his side.

Herata screamed with the raw red pain that filled him. She felt it too, linked as they were, thought to thought. Her cry scaled up over his shout of pain. It was the pain above all that told her this was no dream.

She fought like a wildcat to escape the slab, but men of the Poseideion still held her down. Branek's men flanked him, protecting him as best they could from the many soldiers, and he advanced on the Patriarch, his sword at the ready.

The priests of the Poseideion were no fighters, and they scattered like white-robed birds at his advance. The Patriarch darted for the sacrificial slab, his bloody knife raised high; Herata shrieked, still held fast. But Branek was too fast for him – lunging forward, he snatched at the neck of the old man's white robe, and dragging him close, put the bloody sword at his neck.

His shout filled the chamber. "Let her go!"

A rustle among the stunned watchers in the gallery. The High King arose. "Enough of this, Branek of Lacaon. Put down your sword!"

Branek whirled to face him, the old man held tight, the sword still at his throat. "Release the Lady of Nine Seas to me, or I will slit his throat like a pig's!"

"The Five do not answer to threats," the High King said.

Branek nicked the Patriarch's neck; blood started there and trickled down, red as the mutant crystals, staining the white of his robe. The old man screamed thinly, but he did not die, not yet. "If I kill this Patriarch your transjunction will never take place!" Branek shouted. "You need him to complete the ritual, whereas if you do not give me what *I* need, I will kill him and as many other foul priests as I can before you strike me down. Do you dare try me?"

"If you take her you will both die at the hands of my warriors before you leave this chamber," the King said.

Branek spat in disgust. "That is a better chance than you give my lady on the slab! Now release her!"

The High King gestured to the priests. "Do as he says."

After a moment they let go of Herata's wrists and ankles. She sat up on the slab, dizzy, confused, fear and the drug humming in her head. It had all happened so fast.

She hesitated, fear warring with her desire to flee that chamber of horrors and never look back. Branek! Where had he come from? Why did he do this?

Their eyes met across the blood-stained floor. He saw her fear. Shoving the Patriarch into the hands of one of his men, he held out a hand to her.

"Herata" he said. "It's alright. Come to me."

In her drug-dimmed eyes, he seemed to be lit by a light from above, glowing with a passionate fire, limning his blond hair, his redly gleaming sword. Her golden boy. His eyes blazed with anger and fear, but most of all, love. She could see it in his eyes, could feel it, his love for her, so strong that it would risk death on a moment's notice, forsaking honor, position, life itself, for the chance to touch her a final time, for no better hope than to fight and die at her side.

She ran to him.

With his free arm he swept her up, crushing her to him in a desperate final embrace. She threw her arms around his neck, clinging with the strength of terror. "Branek!" she cried, overcome with equal measures of horror and love. Great wracking sobs shook her. He held her close, his face pressed to her neck; he was trembling too, shaking with passion and rage.

Herata cleaved to him, overwhelmed. He had not played her false. She had misjudged him. There were no words, no words to speak the awe and gratitude that filled her heart to overflowing. But he knew, he knew. Their eyes met, and in that glance passed everything that could not be said.

The blood was sheeting down his side from the sword cut, pattering on the marble floor. It was a bad wound. He held her against his opposite side, but as their skin touched she could feel the pain of it burning like a brand in her own flesh. Gasping, she pressed her hand to it, trying to staunch the bleeding. Blood welled and seeped through her fingers. He groaned at the pain.

He gestured with his sword; his man holding the Patriarch began to edge toward the stairs and freedom. Branek followed more slowly, Herata trying to hold him up, ease the strain on his wound. The soldiers of the Sea Kings circled closer, surrounding them. The glittering crowd in the gallery was silent, riveted, watching this tableau.

"They will never let us go," Herata said. Branek's men surrounded the two of them, swords out, but the soldiers of the Empire thronged closer, and their blades were just as sharp.

"Likely no," he said. "Now, we fight and die together."

The soldiers of the empire fell on Branek's little party, swords high. Battle was joined. Branek's men fought bravely, but they were sorely outnumbered. For every man they took down three more stood to take his place. They would be mown down before they reached the stairs.

Branek killed a man who darted past the ring of their defenders; he died in blood and agony at their feet. Herata could see his life energy flee, spilled with the blood, billowing up in ghostly waves around them. Behind her, Herata could feel the crystal array whirl faster, taking power from that death.

Another soldier crab-stepped up to take the dead one's place. It was hopeless.

"You'll die!" she cried. "You and all your men will die here."

He gave her a wild-eyed sapphire look, and she could read his thought as if it were her own. He would spend the lives of a hundred men, and his own too, at a moment's notice, if there was a chance she herself could walk away.

Overcome, she hid her face against his shoulder. She had done nothing to deserve such love; she had spurned it, even, at the first test. But there it was. He loved her, and he was content to die in that love.

As was she. The hard knot of grief that had dwelled under her heart through her time in the stone circle loosened and unbound. Amid the bloodshed and din of battle, she was overcome by peace. She had tried, and failed; the power had betrayed her in the end. But Branek had not. What else was there? She was willing to die now, with that knowledge in her heart.

Men fell at their feet, their enemies' and their own, and the evil crystals feasted even on those unsanctified deaths. Blood power, earth-power, beat around the temple, whispering raggedly around the room: the remnants of the girl's death, the ghastly energy it had unleashed. Unprecedented power, evoked by unprecedented means. The hinge of the year. The dark of the moon. The burning.

The power that had brooded in her own cells for so long suddenly flared up again, a living flame surrounding her and Branek, hot but unconsuming. And at last she knew the way. She had known it before, deep inside, but she had been too afraid to see it. No longer.

She grabbed Branek's sword hand, forcing it down. "Stop!"

He whipped round to stare at her, a look of astonished dismay. "What are you doing?!"

She called out, and again her voice filed the whole chamber: "*Hold!*"

The High King held up a hand. His soldiers stopped.

Herata took Branek's sword from him and cast it on the floor. "We surrender."

The look he gave her was pure anguish. "Don't do this!"

She could not let him spend his life and the lives of all his men in a futile attempt to rescue her. No. This was the better way.

"Let the King of Lacaon and his men go," She called out to the High King. "I will go to the altar."

"No!" Branek cried.

She took his head between her hands, looking deep into his eyes. "Listen to me very carefully," she said, for his ears alone. "Leave this place. Go to the docks, take ship. Leave the island home as quickly as you can. Don't look back. Do as I say!"

He shook his head in violent denial. "I'll never leave you!"

"You *must*, or else all our deaths will be for nothing. You must do this last thing for me, for love of me." She wrapped her hands around the back of his neck, pulling his forehead down to hers, willing him to understand. "You must trust me – do you trust me, Branek?"

He nodded jerkily. He wept; his tears fell upon her cheeks.

She kissed him, long and deep, their last kiss on this earth. "Then go."

And she pushed him away.

Chapter Twenty-Three

He staggered back, wounded, broken. His eyes devoured her. "I can't," he whispered.

Her cloak of *aum* flared up around her again, screening him from her sight in a haze of golden fire.

"Yes you can," she said. She turned and walked back to the altar stone.

She could still feel him in her mind, like a burning ember, a hot coal of need and fear and tenderness, watching her like a glowing eye in her own head. Which was worse, the pain of the jagged wound, or the soul pain of abandonment and wretched failure? She could not say, for all she felt was an echoing hollowness as she pulled herself within herself and severed that needful link.

Behind her, he groaned pitifully and sank to one knee as what strength he took from their bond was withdrawn. It was a sound of utter despair. Her limbs trembled with her need to go to him, but she kept walking. She finally heard him go as his men dragged him out of the chamber. They left the Patriarch behind.

The fire mantling her retreated into her bones as she smothered it down. Control, control. Not now! Very soon she would have need of it, but not yet.

She reached the slab; priests of the Poseideion reached out to drag her down, but she lifted a hand, forestalling them. If they touched her they would burn. Her rage would spring out and they would be consumed. She was learning to control it, but not that much.

By herself, she lay down on the slab.

Lacaon's minor rebellion was forgotten in the spectacle of a lady of the temples preparing to immolate herself in an act of black sorcery. The crowd leaned forward, staring, their blood rising, fueling the tides of power and lust that swirled in the room.

She lay back, eyes fixed on the vaulted ceiling. The Patriarch came and hovered over her, staring down in mingled satisfaction and doubt.

"Proceed," she said.

The music began again.

They brought her the drug, but again she refused it, and this time they did not force her. Unresisting she lay on the slab, while the priests moved around her and the strange crystal array cycled redly, arching over her head. It sucked at her; she felt the power shudder through her in waves at its call.

She felt both fragmented and strangely at one with herself. One part of her mind yammered in fear, terrified of the knife and the long dark that lay beyond it. Another part of her wept for Branek, gone beyond recall, and for all that might have been. A third part burned with rage at the evil that was being done to her here, and at all that Atlantis had become. But all of these warring thoughts were subordinate to an eerie calmness, that focused itself unflinchingly on what lay immediately ahead: the knife, the pain, the spilling of her lifeforce, raw and coppery as her blood. The sacrifice. A lesser burning to prevent the greater.

Shock – it was shock, she thought mildly, the calmness. If so, she welcomed it.

The rhythm of the ritual reached a peak, the drums booming urgently, the voices of the song-priests fracturing into wordless, eager calls. The crowd in the galleries leaned forward as one, taut with strain, their prurience as much a part of this necromancy as the keen edge of the blade. The array raced through its cycle, a whirling vortex. Far away, like an itch she could not scratch, Herata felt the Trident tremble in its current and began to move.

The Patriarch stood over her.

She lifted her throat to the blade.

The pain surprised her. She shrieked, but it was only a wet and bloody gurgle; her vocal cords were cut. She felt the hot spray of her own blood on her cheek, her chest. She could not breathe. Her windpipe was slashed. Her body bucked convulsively on the slab, fighting to breathe, to live, even as her life energy billowed out of the cut. Her consciousness went with it, sliding out of her ravaged body in a smooth rush, soaring heavenward. She saw her own dying body, bloodied and twisting on the slab below, hands clutching her ruined throat.

Then the arching back eased, the grasping hands fell away, flopping uselessly onto the stone.

Now! Herata-ghost cried, a soundless thunder.

And with the final breath that left her lips came the *aum*.

A torrent of golden power poured from the corpse's body, from the mouth, the eyes, the new wet mouth at the throat, from every orifice, the body's hold on it released at last. A howling fountain of earthlight, of raw power burst skyward, licking the roof of the chamber, plunging down the walls. The priests fell back shouting from the altar slab, dazzled and burned, hiding their eyes.

The stored earthpower that Herata's living form had carried for so many weeks, building up little by little, day by day, in her cells, in her blood, in the leys of her own body -- yes even in her womb, newly opened by Branek's caresses -- poured forth in an instant – *aum* enough to light a city, to stop an earthquake, to change the stars in their courses. Power to move the currents of the earth.

Greedily, like drunkards, the vile stones of the transjunction array sucked down that wild power, drinking it in like morning dew, consuming it utterly. The array whirled faster and faster, power being fed to the giant crystal at its heart, big enough to contain it all and beg for more. Strong enough now, engorged with this power, to reach out with its own infernal lust and pull the Trident to its bosom like a vampire claiming its victim. Shuddering through the earth, the great ley rippled and moved, jumping its ancient bed like a wild river, and with an inexorable rush of light and heat came to nest in the center of the chamber.

Cheers and shouts erupted in the chamber from the celebrants and from the watchers. The first stage of the transjunction was a success!

Disembodied, floating, dead, Herata watched still.

For there was yet more power. The storm of *aum* that had erupted from her dead form had not abated; raw golden power still howled around the chamber like fire, scouring the walls. The sanguinary crystals sucked it in. They whirled still faster, their lights strobing now like a hummingbird's wings. They shivered in their metal frames, humming as if with delight at the feast.

Far away to the northwest, where it joined the Trident in Olmec lands, the ley known as the Feathered Serpent jumped and shivered, and began to move southwards.

Raking the land like a firestorm, boiling the oceans, the Feathered Serpent came to roost in the chamber of the transjunction. With it came the screams of the dead and dying it dragged in its wake, whole villages immolated by the burning flow as the torrent of earthpower crossed miles of ocean and sea, wrenching itself away from its natural flow, disrupting the life that depended on it. Herata saw them, the dead; ghostly shapes like her own, flitting through the storm of power, lost, terrified, wailing.

The chamber hummed with power, the two great leys meeting and conjoining, feeding upon each other, as the greedy blood-crystals fed upon them. The floor shook, the walls shook as the earth itself shuddered at the gout of power flowing through it, where it should not be. The crystal array bucked within its rack, the stones singing, almost shrieking with captured *aum*, blindingly bright so that the whole chamber seemed drenched in blood. The audience was on its feet, shouting with frenzied ecstasy. The dead wailed on the ill wind.

Herata felt herself drifting away. Her part was over; her gift of power had been delivered unasked to the greed and might of the Sea Kings. It was done. A clear light fell around her, coming from nowhere and everywhere, somewhere beyond. She let it fill her, her body forgotten on the slab.

And still the transjunction continued. The array whirled yet, howling, feeding unrestrained on the *aum* of the two great leys. The hair and robes of the watchers billowed in the wind created by the stone's sheer lust, sucking power, gulping it down, reaching out for yet more.

A tremor shook the chamber; the floor bucked and shivered as the Trident, as it had never done before in all the history of earth, reversed its flow and began to run south to north. Crystal lamps on the walls exploded from the strain. The glyphs on the walls writhed like snakes, unhoused by the reversal of power from the stone that contained them. People screamed as the wrenching twist of *aum* took them and shook them like rags; some collapsed, others began to bleed from nose and eyes. When the blood of the earth was reversed in its tracks, no creature that walked its surface could remain unscathed.

Flowing backwards, as unlikely and unnatural an event as the sun rising in the west, the Trident began to draw to it the ley known as the Golden Dragon, the great southwest-northeast ley that ran through Nine Seas temple.

Herata, dissolving in light, nevertheless felt a fleeting hope that Lamike had done as commanded and taken the temple down. Else they would all die, for nothing could contain that destruction.

The hideous pull continued; with a roar and a shock as of an earthquake, the Golden Dragon joined the transjunction. The chamber was shuddering now like a beaten drum; the floor cracked, stones began to fall from the ceiling. A priest was dashed to death by one. The galleries screamed in dismay. The crystals were whirling too fast to be seen, a continuous pulsing swirl of ruby light now. Their shriek scaled up beyond the range of human hearing; people writhed and clasped their ears, pain jabbing them in the little bones inside, from the vibration.

The audience was trapped. The exits were doors above and below the stairway. And who could dare cross the floor, pass in front of the howling array, shuddering in its frame now like a wild beast in a cage? The din was tremendous.

With a groan like a birthing woman, the Trident returned to its normal flow. People were hurled from the balconies by the force of the suction, pulled into the burning array and consumed by the power, screaming. The audience began to panic, running to and fro, climbing over each other, trapped.

The power was too great. The leys had been pulled too hastily, and too far. The junction was not stable. The Feathered Serpent and the Golden Dragon were never meant to join. Their offspring was a monster, a howling vortex of devouring energy, a maelstrom in the body of the earth, sucking power up, spewing it wildly in all directions. The disturbance rippled through the whole web, power backflowing through the violated leys, setting the flows to trembling from here to Hansi.

It could not stand. In her bodiless state, Herata could feel the power as never before, tumbling around and through her, warped, tainted, out of control. The transjunction would unmake itself, violently, and who knew what it would take with it?

This, Herata knew at last, with the clear knowledge of the dead, was her purpose, the fulfillment of her vision. To deliver enough power, by her death, to overpower the transjunction array, to bring the transjunction to its ultimate and hideous conclusion, creating in one night what might have taken many years to occur; the violent implosion of the unstable vortex, by which time the necromantic crystals would have consumed countless lifetimes of *aum*, sucked it up utterly, turning it into mere light and heat, bleeding the very earth dry to feed the lust of the Sea Kings. The flows disrupted and violated all around the world; droughts, ghostfires, poison rain, forests burning, mountains shaking, all to feed the insatiable maw of Atlantis. That, then, was the burning. And this was its antidote.

The mother earth, and the Hexachon her servants, would not see it so. The transjunction could not stand, and as it fell, it would take Atlantis with it. The Sea Kings had at last overreached themselves, and as they used the power, so would it use them. Sow the wind; reap the whirlwind.

The temple began to shake itself apart.

Huge, jagged chunks of stone crashed from the ceiling. The floor split in two. The carved stone panels on the walls crumbled into dust, the protective glyphs obliterated by the maelstrom. People swarmed desperately for the exits, braving the collapsing roof; many were smashed to bits by the falling stones or sucked screaming into the hungry maw of the array, where the raw *aum* consumed them like matchsticks. Others crouched terrified on the stone benches, too afraid to make the attempt, their faces hideous fright masks of blood from nose and eyes.

Still the *aum* whirled around the chamber, unstable, wild, dangerous.

Herata, with her last shred of human consciousness, felt the power grasp her and shake her like a terrier shakes a rat. Her spirit was tumbled like a stone in a raging river, buffeted about the chamber like a scrap of paper before the wind. Startled back to human awareness, she screamed a voiceless scream as the promise of peace escaped her.

She felt a powerful jerk, and suddenly she was beset by sensation, such as she had never known—fear, pain, blinding light. She screamed; her voice was nothing but a breathy hiss. Hideous, jagged pain assaulted her. She could not breathe. Terror swamped her; she thrashed as if she had a body again, for she did. She lifted her eyes heavenward, pleading. Above her, towering blindingly bright, she saw the crystal array, burning and throbbing like the very heart of destruction. Another windless scream ripped her torn throat.

The array quivered in its rack, tensed somehow like a beast poised to pounce. Its light blazed brighter and brighter, impossibly bright, like the sun itself. For a split second, the unearthly wail of its harmonics ceased, like a woman, a dying woman, drawing breath for her last scream.

Then it exploded.

The crystals burst outward in clouds of glowing gas, vaporized by their own energy. A cataclysm of earthpower exploded outwards in all directions, fast as light, bursting with the power of a dying sun. Stone, metal, flesh were consumed in an instant. The power ate through living rock, vaporizing the temple far above and bursting unchecked into the open air of the city.

The lightwave took Herata, enveloping her recovered flesh in the fire of a thousand suns, and then at last, mercifully, she was gone.

Chapter Twenty-Four

Branek's men hustled him out of the transjunction chamber, up and out of the Hall of the Mariners. The passage was a nightmare of jumbled sensations and pain as he hovered on the edge of consciousness.

Herata! he screamed again and again in his mind; if he made any sound, he didn't know it. Oh gods, the knife! How could he just leave her there?

Defend her. The geas the Hexachon had laid upon him thrummed in his veins. He stumbled, fell to the floor; his men pulled him up and on. They had to go back! But no, it was hopeless, she was probably – she was probably already –

"What now, Branek?" Sokar said. They were at the main doors of the Hall, still just as they had found them, riven and blasted off their hinges.

Behind them, deep in the bowels of the Hall, a burst of ruby light flashed, spilling all the way up the stairs and corridors, lighting the entrance hall with a hellish glow. With it came the whoosh-*thump* of some kind of explosion, and -- a sense of *wrongness* somehow, a flood of cold vileness that passed over them all. It felt like the disturbance that had accompanied the Teotihuacan deathwave, but a hundred times worse. The lights in the hallway flickered.

A guttural moan escaped him. He sagged in Sokar's grip. That was it, then. She was gone. He had failed. Herata had failed.

"Bran. Branek!" Sokar grabbed his chin, forcing Branek to look at him. "My king," he said, unusually formal. "We need to leave now. Now! Where to?'

Branek struggled. Grief and pain made it hard to think. What had Herata said? Her dying words.

"The docks," he said. "The ship. We set sail for home."

"As you command, my king," Sokar said, and his men hauled him out the door.

Their sea-going galley, the *Trident*, was docked in the main harbor of the outer ring. Too far to walk for a wounded man. Some of the men-at-arms left to find a gondola while Sokar wrapped Branek's wound in a crude bandage, tearing strips off the hem of his tunic.

Branek struggled to gather his thoughts, turn his mind away from the black pit of despair that threatened to engulf him. The transjunction was occurring, and the consequences would be devastating, of that he was convinced. Herata had always said so. What he had seen in that chamber of horrors made that all too clear. He had to act. *Leave Atlantis,* she had said.

"The people," he told Sokar. "The townhouse. Evacuate. Leave everything behind. Get the people to the galley."

"There isn't room –" Sokar began.

"Just do it!"

Sokar's face was pale with shock, his lips pressed together in a thin line, uncommonly quiet and serious. He had never been a friend to Herata, even less so since Laodice died, but the transjunction ceremony had shocked even him. He tasked two men with overseeing the evacuation of Lacaon's townhouse in the Silver Circle.

The men sent to find a galley did not return. There was no hope for it but to head out across the nearest bridge and start walking, Branek limping, his arm over Sokar's shoulders. The pain of his wound was amazing. He let it wash over him, swamping his consciousness, so he would not have to feel that other, greater pain.

The streets were emptying out of people as they walked, as if the citizenry sensed somehow the wrongness that was occurring under their feet in the bowels of Mariner's Hall. Indeed, there was something in the air, some miasma of evil. Even beyond his pain and confusion Branek felt it. The pavement trembled under their feet. The crystal streetlights glowed a weird green color. With a shiver, he remembered the color of Laodice's crystal during the day of the tsunami in Lacaon. It was like that. Bad magic was afoot here.

"Look," Sokar said. Along the canal came a gondola, piloted by their missing soldiers. They had found one after all.

"Thank the gods," Rames said. The gondola pulled over the edge of the canal and the men bundled Branek into it. Branek let himself slump in exhaustion on the bench. His crude bandages were soaked through with blood. He felt like his will to live, to fight on was leaking out of him with his blood. His family was gone, Herata was dead, murdered. What point was there in going on?

Just then a flash of blinding light swept over them, followed a split second later by the crackling *thump* of a massive explosion. They screamed, blinded and overwhelmed as the shockwave hit, crushing them down into the bottom of the boat. It knocked Rames over the side; he fell screaming as the gondola heeled on the force of the blast and skidded across the breadth of the canal, riding the turbulence as the water in the canal sloshed and heaved.

The gondola slammed into the far wall of the canal, scraped there as the crackling rush of the shockwave passed over them and into the city. The streetlights flickered and buzzed.

Ears ringing, Branek dragged himself up from the bottom of the boat, staring over the side, back the way they had come.

Oh my gods.

Where Mariner's Hall had stood, there remained nothing but a glowing, incandescent fireball, burgeoning hellishly up from within a massive, smoking crater. The building was gone, vaporized, and in its place some dreadful energies roared up from the awful pit that the transjunction had opened in the earth.

The ritual had failed, and Mother Earth's vengeance would be terrible, just as Herata had always prophesied.

Seeing it, Branek was struck again with a searing wave of loss as the last tiny shred of his hope was annihilated. If by any chance Herata had escaped the high priest's knife, been spared at the last, no one could have escaped *that*. Herata was truly gone.

"What did they do?" Sokar gasped, stunned.

"Unleashed the burning," Branek said. "Just as Herata foresaw."

They felt the walls of the canal tremble beside them; chaotic ripples raced hither and yon across the surface of the waters. There was an acrid, bitter tang in the air, as if the very air itself was burning. The buildings adjoining what had been Mariner's Hall caught and ignited in bursts of greenish flame. People fled, screaming, their clothing in rags. The fire grew even as they watched.

Of Rames there was no sign; he had been swallowed by the shockwave and the canal.

"Bran," Sokar asked, almost whimpered, "what –?"

Branek started the tiny crystal motor of the gondola, throttled it up to full speed. It sputtered a moment, then hummed to life and the gondola surged down the canal. "We flee."

"The townhouse …"

There was no time. He had sent them warning, that was all he could do. "We meet them at the docks or not at all," Branek said.

They rounded a corner into a transverse canal that sectioned the city and led to the harbor. Branek set his face toward it and did not look back. There was nothing else to do.

Atlantis was falling. He and his folk would not go with it. It was the only way he could honor Herata's sacrifice.

Chapter Twenty-Five

This time there was not light, but darkness. Darkness and cold. And aloneness, an aloneness so intense her nonexistent throat choked with bitter unsheddable tears.

For a timeless time she existed in that state, not thinking, not remembering, whoever *she* was, for she no longer knew. Only darkness and a sorrow for something she could not name, a loss terrible beyond her comprehension.

Then slowly, sensations began to come to her, one by one, like cats stealing out of the night. Cold, a damp chilly cold. The cold of the grave? But what was a grave? She wondered, trying to remember. The cold seemed to work into her somehow; she shivered, whatever she was.

Then a rushing sound: a ragged howling, its rhythm ever varying but unceasing.

And a touch, light but enveloping, leaving, returning. It brought the cold.

Slowly it occurred to her that the touch mimicked somehow the rushing sound; coming when it came, stopping when it stopped.

Wind. A cold damp wind, blowing over her.

Around her, darkness. Under her, rough dampness, something solid and vast, upon which her body was pressed.

Her body?

Herata screamed.

She was lying on the ground, somewhere outside, a cold wind off the ocean gusting over her. Above her, the starry vault of night.

She gasped, clutching at her throat in panic.

But she could breathe. There was no pain. The flesh of her throat felt whole and smooth to her hands. There was no blood.

She had been healed somehow.

Or had it all been a dream? A nightmare of *aum*, a fever dream of too much power in her blood?

The ground underneath her trembled, shaking; she clutched at it in sudden panic. What was happening?

A low growling rumble came from behind her, like distant thunder. She turned.

Far away over a dark plain, a fire was burning.

A huge fire, a great glowing orb of light, burning with a steady yellow glare. From it came the grumbling sound, the low roar of a vast conflagration. The flanks of the mighty mountains beyond it were lit starkly by the flames.

Now, at last, like the gears of a machine meshing into place, she understood.

The fire was Poseidonis. The Great City was burning.

She was somewhere in the south of the Plains of Gold, near the sea. She must have teleported, ridden the shockwave of exploding *aum* out of the transjunction chamber. Reconstituting, her wounds healed themselves, or had been healed for her, by whatever force had shepherded her until now.

No one else could have escaped. The holocaust of unbalanced power had burst out of the transjunction chamber, searing through tons of rock above, breaking into the open air, boiling along the captured leys. Freed of its bounds, fed by unlimited power from the warped leys, it had begun to burn, consuming all in its path – stone, water, flesh. The ghostfires were loosed in Poseidonis.

And that was not all. Beyond the light of the burning city, another, ruddier glow burgeoned in the mountains. The clouds in the sky were lit by a lurid glow beneath. The fire mountains were waking, shaken into life by the violence of the transjunction.

A light ash was already sifting down. It blackened Herata's face like the ashes of mourning.

She pressed her face into the earth and wept for the dreadful thing she had done.

She was alive. She had never expected to survive. She railed at the cruel fate that had kept her breathing, so that she was forced to see the city burn.

An explosion rocked the city, then another. The ghostfires were reaching the power plants. Nothing could stop them now.

Herata climbed painfully to her feet and began to walk back to the city. Back to the caressing touch of the flames.

The ground trembled and shook. The unholy blaze in the mountains increased.

Then, with a roar that dwarfed even the explosions, Mount Atlan, the greatest of the fire mountains, opened its mighty throat and belched its bellyful of hot ash and gas into the sky. The sound was deafening, even miles away on the Plains of Gold. The clouds above the mountain range evaporated in the heat. The ground shook, then bucked, then rolled like waves of the ocean. Herata was knocked off her feet, tossed hither and yon by the quaking earth, until she could only clutch desperately at the treacherous ground and scream, as the ancient fear of the earthquake overcame her.

Then at last it was over, except for a continuous quivering in the earth like the flanks of a nervous horse. Atlan was crowned with a cap of fire, outshining even the burning city, growling and snarling like a wolf that would devour the sun. A new rain of hot, stinging ash began to fall.

Herata clutched the ground, weeping. The mountains were burning. The ancient fear of the Sea Kings -- that the Old Ones would wake, and undo in an instant what had taken centuries to build. And it was she, Herata, who had awoken them.

Fear hammered her heart, making her breath come fast and shallow. Atlantis would burn! Get off the island – she had to get off the island!

Her earlier deathwish was obliterated by blind instinctive panic. Hardly thinking, driven by an ancestral fear, she staggered to her feet and stumbled south, to the shore, to the ocean and the dubious safety of flight.

The ground continued to shake. From the distant city, rolling over the plains, came the loud continuous *crump* of massive explosions. The crystal nurseries, or perhaps even the Poseideion itself. The city was being consumed. Soon the very island would follow. Herata limped, then staggered, then ran south to the shore.

The wind chilled her to the bone. She tried to conjure some *aum* from inside to warm her, but there was none left. The strange cache of power that she had harbored for so long was utterly spent. She felt very mortal and frail as she lurched south, her bones aching, her skin raw and ripped cruelly by the wind. She sensed everything with a preternatural clarity: the stars above bright as chips of diamond; her thirst, from the blood she had lost, a raging torment. This was the return to normal consciousness, after weeks of being in the *aum*-world.

Nausea heaved at her belly; she fell to her knees and vomited into the grass, spasming on her empty stomach. She had not expected that, not after everything that had happened. At last it stopped and she staggered on.

Another tremor shook the ground; Herata threw herself full length and rode it out. She could not help it; in spite of the horror everywhere around her, something in her wanted to live still. She curled up around her belly, riding the torment of the earth until it mostly stopped. The ground still trembled and twitched: the unbounded wrath of the Old Ones.

Lights appeared ahead of her; she made for them, limping on bare feet. The sound of the sea greeted her; this village was on the coast, perched on cliffs above the rocky beaches of the island home. South and west lay Nine Seas temple. Herata spared a thought for her kin and colleagues, a prayer that they understood the danger and would evacuate. Fresh weeping shook her.

As she neared the village, the villagers ran out to meet her. They clustered around her, staring in dismay at her fine linen robes, torn and stained with her own blood. "Great Lady, what has happened?" they cried. "What has befallen the Great City?"

Herata gaped at them. What could she say?

Before she could speak, another tremendous explosion rocked the Plains of Gold. A blinding light flashed on the horizon, from the direction of the Great City. The ground trembled; people screamed, clutched the walls of buildings and each other. A split second later the shockwave came, a hot gust of acrid, bitter wind smacking them with unholy force, sending people flying and buildings rattling. Herata with the rest groveled on the ground, beat down by the killing hand of the wind, until at last it passed, leaving ashes in its wake.

Sobs and wails rent the restless silence that followed. The infernal glow at the foot of the mountains was brighter than ever, lighting up the southern plains with an uncanny mockery of day.

Herata struggled to her feet. There was no time for explanations now. She cleared her throat painfully, choking on the ash and smoke.

"The City is no more," she said, wiling the villagers to hear and believe. "The Old Ones have awakened. The island home will fall! You must flee Atlantis, now, before it is too late."

They saw the blood on her clothes and the madness in her eyes. They saw the fires on the horizon, and smelled the burning, and they believed.

A line of villagers crept down the cliffs like ants. And among them, people from the Great City began to show up, those lucky ones who had escaped the ghostfires and the volcanoes, on horseback or carriage or on ragged, bleeding feet. Their clothes were burned, they did not speak. Looking into their eyes was like staring into an open grave.

On the shore, the villagers brought Herata to a tiny fishing boat, hardly more than a coracle. They shoved it into the water and then stood back, making way for her. She stretched out a hand, inviting, but as one they backed away, disappearing into the night, seeking other craft. None would sail with her. She was an avatar of destruction. Alone she clambered aboard the tiny skiff.

She struggled to raise the small sail; the winds were gusting fitfully, hot winds from the shore warring with the cold ocean breeze. The waves heaved sickeningly, lurching fore and aft, smacking together. The water showed an oily sheen. Hot ash wafted on the bitter winds.

She set the sail and tacked southeast as best she could. The only safety lay in open water now. When the island went, it would drag down everything around it for leagues in every direction.

Another crashing roar rolled over the water, the angry voice of the mountains. A second later, burning missiles hammered the water all around; red-hot stones from the volcanoes, arching with a whistling roar and plunging into the sea with a fiery hiss. Herata crouched in the belly of the boat, feeling naked and helpless before the wrath of the Old Ones. But there was nothing to do but sail.

The island shook, and the sea lurched heavily in response, long dangerous swells running out from the tortured land. Herata gripped the tiller and prayed to live as fervently as she had prayed to die before.

The rain of molten stone continued. A heavy ash sifted endlessly down from the sky like the tears of dead gods. It lay thick on the waters in sodden clumps, moved turgidly by the waves. It grew hard to breathe. Herata soaked a corner of her robe in the water and wrapped it around her mouth and nose.

The night became as gray as death, shot through with virulent reds in the murk. Occasionally she heard cries, or the slap of oars on water: the sounds of her fellow refugees. But in the miasma it was impossible to tell from where they came. She did not call out. She prayed only that her tiny craft not be overrun by a galley or powered trireme.

The waves showed no discernible current any longer, surging and sinking, shuddering back and forth. Herata tacked, trying to find some current to follow, some tide to carry her. But it was impossible. She was completely disoriented, lost in the hellish gloom. She could be sailing back into the jaws of death and never know.

Her tears left tracks in the mask of ash and smoke on her face.

Then the waves began to surge anew, and did not stop. Crest after crest they built up, running strong and hard in some unknown direction, with deep troughs between. From somewhere came the thunderous roar of a fire mountain, venting its rage upon the world. The end of Atlantis was at hand.

Herata gripped the tiller and the line, knuckles white. She would ride this tide to safety, or she would be swallowed up as what she had wrought worked itself out upon the world.

The drama in the transjunction chamber seemed as distant and fantastic as a dream of another life. Had she done that, lain down on the bloody altar and brought down the Sea Kings? Now she was only an orphaned daughter of the island home, at the mercy of wind and water. Now there was only the sea, the boat and the tiller.

The waves grew taller. Her tiny boat plunged into the troughs, struggled up the crests. She should take down the sail, but she could not spare a hand from the tiller. The mast shrieked ominously, strained by the terrible wind. She could not see beyond the crest of the next wave, looming in the gloom.

Her little boat began to founder in the waves.

Water filled the bottom of the boat. The mast groaned and cracked at the base, collapsing into the sea, dragging the sail dangerously with it, slewing the boat around broadside to the waves with its dead sodden weight. A huge wave smashed into the side of the boat, and it went over. Herata tumbled into the waves.

The end of Atlantis would claim her after all.

The coldness of the Ocean of Storms hit her like a blow, like knives in her chest, sending her breath out in a billowing bubble of pain and shock. She struggled to reach the surface, to gasp one last breath of living air. Her head broke water, and she flailed desperately, grasping for something; the boat, the broken mast, any solid thing to keep from going under. There was nothing; the wicked sea had hurled them far away.

The cold sapped her strength, sucking the life from her limbs. She struggled against the heaving swell. She had no *aum*, no magic left now to strengthen her, and the cold water closed over her head once again.

Like a dream she felt herself falling, sinking in the black waters, as the light left her eyes for the last time.

But then something smooth and strong rose up beneath her, lifting her up, bearing her away across the waves.

She lay draped on a long, arching back, soft and warm as silk in the frigid waves. The clicks and whistles of dolphin speech surrounded her, and she looked down into the bright black eye of Akasha, Prince of the Waters.

"How did you know?" she whispered against the sea prince's silken skin.

"Dolphins watch," Akasha said.

The members of his pod surrounded them, singing with sorrow and awe, songs of the fall of Atlantis.

"Hold on," Akasha sang, and like knives the pod sliced away through the storm waters, away from the dying island, to safety.

Chapter Twenty-Six

Spent, Herata dozed on the back of the mighty beast, safe in the knowledge that he would not let her fall. She felt herself slipping into oblivion.

But she roused when a louder, harsher noise cut through the tumult of the storm. It was the sound of an Atlantean longship, cruising under power of its crystal engines. The dolphins veered toward it.

"No!" she cried weakly, plucking at Akasha's skin. She could not face other humans, Atlantean refugees, not now.

"You belong with your own kind," Akasha sang. "These ones will care for you."

She pleaded, but Akasha was obdurate. "Dolphins know," he said.

The rest of the pod called out in high shrill voices, circling the ship. The longship slowed, and Herata was hauled aboard.

She fell to the deck, her limbs strengthless, unable to hold her. Crewmen crowded around, staring. "She must be someone if the dolphins took her up like that."

"Dressed like a lady, she is – or was."

"Another one, lord!" a sailor called to the ship's master.

"Let's see then," said a weary voice, harsh with ash and fatigue.

Anywhere in the nine seas she would know that voice. She rolled onto her back, looking up at eyes that in this measureless night were somehow still cornflower blue.

"Branek," she said.

He stared down at her. "Herata."

She should be glad, she should be mad with joy, but she could not be. There was no joy left in her now. He was the only one surviving who knew, or guessed, what she had done. When she lay down on the slab she had never dreamed to see him again.

Every time she looked into his eyes she would see what she had done.

He sat down on the deck beside her: fell down, really. Beneath the ash of the destruction his skin was white with shock and loss of blood. A clumsy bandage bound the wound in his side.

"Full speed while you can," he told his pilot, then for a long time no one said anything. There was nothing left to say. All the words would soon be under the waves.

"I prayed," Branek said at last. "The gods must have brought you to me."

"Then I am the gods' fool," Herata said.

She thought she had nothing left, but the tears came and she let them fall. Branek patted her hair absently, as if she were a restive dog beside his dinner table.

The rabid glow of the murky hellish night grew, fed by the fires of the dying island. Roars and thunderclaps chased them across the waters, the sounds of a world ripping itself asunder. The great crystal in the prow of the longship glowed for a while yet, then began to stutter and strobe. The ship eked on its way, drawing the last threads of power from the island continent, to escape before the seas consumed it and everything around it.

Then at last the crystal went dark. A final grumbling roar rose from behind, rising and rising until the refugees collapsed on the deck, smitten by the sound like the bolts of heaven. The light from over the horizon grew and grew, red then yellow then white, so white that Herata, burying her head in her arms, could see the shadow of the bones within her flesh. The sea heaved and rocked like the land under an earthquake.

Then it was gone.

Herata loosed a thin, wretched wail, as something she had held all her life and never knew, was severed forever. Her living bond with the land of her birth. She would never walk the leys again, even in her dreams. The flows were lost to her utterly. Perhaps it was a mercy, she could not know.

"So that is it then." Branek pulled her into his arms and cradled her as she wailed, mewling like a milk-sick infant. She took no comfort in it, but did not fight him either.

"Unship the oars," he ordered. "Best speed to the Inner Sea."

At length Herata stopped keening, her mouth dry as bones.

"Where are you going?" she whispered.

"Home," Branek said. "To Lacaon, to rebuild. The colonies may yet survive." He looked down into her face with a tender pity that slayed her. Pity was worse than scorn. "I will build you a new Atlantis in the Inner Sea. A better one, and you shall be its matriarch."

The cruel fates conspired to make her live, damn their black and pitiless souls. Pain twinged in her belly, pain and a strange pleasure, commingled. She hadn't wanted to believe. But after everything, still, miraculously, it was there.

"I am with your child," she said, looking into his cornflower eyes. The eyes her child would have.

"How?" he whispered, astonished.

"In the stone circle, the very first time. But I never told you because … Because."

Joy sparked in his eyes, joy and sorrow, and he clasped her tight, until she protested weakly that he was crushing her.

"I'm sorry!" he said, and cradled her tenderly as an egg, as if she might crack at the slightest touch.

"We will build a new world in the colonies, Herata," he said. "You will be the mother of gods!"

"I will," she said, "and in ages to come folk will remember me as a terrible destroyer goddess, who swallowed a world. But all I ever wanted to be was a faithful daughter of Atlas."

Branek stood, pulling her up beside him. "No one can argue against the roles that fate has chosen for them. All we can do is take the chances that are given us, and make the most of them while we may. Look." He pointed.

Far away to the east the thick murk of the sky was lightening, graying the smallest bit. Over the limb of the world, the sun was rising, as it would continue to rise every day till the end of time, whether empires rose or fell, kings were toppled or made anew.

"When I went to Mariner's Hall," Branek said, "I never dared pray that I would see another sunrise. But now here we both are, together. I will not let such a chance slip me by -- no, not if a thousand kings have fallen! I will bring you to Lacaon at last. And you will come to love it like I do – not now, not for many years perhaps, but you will. And we will begin again!"

Herata looked into the growing light. The grief and horror were still too heavy on her to answer, but she was glad of Branek's strong arms around her, that she had never thought to feel again. She was glad of the fresh wind in her face.

Leaving the ruins of the old world, they sailed into the dawn of the new.

The End

Kirsten Corby lives with her husband and cats in New Orleans, Louisiana, the newly risen American Atlantis, and works as a librarian by trade. This book arises from a life-long study of history, mythology and lost civilizations. Her work has been published in Marion Zimmer Bradley's Sword and Sorceress X, Realms of Fantasy magazine, and the urban fantasy collection Dirty Magick: New Orleans. Her other interests include Tarot cards, tabletop gaming, and papercrafting. Visit her online at www.atlantisfalling.net.

www.ingramcontent.com/pod-product-compliance
Lightning Source LLC
Chambersburg PA
CBHW070333260626
47160CB00003B/1027